Also by Christian Jacq:

About the translator

Sue Dyson is a prolific author of both fiction and non-fiction, including
over thirty novels, both contemporary and historical. She has also
translated a wide variety of French fiction.

The Mysteries of Osiris
The Way of Fire

Christian Jacq

Translated by Sue Dyson

POCKET
BOOKS

LONDON • SYDNEY • NEW YORK • TORONTO

First published in France by XO Editions under the title
Le Chemin de Feu, 2004
First published in Great Britain by Simon & Schuster UK Ltd, 2005
This edition first published by Pocket Books, 2007
An imprint of Simon & Schuster UK Ltd
A CBS COMPANY

1 3 5 7 9 10 8 6 4 2

Simon & Schuster UK Ltd
Africa House
64–78 Kingsway
London WC2B 6AH

www.simonsays.co.uk

Simon & Schuster Australia
Sydney

A CIP catalogue record for this book is available from the British Library

ISBN-13: 978-0-7434-9223-2
ISBN-10: 0-7434-9223-4

Printed and bound in Great Britain by
Cox & Wyman Ltd, Reading, Berks

The king is a flame on the wind,
reaching the furthermost edge of the sky,
the furthermost edge of the earth . . .
The king rises up in a breath of fire.

Pyramid Texts 324c and 541b.

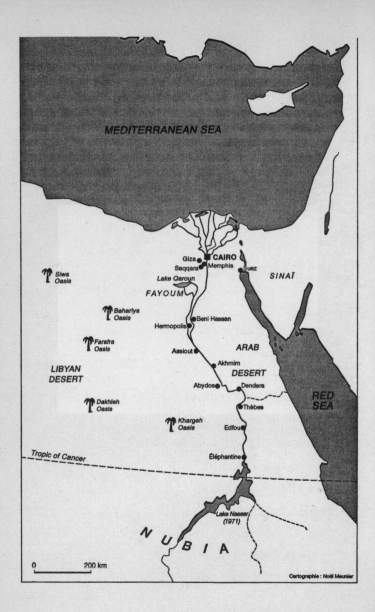

MEDITERRANEAN SEA

SINAÏ

Siwa
Oasis

Giza
CAIRO
Saqqara
Memphis
Suez
Lake Qaroun
FAYOUM

Baharîya
Oasis

Beni Hassan
Hermopolis

ARAB

Farafra
Oasis

Assiout

Akhmim

DESERT

LIBYAN
DESERT

Abydos
Dendera

RED
SEA

Dakhleh
Oasis

Thèbes

Khargeh
Oasis

Edfou

Tropic of Cancer

Éléphantine

Lake Nasser
(1971)

N U B I A

0   200 km

Cartographie : Noël Meunier

ABYDOS

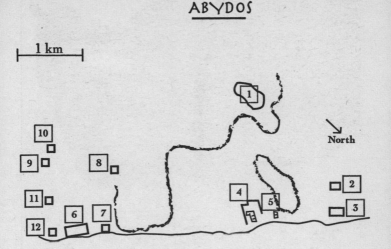

1 Royal Tombs of the first dynasty

2 Ancient Tombs

3 Temple of Osiris

4 Temple of Sethi I and Osireion

5 Temple of Ramses II

6 Towns of the Middle and New Empire

7 Temple of Scsostris III

8 Cenotaph of Sesostris III

9 Cenotaph of Moses

10 Temple of Moses

11 Pyramid of Moses

12 Chapel of Teti-Sheri

1

The owner of the small caravan was congratulating himself on his decision to leave the track controlled by the desert guards. True, there was the risk of attack by sand-travellers, those looters who roamed the whole of Syria and Canaan in search of victims, but his knowledge of the area had enabled him to avoid them. The guards' protection was not free, so he would have had to pay with part of his goods, which would have been examined minutely to check that he was not transporting weapons. In short, it would have meant a lot of trouble and a substantial reduction in his profit.

The caravan was heading for Canaan's principal town, Sichem, where General Nesmontu was based. The rugged old commander of the Egyptian army was determined to combat the small, elusive groups of rebels who were spreading terror. Was the danger genuine, or had it been invented by Nesmontu to justify the military occupation? Sichem had indeed tried to rebel, but that mad venture had ended in brutal repression and the execution of the ringleaders.

In less than three hours, the donkeys would reach the market square and bartering would begin. It was the seller's favourite moment: fix an unreasonable price, see indignation wash over the buyer's face, listen to his outraged protests, start bargaining, and eventually finally reach a compromise which satisfied both parties.

Thirty paces ahead of him a man and a boy suddenly appeared from nowhere.

Without being ordered to, the donkeys halted. One of them began to bray, causing alarm among the others.

'Calm down, my beauties,' said the merchant hastily, 'calm down.'

The man was tall and bearded. He wore a turban and was dressed in a woollen tunic which reached to his ankles.

As he got nearer, the caravan-owner saw that he had an emaciated face and deep-set red eyes.

'Who are you?' asked the merchant.

'The Herald.'

'Oh . . . So you really exist?'

The man merely smiled.

'Is this lad your son?'

'My pupil. Thirteen-Years understands that God speaks to me. From now on, everyone must obey me.'

'No problem. Myself, I respect all gods.'

'I speak not of respect but of absolute obedience.'

'I'd very much like to stand and debate with you, but I'm in a hurry to reach Sichem – market day's sacred.'

'I'm interested in your cargo.'

'You don't look very rich.'

'My faithful need to eat, so you are going to donate all your goods to our cause.'

'I dislike that sort of joke. Go away – and take the lad with you.'

'You must obey me. Have you forgotten that already?'

The merchant became angry. 'I've no time to waste, I tell you. There are ten of us, and one and a half of you. If you want a few blows from a club to knock the sense back into you, we'll be happy to oblige.'

'This is the last warning I shall give you: either you submit or you will be executed.'

The merchant turned to his men. 'Come on, lads, let's teach him a good lesson.'

The Herald transformed himself into a bird of prey, a falcon. His nose became a beak which sank into his victim's left eye, his hands into talons that ploughed into his heart.

Armed with a double-bladed dagger, Thirteen-Years attacked with the speed and precision of a horned viper. The donkey-drivers were rooted to the spot. Taking advantage of their fear, he sliced through tendons, and plunged his weapon into their sides and backs. Soon there was nothing to be heard but the moans and whimpers of wounded and dying men.

Thoroughly proud of himself, Thirteen-Years returned to his master.

'Well done, my boy,' said the Herald. 'You have proved your worth.'

The young Canaanite had been imprisoned after an Egyptian soldier was attacked, and had undergone rigorous questioning before being released. Ever since then he had longed for rebellion and slaughter, and he was convinced the Herald was the most likely person to bring that about, so constantly sang his praises.

He had been spotted by one of the Herald's men and taken to a secret base. There, Thirteen Years had made two wonderful discoveries. The first was the Herald's teaching: he preached the destruction of Egypt and continually repeated the same hate-filled words, to the point where his men became intoxicated by them. The second was intensive military training, from which the boy had clearly benefited.

'Master, may I ask for a reward?'

'You may.'

'These men are just lice – they'd never be able to recognize your greatness. Grant me permission to finish them off.'

His master raised no objection.

The youth carried out his task with ferocity, indifferent to cries for mercy. And thus he became a true warrior in the service of the Herald. Head held high, he led the train of donkeys as it made its way towards the Herald's followers' camp.

The red-haired Shab the Twisted had been one of the Herald's very first followers. Meeting his lord had turned his life as a petty criminal upside-down. The Herald had supernatural powers, and could master the demons of the desert and transform himself into a falcon. He dispensed teachings which would transform the world.

Shab was a hardened killer – he was very skilful with his flint knife, and liked to kill his victims from behind – and he believed that the new doctrine would have to be imposed through violence. But recently he had been succumbing more and more often to flights of mystical fervour in which he found justification for his deeds. Listening to the Herald's sermons plunged him into a sort of ecstasy.

A lookout hurried up from his post on the edge of the camp and reported, 'Caravan in sight.'

'How many men?'

'Just two, Thirteen-Years and the great leader.'

Shab seized him by the throat. 'Learn respect, worm! You must call the Herald "lord" or "master" and nothing else. Understood? Otherwise, you'll taste my blade.'

The Canaanite would not need a second lesson. Shab threw him aside and hurried to meet the caravan.

'Our new recruit did very well,' said the Herald.

'I killed them all!' exclaimed the lad, blushing with pleasure.

'Congratulations, Thirteen-Years. If our lord permits, you shall draw up a list of the booty and then distribute it.'

The lad did not need to be told twice. Not one fighter for the true faith would dare to mock his youth and his small stature. He had a good memory, and retained the master's words better than anyone. And he had just killed a fair few

4

enemies without flinching! His victims might not have been Egyptian soldiers, but Thirteen-Years had gained experience which would stand him in very good stead.

'We could do with a lot more like him,' commented the Twisted One.

'Don't worry,' said the Herald. 'Whole crowds will join us.'

The two men withdrew into the Herald's tent.

'All our spies from Memphis have arrived safe and sound in Canaan,' said Shab, 'apart from those left in place under the Phoenician's control.'

'Have there been any messages from him?'

'The last one was reassuring. None of his people has been arrested or even endangered. The whole palace is afraid. Despite the security measures put in place by Commander Sobek-Khu, Pharaoh Senusret knows he could be murdered at any time.'

The Herald lifted his eyes, as if trying to make out a sign in the distance. 'The king knows no fear. His powers are immense, and he is still our main adversary. Everything he does will be dangerous. One by one his visible and invisible forms of protection must be destroyed, and we shall not sing of victory until the day when both he and the pharaonic institution, whose earthly representative he is, have been annihilated. Our task will not be easy: we shall lose battles, and many believers will die.'

'But they'll go to paradise, my lord, won't they?'

'Certainly they will, my friend. But we must constantly strengthen their desire for victory, whatever the obstacles and the disillusionment. As for the traitors, the cowards and the indecisive, they are to be punished.'

'You can rely on me.'

'Any news of Crooked-Face?'

Crooked-Face had led a raiding-party charged with killing Senusret while he slept, and had very nearly succeeded.

Realizing that he had failed and all his men had been killed, he had fled.

'No, my lord.'

'He knows about this camp. If he has been arrested and has talked, we're in danger.'

'We aren't expecting anyone but him, so let's leave here and go to the second camp. Several Canaanite tribes will join us there.'

'See to the preparations for departure immediately.'

The Herald considered the Canaanites braggarts and cowards, but they were nevertheless a vital part of his plan, which might perhaps lead the pharaoh to make fatal mistakes. Between and within the towns and the villages, between factions and the clan chiefs, the norm had become tumult, underhand tricks, denunciation and conspiracies. The Herald was planning to impose order on this chaos and form some semblance of an army which Senusret would consider a threat. So he must unite several tribes in the name of resistance against the occupying power and the liberation of Canaan, which however could not continue to exist without permanent assistance from Egypt.

A young Asian woman entered the tent, bearing a small scroll of papyrus. No one would ever have been suspicious of this beautiful brown-haired girl, her eyes filled with amorous promise. Yet, by abusing her and mixing his blood with hers, the Herald had transformed her into the Queen of the Night, a formidable weapon which he would use when the right moment came.

'Let me see that,' he said.

Submissively, Bina handed her master the papyrus. It bore a coded text, which he deciphered with interest.

'Is it important news?' she asked.

'You must not ask questions. Be content to obey.'

She bowed.

'Send Thirteen-Years to me.'

As he described his exploits to his master's other followers, the lad crowned himself with success. His convincing response to his lone detractor, a sceptical peasant, was to stab him in the foot. Indifferent to the fate of the buffoon, whose howls of pain made everyone laugh, Thirteen-Years shared out the food the caravan had been transporting.

Conversing alone with the Herald would raise his standing among the men still further. He hurried to the tent.

'Nothing to report, Thirteen-Years?'

'Nothing at all, my lord. People respect me now.'

'Let us pray together. Recite the words of the curse directed at the pharaoh.'

Praying that he might be the one to strike down the tyrant, the boy did so enthusiastically. When he finished, the Herald's red eyes flamed. Utterly subjugated, Thirteen-Years drank in his words.

'To attain the goal ordained by God demands the death of the unbelievers. Alas, many do not understand this. But you will prove yourself worthy of the most vital missions. The one I am going to entrust to you may seem unusual, but carry it out without question. If you do so, you will succeed.'

'May I use my dagger, my lord?'

'It will be indispensable, my child.'

2

Iker, the Royal Son, was walking alone in the luxuriant garden of the palace at Memphis. Anyone watching would have thought that this elegant, well-bred young man was enjoying himself before attending a reception where everyone would congratulate him on his recent promotion, at the same time trying to win his good graces. The former little provincial scribe was obviously enjoying a brilliant and easy career. In fact, the reality was very different.

Iker sat down under the pomegranate tree that had witnessed his declaration of love to Isis, a priestess from Abydos with whom he had been hopelessly smitten since their first meeting. She had granted him only a faint hope by confiding, 'Some of my thoughts will be with you and will never leave you,' a simple expression of friendship, even kindness. But her face never left Iker, who had already been saved from numerous perils by her invisible presence.

He couldn't bear the thought of living out his life far away from from her. And yet he would probably never see her again.

Soon a special mission would take him to Canaan. He must infiltrate the ranks of the Canaanite rebels by pretending to be one of their supporters, discover the lair of their chief, Amu, known as the Herald, and pass on this vital information to the Egyptian army and security guards so that they could take instant action.

The Herald was no ordinary rabble-rouser. Evil forces were conspiring together under his leadership, and had been responsible for putting a curse on the Tree of Life, the Acacia of Osiris at Abydos. Without the pharaoh's magical powers and the daily rites performed by the permanent priests, it would have completely withered away. But how much longer could the protective rituals slow down the tree's degeneration? Only a cure would prove that the Light had been victorious. But the situation was far from hopeful, because the search for the gold that would heal the tree had yielded nothing yet.

That was why it was so vital to catch the Herald. He must be arrested and made to talk, so that they would at last know how he was maintaining the curse.

Iker's mission would enable him to cleanse himself of a great wrong he had done. He had believed the king responsible for his sufferings, and had allowed himself to be used and manipulated like a mere puppet by traitors who secretly served the Herald. They had convinced him that Senusret was a cruel tyrant, and Iker had planned to kill him. Fortunately, his eyes had been opened in time and he had told the king of his intended crime. Instead of punishing him, to everyone's surprise Senusret had appointed him the palace's only ward and Royal Son, to the great displeasure of the many courtiers who had set their sights on these coveted titles.

For Iker, who was solitary, meditative and disinclined to worldly things, such worldly distinction mattered much less than the king's teachings on God, the divinities and Ma'at. By speaking two ordinary words – 'my son' – in a particular way, the pharaoh had put an end to Iker's wanderings.

Never again to leave the way of Ma'at: that was his first imperative, though it was an extremely difficult one to observe. From a true Royal Son, aged only seventeen, the king was demanding an upright, fully formed will, a capacity for perception and understanding, a mind filled with

9

righteous thoughts, the courage to confront fear and danger, and the permanent desire to search for the truth, even at the risk of his life. These qualities alone led to *hotep*, fullness of being and peace of the soul. Iker still felt so far away from it that he thought rather of the words of his first master, an old scribe from Madu, which Senusret had unexpectedly repeated: 'Whatever your ordeals may be, I shall always be by your side to help you accomplish a destiny of which you are as yet unaware.'

Deep in thought, Iker left the garden and the palace grounds, and wandered through the streets of the capital. Despite the recent upheavals and the unsuccessful attempt on the pharaoh's life, Memphis was still joyful and full of colour. The centre of the country's trade since the days of the early pharaohs, it occupied the balancing-point between the Nile Valley, Upper Egypt, and the vast green, watery stretches of the Delta, Lower Egypt.

The priests were fulfilling their ritual duties by giving life to the city's many temples, scribes were carrying out their administrative tasks, craftsmen were making the things needed for sacred and worldly life, traders were bustling about in the markets, dock-workers were unloading goods . . . This bright-coloured, warm society did not know that the Tree of Life, and with it Egyptian civilization, was in danger of dying.

Iker had a horrifying vision: if the Herald won the day and the acacia did die, Memphis – indeed, the whole of Egypt – would be reduced to ruins. He knew very well that volunteering to flush the Herald out was tantamount to suicide, because, despite the military training he had received in the Oryx province, he had no chance at all of succeeding. But the king had not dissuaded him, only advising him to procure weapons from the invisible world.

If Isis had returned his love, perhaps he would have given up. No, it was unworthy to lay any responsibility on her. He must go to Canaan, no matter how afraid he was.

Originally, Iker had wanted only to become first of all a good scribe, then a writer. He enjoyed copying out the texts of wisdom, like the Maxims of Ptah-Hotep, and discovering the treasures of the ancients. They never spoke on their own behalf; they were always determined to pass on Ma'at, without omitting to highlight the human race's particular failings and base elements. And he could not find the words to describe the fullness, the beauty and the profundity of the ritual texts to which he had been given access through his office as a temporary priest of Anubis. Isis had permission to use the libraries of the Houses of Life, so she must know these and many other marvels.

That was the sort of future Iker had dreamt of, not being Pharaoh's special envoy, sentenced to plunge into a cauldron full of curses in which he would soon be burnt to nothing.

Normally, Iker would have been accompanied on his walk by his donkey and confidant, North Wind. But he could not take the donkey to Canaan, so had entrusted it to the care of Isis; the young scribe now felt very alone. He and North Wind had been able to communicate without the need for words, and they had helped each other out of many a tight spot. Parting with his friend had almost broken Iker's heart, but Isis had treated the donkey with such gentleness that she had immediately gained its trust.

Emerging from his sad thoughts, Iker realized he had lost his way. He found himself in a strangely silent alleyway, where there were no children playing, no housewives chatting on their doorsteps, no water-carrier offering his services.

He tried to retrace his steps, but came face to face with a burly, aggressive ruffian armed with a large stone.

'Well,' said the man, 'what a fine kilt and sandals you have – we don't often see that sort of quality around here. Come on, give them to me.'

Iker looked round. At the other end of the alleyway were two more men, equally menacing.

'There's no way out, boy. Just be cooperative, and then you won't get hurt. The kilt and the sandals – quickly.'

Iker had to choose his angle of attack very quickly, before the net closed and the three thieves gave him a beating, putting a premature end to his mission.

He charged at the burly man, who gave a sort of startled squeak, dropped his stone and collapsed, face down. His two henchmen ran up. The faster of them stopped abruptly, as though struck by lightning, and fell over backwards. His companion took to his heels in alarm.

A sturdy fellow with a square face, thick eyebrows and a round belly appeared, casually brandishing a slingshot.

'Sekari!' said Iker. 'Have you been following me ever since I left the palace?'

'And what would have happened if I hadn't been keeping an eye on you? All right, you might have got the better of one of them, or even two, but those fellows are vicious, and they specialize in fighting uncleanly. Whatever got into you, deciding to go for a stroll in a place like this when you're dressed so fine?'

'I was thinking and I—'

'Come and have a beer; that'll set your thoughts straight. I know a rather smart inn where you won't be too noticeable.'

An unbreakable friendship, forged during shared hardships, bound the two men closely together. Sekari came from a humble background and had worked as many different things, including servant, miner, bird-catcher and gardener. His shabby appearance and his love of good beer and wine were deceptive: he was one of Senusret's special agents, and had been ordered to protect Iker in all circumstances. He could move soundlessly and apparently make himself invisible, and could blend in easily with any group of people. Iker suspected that he knew a lot about the Golden Circle of Abydos, the most secret brotherhood in Egypt, but Sekari evaded all questions about it, as if he had been sworn to absolute silence.

The beer was strong and refreshing.

'You don't look very cheerful,' observed Sekari.

'Do you really think I have any chance at all of success?'

'Do you really think the king would send you to certain death?'

The question troubled Iker. 'No, but . . . I'll be so weak, alone in Canaan, which is an unknown world to me, facing enemies I can't pin down. Won't I be easy to catch and kill?'

'Wrong, my friend, absolutely wrong. Your weakness is precisely what will save you. The rebels would easily recognize a strong enemy, no matter how skilful he was at acting his part, but you won't seem dangerous at all. If you can keep them thinking that, you'll achieve an amazing success. Besides, think of what you've already done. Only a madman would have wagered a scrap of rag on your survival when you were kidnapped and taken aboard the *Swift One* as a sacrifice to the sea-god, and then shipwrecked. But now here you are, very much alive and a Royal Son into the bargain. There really is no reason to give up hope, even if your journey is going to be rather dangerous. You know, I've been through things that were nearly as bad and I've lived to tell the tale.'

Iker remembered the question asked by the giant serpent that had appeared to him on the Island of the *Ka* after the shipwreck: 'I could not prevent the end of this world. And what of you – will you save yours?'

Sekari broke into his thoughts, asking, 'Do you remember the queen of turquoises, which we discovered together? If the Herald's got it, what will he use it for? A stone like that must have formidable powers. Supposing it can heal? If it can, it would be very useful to us.'

'Perhaps it's kept in the acacia-wood box made for the Herald?'

'No, that holds other secrets – and you, Iker, are going to find them out. And you're also going to find out if the Herald

13

killed my master, General Sepi. Royal justice will be done sooner or later, and I'd very much like to be the one to execute it. What a delightful prospect!'

Sekari was making great efforts to be reassuring, but neither he nor his friend was deceived.

'We must go back to the palace,' decided Iker. 'I want to give you my most treasured possession to look after while I'm away.'

The two men did not use the official entrance. Sekari, whose true role was known to only a handful of people at court, was as discreet as a shadow. After taking a roundabout route, he joined Iker in his apartments, which were near those of the king.

'The king was wise to appoint Sobek the Protector head of all the country's guards,' said Sekari. 'He's trained his men well: they're so thorough and conscientious that even I had difficulty getting though unnoticed – Pharaoh's safety's in good hands, so I'm less worried about it. But I am worried about the bogus desert guard who tried to kill you. Who was he working for? If it was the Herald, there's no problem. But if it wasn't, there certainly is: to me, it would imply that there's another traitor about, perhaps inside this very palace.'

'Do you think it might be Sobek-Khu himself?' asked Iker.

'That would be terrible, but I shall carry out my investigation without ruling anything out.'

'Don't forget that Sobek will be the first to hear my information from Canaan.'

'Don't worry, I shan't let him harm you.'

Iker handed his friend a set of remarkably fine scribe's materials. 'They were a gift from General Sepi. I shan't need them in Canaan.'

'I'll keep them safe for you, and they'll be waiting for you when you get back. Talking of keeping things safe, what weapons are you taking with you?'

'An amulet shaped like the *was*, the Sceptre of Power, and the guardian spirit's knife that the king gave me.'

'Never let your guard down, don't trust any one, and always expect the worst. That way you'll never be caught unawares.'

Iker went to the window and gazed up at the brilliantly blue sky. 'How can I ever thank you for your help, Sekari? Without you, I'd have been dead long ago. But now we must part.'

Sekari turned away to hide his feelings.

Iker went on, 'Your loyalty to the king is unshakeable, isn't it?'

'You can be sure of that.'

'I dare say you've never once thought, even for a moment, of disobeying him.'

'Not for a moment.'

'Then you must stay in Memphis and not follow me into Canaan.'

'Now that, that's another thing—'

'No, Sekari. I must act alone: succeed alone or fail alone. This time, you can't protect me.'

3

Being away from Abydos caused Isis great pain. Whatever the charms of Memphis might be, or those of any other place to which her duties as a priestess called her, all she thought of was returning as soon as possible to the country's spiritual centre, the great Land of Osiris, the isle of the righteous.

As soon as the boat neared Abydos, and she saw the cliff, the houses along the canal and the monuments that dotted the desert around the town, her heart soared. In this sacred place stood Osiris's house of eternity and temple. A processional roadway led up to it, bordered by shrines and stelae. Here stood the Tree of Life, the focal point of the whole world.

Abydos had recently been blessed with two great works of art, Senusret's temple and his vast tomb, where Isis had completed a major stage in her initiation into the great Mysteries. A small town, Enduring Places, completed the group of buildings. Here lived craftsmen, scribes, the permanent priests and priestesses of the Temple of Osiris, and temporary priests who came to work there for anything from a few days to several months.

Besides the curse on the Acacia of Osiris, there had been attacks on the town of Kahun and on Dahshur, location of the royal pyramid: Egypt's enemies were determined. Abydos was therefore protected by a strong force of security guards.

All through her journey, Isis's mind had been troubled.

This was not because of the number and difficulty of the tasks imposed by the pharaoh – though they would have daunted the most resilient person. Her tasks were inspiring, and provided her with hitherto unsuspected strength. However, the meagre results obtained against the forces of darkness inclined her to pessimism. But the acacia was still alive. Two branches had even grown green again, and each re-conquest, even a modest one, persuaded Isis that they would win in the end.

No, her troubled thoughts were the result of a declaration of love by Iker, the Royal Son. His love was so intense that it frightened her, to the point of preventing her from answering a crucial question: did she, Isis, love Iker?

Up till then her life as a priestess, her efforts to deepen her knowledge of the Mysteries and the rites, had made her forget the maze of feelings and passions.

Since she had met Iker, Isis felt different. She was experiencing strange sensations, very different from those she had felt during her spiritual experience. To outward appearance there was nothing contradictory, but the prospects were unknown. Ought she to explore them?

By her own admission, some of her thoughts remained with Iker. It did not matter if he was the Royal Son, a provincial scribe or a servant. All that mattered was his authenticity and sincerity. Iker was an exceptional person.

When she left him, Isis had been afraid. Afraid she would never see him again, because he was setting off on an venture from which he would probably not return. And her fear was transformed into sadness. Ought she not to have spoken to him differently, talked of the difficulties of a priestess's life, been more friendly?

Friendship, mutual respect, trust . . . Were these the right words? Or were they simply masks for a feeling which she refused to name because it would divert her from her destiny?

An insistent muzzle reminded her that she must descend

the gangplank. Isis smiled, and North Wind contemplated her with his big brown eyes. They had understood each other from the first. Very much affected by Iker's departure, the big donkey found the comfort he needed with this young woman, so gentle and radiant. Thoughts passed between them without difficulty, and neither of them tried to disguise the reality: the Royal Son's chances of survival seemed infinitely small.

The first checkpoint posed no problems. The soldiers knew Isis, and were delighted to see her again. Abydos had seemed a bit colourless while she was away. Her reception at the second checkpoint, though, was very different. The guards hesitated to question her, but a temporary priest could not restrain his indignation.

'A donkey in Abydos? A donkey, the creature of Set? Look at its neck: there's a tuft of red hair! This animal is the incarnation of the spirit of evil! I shall inform the Shaven-headed One at once.'

Isis patiently awaited his arrival.

The Shaven-headed One was Pharaoh's official representative at Abydos, and never took any decision without the king's express agreement. Senusret had appointed him to lead the permanent priests and to watch over the temple's sacred library and archives, to which only he could grant access. He was now sixty years old, gruff, stubborn and wholly lacking in tact and subtlety. He never left the domain of Osiris, laughed at worldly honours, and would not tolerate a single mistake in the carrying out of ritual tasks. His watchword was thoroughness, and he punished each breach of the Rule, regarding good excuses as bad.

'A donkey with a tuft of red hair?' he exclaimed in astonishment. 'You never stop surprising me, Isis!'

'North Wind was entrusted to me by Iker, the Royal Son. He will live close to my official dwelling and will not disturb the sacred area. After all, one of our duties is to control the strength of Set. I don't dispute that the donkey is one of its expressions, but the priestesses of Hathor are called upon to pacify its fire, aren't they?'

'Set was condemned to carry Osiris on his back,' agreed the Shaven-headed One. 'Will this animal be able to be silent at all times?'

'I'm sure of it.'

'At the first sign of disobedience, at the very first bray, it will be expelled.'

'Did you understand that?' Isis asked the donkey.

North Wind raised his right ear as a sign of agreement.

The Shaven-headed One muttered something inaudible and stroked the donkey's head. 'Settle him in and then join me in the pharaoh's temple.'

The king's temple of a million years was a mighty building surrounded by a curtain-wall. It was designed to produce *ka*, which strengthened the magical defences of the Tree of Life. A paved roadway and a pillared gateway led to it. Equipped with a complex system of channels to carry away the water from purifications, this vast, squarish structure seemed to guard the whole desert around it.

Isis entered the courtyard, next to which stood a roofed portico supported by four pillars, then the covered hall. Here, a profound silence reigned, inhabited by the words of the gods to whom the king made offerings. The ceiling depicted the starry sky.

The Shaven-headed One was meditating before a relief carving of Osiris.

'What are the results of your research at the great library in Memphis?' he asked when Isis joined him.

'They confirm what we thought: only the purest gold, from the belly of the divine mountain, can cure the acacia.'

'We need it for the celebration of the great Mysteries, too. Without it, the ritual will be ineffective and Osiris will not be reborn.'

'That is our enemies' true goal,' said Isis. 'Despite General Sepi's death, His Majesty is intensifying the search, but no one knows the location of the City of Gold or the land of Punt.'

The Shaven-headed one gestured dismissively. 'Those are simply poetic names.'

'I shall continue to investigate, in the hope of finding something significant.'

'What has the pharaoh decided?'

'The man responsible for our misfortunes is probably a rebel who calls himself the Herald and is operating in Canaan. Senusret is sending Royal Son Iker there to try to find him. Only the inner circle of His Majesty's most loyal friends know this, and now the two of us.'

Isis had a particularly delicate mission to fulfil: to be constantly vigilant and make sure that none of the permanent or temporary priests of Abydos was an accomplice of the enemy. As he had complete trust in his official representative, the king had authorized her to take the Shaven-headed One into her confidence.

'I did not notice anything unusual while you were away,' said the Shaven-headed One. 'Everyone is carrying out his or her duties to best effect. How could an evil demon possibly have infiltrated our ranks?'

'The workshop of the Temple of Hathor in Memphis gave me something that may help. I should like to check whether it does.'

They left Senusret's temple and went to the Tree of Life, which stood at the heart of the sacred wood of Peker. The small group of permanent priests who tended it were scrupulously carrying out their duties, as they did every day. To maintain the spiritual energy with which the place was imbued, and the vital link with the beings of Light, the Servant of the *Ka* was celebrating the cult of the ancestors. The priest charged with pouring the libation of fresh water did not miss a single offering-table. The priest who saw secrets made sure that the rituals were carried out properly, and the one who watched over the wholeness of the great body of Osiris checked the seals placed on the door of his tomb. The seven female musicians whose task was to enchant the divine soul made music which was an echo of the celestial harmony.

The pharaoh was the Bearer of the Golden Palette, which bore the words of knowledge revealed in Abydos. Wherever he was, he intoned them every day in an innermost shrine, thus ensuring there was no break in the chain of revelations.

The Shaven-headed One and Isis poured water and milk at the foot of the Acacia of Osiris. Only a few traces of life now remained in it. Four young acacias had been planted round it, one at each point of the compass, creating a protective forcefield. And there had been performed a ceremony in which ritually made and dedicated clay balls had been assimilated into the eye of the sun, thus strengthening the magical protective barrier. No waves of evil could now cross it, but had those precautions been taken too late?

'May you continue to dwell within this tree, Osiris,' the Shaven-headed One prayed. 'May it maintain the bond between the heavens, the earth and the depths; may it grant light to the initiated and prosperity to this land, beloved of the gods.'

Isis held up a beautifully wrought mirror. It was made from a thick disc of silver and had a handle of jasper, decorated with a likeness of Hathor; fine strips of gold surrounded inlays of lapis-lazuli and cornelian. She raised it high, so that it reflected a ray of sunlight which caressed the trunk of the acacia. It was a delicate task, which had to be performed with great care so that the sun's heat warmed the tree but did not burn it.

Isis placed the mirror in one of the shrines of the Temple of Osiris, the one reserved for the ship used during the ritual of the great Mysteries. According to the Shaven-headed One's observations, its heavenly counterpart was no longer moving normally. So, in order to avoid fragmentation, Isis had been charged by the king with naming each of its parts and thus preserving its unity. This would keep alive one of the fundamental symbols of Abydos, the guarantor of the energy vital to the process of resurrection.

Enduring Places had been built strictly according to Senusret's plan. Each street was five cubits wide, with separate blocks of houses, and each brick-built dwelling comprised a courtyard, a reception room and private apartments. Fine houses looked out over at the desert. At the south-western corner of the town stood the mayor's huge house.*

Isis lived in a four-roomed house whose wooden door had an ornamental limestone surround. There was a striking contrast between the whiteness of the outside walls and the vibrant colours of the interior. The furniture was simple and robust, the dishes and plates were made of stone and pottery, and the bedding was linen: the priestess's material goods were amply sufficient for her needs. Because of her rank, a cleaning-woman with excellent cooking skills relieved her of domestic cares.

North Wind was standing at the threshold, watching over his mistress's house. Already, all of Abydos knew that a creature of Set had been granted the status of temporary resident, on condition that it observed a strict religious silence.

'You're very hungry, aren't you?' said Isis.

The donkey raised his right ear.

'It won't be a very good supper this evening, I'm afraid. But from tomorrow I'll prepare proper meals for you.'

*It measured 82 metres by 53.

Together, they walked along the edge of the desert, gazing at the sunset, whose rays tinged with pink an old tamarisk tree. Its name, *iser*, was reminiscent of *Usir*, 'belonging to Osiris'. From time to time, branches from this tree were placed inside a sarcophagus to facilitate the mummy's transformation into a body of Osiris. The hardy tamarisk triumphed over the desert's dryness, for its roots plunged deep to draw up water.

Isis made a silent prayer that Osiris would protect Iker and enable him to walk blamelessly across the perilous land where he would risk his life to try to save both Abydos and all Egypt.

4

Medes was an energetic forty-year-old with jet-black hair cut close to his round head, a moon-shaped face, a broad chest, short legs and pudgy feet. As secretary of the King's House, a vital centre of power in Egypt, he wrote out the decisions taken by the pharaoh and his council, then had them distributed throughout the entire country.

Although he was extremely proud of his post, which made him one of the most important men in the state, Medes harboured fierce secret ambitions, notably to become a member of the King's House, not in order to serve it better but to destroy it. It would be far from easy to dispose of Senusret; the failure of the last attempt on his life had demonstrated the extent of the king's magical protection. But Medes was not one to give up easily, especially since he had entered an alliance with the Herald, a strange and dangerous man who was determined to bring down the throne of the pharaohs.

Medes demanded the highest standards of his staff and he led by example. He was always the first to arrive at his secretariat's offices and the last to leave. In short, he acted the part of a responsible, hard-working official who was beyond reproach. However, the king had recently limited the influence of the secretary of the King's House by re-establishing the post of tjaty, which he had entrusted to

Khnum-Hotep. The new tjaty was fulfilling his duties exceptionally well, displaying absolute loyalty to a sovereign he had once opposed. Medes was a cautious man. He hid his resentment and took care not to trespass on Khnum-Hotep's domain, to obey him without question, and to give him no grounds for complaint, for the new first minister had the king's ear.

Medes bustled around, thinking of the meeting arranged for midnight, which was as important as it was risky. The approach of the meeting made him even more irritable than usual, and he actually man-handled several scribes whose work was too slow for his liking.

He was reading an official document when High Treasurer Senankh, director of the Double White House and minister for the country's trade and finances, paid him an unexpected visit.

Medes hated Senankh. The High Treasurer was a lover of the good things in life, which had led to plump cheeks and a rounded belly. But his appearance was deceptive. In fact, he was not only expert at safeguarding Egypt's wealth but a feared leader of men. Himself wholly impervious to flattery, Senankh did not hesitate to bully courtiers, or the lazy and incompetent. Medes had tried his utmost to discredit him and force him to resign, but in vain. Senankh was as cunning as a fox. He could scent vicious attacks and responded vigorously.

'Any serious problems on the horizon?' asked Senankh.

'No, none, High Treasurer.'

'Your department's finances look very healthy.'

'I watch out for the smallest sign of waste. It is an never-ending task, I'm afraid. If one's attention wavers for even a moment, people take advantage of it.'

'You are an excellent manager – the secretariat of the King's House has never functioned so well. And I have some good news for you: your request has been granted, and you are to have five additional fast boats at your disposal. Take on as many scribes as you think necessary and ensure that information circulates more quickly.'

'Nothing could make me happier, High Treasurer! With the extra boats, I shall be able to disseminate the royal decrees much more efficiently.'

'Thus strengthening the unity of the Two Lands still further,' commented Senankh. 'But you must not slacken your efforts under any circumstances.'

'Have no fear: I shan't.'

As he made his way home, Medes wondered if the High Treasurer suspected anything. Neither his words nor his behaviour had suggested that he did, but Senankh was clever enough not to betray any sign of his true intentions, and Medes knew he must never lower his guard. Whatever the case, Medes had got what he wanted. His new employees – messengers and sailors alike – would be drawn from his network of informants. When he needed to get information to the rebels, it would now be simple.

Medes lived in a superb house in the centre of Memphis. On the side facing the street were a service entrance and a double main door, where a guard was permanently on duty. On both floors there were tall windows, with wooden openwork. A covered balcony, with small pillars painted green, opened on to a garden.

Medes had scarcely entered the reception room when his wife threw herself at him. 'I'm ill, my darling, so ill! You leave me alone too much.'

'What's wrong with you?'

'I have attacks of nausea, my hair is falling out and I have no appetite . . . Send for Doctor Gua straight away.'

'I'll see to it tomorrow.'

'But it's urgent – very urgent!'

Medes pushed her aside. 'I have something even more urgent to deal with first.'

'You want me to die!'

'You'll live until tomorrow. Have my dinner served and then tell your personal maid to give you a massage. That will relax you.'

After he had eaten, Medes waited until nearly midnight before leaving the house, the hood of his cloak pulled well over his head. He stopped and turned round several times, to make sure no one was following him. Even then, he retraced his steps and circled round and round before going to his destination.

He knocked at the door of a wealthy-looking house, hidden in a modest district. He handed the forbidding guard a small piece of cedar-wood, on which was engraved the hieroglyph of the tree.

The door opened, and Medes walked up to the first floor, where he was greeted by a talkative man who looked rather like a heavy wine-jar, and who was over-perfumed and dressed in a long, richly-brocaded robe.

'My very dear friend, what a pleasure to see you again. Will you sample a few sweetmeats?' The Phoenician merchant was trying to control his weight, but his huge reception room was still full of low tables laden with cakes, each more tempting than the last.

Medes pushed back his hood and sat down. 'Give me some date-wine.'

'At once.'

The silver goblet the Phoenician held out to his guest was a small marvel. 'It was a gift from a ship-owner who tried to swindle me,' he explained. 'Before dying in dreadful pain, he bequeathed all his possessions to me. Even bad men sometimes revert to good sentiments.'

'I'm not interested in how you settle your accounts,' said Medes. 'Iker has left the palace. I am convinced that he isn't going back to his native province but is heading for Canaan.'

'My network has already been alerted about that, but why would he go to Canaan?'

27

'To discover the Herald's lair and inform the Egyptian army.'

The Phoenician smiled. 'The Royal Son's as weak as he is presumptuous, don't you think?'

'Don't underestimate him. He's already escaped death several times, and his ability to harm our cause is well known. However, he has made the mistake of venturing into our territory, believing that he'll pass unnoticed, so let us take advantage of that fact.'

'Why are you so worried?'

'Because Iker must have been given his mission by the pharaoh himself, and must therefore be endowed with very special powers. Senusret does not act lightly. If the Royal Son has been ordered to infiltrate the ranks of the Canaanite rebels, he must have a chance of success.'

The argument carried much weight. 'So do you wish me to arrange an ambush?'

'If I'm not mistaken, Iker will go to Sichem. Have your spies inform you as soon as he arrives. We'll let him enter one of the clans there, and they can kill him at their leisure, once they've interrogated him – he may supply us with interesting information about the enemy's plans.'

The Phoenician stroked his chin. 'That might be one way to proceed.'

'Arrange things however you like, but kill Iker. His death will weaken Senusret.'

'I'll deal with the lad,' promised the trader. 'Now, shall we talk about our business affairs? I must remind you that a new cargo of precious wood has just left Phoenicia. The trade-control officers must turn a blind eye to it.'

'The arrangements will be made.'

'And we must switch storehouses.'

'I haven't forgotten that. What about the . . . the "special" oils?'

'When the time comes, I'll tell you.'

Evil was about to strike. If they succeeded, the Phoenician's monstrous plans would cost the lives of hundreds, perhaps even thousands, of Egyptians. Medes was momentarily shaken by that thought, but soon yielded once again to the allure of the new future. Yes, violence and suffering would be widespread, but the conquest of power justified that: to defend Ma'at as Senusret did was to venerate an outdated past. Medes had chosen his side a long time ago, and any hesitation now would be harmful. Meeting the Herald had given him an undreamt-of opportunity to overcome obstacles he had thought insurmountable. Selling his soul to a demon from the darkness would bring him glory and wealth.

'Have you had any problems?' asked Medes.

'Sobek the Protector's men haven't been by any means idle, but they haven't caught any of my people. I congratulate myself on having kept only the best of them in Memphis, where they are fully integrated into Egyptian society.'

On the orders of the Herald, most of whose troops had withdrawn into Canaan, the Phoenician was directing a network of spies disguised as shopkeepers, itinerant traders and barbers, all of them past masters in the art of spotting inquisitive folk and, if necessary, killing them. The spies were kept strictly separate from one another, so that if one of them was caught, or changed sides, he could not endanger the whole group.

The Phoenician would never deceive or betray the Herald. Once – and only once – he had lied to him. The preacher with the eyes like burning coals had almost torn out his heart, leaving a scar in his flesh that served as a permanent warning. The Phoenician knew he would never escape the falcon-man's talons.

'And what about you, Medes?' he asked. 'Does anyone suspect you of anything?'

Medes took time to think. 'I'm not stupid, and I ask myself

that question constantly. There are no worrying signs, but I'm wary. Whenever High Treasurer Senankh accepts one of my proposals, I ask myself whether he's concerned with the interests of the state or putting me to the test. Both, probably.'

'We cannot relax our vigilance in the slightest,' the Phoenician reminded him, 'or we shall have to cancel our plans. If one of Senusret's loyal supporters gets too close to you, let me know without fail; we can then act quickly. And remember, Medes, if we fail the Herald won't forgive us.'

5

Hordes of workmen were engaged in extending the King's Walls, a line of forts intended to strengthen Egypt's north-eastern frontier and to discourage invasion by rebellious Canaanite or Syrian tribes. The old forts were being strengthened, and new ones built; they communicated with one another by means of visual signals and carrier-pigeons.

The garrisons, made up of soldiers and trade-control officials, checked goods and travellers' identities meticulously. After the attempt on Senusret's life, they had redoubled their vigilance. A few Canaanite rebels had been killed, but others would certainly try to get into the Delta and avenge their comrades, so the soldiers searched suspects and undesirables, and gave out passes only after detailed questioning. 'Whoever crosses this frontier', proclaimed the pharaoh's decree, 'becomes one of my sons.'

Leaving Egypt to go to Canaan was subject to strict rules: one must give one's name, the reasons for the journey, and the exact date of one's return. Scribes built up files, which were constantly updated.

For Iker, crossing the border would be difficult because he must leave no trace that he had done so. This first test would not only be important in itself but would also enable him to tell the rebel Canaanites that he was fleeing from Egypt, where he was being hunted by the security guards. If, as he

31

assumed, they had informants among the people working at the King's Walls, they would be able to verify that no official pass had been issued to him and that he was indeed behaving like a fugitive.

Iker noted the extensive security measures. There were many archers on the battlements of the keeps and many troops on the ground; both were permanently ready for action. No raid could possibly succeed. A fort under attack would have time to warn the neighbouring ones, news of the attack would spread rapidly along the Walls, and reinforcements would arrive almost immediately.

Without inside information, Iker would have stood not a chance of getting past the King's Walls. Fortunately, though, Sehotep, Bearer of the Royal Seal, had given him a detailed map, indicating the last weak spot in the fortifications. So, as night fell, the young man set off into an area of undergrowth.

In front of him was an old, isolated fort, which was being restored. Torches would be lit when it was time for the guard to be changed. Iker would have a few minutes' grace in which to run full-tilt across the border into Canaan.

The commander of the fort was not pleased with his new appointment. He missed the barracks in Memphis, and the capital city and its countless distractions. Here, time hung heavy. Fortunately, General Nesmontu, head of all Egypt's armies, was an experienced officer. He had ordered exercises to be carried out every day, but he also authorized plenty of leave and often changed part of the garrison in order to prevent the men getting bored and slack. With a leader of that stamp, the soldiers enjoyed their work.

First thing tomorrow, the commander decided, he would have the undergrowth around the fort burnt off. Once the area was cleared, anyone who ventured into it would be spotted immediately, and if he tried to run away the archers would be ordered to fire.

It was time for the guard to be changed.

At the head of ten archers, the commander headed for the watchtower, where torches were being lit. The change was usually carried out quickly, the guard gladly changing places with their replacements and heading for the dining-chamber at top speed.

Tonight, however, something most unusual was going on. The archers still on guard were talking in raised voices, apparently on the verge of an argument, and did not come down.

'What's going on up there?' demanded the commander.

'Come up here, sir. We're not coming out.'

The officer climbed the steps four at a time.

In the watchtower a soldier with a bloody nose was lying flat on his back. Two of his comrades were having great difficulty in controlling his attacker, who was foaming at the mouth like a mad bull.

'Do my eyes deceive me?' said the commander furiously. 'Have you been neglecting your duty and fighting among yourselves?'

'It was him,' mumbled the injured man, 'it was him. He's crazy – he hit me for no reason.'

'Not for no reason!' roared the other man. 'You stole from me, you piece of filth!'

'I don't want to hear another word,' snapped the commander. 'You will both appear before the military court, and we shall find out what really happened.'

One of the other archers turned for a last look across the plains of Canaan. What he saw in the moonlight astounded him.

'Commander,' he said urgently, 'look over there. There's a man running away.'

'Fire,' ordered the officer. 'All of you fire – and don't miss him!'

*

Ikcr was still close to the fort when the first arrow whistled past his ear. A second later another grazed his shoulder. He was glad he had been trained as a runner in the harsh terrain of the Oryx province, because it meant he never got out of breath. Zig-zagging as he ran, he forced the pace by concentrating on the distance.

The sinister whistling of arrows became more spaced out, and the intensity diminished. Then there was nothing but the regular sound of his feet striking the ground. Iker had made it across the border, safe and sound!

He did not slacken his speed, in case a patrol was sent after him. But he thought that unlikely: it was dark, and the commander would not leave himself short of men, for he would be on watch for others trying to find a way through.

All he had to do now was reach Sichem.

By biting him on the face, the giant ant woke Iker up, thus saving his life.

Two unshaven men were approaching the bush in whose shelter Iker had slept for a few hours. They thought they were being cunning, but they couldn't keep silent.

'There's something there, I tell you,' said one of them.

'A heap of rags, probably.'

'And supposing there's a man inside the rags? Take a closer look.'

'It looks like somebody with his travelling-baggage.'

'That's more like it.'

'He may not want to give it to us.'

'Would you want to give your things away?'

'You're out of your mind!'

'There's no need to talk to him. Just knock him out and see if there's anything worth taking. If we hit him hard enough, he won't remember a thing.'

Just as the men were preparing to spring, Iker stood up, brandishing the guardian spirit's knife.

'Don't move,' he ordered, 'or I'll cut your hamstrings.'

One man fell to his knees in alarm, while the other took a step backwards.

'You look as if you're serious! You're not a desert guard or a soldier, are you?'

'No, but I know how to handle weapons. Were you really going to rob me?'

'Oh no!' exclaimed the fellow on his knees. 'We just wanted to help you.'

'Don't you know that thieves are sentenced to hard labour and murderers to death?'

'We're only poor peasants looking for something to eat. It's not much fun around here, you know.'

'I thought General Nesmontu had made this area prosperous again.'

The two crooks exchanged worried looks. 'You're . . . you're Egyptian, aren't you?'

'Correct.'

'And you work for the general?'

'Incorrect.'

'Then what are you doing here?'

'I'm trying to escape from him.'

'You mean you're a deserter?'

'Something like that.'

'Where do you want to go?'

'To join the men who are fighting against the general and for the liberation of Canaan.'

'That's more than a little bit dangerous!'

'Aren't you supporters of the Herald?'

The man on his knees got up and huddled against his partner in crime. 'We don't get too involved in things like that.'

'A little bit involved though, eh?'

'A very little bit – a very, very little bit – even less than that.'

'Your "less than that" might earn you a fat fee.'

'Could you be more specific, friend?'

'A copper ingot.'

The two crooks almost drooled. An absolute fortune! They could drink to their hearts' content and enjoy all the girls in the ale-houses.

'This is your lucky day, friend.'

'Take me to the Herald's camp,' said Iker, without too much optimism.

'Are you dreaming? Nobody knows where it is.'

'You must know some of his supporters.'

'We might . . . But how can we be sure you're an honest lad?'

'Because of the copper ingot.'

'Nobody can say your arguments aren't convincing.'

'Then lead on and I'll follow you.'

'Give us the ingot first.'

'Do you take me for a fool? First you guide me to the Herald's supporters, and then I pay you. Otherwise, it's goodbye and I'll manage on my own.'

'We'll have to discuss it.'

'All right, but do it quickly.'

The pair began a lively discussion. One advocated caution, the other profit. Eventually they reached a compromise.

'The best place,' said the cautious one, 'is Sichem. In the countryside there's a risk of nasty surprises, but in town we have our hiding-places.'

'Don't the guards and the army patrol the town?'

'Of course they do, but they can't keep watch on every single house. We know people in Sichem who'll be able to take you to the Herald.'

'Let's go straight there, then.'

'Keep your distance, friend – we know what Egyptians are like. And if you're caught and arrested, we don't know you.'

'Bearing in mind what you're earning, let's not say things like that.'

'What are you thinking of? If you're caught, we'll have worked for nothing!'

This cry from the heart reassured Iker.

They travelled by an indirect route, made numerous stops and, once in sight of the town, actually moved away from it, before entering via a humble district where the hovels rivalled each other in poverty.

The two men greeted old men seated on the doorsteps of their poor dwellings, and the old folk returned the courtesy. It was clear that the pair were not unknown here.

Suddenly, several children surrounded Iker. 'You aren't from here, are you?'

'Stand aside.'

'Answer, or we'll stone you.'

Iker had no wish to fight children, but these did not seem to be joking.

One of the crooks dispersed the mob with a series of kicks. 'Keep watch further off,' he ordered. 'This one's with us.'

The children immediately scampered off.

Iker followed his guides to a house with dirty walls. Outside was a heap of manure, on which an old woman was crouching, empty-eyed and covered in rags. A donkey was tied to a stake in the burning sunshine, with a rope so short it could scarcely move.

'You should at least give it something to drink,' said Iker.

'It's only an animal. Go inside.'

'Who lives here?'

'The people you're looking for.'

'I'd like to be certain.'

'We're honest fellows. Now you must pay us.'

The situation was becoming tense. Iker took a copper ingot from his bag, and a greedy hand seized it at once.

'Go on, go inside.'

Iker opened the door and saw a dirty room with a beaten-earth floor. It smelt so bad that he paused on the theshold, trying not to breathe in. But a hard shove in the back thrust him into the room and the door slammed shut behind him. In the half-light he saw ten Canaanites, armed with forks and mattocks, facing him.

A bearded man with a mop of filthy hair addressed the new arrival. 'What's your name?'

'Iker.'

'Where have you come from?'

'From Memphis.'

'Are you Egyptian?'

'Yes, but I oppose Senusret's tyranny. I helped my Asian friends in Kahun, and tried to kill Senusret, but I failed. Since then I've been in hiding, hoping for a chance to find my friends again one day. The only way I could escape from the guards hunting me was to get through the King's Walls and take refuge in Canaan. I want to take up the fight against the oppressor again. If the Herald will accept me as one of his followers, I won't disappoint him.'

'Who told you about him?'

'My Asian friends. His reputation is growing and growing everywhere – the pharaoh and his circle are beginning to be afraid. Many other Egyptians will soon rally to the Herald's cause.'

'How did you get through the King's Walls?'

'I chose an isolated fort and crossed at night. The archers fired at me, and I was grazed on the left shoulder,' and he showed the men his wound.

'He must have done it on himself,' said a Canaanite accusingly. 'I don't like the look of this Egyptian – he's probably a spy.'

'If I were,' said Iker, 'would I have been stupid enough to throw myself into the jackal's mouth like this? I've risked my life several times to defend your country, and I'll never give up as long as it remains oppressed.'

One of the mob of children appeared and whispered a few

words in the leader's ear, then ran off again.

'Well, you did come alone, and nobody followed you,' said the bearded man.

'That doesn't prove anything,' argued one of the others. 'Let's be sensible and kill him.'

The atmosphere became menacing.

'Don't do anything hasty,' warned Iker. 'I'm a scribe, and I know a lot about about what goes on in Memphis and about palace customs. I can give you valuable help.'

This caused disagreement among the Canaanites. Several judged him sincere and declared themselves willing to accept him, but two hot-heads continued to demand his execution.

'We need to think about this,' the bearded man told Iker. 'Until we've made our decision, you're our prisoner. If you try to escape you'll be killed.'

6

Isis entered the shrine in Senusret's temple where the golden ship of Osiris had been placed. The shrine was permanently guarded, and provided a secure shelter. Only the royal couple, the permanent priests and the young priestess had access to the shrine to carry out rites there. In the absence of Pharaoh and the Great Royal Wife, Isis brought back life to the ship which, because of the acacia's sickness, lacked energy vital to the celebration of the Mysteries. Only the call to the voices of its different elements was keeping it alive.

Gently and reverently, Isis removed the cloth veiling the matchless relic.

'Your prow is the torso of the Lord of the West, Osiris reborn, your deck that of the god Min, the regenerative fire. Your eyes are those of the spirit capable of seeing the Great One. Your rudder is made up of the divine couple of the city of God. Your double mast is the single star that rends the clouds, your fore-rigging the great brightness, your aft rigging the mane of Mafdet the she-panther, guardian of the House of Life, your starboard rigging the right arm of the Creator, Atum, your port rigging his left arm, your cabin the sky-goddess, equipped with her powers, your oars the arms of Horus when he travels.'[1]

[1]Indications given by Chapter 398 of the Sarcophagus Texts (in Paul Barguet's translation).

40

For a few moments, the gold seemed to be brightened by an intense light. The entire shrine was illuminated, the ceiling was transformed into a starry sky, and the ship once more sailed across the heavens. Then darkness fell again, the gold grew dull and the movement stopped.

Until the acacia grew green again and Abydos possessed the gold of the gods, Isis could do no more. At least the words of knowledge were preserving the unity of the ship and preventing it from disintegrating.

Her task completed, Isis went to check that North Wind had enough food. Then, as she did every day, she went for a long walk with him along the edge of the fields. Always willing to carry a load, the donkey was finally winning round even the hardened doubters. He, the creature of Set, was establishing himself as a good spirit protecting the site, and everyone recognized that Isis had been right to attempt the experiment.

'Iker must have passed through the King's Walls,' she ventured.

North Wind raised his right ear.

'So he is in Canaan.'

The donkey confirmed that this was so.

'He is alive, isn't he?'

The right ear sprang vigorously up again.

'You never lie. So he's alive, but is he in danger?'

The answer was, again, in the affirmative.

'I shouldn't be thinking of him,' she whispered, 'at least, not so much . . . And he asked me for an answer. Is it reasonable to love a priestess of Abydos? And do I have the right to love a Royal Son? My life is unfolding here, and nowhere else, and I must carry out my duties unfailingly. Do you understand, North Wind?'

There was great tenderness in the big brown eyes.

Bega contemplated the palm of his right hand, in the hollow of which a tiny head of Set was permanently imprinted, with its large ears and characteristic snout. This emblem united the three confederates of the god of destruction and violence, Bega himself, Medes, secretary of the King's House, and Medes's henchman Gergu.

Bega was a permanent priest at Abydos. He, who had sworn to serve Osiris all his life, was betraying his god. The pharaoh had humiliated him by not appointing him superior of Abydos and entrusting him with the key to the great Mysteries, even though Bega deserved it. He had led an exemplary life, his skills were acknowledged by everyone, and his austerity and meticulousness were worthy of the highest praise. Nobody, not even the Shaven-headed One, could equal him.

Senusret's failure to recognize Bega's talents was an intolerable insult, for which he would pay dearly. Bega, breaking his solemn vows, hating what he had once worshipped, now burnt to see the tyrant dead. And the king's death would be followed by that of all Egypt, following the annihilation of Abydos, the country's living heart. Icy as a winter wind, tall, his unattractive face dominated by a prominent nose, Bega gloated over how his vengeance would destroy Osiran spirituality, the base upon which each pharaoh built his people and his country.

In the depths of his rage and bitterness, Bega had met the Herald and, with the brutal force of a storm, evil had taken control of his mind. Bega felt nothing but contempt for his allies, Medes and Gergu, even though Medes was both forceful and determined in his perverted way. However, when faced with the Herald he had behaved like a frightened little boy, submissive and compelled to obey. He, Bega, despite his age and experience, had offered not the slightest resistance: the greatness of the power of Set was far beyond anything he could imagine.

Since his act of allegiance to the darkness, the priest had felt reassured. By placing a curse upon the Acacia of Osiris, the Herald had demonstrated his powers: he alone would be able to bring down the pharaoh and empty Abydos of its substance. Because he knew part of the secrets of Osiris, Bega was a privileged participant, and was playing a key part, in the conspiracy of evil.

When he came out of the shrine after performing his ritual service, he saw Isis going towards the library of the House of Life.

He went over to her and asked, 'How are you progressing with your research?'

'More slowly than I could wish, but I haven't given up hope. The ancient texts have already provided me with valuable clues.'

'Fortunately, the acacia has not degenerated any more. We all admire what you have achieved.'

'I have done very little,' said Isis. 'It is the mirror of Hathor that deserves our admiration: its radiance ensures that the sap continues to circulate.'

'Nevertheless, I am delighted to say that your reputation is growing all the time.'

'My only concern is the survival of Abydos.'

'You are becoming a vital element in this relentless war against the forces of darkness.'

'All I do is carry out the wishes of the pharaoh and the Shaven-headed One. If I fail, another priestess of Hathor will replace me.'

'We are all concerned about the condition of the ship of Osiris,' said Bega. 'If it stays motionless, how will the energy of resurrection be diffused?'

'We must deal with the most urgent matter first, by preventing its disintegration.'

'But the results so far have been meagre, we must admit.'

'At least the ship's soul is still present among us. What more can we hope for at present?'

'It is difficult not to give up and lose hope. But thanks to you, Isis, the permanent priests still want to believe that all is not lost.'

'We benefit from the unshakeable determination of an exceptional king. As long as he reigns, victory will be within our reach.'

'May Osiris protect us!'

Bega watched Isis enter the library. She would work there for the rest of the day and part of the night, leaving the coast clear for him to prepare for his next transaction: today Gergu, Medes's henchman, was arriving.

To stave off the boredom of the journey, Gergu had got drunk on strong beer. Before he left, a Syrian prostitute had relieved his tension a little, though she had protested at the few slaps he gave her. He thoroughly enjoyed beating women and, had Medes not intervened on his behalf, the official complaints lodged by his three successive wives – all of whom had divorced him – would have ensured that he went to prison. Medes had formally forbidden him to marry again, so he had to make do with low-ranking whores who were in no position to make a fuss.

Initially a collector of taxes and levies, Gergu had been appointed principal inspector of granaries, again thanks to Medes, whose faithful and devoted servant he was. This post enabled him to hold honest managers to ransom by threatening them with all manner of penalties for non-existent faults, and also to build up a network of petty criminals which was earning him a small fortune through thefts of grain. A heavy eater and drinker, Gergu would have been happy to carry on living this easy life, but Medes had other ambitions.

Since meeting the Herald, Medes wanted not only to overthrow Senusret but also to seize the country's riches and promote the all-powerfulness of a new god, whose worship had the advantage of ensuring that women were reduced to their true status, that of inferior creatures. This highly dangerous plan terrified Gergu. However, it was out of the question to disobey Medes – and much less the Herald, who executed traitors with appalling savagery. He must therefore follow the movement while taking as many precautions as possible so as not to leave himself too exposed.

Gergu went so regularly to Abydos that he had been granted the rank of temporary priest there. This made it much easier to carry on the illicit trade devised by his accomplice, Bega. Gergu would never have dreamt that a man initiated into the Mysteries of Osiris would be overcome by greed, but this was the most profitable business deal of his whole career, so he was not going to turn up his nose at it.

When the boat pulled in to the landing-stage at Abydos, Gergu greeted the guards. They exchanged friendly words, congratulating themselves on the fact that all was quiet. Given the strict and extensive security system imposed by the king, they agreed, Abydos really had nothing to fear.

As usual, Gergu was overseeing a delivery of food, pieces of fabric, ointments, sandals and other necessities for the town and temple, which Bega had officially requested. The two men had long meetings, ostensibly to check the list of goods delivered and prepare for the next order. In reality, they spent most of their time dealing with a trade which was absolutely secret and much more lucrative.

When the lists of goods had been dealt with, Bega took Gergu to the terrace of the Great God. They walked along the processional way, which was deserted outside festival periods. The festivities would not be celebrated again for a long time – if ever.

On either side of the roadway leading to the staircase of Osiris were many shrines. They contained statues and stelae whose purpose was to link their owners' souls to the eternity of the Reborn One. Only a select few people were authorized, after being initiated, to live on in this way: by forming Osiris's court in this world and the world beyond.

Silence and tranquillity surrounded the shrines, which were anchored in the invisible world. No outsider, no member of the forces of order, ever disturbed the quiet of the place. So a devilish idea had come to Bega: to smuggle out of Abydos small consecrated stelae, of inestimable value, and sell them for enormous prices to the best buyers, who were only too happy to acquire their share of immortality. And he did not stop there: by giving his accomplices a seal and revealing the words to be engraved on the stelae, he enabled them to make clever imitations, which they sold without difficulty.

Bega no longer had any doubts about what he was doing. On one hand, he was at last getting rich, after many years of asceticism in the service of Osiris. On the other, by removing some sacred stones, albeit modest ones, he was weakening Abydos's magic.

'This burial-ground always makes me uneasy,' confessed Gergu. 'I feel as if the dead are watching me.'

'If you're afraid of them,' said Bega scornfully, 'stop trading with me. But even if they are watching there's nothing they can do to you – I've proved that. Believe me, Gergu, they have no power. They're inert, reduced to the state of rocks and ores, whereas we are very much alive.'

Despite this encouragement, Gergu was eager to get away from the terrace of the Great God. Osiris always watched over his faithful, and thefts from them would certainly arouse his anger.

'How shall we go about it?'

'In the usual way,' replied Bega. 'I've chosen a superb little stele in the middle of a group of twenty right at the back of a shrine – no one even remembers they're there. Come with me, and we'll remove it.'

Although the monuments, which were fronted by small gardens, contained no mummies, Gergu felt as if he was desecrating a tomb. He wrapped the hieroglyph-covered stone in a white cloth and carried it a little way out into the desert. Sweat stood out on his brow, not because of the effort but because he was afraid that the magic with which the stele was imbued might attack him. Hurriedly, he buried it in the sand and rejoined Bega.

'I trust,' said Bega, 'that there will be no problem with the next stage?'

'No, no,' promised Gergu. 'I've bribed the guard who'll be on duty tonight. He'll dig up the stele and pass it on to the captain of a boat heading for Memphis.'

'I'm relying on you, Gergu. Don't make any mistakes.'

'I shan't – there's a lot of money at stake.'

'Don't let yourself be blinded by profit. The objective the Herald has set us is much more lofty, and you had better remember that.'

'But if we aim too high, isn't there a risk of missing the target altogether?'

Suddenly Gergu's right hand became painful. He looked at it and saw that the tiny head of Set on his palm was turning red.

'Don't even think of betraying us,' warned Bega, 'or the Herald will kill you.'

7

The third session of Iker's interrogation was beginning, led
by the Canaanite rebel who was most hostile to him. In their
first two sessions, his captors had not been able to reach a
final decision about him.

Iker was growing no more accustomed to the stench and
the filth of his surroundings. His adventure had begun badly
and seemed likely to end prematurely.

'Confess that you're a spy in the pharaoh's pay,'
demanded the Canaanite.

'You won't change your mind, no matter what I say, so
what is the point of denying it?'

'What is your real mission?'

'I won't know until the Herald entrusts me with it.'

'Do you know where he is and how many men he has?'

'If I knew, I'd be with him.'

'What are General Nesmontu's battle plans?'

'I'd like to know, so that I could disrupt them.'

'Tell us about the palace at Memphis.'

'I'll give that information to the Herald and to nobody else.
When he learns how you've treated me, you'll pay for it. By
keeping me here, you're losing our cause precious time.'

The Canaanite spat on Iker, then tore off the amulet the
young man wore round his neck and stamped on it in fury.

'Now you haven't got any protection, you filthy traitor!

Right, men, let's torture him. Bring me the knife he was hiding. He'll soon talk – you'll see.'

Iker shivered. Dying was frightening enough, but to suffer like that . . . However, he would not talk. Whatever he said, his torturer would persevere. Best to let him believe he was mistaken, and perhaps attract the sympathy of the other rebels.

The Canaanite brandished the knife and passed its blade under the young man's nose. 'You're afraid, aren't you?'

'Of course I am. And I don't understand why I'm being put through all this.'

'First I shall slash your chest. Next I shall cut off your nose. Lastly, I shall cut off your testicles. When I've finished, you will no longer be a man. So, traitor, do you confess?'

'I demand to be taken to the Herald.'

'You're going to tell me everything, you dog of a spy!'

The first bloody gash tore a cry of pain from the Royal Son. He was bound hand and foot, and could do nothing to defend himself.

The blade was slicing into his flesh again when the door of the rebels' hiding-place burst open and the lookout shouted, 'Soldiers! Run for it, quick—' An arrow took him between the shoulder-blades, and he fell to the ground.

Twenty soldiers poured into the stinking building and cut down every single one of the Canaanites.

'What do we do with this one, sir?' asked a soldier, pointing at Iker.

'Untie him and take him with us. The general will welcome the chance to interrogate a rebel fighter.'

Officially, Iker was being held at the main barracks, where General Nesmontu, delighted to have captured one of the Herald's supporters at last, was interrogating him so brutally that nobody else was allowed to be present.

The old general had been a soldier all his adult life. He was a stocky man, gruff and plain-speaking, who was indifferent to honours and liked to live among his men. He never balked at hard work, and despite his years he often wore out men much younger than himself.

'It's only a superficial wound,' he told Iker, applying an ointment to it. 'With this, you'll soon heal.'

'If it hadn't been for you . . .'

'I know these barbarians' practices and I was beginning to worry about how long they'd held you – evidently you hadn't convinced them. You were lucky: my men might have arrived too late.'

The young man's nerves gave way, and his shoulders began to shake.

'Cry if you need to,' said Nesmontu. 'It will make you feel better. And don't worry, even heroes panic when faced with torture. Now, drink this fine old wine from my vineyard in the Delta. No sickness can hold out against it. Drink two cups a day, and you'll be fortified against fatigue.'

The wine did indeed fortify Iker, and he gradually stopped shaking.

'You don't lack courage,' said the general, 'but you're up against fearsome enemies – they're worse than savage beasts – and you don't seem to me to be cut out for this kind of mission. All the volunteers who've tried to infiltrate the rebel ranks have died hideous deaths, and you almost did, too. I strongly advise you to go back to Memphis.'

'But I haven't achieved anything yet,' protested Iker.

'You've survived, and that's an achievement in itself.'

'I think I can turn this incident to my advantage, General.'

Nesmontu was surprised. 'How?'

'I'm a rebel, and you arrested, interrogated and sentenced me. Have it made known, so that nobody doubts my commitment to the Canaanite cause. My allies will probably try to free me from prison before I'm executed.'

'You're asking too much. My prison is secure, and its

reputation must not be damaged. There's a simpler solution: the cage.'

'What's that?'

'You'll be sentenced to forced labour, and you'll have to be transported from Sichem to the place where you'll serve your sentence. Before that's done, you'll be shut in a cage, which will be pulled through the town so that everyone is made aware of what will happen to them if they attack the Egyptian authorities. The cage's armed escort will leave it unguarded for a little while during a halt. If the rebels want to free you, that will be the ideal opportunity.'

'It's perfect, General.'

'Listen, my boy, I could be your grandfather. You may be the Royal Son, but I won't bow and scrape, or waste time on false reassurance. First, your plan will never work. Second, even if it did, you'd be plunging into the heart of an absolute furnace. Wasn't your recent experience enough for you? Give up, and go back to Egypt.'

'I can't, General.'

'Why not?'

'Because I must expiate my past wrongs, obey the pharaoh and save the Tree of Life. As things stand, the only hope we have is finding the Herald.'

'My very best men have tried, but they all failed.'

'So we must use a different method, and that's why I'm here. My first efforts weren't very successful, I admit, but how could they be otherwise? Actually, on reflection, I don't think the results are so bad: when your men rescued me they wiped out one of Sichem's rebel groups, didn't they? I think your suggestion of the cage is an excellent one. Everyone will know I'm a hero of the Canaanite cause, and they'll free me when they see their chance.'

'But will they take you to the Herald?'

'Everything in good time, General. Let's take this step first.'

'This is completely insane, Iker!'

'My father trusts me to carry out this mission, and I shall do it.'

His seriousness impressed the old soldier. 'I shouldn't say this, my boy, but in your place I'd do the same.'

'Did you find the knife the Canaanite was torturing me with?'

'Yes – and anyone would think it was the weapon of a guardian spirit. It burnt the hand of the soldier who picked it up.'

'But you can hold it without being harmed?'

'Yes, I can.'

'Isn't that a privilege granted only to the members of the Golden Circle of Abydos?'

'Where did you get that idea? It's merely that my soldiers are afraid of sorcery whereas I am not. You're interested in Abydos, are you?'

'It's the spiritual centre of Egypt.'

'So people say.'

'I'd dearly love to get to know it.'

'Well, you aren't going the right way about it.'

'Who knows? Today, my path takes me by way of Canaan.'

Nesmontu handed him the knife. 'And it doesn't burn your hand, either?'

'No,' said Iker. 'In fact, it gives me new energy.'

'Unfortunately, you won't be able to take it with you. After interrogation, a rebel is put naked into the cage and he may be rather knocked about. Are you still determined to go through with it?'

'More than ever.'

'If you come back alive, I'll return the knife to you.'

'When I've found the Herald's lair, how will we communicate with each other?'

'By any and every means we can think of – though none of

them will be without its risks. If you're admitted into a Canaanite clan, it's bound to be nomadic. At each encampment leave a message in coded writing. Only I will be able to read it, and I'll pass it on to Sobek the Protector, who will give it to His Majesty. Write on anything – a tree-trunk, a stone, a piece of cloth – in the hope that you won't be spotted and that the desert guards will find your message. Try to bribe one of the nomads and promise him a generous fee. If he's loyal to the king, he may come to Sichem to warn me. But if you choose someone who's loyal to the Herald, you'll be a dead man.'

Iker felt hope ebbing away. 'In other words, nothing is sure.'

'Nothing at all, my boy.'

'So I may succeed and fail at the same time – find the Herald but not be able to tell you.'

'That's right. Still determined to try to do the impossible?'

'Yes.'

'We'll have our midday meal here, under the pretext of continuing the interrogation. After that, you won't go to prison but will be put directly into the cage. From that moment, there will be no going back.'

Iker thought about that for a minute. Then he said, 'General, do you trust Sobek-Khu?'

Nesmontu's stomach turned over. 'Like my own self. Why do you ask?'

'He dislikes and distrusts me and—'

'I don't want to hear any more! Sobek is integrity personified and would gladly give his life to save the king. So he's suspicious of you – what could be more normal? By your actions, you'll convince him you deserve his respect. As for the information you and I pass on to him, it won't be divulged to anyone but the king. Sobek loathes the flatterers and deceivers at court, and with good reason. And now enough of that. Let us eat.'

As he ate a succulent rib of beef and drank a fine red wine, Iker came to the conclusion that the general was right: the plan was indeed insane. There were so many hazards and imponderables that he had no chance whatever of succeeding.

8

The cage was placed on a wooden sledge, pulled by two oxen, and displayed in every part of Sichem. It was so constructed that Iker could neither sit down nor stand upright but had to crouch; he gripped the bars and looked covertly at the Canaanites who were watching this dismal sight.

Bruises, skilfully painted, covered the young man's body and showed how cruelly he had been tortured. But General Nesmontu's men had not raided any of the sensitive districts, so the unfortunate prisoner had obviously not talked.

The soldiers in charge of the procession were in no hurry. Every single citizen of Sichem must be made aware of the fate that awaited rebels.

'That poor boy hasn't experienced the worst yet,' whispered an old man. 'Now they're going to send him off to forced labour. He won't last long.'

A heavy silence surrounded the cage as it passed through the town. Some of the Canaanites would have liked to attack the guards and free the prisoner, but nobody dared do it, for fear of terrible reprisals.

Iker kept hoping for a promising sign of future action: a quick gesture or a significant look.

But he saw nothing. Worn down by feelings of powerlessness, the spectators did nothing.

At the end of the cage's circuit, the prisoner was allowed a little water and a stale flatcake. Then the soldiers left Sichem and headed north.

The Herald's two supporters disagreed about what they should do.

'Orders are orders,' the nervous one reminded his companion. 'We must kill the spy.'

'Why should we run such risks?' argued the fair-haired lad. 'The Egyptians will do it for us.'

'You don't know everything.'

'Then tell me.'

'The Herald told me that this man Iker is in league with the Egyptians.'

'That's hardly likely.'

'According to information from Memphis, there is no doubt about it. Not only that, but he's a Royal Son sent here by Senusret to infiltrate our ranks.'

'But he was tortured and put in the cage!'

'That was a ruse arranged by Nesmontu so that the people would think Iker's given his life for our cause.'

The fair-haired lad was devastated to hear this, but had to hide his feelings. He was the only one of Nesmontu's agents to have succeeded in infiltrating a Canaanite clan. He had never met the Herald and was beginning to wonder if he was a mirage. But the rebels' activities were certainly no mirage. Soon, the fair-haired lad would send Nesmontu information which would prevent murders and enable many arrests to be made.

But in the immediate future, he must carry out a mission he had not been expecting. And what he had just learnt had made his task infinitely more complicated.

'You aren't thinking of attacking the convoy, are you?' he said to the nervous man. 'There are only two of us.'

'They won't be watching the cage all the time, because this bogus prisoner is hoping we will intervene. When they pitch camp at nightfall, we'll free him.'

Nesmontu's spy could not oppose an order from the Herald, on pain of being suspected himself. How could he solve this insoluble problem? Either he must take part in the murder of a fellow Egyptian and ally – and a Royal Son to boot – or else he could save him; in which case all those months of effort would have been for nothing, because it would be impossible for him to go back to the clan he had betrayed.

At dusk, the convoy halted near a little wood, and the solders placed the cage at the foot of a tamarisk. They ate their evening meal amid much joking, then fell asleep. There was a sentry on guard, but before long he dozed off.

'You see?' said the nervous man. 'Now's our chance.'

'They might be setting a trap for us,' said the fair-haired lad worriedly.

'Surely not. Everything's happening just as the Herald said it would – he's never wrong.'

'Shouldn't we kill the soldiers first?' The spy hoped that an attempted attack would end in their having to make a hurried escape. But he still had to find a way of warning Iker that he'd been denounced and must abandon his plan.

'Definitely not. They're pretending to be asleep. Let's free the Egyptian.'

The fair-haired lad made up his mind. After they'd freed the Royal Son, he'd kill the nervous man and reveal his true identity. His mission, like Iker's, would have to be aborted, but at least they'd both be alive.

His semi-crouched position was exhausting, but Iker held fast by remembering the words of the sages and thinking of Isis. From time to time, he even felt the urge to laugh: if she could see him in this state, what would she think of his declaration of love?

And then fear returned, insidious and obsessive. What would the rebels do, and how? Would they carry out a massacre? Being confined like this set his nerves on edge. Unable to sleep, he listened for the slightest sound.

Despite the sentry's snores, he heard two men crawling towards him.

The rebels reached the cage and stood up, gesturing to Iker to make not a sound. Then they cut the thick ropes that held the wooden poles together.

At last the Royal Son could emerge from his prison!

Just as the prisoner, his cramped limbs shaking, was preparing to climb out of the cage, the fair-haired lad drew back and stepped behind the nervous man. He drew his knife, but before he could plunge it into the rebel's back, he felt a terrible burning pain in the nape of his neck.

The pain was so fierce that he opened his mouth but could make no sound. He dropped his weapon and fell to his knees. Almost instantly, the same blade slit his throat. Thirteen-Years killed swiftly and well.

'That filth was a traitor in the pay of Nesmontu,' he told the thunderstruck nervous man. 'I am a follower of the Herald.'

'Are you the boy who took a caravan single-handed?'

'I am indeed, but I am not a boy. Bring the traitor's body and let's get away from here.'

'Why bother with the body?'

'I'll explain later.'

Taking Iker with them, they hurried away.

As last they felt they were safe, and stopped to rest. Exhausted, Iker lay down on the ground and closed his eyes, unable to fight off sleep. He must sleep, even if it was only for an hour. He was physically drained, and did not have the strength to fight.

The nervous man dropped his burden on the sand and looked at Iker. 'It'll be easy,' he said.

'What do you mean?' asked Thirteen-Years.

The nervous man drew him aside. 'I have my orders.'

'What orders?'

'Let me carry them out and don't interfere.'

'I want to know what they are.'

'Listen, youngster, you may give yourself airs, but the Herald is our supreme leader.'

'Well, we agree about that.'

'You've killed one traitor, and I am going to kill another.'

'You mean . . . ?'

'This Egyptian isn't a real prisoner. He's loyal to the pharaoh and he's acting a part to make us trust him. Fortunately, we know the truth. He's been freed from his cage only to die. As he's asleep, he won't offer any resistance at all.'

He went over to Iker and knelt down. Just as he was preparing to stab him through the heart, a knife-point sank into his back. His tongue shot out of his mouth like a rearing snake, his limbs stiffened, and he collapsed beside Iker.

'The Herald is indeed our supreme leader,' agreed Thirteen-Years, 'and he ordered me to save Iker.'

The first rays of the rising sun awoke the Royal Son. He was so stiff and sore that he had difficulty standing up. When he did, the first thing he saw was a boy chewing a piece of bacon. The next was two dead bodies, one of which was horrifyingly disfigured: there was only a bloody mess where its face ought to have been. Iker's stomach churned, but there was nothing in it to vomit up.

'What happened?' he asked.

'The fair-haired one was one of General Nesmontu's spies,' said the boy. 'He'd belonged to a Canaanite clan for over a year, but we unmasked him. That's why I killed him.'

Iker shuddered. 'And the other one?'

'A good worker, but very limited. He was going to kill you.'

'And you saved me?'

'I had my orders. I'm called Thirteen-Years, for I shall always bear the age of my first exploit. I'm a loyal follower of the Herald, and have the honour of carrying out delicate and confidential missions for him.'

'And do you know who I am?'

'Your name is Iker, and you're a Royal Son of Senusret, whom you wanted to kill. You were in danger of being arrested in Egypt, so you came to Canaan, hoping to join the rebels.'

'Are you willing to help me?'

'I'll take you to my clan. You can fight with us against the oppressor.'

Iker couldn't believe his ears. This was only a first step, but it was most encouraging.

'Why did you disfigure that man?' he asked.

'Because we only need his body. Take a careful look: same size as you, same build, same type of hair. The only difference is the face, so it had to be destroyed. And I haven't forgotten your two scars: one on the shoulder, the other on the chest. When the Egyptian soldiers find these two bodies, they'll think that both their spies are dead.'

Iker shuddered again. 'Do you think I'm a spy?'

'My clan will transform you into a Canaanite rebel. Iker the Royal Son no longer exists. Your new life is beginning, and it will be devoted to the service of the cause.'

Iker felt sure he'd be able to kill the boy and get back to Sichem. But Thirteen-Years' cruel smile froze him where he stood. Then, as if from nowhere, twenty Canaanites appeared, armed with daggers and spears, and surrounded him.

The soldiers of the main Sichem barracks gazed in horror at the two corpses lying in the courtyard.

Although he had seen many worse sights, General Nesmontu was almost overcome. He had liked the fair-haired lad; an extremely courageous volunteer who had been on the point of reaping the well-earned rewards of his work. But the lad must have made a fatal mistake and given himself away. Infiltrating the Canaanite rebels seemed utterly impossible, and the presence of the second corpse reinforced this feeling of failure.

How could anyone be so cruel as to mutilate a human being like that, even if he was an enemy? The tortured man no longer had a face, but Nesmontu knew only too well who he was.

A lump in his throat, an officer covered the bodies with a white sheet. 'What are your orders, General?'

'Search all suspects in Sichem, and double the patrols in the countryside. As for these two brave fellows, they are to be mummified quickly, then sent home to Memphis.'

'I knew the fair-haired man well,' said the officer, 'but who is the other one?'

Nesmontu walked slowly back to his office to write the message informing Pharaoh Senusret of the tragic death of Iker, the Royal Son.

9

'There's nothing whatsoever wrong with you.'

'But, Doctor Gua,' protested Medes's wife, 'I'm suffering terribly!'

Gua was a small, thin man, who always carried the heavy leather bag that contained his remedies and instruments. It was only with the greatest reluctance that he had left his home in Khemenu, capital of the Hare province, and accompanied the province's former governor, Djehuty, to Memphis; but he was now one of the city's most famous doctors. He was stern with his patients, and constantly criticized their way of life and eating habits, but he treated them nevertheless and the results he obtained meant that his reputation continued to grow.

'You aren't suffering, you're merely experiencing some discomfort because you abuse your body – which is far too fat. If you don't stop eating morning, noon and night, your liver will become blocked, and then, as sure as Ma'at dwells within, you really will suffer: from dizziness and sicknesses, among other things.'

'Please give me some medicine, Doctor,' she begged, 'some pills and soothing draughts.'

'They would be of no use unless you were to adopt a strict diet. Discipline yourself, and then we shall see.'

Gua refused to give in to his patient's pleas and

recriminations, and when she began to scream and cry he simply marched out of the house.

It took all Medes's skill to calm and soothe his wife, but at last she fell asleep. After taking the precaution of locking her bedchamber door, he went to the room he used as an office, where he received his faithful servant Gergu, who had just returned from Abydos.

'Well, Gergu,' he said, 'is our friend Bega still proving cooperative?'

'He wants to get rich, but that isn't enough for him. His bitter hatred for the king is strengthening his determination, but . . .'

'He seems steady enough to me,' objected Medes. 'In fact, his true nature is being revealed: he's being eaten up by greed. Once, he deceived himself by thinking he was serving Osiris and being content with little worldly reward. And now his only master is the Herald. Evil fascinates me, Gergu, for it can do anything at any moment. In an instant, it destroys what it takes Ma'at years to build. When this country, its temples and its society are nothing more than a field of ruins, we shall be able to act as we please.'

Gergu slaked his thirst with some cool white wine. When Medes opened his heart like that, he preferred not to hear. If a court of the afterlife existed, Gergu wanted to be able to tell the judges he hadn't known anything, and that way he would obtain their mercy.

'What have you brought back this time?' asked Medes.

'A magnificent stele depicting Osiris and the sacred words of Abydos linking the deceased to the cult of the ancestors. We'll get a fortune for it!'

'Are your channels completely secure?'

'They should be: they cost enough! I had to buy one of the guards in Abydos, and also to pay one of your messengers – he's transporting the stele on one of your message-service boats, and he wasn't cheap. And Bega insists that we

63

must be cautious and never remove more than one stele at a time.'

'When this transaction is completed, don't forget to oil the hands of our friends the trade-control officers. And you must choose a new storehouse for the timber from Phoenicia.'

Gergu enjoyed the smuggling trade. It involved neither gods nor demons, only a good knowledge of the port administration and of a few indiscreet or corrupt officials.

The sombre atmosphere in the palace surprised Medes. Certainly the pharaoh demanded that scribes and servants should behave correctly, but usually they smiled and were friendly. Today, though, their faces were blank and the silence weighed heavy.

As usual, Medes went to see the Bearer of the Royal Seal to receive his instructions. He found that Sehotep was not in his office, so he asked to speak to High Treasurer Senankh. But Senankh was not in his office, either. His curiosity aroused, Medes requested an audience with the tjaty, who received him almost immediately.

Khnum-Hotep had formerly been governor of the Oryx province and a fierce opponent of Senusret. However, he had eventually come to see the need for the union of Upper and Lower Egypt under the pharaoh's authority, and was now one of that pharaoh's most loyal subjects. An excellent administrator and a hard worker, the tjaty staved off the advance of old age by serving his country with a devotion and skill which everyone admired.

Khnum-Hotep mixed three old wines in his favourite cup, which was decorated with gold leaf and ornamented with lotus petals. Thanks to this youth-renewing potion and to hearty meals, he had more energy than most of his subordinates, who were often unable to keep up with him.

His three dogs, a lively male and two plump bitches, were always with him. Twice a day, they were given a long walk and followed their master who, comfortably seated in a travelling-chair with an adjustable back, continued to work compulsively on his files.

'What is the reason for this visit, Medes?'

'Sehotep and Senankh are both away, and I should like to know if there is anything urgent that I should be doing.'

'Confine yourself to expediting current matters. There will be no meeting of the King's House today.'

'Has something serious happened? The whole palace seems weighed down with sorrow.'

'There has been very bad news from Canaan, and His Majesty is undergoing a terrible ordeal. That is why nobody has the heart to smile.'

'Another rebel uprising?'

'No,' said the tjaty. 'Royal Son Iker has been murdered.'

Medes put on a suitable expression. 'It is my only wish that the guilty parties be caught and punished.'

'General Nesmontu will not be idle, and the king will break the backs of the insurgents.'

'Am I to see to bringing the body home?'

'Sehotep is taking care of it, and Senankh is having a tomb prepared for Iker in Memphis. The funeral ceremonies will be discreet; the enemy must not know how deeply wounded His Majesty is. You and I must see that nothing disturbs the proper functioning of the state.'

As he emerged from Khnum-Hotep's office, Medes felt like singing and dancing. Now that he was rid of Iker, whom he had considered a real danger, he could envisage the future with a much lighter heart. And the Herald, free from the threat of a spy, no longer risked being unearthed.

His hands bound behind his back, Iker had merely changed one prison for another, with no chance of escape. Since Thirteen-Years knew everything about him, his fate was sealed: he faced interrogation, torture and execution.

However, the boy showed no hostility, and even offered his future victim food and drink.

'Don't worry, Iker, you're going to be re-educated. Up to now, you've believed in false values. I haven't saved you for nothing.'

'Before I die, may I at least meet the Herald?'

'You aren't going to die – at least, not today. First you must learn to obey. Then you will fight properly against the tyrant. When you're killed, you will go to paradise.'

The Royal Son pretended to be a broken man. If Thirteen-Years thought him cowed, he might get a chance to escape.

'The pharaoh says the Herald's a criminal,' he said in a deadened voice, 'and that only Egypt can ensure Canaan's prosperity.'

'He's lying!' said Thirteen-Years furiously. 'It's the pharaoh who's the criminal! You've been deceived, but when you join my tribe you'll soon become a new man. Bina says that at first you were a good man, but then you strayed. Either you convert and follow the Herald, or else you'll be fed to the pigs.'

Iker did not doubt it. Trying to make friends with the boy seemed impossible. He was a frightening creature, cruel by nature, and knowing neither remorse nor regret; he killed like a wild animal. It was clearly dangerous to contradict him, because it made him angry. Iker would have to try to deceive him by agreeing with his fanatical words.

The little band carefully avoided contact with the Egyptian desert patrols. It travelled rapidly northwards, thus moving further away from the area more or less controlled by Nesmontu.

Dead and forgotten, Iker walked forward into nothingness.

The landscape resembled neither the Nile Valley nor the Delta. Hidden deep within a forest of thorn-trees, where there was plenty of water, the members of Thirteen-Years's clan lived on game and berries. The women rarely emerged from their huts.

After his recent exploits, the boy had acquired the status of a hero. Even the chief, a bearded man with a squashed nose, hailed him.

'Here is an Egyptian I have captured on the orders of the Herald,' Thirteen-Years declared proudly.

'Why didn't you kill him?'

'Because he's been sentenced to help us.'

'An Egyptian, helping Canaanites?'

'The Herald has decided to re-educate him and transform him into a weapon for use against his own countrymen. You will be in charge of his education.'

An enormous hound loped up to its master. Staring at the stranger, it growled so menacingly that even Thirteen-Years was worried.

'Calm down, Flesh-Eater,' said the chief.

The dog did not take its eyes off the prisoner, but it growled a little more quietly.

'I'm not interested in all these stories,' said the chief. 'What I need is a slave who can make bread with the grain we steal from the Egyptians. If he can't do it, I'll give him to the dog.'

Iker had been brought up in the village of Madu in the countryside, and had performed many of the tasks of daily life. He had often helped the baker in Madu to prepare flatcakes.

He said, 'Give me the things I need.'

'Don't disappoint me, boy.'

'I'm going back to the Herald,' announced Thirteen-Years.

'Get to work, slave!' snapped the chief, delighted with this unexpected help.

Hour followed hour, each more exhausting than the last. With the aid of a bushel, Iker measured out the necessary quantity of grain, which he sieved into an earthenware mortar. Then, with a coarse pestle, he crushed the grains to separate them from their husks and produce flour – its quality, despite several siftings, left something to be desired. Next, he moistened it and kneaded it for a long time until he obtained a rather unsatisfactory dough. The delicate phases were the addition of the right amount of salt and the baking, on carefully tended coals. As for the shape of the loaves, that depended upon the cracked moulds, which had been stolen from caravans. He had neither the right equipment nor the touch of a real baker, but as the days passed he tried hard to improve.

His daily work also included carrying water and cleaning the camp. By the evening Iker was half dead with tiredness, and he slept heavily until he was dragged out again as soon as dawn broke.

Several times he almost gave up hope, convinced that he could not go on. But he still had a grain of willpower left and, watched with amusement by the Canaanites, he began his pitiless toil once again. However, at the end of one stifling day, he was so exhausted that he collapsed in front of the bread oven, almost serenely awaiting the fatal blow that would deliver him from this abominable existence.

A soft tongue licked his face. In his own way, Flesh-Eater was comforting him. This unexpected demonstration of friendship saved the Royal Son. He got up, and from that moment his body bore the ordeal more easily. Instead of destroying him, the forced labour made him harder.

When the chief saw his dog accompanying the prisoner and defending him against one of his henchmen, who wanted to beat him, he was stunned. A born killer, Flesh-Eater ought to have torn the slave apart. To have tamed him like this, Iker must have magical powers. Moreover, Iker should long since have collapsed and died, but he had not . . .

Nobody, not even the chief of a Canaanite clan, made mock of a magician, for at his death he would be bound to put a spell on his torturers. Iker would have to be treated a little less harshly, though without the chief losing face. The tribe would be moving to another refuge soon – they had stayed here too long already – and the right opportunity might arise then.

Iker was ordered to prepare the provisions for the journey. He obeyed with his usual docility. If he had any thoughts of escape, he was making a big mistake. Flesh-Eater ate fugitives.

10

Using the secure and efficient network set up by Gergu, a new stele had been removed from Abydos without anyone noticing. Bega knew all the shrines and their contents, so he could lay hands on many treasures to sell. And at some time in the future, he would sell some of the secrets of the Mysteries of Osiris. Doing so would be a final, irrevocable violation of his oath, but that did not trouble him now that he was a confederate of Set and follower of the Herald. When the priesthood was wiped out, he would be the first to know the ultimate secrets, to which he did not yet have access.

Within the sacred city, nobody suspected him. The Shaven-headed One approved of his diligence, and did not suspect for a moment that his main desire was to destroy Abydos.

The person Bega was most wary of was Isis, whose rise was far from over. She seemed indifferent to power and honours, but would her attitude change? To prevent any unpleasant surprises, Bega watched her closely. He saw nothing unexpected: she carried out her ritual tasks, spent long hours in the library of the House of Life, meditated in the temple, conversed with her colleagues and looked after her donkey, who had not yet misbehaved once.

She went to Memphis sometimes, but otherwise she never left the domain of spirituality. Soon, Bega was resolved, that domain would be reduced to nothing. The pharaoh owed most of his power to the Mysteries of Osiris. Once the Tree of Life was dead and the sacred ship had disintegrated, Senusret would be no more than a vacillating, vulnerable despot, to whom the Herald would deliver a fatal blow.

If the king had recanted his mistake, and recognized Bega's true worth, the latter might perhaps have given up his quest for vengeance. But since the meeting with the Herald, it was too late to go back.

'You are on duty in Senusret's temple,' the Shaven-headed One informed him.

'Will the other permanent priests be on duty, too?'

'Each will work in the place I have assigned to him. Tomorrow morning we shall resume the normal course of the rites.'

Bega understood: the Golden Circle was to meet. Why had the brotherhood not coopted him? This additional humiliation strengthened his determination to prove his own importance, even if the path he took drew him once and for all away from Ma'at.

The moment Senusret appeared, everyone knew that this was the pharaoh. He was a giant of a man with a stern face, big ears, heavy eyelids and prominent cheekbones; and his gaze was so piercing that nobody could bear it.

Sobek the Protector, the commander of all the guards forces in the kingdom, had tried in vain to persuade the king not to travel. Ensuring his safety in Memphis was difficult enough, but travel posed insoluble problems. Six hand-picked officers, rigorously trained by the Protector himself, guarded the pharaoh at all times. They would intercept anyone who might threaten the king.

It was another source of worry when Senusret celebrated the rites alone in the innermost shrine of a temple, or gave private audiences. In Sobek's eyes everyone was suspect, and

71

the two attempts on the king's life had reinforced his attitude. Perpetually wary, and a light sleeper, he did not want to leave anything to chance.

Sobek-Khu knew that his enemies hoped to sully his reputation and discredit him in Senusret's eyes. The last scheme, probably hatched by a circle of courtiers whom he hated every bit as much as they hated him, had failed, and he had been retained and even strengthened in his post.

Sobek was furious that he could not dismantle the network of Canaanite rebels who, he was sure, were continuing to establish themselves in Memphis and perhaps elsewhere, too. A good many of these criminals had, it was true, gone back to their native land, but others remained integrated into the general population. So far they were acting with the utmost caution, but how long would they be content to stay crouching in their lairs? What hideous crimes were they planning?

One particular dignitary had always annoyed the Protector a great deal: the scribe Iker. The young man had once tried to kill Senusret, and his subsequent repentance seemed thoroughly unconvincing. Although Iker had been awarded the prestigious title of Royal Son, Sobek was deeply suspicious of him, and believed that he was still in league with the Canaanites.

Now, however, that threat at least had disappeared, because Iker's mutilated body had just been interred in the burial-ground at Memphis.

Sobek checked that the area was cordoned off. No temporary priest would enter it while the permanent priests were officiating in Senusret's temple of a million years. Moreover, the guards would be patrolling the streets of Enduring Places.

The king could therefore safely hold a meeting of the Golden Circle in one of the halls of the Temple of Osiris.

Four offering-tables had been placed at the four cardinal points. To the east sat Pharaoh and the Great Royal Wife; to the west were the Shaven-headed One, Djehuty, mayor of Dahshur, where the royal pyramid was being built, and the empty chair of General Sepi; to the south, Tjaty Khnum-Hotep, High Treasurer Senankh and Sekari; to the north were Royal Seal-Bearer Sehotep and General Nesmontu.

The king gave the Shaven-headed One permission to speak.

'No new curse has damaged the Tree of Life,' he said, 'but it is not recovering. The magical defensive measures we are taking have proved effective, but I fear that our enemy will eventually break through them.'

'Has Isis's intervention helped?' asked the queen.

'Yes, Majesty. With the mirror of Hathor, she has managed to give a little energy back to the acacia. But all our care has produced only partial results, and I fear that the tree may suddenly degenerate further.'

The Shaven-headed One's gloomy words did not dim the basic optimism of the elegant and well-born Sehotep, whose handsome face and sparkling eyes had seduced many of the prettiest women in the land. He safeguarded not only the secrets of the temples but the prosperity of the country's livestock. He could see the link between spiritual and material preoccupations, as he did in his other role as overseer of all Pharaoh's building works. And in that capacity he had some reassurance to offer the Circle.

'Thanks to Djehuty's hard work,' he said, 'the work at Dahshur will soon be completed. The pyramid emanates *ka*, which ensures the stability of the pharaoh's reign and nourishes the Tree of Life. We have certainly taken harsh blows, some of which could have been fatal, but now we have moved on to the offensive. By building the pyramid, we have weakened the enemy.'

Djehuty had once been governor of the Hare province. He was old now, and suffered from aching joints; and he felt the cold, so he was always wrapped in a large cloak. He kept death at bay by placing himself at the service of the king. Every night when he went to bed he was sure he would never be able to get up again. In the morning, the desire to continue his work gave him new strength, and he went back to the site with undiminished enthusiasm. Initiation into the Golden Circle had strengthened his heart, and he, supervisor of the Mysteries of Thoth and a priest of Ma'at, marvelled at the sheer extent of the Osiran secret. By granting him this immense privilege, Senusret had lit up the twilight of a long life.

He said, 'My work is nearly done, Majesty. Dahshur has been brought into the world according to the plan drawn by your own hand, and you shall shortly consecrate its birth.'

'The site's security seems assured,' added Tjaty Khnum-Hotep. 'I consulted General Nesmontu over the choice of officer to command the garrison, and I guarantee that a rebel attack would fail.'

Knowing how much Khnum-Hotep hated boastfulness, the Golden Circle was reassured.

The king asked, 'Has there been any progress in the investigation into the death of General Sepi?'

'Unfortunately not,' said Senankh. 'Our teams of miners are hoping to gather information and discover the location of the healing gold, but so far they have had no success.'

It was Nesmontu's turn to speak; there were deep new lines on his sunburnt face. 'The plan devised by Royal Son Iker has failed. We were aware of the dangers of his mission, and I tried to dissuade him, but he was immovable. We therefore decided to attempt the venture by making him pass as one of the terrorists' allies.'

'How?' asked Sekari, very sadly.

'By subjecting him to the humiliation of being displayed in a cage drawn through the streets of Sichem. We reserve this treatment for fanatics, so the Canaanites could have been in no doubt that Iker was one of their own.'

'What happened next?' asked the king.

'Like any criminal sentenced to forced labour, Iker was to be transferred to a camp where he would work out his punishment. The guards had been ordered to let the Canaanites free the prisoner. The plan worked well up to that point, but what happened afterwards was a disaster.'

'How did that come about?'

'I do not know the details, Majesty. A desert patrol discovered the bodies of Iker and the only one of my agents to have infiltrated the Canaanite ranks. I must add, alas, that the Royal Son had been tortured with savage cruelty.'

'Does someone want us to believe they killed each other?' asked Sehotep.

'Probably. I assume that they were ambushed, and my agent had no doubt been ordered to kill Iker if they were identified. After his execution, the Canaanites abandoned the bodies in plain sight, to demonstrate that no Egyptian can deceive them. Of course, after this terrible failure, I am presenting my resignation to His Majesty.'

'And I am refusing it. Your agent and Iker knew the risks, and you are in no way responsible for this tragedy. Driving you from your post would demoralize our army.'

All the members of the Golden Circle agreed.

'There can be no doubt,' said Senankh, 'that these two brave men were betrayed.'

'That's impossible,' objected Nesmontu. 'I was the only person who knew of their mission.'

'In that case,' retorted the High Treasurer, 'either your agent did something unwise, or else a Canaanite identified him. As for Iker, many courtiers must have noticed his absence. A Royal Son, especially one only recently appointed, does not leave the court without serious reasons.'

'Yes,' said Sehotep, 'but from that to concluding that he had been sent to Canaan is an enormous step.'

'Not so enormous if there is a rebel network in Memphis.

It would be aware of everything we do, and Iker's absence would certainly not go unnoticed. In their place, I would have informed my allies and told them to watch for him.'

'If you are right,' said the tjaty, 'Iker's mission had failed before it even began. Moreover, we would have to assume that the enemy has informants at court. Are they acting deliberately, or are they merely stupid?'

'I think the second possibility is more likely,' said Sehotep, 'but we cannot exclude the first.'

'Clearly,' said Sekari, 'it is absolutely vital to root out the traitors.'

'That task falls to Sobek,' said the king. 'I must remind all of you of the need for secrecy, without which nothing of significance will be accomplished.'

'It's impossible to convince the court of that,' said Senankh. 'They love to gossip, and nothing will change their bad habits.'

'Whoever the miserable wretch is that caused Iker's death,' promised Sekari, 'I shall punish him with my own hands.'

'Do not usurp the place of justice,' advised the tjaty. 'The guilty man must be judged and sentenced according to the Law of Ma'at.'

'What is your assessment of the situation in Canaan?' the pharaoh asked Nesmontu.

The old soldier did not try to hide his anxiety. 'Despite the best efforts of my men – and they are not holding back – the Canaanite rebellion continues. I have made many arrests, and have succeeded in dismantling a few small groups in Sichem and the surrounding area, but I have not caught a single major figure and have no serious clues to the Herald's lair. The men close to him are totally devoted to their leader, and surround him with an unbreachable wall. So it seems pointless to me to send a new agent, for he would have no chance of infiltrating the enemy ranks.'

'Then what do you advise?'

'First, strengthen the King's Walls; next, cleanse Sichem of rebels as completely as possible; lastly, try to give the Canaanites work, so that they get a taste of prosperity. However, those measures on their own won't be enough, and I don't want to send patrols too far north, in case they fall into enemy ambushes. I therefore propose allowing the monster to grow and to think we cannot destroy it – feeding its vanity will spare us many losses. When the Herald's troops eventually emerge from their hiding-place, certain of conquering Sichem, I shall attack them openly.'

'Isn't that plan rather too ambitious?' asked Khnum-Hotep worriedly.

'I believe it to be the one best suited to the terrain and the circumstances.'

Before returning to Memphis, the king had to carry out a painful task. At nightfall, he joined Isis, who was walking with North Wind along the edge of the desert.

'This is Iker's donkey, isn't it?' he said.

'He entrusted him to my care, Majesty. It was not easy to have him admitted to Abydos, but North Wind respects our Rule.'

'I have terrible news for you.'

The donkey and the young woman halted. North Wind raised his eyes to the king's face.

'Iker has been murdered by Canaanite rebels.'

Isis felt as though an icy wind had enveloped her. Suddenly, the future seemed empty of meaning, as if the young scribe's absence took away her own existence.

The donkey's left ear pricked up, firm and stiff.

'Look, Majesty! North Wind thinks differently.'

'General Nesmontu identified the body.'

The donkey's ear remained as straight as a spear-shaft.

'The reality is appalling, Isis, but it must be accepted.'

'Can we ignore what North Wind is saying? I think he is capable of telling whether his master is alive or dead.'

'And what is your own feeling?' asked Senusret.

She gazed at the setting sun, which was covering the west with gold and red. Then she closed her eyes and relived that intense moment when the Royal Son had declared his love for her.

She said, 'Iker is alive, Majesty.'

11

For three days and three nights, the tribe advanced at a forced march, allowing themselves only brief stops. They crossed a forest, a plain, a desert area, then travelled along a dry river-bed before turning off towards a lake. Flesh-Eater paddled in it, but only Iker did likewise: the Canaanites feared that a bad spirit from the depths of the water would drown them.

Then it was back to the daily routine: Iker had to turn back into a baker and a cook, under the yoke of his torturers.

In Egypt, everyone must believe him dead. Everyone except, he was certain, his sole confidant, North Wind. And, as the donkey was living with Isis and must be communicating with her, she might also doubt that Iker was dead. The Royal Son clung to this slender hope. Who would ever find him, so far from Sichem, in a harsh land where no Egyptian patrols went?

A few Canaanites wanted to whip the Egyptian for amusement, but Flesh-Eater's bared fangs dissuaded them. The dog's attitude amused and reassured the chief, for the prisoner could not be better watched.

They set off again, northwards. Suddenly, faces hardened, there were no more jokes, and nobody tormented the slave any more. Flesh-Eater growled and bared his teeth.

'Over there, Chief! A cloud of dust!' shouted the man at the front.

'Must be sand-travellers.'

'Are we going to fight them?'

'That depends. Let's prepare for the worst.'

From time to time, tribes parleyed and came to an understanding. Generally, after acrimonious discussions, fighting broke out.

This time, there weren't even any preliminaries. Armed with slingshots, clubs and staves, the troop of hungry sandtravellers charged straight at the intruders.

The chief hurled himself into the thick of the fighting, but some of his men took to their heels.

'Come back,' yelled Iker, 'and fight!'

Most of them obeyed this unexpected order. The others fell victim to sharp flints hurled by the enemy's slingshots.

'Use this,' the chief told Iker, handing him a throwingstick.

The Royal Son aimed at the leader, an excitable fellow who was encouraging his comrades with shouts that sounded like the cries of a wild beast. He did not miss.

The sand-travellers, who had thought they would win an easy victory, wavered for a moment, and the Canaanites immediately took advantage of it. Wielding a heavy club, Iker knocked out an enraged man covered in blood. The fight began to go their way, and was soon over.

The scramble for the spoils was terrible. Drunk with violence, the victors gave no quarter.

'Our chief . . . He's dead!' exclaimed a Canaanite.

The warrior was lying between two sand-travellers, his brow smashed in. Flesh-Eater was gently licking his face.

'Let's get away quickly,' suggested the most senior member of the tribe. 'There are likely to be other sandtravellers in these parts.'

'We must bury the chief first!' protested Iker.

'There's no time. You know, you fought well. We'll take you with us.'

'Where are you planning to go?'

'We're going to join Amu's tribe and place ourselves under his protection.'

Iker suppressed a joy that was mixed with fear. Amu: the Herald!

Amu was tall, thin and bearded. Around him stood Syrian warriors armed with spears.

The Canaanites laid down their weapons and bowed very low, in a sign of submission. Iker did likewise, at the same time observing this individual with the indecipherable face, the man responsible for the curse that had struck down the acacia.

Having found him was a miracle, but Iker must yet be certain of his guilt, then find a way to pass the information on to Nesmontu. Would the Herald give him time to do so?

'Where have you come from?' demanded Amu aggressively.

'From the bitter lake,' replied the eldest Canaanite in a trembling voice. 'Sand-travellers attacked us, and our chief was killed. Had it not been for this young Egyptian, our prisoner, we would have been massacred. It was he who called back the men who had run away and regrouped our fighters. We have made a good slave of him; he will serve you well.'

'How did you get here?'

'The chief knew you were camping in this region. He wanted to sell the hostage to you. I am offering him to you as a token of friendship.'

'So you ran away in the face of the enemy!'

'The sand-travellers attacked us before we had parleyed. That is not the custom.'

'The customs of my tribe stipulate that cowards must be killed. Cut their throats – all except the Egyptian.'

Flesh-Eater pressed close to Iker's legs and bared his teeth, forbidding anyone to approach him.

The Syrians cheerfully executed the Canaanites. There was

neither respect nor friendship between the two peoples, so Amu never missed an opportunity to eliminate this scum. The bodies were robbed and abandoned for the hyenas.

'Your guardian is impressive,' Amu said to the foreigner. 'Even when wounded by several arrows, a hound like that will fight on. What is your name?'

'Iker.'

'Where did those rats kidnap you?'

'They freed me.'

Amu frowned. 'Who had arrested you?'

'The Egyptians.'

'Your own countrymen? I don't understand.'

'After trying to kill Pharaoh Senusret, I became their sworn enemy. I managed to get out of Memphis, and through the King's Walls, but Nesmontu's men caught me in Sichem and imprisoned me. I was hoping the Canaanites would let me join the resistance again, but instead of helping me they enslaved me.'

Amu spat. 'Those cowards are worthless. Allying oneself with them always leads to disaster.'

'I have set myself a goal: to serve the Herald,' said Iker.

Amu's little black eyes glittered with excitement. 'The Herald stands before you. And I keep my promises.'

'Are you still determined to overthrow Senusret?'

'His throne is already beginning to totter.'

'Yes, but the curse on the Tree of Life isn't working.'

'I shall put other curses on it. The Egyptians have been trying to catch me for a long time, but they'll never succeed. My tribe dominates the region, and the women give me many sons. Soon they'll form a victorious army.'

'Have you never thought of uniting the clans? Then you could launch an offensive capable of sweeping away General Nesmontu's troops.'

Amu looked angry. 'A tribe is a tribe, and a clan is a clan. If we begin to change that, what will become of the region?

The best leader imposes himself upon the others: that is the single and only law. And the best leader is myself. Do you know how to handle the throwing-stick, my boy?'

'Fairly well.'

'You have two days to perfect your skills. Then we shall attack an encampment of sand-travellers who have just pillaged a caravan. In my territory, I am the only one entitled to steal and kill.'

Protected by the hound, Iker dozed. He had trained for hours with the throwing-stick, practising hitting targets which got progressively smaller and further away. He was being watched, and must not prove unskilled. Concentrating hard, his style firm and sure, he lived up to his words.

Amu allowed him to move around freely, but Iker knew that he was watched all the time. If he tried to run away he would be struck down. The tribe would judge him during the fight against the sand-travellers. If he was not to suffer the same fate as the Canaanites, he must show himself to his best advantage.

What was Isis doing now, in Abydos? he wondered. She might be celebrating the rites, or meditating in a temple, or reading a text telling of the gods, of sacred things and of the fight of the Light against nothingness. Clearly she was not thinking of him. Had she been moved, even for a moment, by the news of his death?

And yet a few of her thoughts remained with him . . . In his worst moments, only this very tenuous bond saved him. In the depths of his loneliness, Isis continued to give him hope: the hope of telling her, with all the force of his love, that he could not live without her.

Amu's voice broke into his thoughts. 'Wake up, my boy, it's time to leave. My scout has just told me where the sand-travellers' camp is. Those fools think they're safe.'

*

Amu did not bother with strategy. On his order, everyone charged. As most of the sand-travellers were sound asleep, their ability to defend themselves was minimal. Accustomed to robbing unarmed traders, they put up only a feeble resistance to a band of wild-eyed Syrians.

One of the sand-travellers managed to escape the massacre by crawling towards the middle of the camp, then pretending to be dead. Out of the corner of his eye, he saw Amu strutting up and down, right next to him. The survivor wanted to avenge his comrades. He was ideally placed, and all he had to do was plunge his dagger into Amu's back.

Appalled by the savagery of his new companions, Iker had not taken part in the slaughter. From his place in the background, he saw a supposedly dead man get up and prepare to strike. He hurled his throwing-stick, hitting the sand-traveller on the temple.

In fury, Amu trampled on the wounded man, staving in his chest. 'That vermin tried to kill me – *me*! And you saved me, Egyptian.'

For the second time, Iker had flown to the aid of the enemy. Allowing the Herald to die without obtaining as much information as possible would have been disastrous. Iker must win his trust and find out how he was cursing the Acacia of Osiris.

While his men were sacking the camp, Amu led Iker towards the only tent still intact; the others were burning. With his dagger, the chief slashed the fabric, creating a way in.

At once there were cries of fear. Huddled together inside were ten women and about the same number of children.

'Just look at these women! The most beautiful will enter my harem and replace the ones I don't desire any more – my men can have those.'

'Will you spare the children?' asked Iker worriedly.

'The strong ones will serve as slaves, but the weaklings will be killed. You bring me luck, my boy! I've never known such an easy victory. And I shan't forget that I owe you my life.'

Grinning, Amu grabbed a young and pretty girl by the hair and forced her against him. 'I'm going to show you right now what a virile man is like.'

The clan set off along a dried-up river which had long ago hollowed out its bed between two cliffs; it seemed to lead nowhere. A scout walked a long way in front, while others guarded the rear.

'I am granting you an enormous privilege,' Amu informed Iker. 'You will be the first foreigner to see my secret encampment.

Iker did not regret having used his throwing-stick. By winning the Herald's good graces, he was at last going to discover his lair.

The place was both well-hidden and easy to guard. Deep within an arid desert region, a small oasis provided water and food. Assisted by slaves, those who lived there permanently grew vegetables, and there was a well-stocked poultry-yard.

'Here Syrians and Canaanites live together,' said Amu, 'but this place is exceptional. These Canaanites have learnt to obey me without question and to stop snivelling.'

'Wouldn't it be necessary to form a great coalition to attack Sichem?' asked Iker again.

'We'll talk about that later. First, let us celebrate our victory.'

All the members of the tribe were engaged in acts of devotion to their leader, who was massaged, anointed with scented oil and settled on soft cushions, in the shade of a huge tent. A procession of Canaanite slaves brought dishes of food, and date-wine flowed freely. At length, four submissive, well-built women led Amu to his bed, stuffed with food and dead drunk.

Iker had not imagined that the Herald would be like this.

85

12

Dressed in a long white robe with a red belt, her hair falling freely about her shoulders, Isis followed the pharaoh to his temple of a million years.

They entered a shrine whose ceiling was covered in stars and which was lit by a single lamp.

'Travelling the path of the Mysteries means passing through a new door,' said the king. 'It is a dangerous step for, in order to confront the criminal who is wielding the strength of Set against Osiris, you must become a true magician. So the sceptre I gave you will become dazzling speech and effective light, able to fend off the blows of fate. Do you agree to run this risk?'

'I do, Majesty.'

'Before uniting yourself with the powers of the Pesedjet, rinse your mouth with fresh natron and put on white sandals.'

Once this rite had been carried out, the king pressed a statuette of Ma'at to Isis' lips. 'Receive the secret words of Osiris,' he said. 'He spoke them when he reigned over Egypt. They enabled him to create the golden age and to pass on life. Now penetrate the darkness.'

He raised a vase above Isis's head. Out of it flowed a luminous energy which enveloped the priestess's body.

At the far end of the chamber, a royal cobra reared up on the roof of the innermost shrine, poised to attack.

'Touch its throat and make it submit,' ordered Senusret.

Isis was deeply afraid, but nevertheless stepped forward. The snake made ready to strike.

Isis was thinking not of herself but of the battle for the Tree of Life. Why should the spirit of the subterranean world, a fearsome and fascinating reptile, belong to the destroyers' camp? Without it, would the soil not be sterile?

She slowly held out her right hand; the cobra did not move. When she touched its throat, a halo of light surrounded its head and formed the shape of the White Crown.

'The creative force of the Great One of magic flows in your veins,' declared the king. 'Make it active: play the sistra.'

He handed her two gold objects, the first shaped like an innermost shrine flanked by two spiralling rods, the second made up of uprights pierced with holes into which metal rods were fixed. He said, 'When you make them ring out, you will hear the voice of Set, which brings to life the four elements, and you will thus dissipate inertia. Thanks to the sistra's vibrations, the vital powers will awake. Only an initiate can attempt such an experiment, for these instruments are dangerous. They are repositories of the perpetual movement of creation, and they strike bad musicians blind.'

Isis took the sistra by their cylindrical handles. They felt so heavy that she almost dropped them, but her wrists held firm and a strange melody was born. From the rattle sistrum came forth sharp, piercing notes; from the shrine-shaped sistrum came a soft, enchanting song. Isis sought the right rhythm, and the sounds mingled harmoniously.

For a few moments, her vision clouded. Then the music swelled, so much so that it made the stones of the temple vibrate, and the priestess experienced a perfect feeling of well-being.

She handed the sistra back to the king, and he led her to the edge of the sacred lake.

'By appeasing the Great One of magic,' he said, 'your eyes

see what outsiders' eyes cannot. Gaze at the centre of the lake.'

Little by little, the lake took on immense dimensions, until it became one with the sky. The *nun*, the ocean of energy from which everything was born, was revealed to Isis. A fire lit up the water and, just as in the first time, the golden lotus with lapis-lazuli petals was born from the burning isle.

'May it rise each morning in the valley of light,' prayed the king. 'May this great living god be reborn, he who came from the isle of flame, the golden child who came forth from the lotus.' He paused, then said, 'Breathe it in, Isis, as do the creative powers.'

A sweet, enchanting scent spread over Abydos.

The lotus vanished, and the sacred lake took on its usual appearance. On the surface of the water a face appeared, only to be quickly washed away by the waves created by the wind.

But Isis had recognized it: it was Iker. 'He is alive,' she whispered.

'Lie flat on your belly,' ordered Amu.

Imitating the Syrian warriors, Iker flattened himself on the hot golden sand.

'Do you see them, my boy?'

From the top of the dune, the scribe looked down on the camp of the sand-travellers, who were certain they were safe. The women were cooking, the children playing, the men sleeping, apart from a few sentries.

'I hate this tribe,' Amu confided. 'Its chief stole from me a superb woman who would have given me strong sons. Besides, he owns the best well in the region – its water is always sweet and fresh. I'm going to seize it and add to my territory.'

That plan's fully worthy of the Herald, thought Iker. His doubts were constantly growing. Amu spent his time dallying with the beauties in his harem, drinking and eating. He never mentioned the conquest of Egypt and the annihilation of the pharaoh. Instead, cosseted by his women and worshipped by his warriors, he led the easy life of a rich brigand. But at last he had decided to take action.

'Let's kill the sentries first,' suggested Iker.

'There's an Egyptian's plan for you!' snorted Amu sarcastically. 'Me, I don't waste time on precautions like that. We'll charge down the dune, yelling, and slaughter the whole lot of this rabble.'

No sooner said than done.

The flints flew out of the slingshots and struck down most of the sand-travellers, so that the attackers met only weak opposition. The Syrians amused themselves by putting out the eyes of the few survivors, who died slowly and in agony. Even the children were all killed, and Amu's harem was full to bursting so he did not spare a single woman.

'I shan't miss them – they were too ugly,' he confided to Iker, who was almost fainting with horror. 'Doesn't this sort of thing agree with you, my boy?' He tapped Iker on the shoulder. 'You've got to harden up. Life is a harsh struggle. Those sand-travellers were nothing but thieves and criminals. If General Nesmontu had found them before I did, he would have ordered his archers to kill them. I'm cleansing the region in my own way.'

'When will you finally unite the tribes to drive out the occupying army?'

'You're obsessed with that plan, aren't you?'

'It's the only one that really matters.'

'The only one, the only one . . . Let's not exaggerate. The most important thing is for me to reign supreme over my territory. Now, there are a few lice who still dare to doubt my supremacy. We must take care of them, my boy.' He handed Iker a new throwing-stick. 'The spirits of the dead are embodied in it. It crosses lakes and plains to strike the foe, then returns to the thrower's hand. Take care of it and use it wisely.'

Iker thought of Senusret's advice: to procure weapons from the invisible world. This was the first he had procured – and it was a gift from the enemy.

'We'll eat now,' decided Amu, 'and then continue the cleansing.'

Relentless and cruel, the Herald wiped out the small groups of Canaanites and sand-travellers one by one, holding them guilty of drinking at his wells or stealing one of his goats. All this time, Iker was apparently free to move around, but always he was watched, as well as protected, by Flesh-Eater. He was careful to do nothing that might arouse the suspicions of his new comrades in arms. As the days passed, he made himself both forgotten and accepted.

Amu never varied his tactics. He charged down on his victims like a sandstorm, and filled them with such fear that it undermined their ability to defend themselves.

Iker was still perplexed. Powerful, violent, merciless, tyrannical . . . the Herald was certainly all those things. But why was he avoiding announcing his real intention? Was he still suspicious of the Egyptian, whom he ought to have killed, and watching him for the first mistake? Iker must therefore be of use to him, one way or another. Perhaps he was meant to pass on false information to Nesmontu, thus precipitating the defeat of the Egyptian army? So he did not even try to send any messages, however small. First, he must get accurate information.

While the leading warriors of the tribe were gathered round the campfire, eating spit-roasted lamb, Iker went over and sat down beside the Herald, who was half drunk.

He said, 'You must have magical protection.'

'What kind, do you think?'

'The queen of turquoises.'

'The queen of turquoises?' repeated Amu stupidly. 'What's that?'

'It's an amazingly beautiful stone. I found it in a mine in

Sinai, where the pharaoh had sent me as a slave. Normally, it would have belonged to me, but a band of marauders attacked the mine, killed all the guards and miners, and stole the turquoise.'

'And you want to get it back . . . Well, I'm not the one who has it. It was probably taken by sand-travellers, so with a little luck you'll find your queen of turquoises again. If it's as beautiful as that, you're bound to hear someone talk about it.'

'A senior Egyptian general, Sepi, was killed in the middle of the desert. You killed him, didn't you?'

The Syrian's astonishment looked genuine. 'Me, kill a general? If I had, I'd boast about it. The whole region would have acclaimed me, and dozens of tribes would have prostrated themselves before me.'

'But everyone thinks the general was killed by the Herald.'

Annoyed, Amu stood up and seized Iker by the shoulder. Immediately, Flesh-Eater growled at him.

'Make that animal behave itself.'

A look from Iker calmed Flesh-Eater.

'Come into my tent.'

The dog followed them in.

With a kick in the ribs, Amu awoke a Canaanite girl, who hurriedly dressed and left, then poured himself a large cup of date-wine.

'I want to know what you're really thinking, my boy.'

'I am wondering if you are really the Herald or if you're merely playing the part.' By speaking so frankly, Iker was playing for high stakes.

'You've got cool nerves, haven't you?'

'I just want to know the truth.'

Pacing round and round like a bear in a cage, Amu avoided the young man's gaze. 'What if I wasn't the Herald? What would it matter?'

'I risked my life to put myself in his service.'

'Isn't it enough for you to be in mine?'

'The Herald wants to destroy Egypt and take power. You're content with your own territory.'

The Syrian sat down heavily on his cushions. 'Let's talk frankly, my boy. You're right: I'm not the Herald.'

So Iker was the prisoner of a miserable leader of a band of killers and looters! 'Why did you lie about it?'

'Because you could be one of my best warriors. You wanted to believe I was this Herald, so it would have been stupid to discourage you. What's more, you weren't entirely wrong.'

'What do you mean?'

'I'm not the Herald,' repeated the Syrian, 'but I know where he is.'

13

One question, to which he desperately sought an answer, haunted High Treasurer Senankh: was there a traitor hidden among his staff? He himself appointed all the scribes working in his secretariat, having carefully studied their professional careers and checked their skills. He found a few very small errors, but nothing to make him suspicious of any of them.

Senankh checked again, yet more thoroughly, viewing each of these model scribes as a suspect. He even set a few traps, but they yielded no results. So he decided to consult Sobek-Khu.

The Protector had recently tightened the rules on river navigation, which he had considered too lax, and was always on the alert. He went to great efforts to ensure the pharaoh's safety and to guarantee the free movement of people and goods, while at the same time hunting down miscreants of every type. No case was beneath his interest, and he was kept informed of every single inquiry in progress. If progress was too slow, his wrath descended on the head of the person at fault.

But Sobek's fiercest wrath was directed at himself: he had still not succeeded in uncovering and destroying the rebels' network of spies in Memphis. He had not the smallest clue, not a single suspect. Could it really be that the enemy was no more than a bad dream? No. The truth was that they were taking care to keep out of sight and, sooner or later, would strike again. The Protector therefore well understood the High Treasurer's concern.

'I've failed completely,' said Senankh. 'From one point of view, I'm glad: as far I can tell, there is no disloyalty among my scribes. But I'm not a trained investigator, so it simply may be that I did not see it. I take it that you have investigated them yourself?'

'Of course.'

'And what was your conclusion?'

'The same as yours.'

'You might have warned me!' protested Senankh.

'I answer only to the pharaoh. He alone is informed of all I do.'

'Have you by any chance investigated . . . me?'

'Of course.'

'How dare you suspect a member of the King's House!'

'It is my duty.'

'Have you also spied upon Sehotep and Tjaty Khnum-Hotep?'

'I do my duty.'

Senankh could hardly tell Sobek, who did not belong to the Golden Circle of Abydos, that its members were above suspicion.

'I'm still convinced,' the Protector went on, 'that there are one or several traitors at court, among that band of vapid, jealous, pretentious parasites. If there's even the smallest incident, they shout and scream about it, and blame my men for everything. Those people are incompetent, and they have no courage or honesty. Fortunately, His Majesty doesn't listen to them, and I hope he'll reduce their number to a minimum.'

'What about Medes and his secretariat?'

'They're under control, like all the others.'

Sobek had introduced one of his men into Medes's staff in

order to observe his conduct at close hand. By having eyes and ears everywhere, the Protector was bound to find some clues eventually.

Every evening Sehotep, Bearer of the Royal Seal, held a lavish banquet at which his steward served the best foods and wines. Everyone at court was eager to receive an invitation from this influential man. Few women were impervious to his charm, and many husbands spent an anxious evening worrying about their wives' future conduct. However, there were no scandals to deplore, for Sehotep was careful to keep his adventures discreet.

This worldly activity, which some of his critics considered frivolous, enabled him to get to know the courtiers well and gather a great deal of useful information: the plentiful wine and good food loosened people's tongues.

On this particular evening, Sehotep was entertaining the principal archivist, his wife and daughter, and his three most senior colleagues and their wives. As usual, the light-hearted, sparkling conversation covered a thousand and one subjects, despite the threats weighing heavy upon Egypt. The Bearer of the Royal Seal created an atmosphere of celebration which invited confidences.

His guests did not seem likely suspects. They carried on their careers peacefully, never acted on their own initiative and, at the slightest difficulty, placed themselves under the protection of a higher authority. They would willingly have behaved like petty tyrants to their subordinates, but the tjaty was keeping watch.

At the end of the reception, the principal archivist's daughter came over to Sehotep; she was rather stupid, talkative, and very pretty.

'Your terrace is said to be the most beautiful in Memphis. I'd love to see it.'

'What does your father think?'

'I'm rather tired,' replied the archivist. 'My wife and I would like to return home. If you will grant my daughter this privilege, we should be very flattered.'

Sehotep pretended not to notice the trap. Several courtiers had already thrown their eldest daughters at him, hoping it might lead to marriage. The idea horrified him, so he always took precautions to ensure that the young lady concerned did not become pregnant and that her only memory was of a beautiful night of love.

The archivist's daughter waxed lyrical as she gazed out at Memphis. 'What a wonderful city it is. And you're wonderful, too, Sehotep.'

With a tenderness that a well-brought-up man could not reject, she rested her head gently on his shoulder. He took off her light wig and stroked her hair.

'Don't leave too soon,' he said. 'Would you like to go on admiring Memphis for a long time?'

'Yes – I mean no. Will you show me your bedchamber?'

Senankh was happy to oblige.

He undressed her slowly and quickly noted that the young lady lacked neither sensuality nor experience. Their games were joyful, their pleasure shared. At the end of a delicious joust, Sehotep thought she would make an abominable wife, possessive and capricious.

'Aren't you worried about the future?' asked the girl.

'Egypt is ruled by a great king. He will be able to ward off the evil.'

'That isn't what some people think.'

'Doesn't your father like Senusret?'

'My father likes any superior provided he's paid well and isn't overworked. But my last suitor didn't agree with you.'

'Who was he?'

'Eril, a foreigner in charge of the public scribes. His ambition oozes from every pore. With his little moustache, sugar-sweet voice and friendly ways, he tries to pass himself off as the gentlest of men. In fact, he's as dangerous as a horned viper. All he thinks about is scheming to ruin his competitors' reputations.

'The little rat wanted to marry me, can you believe? And my father, the coward, actually agreed, though when I flatly refused he didn't insist. The thought of Eril's hands on my skin, as slimy as a slug – how horrible! I had to slap him hard before he at last realized that he'd never have me.

'And that's not all. He's corrupt and a corruptor, and he sells his services to the highest bidder. But spreading his poison isn't enough for him. He criticizes the pharaoh, too.'

Sehotep's interest was aroused. 'Are you sure of that?'

'Of course, or I wouldn't say it.'

'What sort of thing does he say?'

'I can't remember exactly. But it's a crime to malign the pharaoh, isn't it?'

'Did Eril ask you to help him or do something for him?'

The girl was surprised. 'No, nothing like that.'

'Then forget those bad moments,' advised Senankh, 'and enjoy the present moment. Unless you want to go to sleep . . . ?'

'Oh no!' she exclaimed, and she stretched out on her back, desirable and available.

Every morning, Sekari looked at Iker's writing-materials, precious tokens of his friend. He would so have loved to give them back to him on his return from Asia. Abandoning Iker like this filled him with angry dismay, but the pharaoh had forbidden him to go to Canaan to try to find him.

Sekari refused to acknowledge the void that Iker's absence left. By accepting it, he would have sanctioned his friend's death and killed hope. Now, in the deepest part of himself, he did not believe that Iker was really dead. He might be a prisoner, or perhaps wounded, but he was alive.

Sekari had carried out his own checks on the measures taken by Sobek to ensure the king's safety, and had not found any flaws. However, he had serious doubts about Sobek-Khu, who had been so pleased by Iker's death. Supposing the traitor at court was none other than Sobek himself? Why did he hate Iker, if not because of the threat that the Royal Son might realize what his true role was? And wasn't the Protector the person best placed to order a guard to kill the young scribe?

The answer to these horrible questions seemed obvious. Too obvious. So Sekari needed irrefutable proof before he went to the king, and until he found it the king was in great danger. The only reassuring thing was that the guards responsible for Senusret's close protection worshipped the pharaoh.

Yet again, Sekari resolved that, if Sobek the Protector had sent Iker to his death, he would pay for it.

Medes enjoyed his position as secretary of the King's House. He did not dislike hard work – quite the contrary, in fact. He was an extremely well organized man, who quickly assimilated complex cases, and his excellent memory retained every important fact. Capable of attending meeting after meeting without feeling tired, Medes demanded such a taxing rate of work from his employees that some of them could not bear it. So each month he was obliged to take on four or five new scribes, whom he put to a harsh test. Very few lasted the distance. In this way he formed disciplined, efficient teams. Neither the king nor the tjaty made even the smallest criticism of his work.

He also had another, parallel organization, which was devoted exclusively to him. Made up of scribes, messengers and sailors, it provided him with information and passed on his instructions throughout the land. Each new member of the network was given a specific job to do and reported only to him. The men were kept strictly separate, and of course nobody suspected Medes's true aim. When the Herald's uprising occurred, this organization would be an invaluable weapon.

Medes was preparing to assign work to a conscientious scribe who had been employed for several months, when Gergu was shown into his office.

'Is there a problem?' asked Medes.

'The Phoenician wants to speak to you immediately.'

'In broad daylight? It's out of the question.'

'He's walking around the market. He says it's urgent and serious.'

The arrangement was as unusual as it was worrying, but Medes hid his uneasiness and went to meet the Phoenician.

In the crowd of passers-by, they went unnoticed. Standing side by side at a leek-seller's stall, they conversed in hushed voices without looking at each other.

The Phoenician asked, 'Have you recently taken on a scribe from Imau, aged about thirty, unmarried, rather tall, clean-shaven, with a scar on his left forearm?'

'Yes, I have, but—'

'He's one of Sobek's men – my best agent saw him coming out of Sobek's office. He's probably been sent to spy on you.'

Medes flinched. Had it not been for his ally's vigilance, he might have made a fatal mistake. He said, 'Gergu will get rid of him for me.'

'Certainly not. Now that we've identified him, let's use him to reassure the Protector about you. But this setback should make you even more careful.'

14

Amu was followed by only ten of his most experienced men. All wore solemn expressions, as if their chief was leading them to disaster.

'Where are we going?' asked Iker.

'To the Herald.'

'Your men don't look very happy about it.'

'He's our worst enemy and has sworn to destroy us.'

'Then why are you running into the monster's jaws like this?'

'I must challenge him to single combat. The victor will take over the loser's tribe. In that way, we'll avoid a lot of deaths.'

'Do you think you can win?'

'It will be difficult,' admitted Amu, 'very difficult. The Herald has never been brought down. The only weapon that might work is cunning, and he'd have to give me time to use it.'

'Is the Herald some sort of giant?'

'You'll see soon enough.'

Contrary to his usual custom, Amu marched openly and lit fires which would be visible from a long way off. By signalling his presence, he was informing the enemy that he was planning not to attack but to parley.

At dawn on the fourth day, Flesh-Eater growled. A few

minutes later, some sixty Canaanites armed with bows and spears encircled the little band. The big hound planted itself in front of Iker.

A short, square-shouldered man stepped forward. 'You are my prisoner, Amu.'

'Not yet.'

'Do you really think you can defend yourself with this small band of frightened men?'

'Your master's afraid of us. If not, why hasn't he killed us? He's nothing but a weakling, a girl-child, an empty head, and his arms are soft and feeble. Let him come and prostrate himself before me, in this very spot, first thing tomorrow. I shall spit on him, and he will weep as he begs for mercy.'

The Herald's man boiled with rage. He would willingly have cut out Amu's tongue, but he had to respect the rules of the challenge thrown down by the Syrian. His master would be delighted to tear Amu limb from limb. Still raging, he ran off to alert him.

'All we have to do now is prepare ourselves,' said Amu.

In the middle of the night, the chief's belly was racked with spasms of fierce pain. It was so bad that all he could do was lie on his side with his legs drawn up. One of his men gave him an evil-smelling potion, but it did not help. Clearly, Amu would be unable to fight.

'We're lost,' said the temporary doctor. 'The fight cannot be renounced for any reason whatsoever. We must make our escape immediately.'

'Those savages would catch us and slaughter my whole clan,' objected Amu. 'We must take our chances, however slim they may be.'

'But you can't even stand up!'

'I have the right to name a replacement. One of you will fight in my name.'

'Who?'

'Iker.'

The Syrians were appalled. 'He won't last ten seconds!' said one.

'He's the fastest of us all.'

'It isn't just a matter of running and ducking, it's about killing a giant.'

Unperturbed, Iker himself said nothing. The hour of truth was approaching. Soon he would meet the Herald, with only one choice: conquer or die.

'Say no,' one of his travelling companions advised him. 'Nobody else will agree to take Amu's place. The only answer is to run away.'

'I accept.'

'You're mad!'

'It's going to be a tiring day. I'm going to rest while I wait for the fight.'

Although his hands were free, Iker felt as if he were once again tied to *Swift One*'s mast. This time no wave would come and save him from his fate, but at least he could fight. Aware that his chances were non-existent, he vowed that he would not die pointlessly. So, on the inner surface of a fragment of bark, he scratched a hasty message in a code which only Nesmontu could decipher:

Amu is not the Herald. The Herald is some kind of monster who is hiding less than one day's march from here, probably to the north. I am going to fight him in single combat. Long live the pharaoh.

Then he buried the piece of bark and covered the hiding-place with dry stones. He stood one up vertically, after drawing an owl on it with the aid of a flint. This hieroglyph meant 'inside; in the interior'. If an Egyptian patrol passed by, it was sure to take notice.

He leant against the trunk of a tree, and Flesh-Eater lay

down at his feet. If danger threatened, the dog would warn him immediately. Unable to sleep, Iker thought of all the inaccessible sources of happiness: seeing Isis and declaring his love again, trying to make her love him, building a life with her, serving Pharaoh, discovering the Mysteries of Abydos, passing on Ma'at through writing, understanding more clearly the radiant power of the hieroglyphs . . . These dreams were shattered by a merciless reality: the Herald.

The next morning was misty.

Amu had vomited a good deal during the night, and was now sleeping.

'There's still time to withdraw,' one of the Syrians told Iker.

'No, there isn't,' objected another. 'The monster will be here soon, and if we haven't got an opponent for him he'll cut our heads off.'

'And what if I lose?' asked Iker.

'We'll become his slaves. Here are your bow, your quiver of arrows and your sword.'

'What about my throwing-stick?'

'It would only scratch him.'

'Here they are!' shouted the sentry.

The Herald was marching at the head of his whole tribe, women and children included, for nobody wanted to miss the spectacle.

For a few moments, Iker was speechless. Never had he seen such a mountain of flesh and muscle. Even Senusret himself would have seemed small beside this incredible giant of a man.

Low-browed, with tousled hair and a very prominent chin, the Herald was one-eyed; a greyish strip of fabric covered his dead eye. He was armed with an axe and an enormous shield.

He halted a good distance from the enemy encampment and shouted, 'Come out of your tent, little woman! Come and face me, Amu the coward, whose enemies see only his backside! Come and taste my axe!' His voice was ludicrously high and shrill for such a huge body, but no one laughed.

Iker stepped forward. 'Amu is ill.'

The giant sneered disdainfully. 'I'll wager fear is emptying his bowels! All the same, I'll cut you into pieces.'

'You'll have to fight first.'

'Amu's chosen a champion, has he? Good, then we'll have our fun. Let this hero show himself.'

'I already have.'

The giant gazed incredulously round the Syrian camp, then burst out laughing. The rest of his tribe followed suit.

'You must be jesting, little man!'

'What are the rules of this fight?'

'There is only one: kill or be killed.'

With a speed that amazed the watchers, Iker fired three arrows in succession.

The enormous shield blocked them: there was nothing wrong with the giant's reflexes.

'Good try, little man. Now it's my turn.'

The axe came down with such violence that the wind from it knocked Iker over, saving his life. He leapt up and started running in a zig-zag pattern, so that the monster could not strike a decisive blow.

At each step the giant took, the ground trembled. Despite his size he was agile, and whirled his weapon round so skilfully that several times he almost decapitated Iker. But the young scribe was an excellent distance runner, and managed to tire his opponent.

Panting, the giant threw his shield away from him. 'I'm going to crush you, runt!'

Iker moved back towards the Syrians, who were astonished to see him survive so long.

'My throwing-stick, quickly!'

Dizzy but on his feet again, Amu handed him the weapon.

As the Herald charged at Iker, Flesh-Eater leapt forward and sank his teeth into his leg. Roaring with pain, the giant raised his axe, ready to cut the dog in half. Just as the blade began to descend, the pointed edge of Iker's throwing-stick plunged into his eye. He dropped his axe and clasped his hands over the horrible wound. The pain was so unbearable that he fell to his knees.

Staggering forward, Amu seized the axe and, with all his strength, sliced through the neck of his sworn enemy.

Flesh-Eater opened his jaws and was stroked and praised by Iker, who was soaked in sweat. The Syrians gave shouts of victory, but the Canaanites wept.

Amu ordered the slaughter of the old, the sick children, one hysterical woman and two men whose faces he did not like. The rest of the Herald's tribe would obey him without question from now on.

'May the gods bless my bowels!' he told Iker. 'If I hadn't been ill I'd have lost. And may they bless your inexhaustible breath: only you could have tired out that brute and forced him into a fatal mistake.'

'Don't forget Flesh-Eater. We wouldn't have won without his help.'

The dog looked up at Iker with eyes full of affection.

'To be honest, my boy, I didn't think for a moment that you'd win. A little man bringing down a giant – what a marvel! In a few hundred years, people will still be speaking of you. From now on, everyone will regard you as a hero. And there are more surprises in store for you yet. Let's go and take control of the monster's territory.'

Iker felt profoundly dissatisfied. Yes, he was alive. Yes, he had helped kill the Herald. But his mission was to find out how the Herald had cursed the Tree of Life and then find out how to break the curse. Now he would not be able to find the answers to these crucial questions.

Could it be that the death of that malevolent creature would be enough to heal the acacia? There was one last hope: in the dead man's lair, Iker might perhaps find important clues, so he obediently followed Amu.

He was expecting to find an entrenched camp, but he could not have been more wrong. The land the Herald had ruled was planted with vines, fig and olive trees. Herds of cows and flocks of sheep prospered there, and a pretty village occupied the centre. The tribe's new master was offered wine, beef, spit-roasted fowls and cakes cooked in milk.

'Thanks to you, Iker,' acknowledged Amu, 'we now own a real little paradise, so it's only right that you should be rewarded. It is true that I have a few children here and there, but they're lazy and incompetent. You're different. It's only fitting that a great hero should succeed me, so choose a wife, and I'll give you a farm and servants. You'll have several sons, and we'll rule this huge territory together – it will make us very rich. Given your reputation, nobody will dare bother us, and from time to time we can arrange a little skirmish to amuse ourselves. There's a glowing future in store for you.'

Amu paused and scratched his head. 'After what you've done, I owe you the truth. I'd wanted for a long time to kill that brute. He was threatening my tribe, so I'd decided to fight him, despite the risks. And you brought me luck.'

'Do you mean . . . ? Are you saying that man wasn't really the Herald?'

'I don't know if the Herald really exists or is just a legend. In any case, he doesn't prowl around in this region. Forget about him and enjoy your good fortune. You'll be happy here.'

Iker was devastated. So he had risked his life for a mirage and passed on false information to General Nesmontu. And his 'glowing future'? It would simply be a new form of captivity.

15

The small patrol of desert guards did not usually venture into this lost corner of Canaan, but its commander, an inveterate hunter, was hot on the trail of a wild boar. After crossing a tamarisk wood and fording a dry riverbed, the animal had shaken off its pursuers.

'We ought to go back, sir,' said one of the guards. 'This place isn't safe.'

The officer could not disagree. If they encountered a band of sand-travellers determined to kill Egyptians, they would not stand a chance. 'We'll go as far as the end of this valley,' he decided. 'Keep your eyes and ears open.'

There was no trace of the boar, but one of his men said, 'Look there, sir. It's rather odd.' He gestured at a heap of stones that looked unnatural. 'There's the sign of the owl on that vertical stone.'

'Interesting,' said the commander. 'The letter M, meaning "in the interior" or "inside". Clear those stones away.'

The officer helped dig away the soft sand, and before long he unearthed a piece of bark with hieroglyphs cut into it.

'That's strange,' he said. 'Each sign is expertly written, but the text doesn't mean anything.'

'Might it be one of those coded messages we were told to collect?'

*

Frozen to the marrow, Djehuty pulled his big cloak round him more closely. Although the cloth was thick, it scarcely warmed him at all. Yet the air was quite warm, and no wind was blowing through Dahshur. Strangely, his joints no longer ached so atrociously, but his illness was eating away at what little strength he still had.

But that mattered little, for he was witnessing the completion of the royal pyramid. Thanks to the builders' great enthusiasm and skills, the work had not taken as long as expected. Several times, High Treasurer Senankh had intervened fast and efficiently to meet the craftsmen's demands.

Seated in his travelling-chair, Djehuty toured the curtain-wall, which with its bastions and redans imitated that of Pharaoh Djoser at Saqqara. The whole structure bore the name of *kebehut*, 'cool celestial water', from which emerged the pyramid called *hotep*, 'completion'. Thus was embodied the myth according to which life, born from the first ocean, manifested itself in the form of an island on which a first temple had been built, out of the primordial stone.

'You may be proud of your work,' said a grave voice.

'Majesty! I was not expecting you so soon. The custom—'

'Forget it, Djehuty. In scrupulously following my plans, you drew the lines of force that enable this monument to emit *ka*. Thus the victory of Ma'at over *isefet* is declared.'

The faces of the pyramid were dazzling white, clad with limestone from Tura which had been polished to perfection and reflected the sunlight. The triangles of light lit up the sky and the earth.

Accompanied by Djehuty, the king proceeded to open the mouth, eyes and ears of the temple. There, the festival of the royal soul's regeneration would be eternally celebrated. Giant statues depicted Pharaoh as Osiris, charged with receiving the divine life and passing it on. So long as a dwelling was built to house it, Egypt would resist the darkness.

Each day, in the king's name, priests would carry out the

rites bringing to life the processions of offering-bearers and making real the dialogue between the monarch and the gods.

Then Senusret entered the underground part of the pyramid and made his way to the sarcophagus chamber, the red granite boat in which his body of light would sail. The supernatural peace of the place strengthened Senusret's will to battle against the demon who was trying to prevent the resurrection of Osiris.

As he gazed upon this stone of eternity, the king forged a new belief: Iker was not dead.

Eril was half Phoenician and half Syrian, but had lived in Memphis for about ten years. He was the head of a team of public scribes made up of men who were not capable of reaching the highest offices but were very skilled in their field: the settlement of litigation between individuals and the government.

Without a good number of crafty tricks and a thorough knowledge of corruption, Eril would never have obtained this post, which he had coveted for a long time. He had flourished in the shadow of his predecessor, a vain, petty tyrant with connections at court, and had used his time to learn from this good teacher the art of eliminating his rivals while making himself a reputation as an honest man.

Eril was congratulating himself on reaching a new peak of success. He, the foreigner, the man of the shadows, had been recognized as someone of importance: Sehotep had invited him to tonight's banquet!

The whole day had been taken up by having his hair and his little moustache trimmed, inspecting the wares of perfume-makers and clothes-makers, and having his hands and feet tended to, in order to turn himself into an elegant notable. Everyone knew that the Bearer of the Royal Seal detested errors of taste, but the people working on Eril were so skilled that he was sure he had nothing to worry about.

One thing did bother him, though: who would the other guests be? Unlike Sehotep, Eril loathed the company of women. There were bound to be several there, and he would have to put up with their simpering and their chatter. Still, eating at the table of a member of the King's House outweighed these minor displeasures. This evening would probably lead to promotion for him. He might even have a chance tactfully to reveal some of his ambitions.

Rumour had not lied: Sehotep's house was an absolute marvel, whose smallest detail beguiled the eye, and the luxuriant garden took one's breath away. Jealousy brought bile to Eril's throat. Why shouldn't he, too, live in splendour like this? All things considered, did he have fewer qualities and merits than the son of a prosperous family who had been favoured by chance?

A servant greeted Eril deferentially and showed him into a huge reception chamber filled with the sweet scent of lilies. Sweetmeats, fruit juices, beer and wine were set out on low tables.

'Please be seated, sir,' said the steward.

But Eril was tense and preferred to pace up and down the room while he waited for his host. He nibbled a fresh onion dressed with bean paste as he admired the wall-paintings depicting cornflowers, poppies and chrysanthemums.

'I am sorry for the delay,' Sehotep apologized when he joined his guest. 'I was kept late at the palace – affairs of state must always take priority, of course. Would you care for a little wine?'

'Indeed I would, my lord. But I think I must be early, because the other guests haven't arrived yet, and—'

'This evening you are my only guest.'

Eril could not hide his amazement. 'It's an honour, my lord, a great honour!'

'For me it's a great pleasure. Shall we eat now?'

Eril felt very ill at ease. Neither the quality of the food nor the vintage wine, not even the master of the house's friendly manner, could make him forget the surprising nature of this intimate meeting.

'You practise a delicate profession,' remarked Sehotep, 'and it seems you acquit yourself rather well.'

'I do my best, my lord.'

'Are you satisfied with your results?'

Eril's stomach turned over. Above all, he must not rush things and must manoeuvre skilfully. 'Under the tjaty's leadership, the Memphis government is improving all the time. There are still a few problems, but I and my team are trying to resolve them in the interest of the individuals concerned.'

'Would you not like a more . . . lucrative job?'

Eril relaxed. So his performance had attracted the attention of the authorities! And the Bearer of the Royal Seal was going to offer him a post at the heart of his government and entrust him with senior responsibilities.

Sehotep contemplated his cup, which held a superb red wine from Imau. 'My friend High Treasurer Senankh has carried out a detailed investigation into your fortune – your real fortune, of course.'

Eril turned pale. 'What . . . what do you mean, my lord?'

'That you are corrupt and a corruptor.'

The accused man sprang to his feet in indignation. 'That is untrue, totally untrue, and—'

'Senankh has irrefutable proof that you are exploiting your clients shamefully and are involved in many dubious operations. But there are much more serious matters involved.'

Taken aback, Eril sat down again. 'I don't understand.'

'I think you do. For your dishonesty, you will go to prison. For your participation in a plot against the king, you will receive the death penalty.'

'Plot against the pharaoh? Me? How can you possibly think—'

'Stop lying. I have a witness. If you want to escape execution, tell me the names of your accomplices immediately.'

Losing all dignity, the little man threw himself at Sehotep's feet. 'Someone must have misunderstood something I said. I'm a faithful servant of the king.'

'That is enough, you miserable creature. You belong to a network of rebels who have infiltrated Memphis. I demand the names of all your contacts.'

Eril raised eyes filled with fear. 'Rebels? No, you are mistaken! I just know about ten . . . understanding officials and courtiers.' He named them, explained in detail how his schemes worked, and poured out lamentations interspersed with regrets.

Sehotep listened in deep disappointment. Clearly he had unmasked a petty swindler, not a supporter of the Herald.

'The moment I deciphered the message, Majesty,' said General Nesmontu, 'I left Sichem to inform you of its content. There can be no possible doubt, Majesty: Royal Son Iker is alive. Someone tried to trick us by using another man's dead body.'

'How is it that you can be certain?' inquired Senusret.

Sobek the Protector, who was standing beside the king, was visibly sceptical.

'Iker and I agreed on a code which only I could decipher,' said the general.

'And what does the message say?' asked Sobek.

'Iker has found the hiding-place of the Herald, a monster against whom he is going to fight in single combat.'

'That's ridiculous!' declared the Protector. 'The Royal Son was forced to write that, in order to lure our soldiers into an ambush.'

'Even if that's true,' said Senusret, 'Iker is alive.'

'Most unlikely, Majesty. After writing the message he'd have been executed.'

'Wouldn't the Herald have kept him as a hostage?' asked Nesmontu.

'No, because he was no longer useful.'

'I disagree,' said the general. 'He could have continued to deceive us with other messages. I think the truth is much simpler: the Royal Son has succeeded in his mission and at this very moment he is trying to get back to Memphis.'

'A pretty tale, but unlikely!' scoffed the Protector.

'In which region is the Herald supposedly hiding?' asked Senusret.

Nesmontu grimaced. 'One of the least-controlled ones, on the border of Canaan and Syria. Forests, swamps, ravines, wild animals, no roads – an ideal place for a rebel because troops can't deploy properly. It is an uncharted area on our maps, without any points of reference.'

Sobek was triumphant. 'The perfect place for an ambush! What does General Nesmontu recommend that we do?'

'We should send a patrol of volunteers who are familiar with the Syrian terrain.'

'That would just be condemning experienced soldiers to death,' said Sobek angrily. 'Let us face up to the evidence: Iker cannot have survived unless he is in league with the rebels.'

'Prepare to send out that patrol,' the king ordered Nesmontu. 'But it is not to leave until we receive a second message confirming the first.'

16

Crooked-Face and his band of marauders approached an isolated farm. They were once again going to extort food and livestock from one of the peasant families they were 'protecting'. The farmers were terrified of the ruthless Crooked-Face, and did not dare inform the soldiers or desert guards for fear of terrible reprisals.

Since the failure of his attempt on Senusret's life, Crooked-Face had been in hiding. His men had begged him to rejoin the Herald but he felt capable of getting by on his own, though since his break with the 'great leader', his luck seemed to have taken a turn for the worse. He secretly mocked the Herald's sermons, but realized that the preacher was clever and cruel enough to triumph in the end.

He would not admit it, even to himself, but Crooked-Face, who was afraid of neither gods nor devils, was afraid of the Herald. He dared not reappear before him following the botched attempt to kill the pharaoh, for which the Herald would hold him to blame. The man-falcon would probably tear him apart with his talons, in a paroxysm of rage.

Crooked-Face had to think about feeding himself and his men. These peasants would provide him with a meal fit for a king, and then he would rape the farmer's wife. It would destroy the peasants' will to resist, besides which Crooked-Face enjoyed humiliating his victims.

His hunter's instinct saved him from disaster. Two hundred paces from the farm, he halted.

His men did likewise. 'What's the matter, chief?' asked one of them.

'Listen, you fool.'

'I can't hear anything.'

'Exactly. Don't you find it odd, this silence? There isn't even any noise from the poultry-yard.'

'So . . . ?'

'So it means that the farmer we've been protecting has left. It won't be peasants waiting for us. We're getting out of here.'

When the guard on lookout saw the raiders running away, he gave the signal to attack. But it was too late. Crooked-Face's band was already out of range.

Honest, helpful, well-liked in his part of Memphis, the sandal-seller had made people forget his foreign origins and had been absorbed into the mass of working people in the city. Nobody would ever have suspected that he belonged to the Herald's network of spies.

One evening, as he was going home at dusk, an enormous arm encircled his neck.

'Crooked-Face!' exclaimed the shopkeeper. 'What are you doing here? We thought you were dead.'

'Where is the great leader?'

'I don't know. I—'

'You may not, but your superior certainly will. My men and I are going to rejoin the Herald. If you don't help me, I'll kill all his followers, beginning with you.'

The sandal-seller did not take the threat lightly. 'I will help you.'

The landscape south of Sichem was sinister. Dried-up trees, red, sterile earth, a dry riverbed full of stones, traces of snakes.

'It can't be here, chief,' said one of the brigands.

'On the contrary,' said Crooked-Face, 'this is just the sort of country he likes. He isn't like anyone else, my lad. We'll settle ourselves in and wait.'

'But supposing it's a trap?'

'Post four sentries.'

'Look! There's someone down there.'

A tall man dressed in a turban and a long woollen tunic appeared from nowhere, and stood gazing at the small band.

'I am happy to see you again, my friend,' said the Herald in a voice so soft that it gave Crooked-Face gooseflesh.

'So am I, my lord.' Wisely, the ruffian prostrated himself. 'It wasn't my fault,' he said. 'I tried to get some food, but the guards chased me away. Some damned peasant must have denounced me – can you believe it? Basically, I was leading a boring life. I and my lads need action, so here we are.'

'Have you finally decided to obey me?'

'Yes, my lord. I swear it on pain of death.'

The Herald had set up his headquarters at the heart of a network of caves linked by galleries. In the event of an attack, he would have more than one way to escape. Several springs supplied this desolate place with water, and lookouts were posted around it to ensure its security.

The Herald occupied a small house. A huge cave served as a teaching-place where, each day, his faithful listened attentively to his preaching, which constantly hammered home the same message: the forced conversion of unbelievers, the suppression of the pharaonic institution, the submission of women. These themes were repeated until they were engraved in people's minds. Shab the Twisted watched for those who were not fervent enough, and if they did not show greater devotion they suffered a brutal death. With his flint knife, he sliced open the neck of the condemned man, whose corpse served as an example. On the path to conquest, no weakness could be forgiven.

Thirteen-Years, the Herald's youngest follower, had an unfailing instinct for flushing out cowards. Shab gladly gave him permission to torture them and then summarily execute them, knowing that the work would be done well. The only ones who deserved to survive were those who committed themselves to dying for the cause.

The young and beautiful Bina was shut away from men's sight, and rarely emerged. In the service of her lord and master, her fame was growing. She enjoyed the extraordinary privilege of being close to the Herald.

This situation deeply displeased Ibcha, a former metal-worker and commander of the Asian raiding-party. He was in love with the pretty brown-haired girl, and waited longingly for her fleeting appearances. Although he had led two unsuccessful attacks, at Kahun and Dahshur, his fellow countrymen still trusted him. To everyone's surprise, the Herald had not reproached him in any way, and Ibcha remained a member of his inner council.

'You look worried, Thirteen-Years,' said Ibcha.

'Aren't you? The lord ought not to have gone off on his own.'

'Don't worry. The Herald can control the demons of the desert, can't he?'

'We must all worry about his safety. Without him, we'd be nothing.'

Thirteen-Years had been furious to learn, from a sand-traveller who had suffered from Amu's cruelty, that Iker was dead. Not that the boy felt any affection for Iker, but he would have liked to break his soul and transform him into a vengeful puppet, eager to fight against a pharaoh who had abandoned him. By slaughtering the Canaanite tribe charged with Iker's re-education, Amu had destroyed that fine project, and he was famous for his hatred of Egyptians so there could be no doubt about the Royal Son's fate.

'Next time,' promised Thirteen-Years, 'I shall follow the Herald. If anyone dares threaten him, I shall take action.'

Ibcha stroked his beard. 'Shouldn't you obey his orders?'

'Sometimes disobedience is necessary.'

'That's a dangerous slope, my boy. You might slip and fall.'

'He'll understand – he always understands.'

The fanaticism of the boy and of those close to the Herald was beginning to worry Ibcha. Of course they must drive out the Egyptian occupier and liberate the land of Canaan, but what kind of rule would then be imposed upon the region? This boy dreamt of killing people, while his master wanted to conquer Egypt, Asia and even more. There was a danger of sinking into a murderous madness which would result in nothing but ill fortune. Ibcha would have liked to confide in Bina, and ask her advice, but she remained inaccessible. She, once so wild and so free, now behaved like a slave. Was that the fate in store for all the faithful who hung on the predator's every word?

'Here he is!' shouted Thirteen-Years. 'He's coming back!'

The Herald entered the camp walking calmly at the head of a small band of men. 'Give food and drink to the warriors of the true faith,' he ordered.

Shab the Twisted tapped Crooked-Face on the shoulder. 'Well, you took your time about it, but you understand now, do you? You belong here with us, and nowhere else. If you leave the lord you'll meet only failure, but under his command you'll triumph.'

'Maybe so, but I don't want a sermon from you about it.'

'One day your spirit will open to the Herald's teachings.'

Shab's devotion exasperated Crooked-Face, but this was no time for an argument. Only too happy to have come through so well, the ruffian ate and drank greedily.

As he did, he observed the great leader's headquarters. 'Astute, very astute,' he said. 'You can't be taken by surprise.'

'The Herald is never wrong,' the Twisted One reminded him. 'God expresses himself through his mouth and dictates his actions.'

A pretty brown-haired girl emerged from the main cave, knelt before the Herald, and presented him with a cup of salt.

'What a superb creature,' said Crooked-Face, his lust aroused.

'Whatever you do, don't go near Bina. She's the servant of the Herald.'

'He doesn't waste his time, eh?'

Shab's face hardened. 'I forbid you to talk of the lord like that.'

'All right, don't get angry. A woman's still a woman, even if she is Bina. Let's not make a fuss about it.'

'She's different. The Herald's training her to do great things.'

That's all we need, thought Crooked-Face as he munched a flatcake filled with hot beans. Out of the corner of his eye, he saw a bearded man go up to Bina, as she was going back into her cave.

'I want to talk to you,' said Ibcha in a low voice.

'There's no point.'

'I've fought under your leadership, and I—'

'Our only leader is the Herald.'

'Bina, do you believe—'

'I believe only in him.' With that, she disappeared into the cave.

Shab had also witnessed the little scene, and he went straight to inform his master. 'My lord, if that man Ibcha is bothering your servant—'

'Don't worry about him. After his two dismal failures, I'm planning to entrust to him a role that fits him somewhat better.'

*

There were no fewer than thirty of them. Thirty chiefs of Canaanite tribes, large and small, had answered the Herald's call. Some were curious, others were determined to reaffirm their independence, but all wanted to meet this man, whom most of them had thought was a spectre, a phantom invented to disturb the Egyptians' sleep.

The first to speak was a small, fat man with a red beard. 'I, Dewa, speak in the name of the oldest tribe in Canaan. Nobody has ever defeated us, and nobody gives us orders. We rob anyone we like, when we like. Why have you called this assembly?'

'The divisions among the tribes make you weak,' replied the Herald calmly. 'The enemy army is vulnerable, but to defeat it you must be united. Here is my proposition: forget your quarrels, place yourselves under the command of a single leader, and liberate Sichem. The attack will take the Egyptians by surprise, and they will be wiped out. The pharaoh will be paralysed by such a demonstration of strength.'

'No, he won't,' argued Dewa. 'He'll send all his armies against us.'

'He will do nothing of the sort.'

'How do you know that?'

'Egypt is about to experience serious internal trouble. The king will be busy dealing with it.'

Dewa was shaken for a moment, but soon regained his composure. 'You don't know General Nesmontu.'

'He's an old man nearing the end of his career,' the Herald pointed out. 'He has given up trying to conquer your lands, because he is afraid of you and does not believe he will ever force you to submit. By terrorizing Sichem, he makes Senusret believe that Egypt rules Canaan. And you yourselves are strengthening that illusion.'

Several tribal chiefs nodded.

'Together,' the Herald went on, 'you will outnumber Nesmontu's worn-out troops by three to one. The Canaanite army of liberation will sweep away everything in its path and give birth to a strong, independent state.'

Despite his opposition to the plan, Dewa sensed that he could not dismiss it with a wave of the hand. 'We must discuss the matter.'

17

'My lord,' ventured Shab the Twisted, 'can this collection of braggarts really form an army worthy of the name?'

'Of course not, my friend.'

'But then . . .'

'Pharaoh cannot afford to disregard them. While these worthless creatures are occupying Canaan, we shall launch the real offensive. Canaan will remain what it is: a region of infighting, more or less latent conflicts and interminable quarrels, punctuated by devious tricks. When I have finished with Egypt, I shall make the true religion reign here, and no one will disobey me.'

'But what if the tribes refuse to unite?'

'They won't refuse this time, Shab. Sichem tempts them too much.'

The stormy deliberations lasted all night.

At dawn, Dewa hailed the Herald, and asked, 'What share of the booty do you want?'

'Nothing.'

'Ah. That makes things easier. And you want to lead our troops.'

'No.'

Dewa was astounded. 'Then what do you want?'

'The defeat of the Egyptians, and your victory.

'I shall lead the Canaanite army.'

'No,' said the Herald.

'What do you mean, "no"? Do you think I can't do it?'

'No one tribe must hold sway over all the others. I advise you to choose a very clever commander, Ibcha, who is accustomed to this kind of fighting. After your victory you can reward him according to his merits and choose the new king of Canaan.'

The proposition met with enthusiasm from the tribal chiefs. They were immediately served date-wine, and sealed their union.

'I was not expecting such an honour,' Ibcha confessed to the Herald, 'especially after my two previous failures.'

'The circumstances were against you, and you did not have enough men or weapons. This time it will be different. A whole army of hardened warriors will follow your orders, and you will have the advantage of numbers and surprise.'

'I shall succeed, my lord!'

'I am certain of it, my faithful servant.'

'Will you permit me not to take prisoners, even if the Egyptian soldiers surrender?'

'Don't encumber yourself with any useless mouths.'

Ibcha would have liked to talk to Bina about this marvellous promotion, but it was more important to talk to the Canaanite chiefs and work out a battle-plan.

'Come here, Thirteen-Years,' ordered the Herald.

The youth raised worshipful eyes to his master. 'I have disappointed you, my lord. I wanted to turn Iker into a bloodthirsty warrior devoted to our cause, and he stupidly got himself killed by Amu.'

'That is of no importance, my young hero. You have rid us of him, and I congratulate you.'

'Then . . . you aren't angry?'

'On the contrary, I'm going to trust you with a vital mission.'

Thirteen-Years trembled from head to foot.

'You know General Nesmontu, I believe?'

'When that vermin interrogated me and humiliated me, I swore to have my revenge.'

'The time is coming, Thirteen-Years. Victory is proclaimed when the enemy's head is cut off. So your new mission is to kill Nesmontu, cut off his head, and brandish your trophy before the Canaanites.'

To Ibcha's great surprise, the discussions had not gone on for ever. Won over by his determination and seriousness, the tribal chiefs gave up their usual demands. Each agreed to bring his men to the appointed gathering-place, two days' march from Sichem, in a hostile region where Nesmontu's soldiers did not venture.

Several scouts were sent out to locate the enemy's positions. Several Egyptian encampments would probably have to be destroyed before the Canaanites could attack Sichem, whose fortifications were bound to have been improved.

Ibcha was not worried about anything. Thanks to the Herald, he had become a real general and would prove his worth. A chance like this was so unhoped-for that it would make him invincible.

Another source of surprise was the fact that none of the tribal chiefs withdrew from the coalition. On the given day, they all gathered with their warriors, ready to fight.

'What is the news from the scouts?' asked Ibcha.

'It's very good,' replied Dewa. 'As the Herald predicted, the Egyptians have withdrawn and shut themselves up inside Sichem. Those cowards are afraid of us! And here are the remnants of their main defence.' He emptied a basket at Ibcha's feet: broken amulets and scarabs, torn papyri, pieces of slate tablet covered in curses. 'Baubles, pathetic baubles! Those Egyptians are children. They think that their magic will stop us, but ours is stronger than theirs: we easily found and destroyed these feeble defences.'

'And there is not a single one of Nesmontu's soldiers between Sichem and our army of liberation?'

'Not one.'

'What about the town's fortifications?'

'They're equally feeble,' scoffed Dewa. 'The general has strengthened only the northern part; all we have to do is go round it. We must attack quickly and in force. Nesmontu believes the Canaanite tribes are incapable of uniting, so the surprise will be total.'

'Is everything in place?' Nesmontu asked his assistant.

'Yes, General.'

'Did the enemy scouts find the decoys?'

'Their sorcerers did. Judging by their shouts of joy, they think there's not a single obstacle left on the road to Sichem.'

'Then the attack is probably imminent. Given our evident weakness and the feebleness of our fortifications, the Canaanites will throw all their forces into the battle. At last the moment we've been waiting for has come. We had to make them leave their damned hiding-place, where any sizeable battle would have been impossible: too many water-courses, too many hills, too many trees, too many tracks impassable for an army. Here they'll be out in the open, and I shall apply the good old methods. Put the men on the highest alert.'

Nesmontu had been right to rely on Dewa's greed. Sneering at Canaanite unity and thinking only of making himself rich, the chief had sold the general invaluable information in exchange for immunity and vast lands.

Now they could only hope that the little rat had not told too many lies.

'Isn't she beautiful?' Amu asked Iker.

Her face exquisitely painted, perfumed, her hair plaited, the small, slender Syrian girl was delightful. She dared not look at her future husband, so kept her eyes lowered.

125

'The prettiest virgin in the land,' declared Amu. 'Her parents own a flock of goats, and they're offering you a house and fields. You see, you've become a leading citizen, Iker. And I shall keep my promise. Help me manage my possessions, and you will succeed me as chief.'

Iker thanked him with a weak smile.

Amu patted him on the shoulder. 'So you aren't a woman's man! Don't worry: this little girl will satisfy you. Inexperience is not without its charm, and you'll manage eventually. Your marriage tomorrow will be the opportunity for a drinking-party that everyone will remember. Don't forget to hide your wife safely away before the end of the feast, because I can't answer for my men's morality – or mine, come to that!'

Laughing heartily, Amu took the girl back to her parents. At the end of the wedding night, the proof of her virginity must be produced in the sight of the tribe.

Disconsolate, Iker wandered aimlessly around, Flesh-Eater at his heels. The Herald was still alive, his hiding-place could not be found, and Iker was condemned to an unbearable future. This forced marriage disgusted him. He loved only one woman, and would never be unfaithful to her.

There was only one solution: to run away this very night and try to get back to Egypt, even though his chances of survival were infinitesimal. So he must persuade his ally and guard to let him go.

He said, 'Listen to me carefully, Flesh-Eater.'

The huge hound lay down, stretched out, got up, then sat down and gazed deep into its master's eyes.

'I want to go away from here – far, far away. You can stop me and sound the alarm by barking. Since I'll never accept the sentence Amu is imposing upon me, I'll fight him and his whole tribe, in the name of Senusret. Alone against all Amu's fighters, I won't hold out for long, but at least that death will seem sweet to me. If you agree to help me, stand guard in front of my tent so that people will think I'm asleep. By the time Amu realizes I've gone, I'll have something of a start and will have a chance of escaping. I can't take you with me, Flesh-Eater, but I won't forget you. It's up to you: you can either help me or denounce me.'

At last the excitement was dying down a little. The preparations for the wedding were finished, and everyone was in a hurry to get to bed. They must awake fresh and ready for an unforgettable day of carousing, followed by a hot evening during which the young married couple would not be the only ones to enjoy pleasure.

After dining with Amu, who was in talkative mood and continued to promise him the world, Iker went to bed.

In the middle of the night, he emerged from his tent. He found Flesh-Eater on guard in front of it.

'I'm going now, Flesh-Eater,' he said. He kissed the dog on its head and stroked it for a long time. 'Do as you see fit If you stop me, I shan't hold it against you.'

Bent double, he headed for the southern edge of the camp, which was watched by only a single sentry. By crawling, Iker could avoid him. And then it would be the unknown: a long road, leading no doubt to the abyss.

Very slowly, the enormous hound lay down in front of Iker's tent. It made no sound except for a little whine of sadness.

'What a beautiful day!' exclaimed Amu as he walked through the camp, which would soon be transformed into a prosperous village run by Iker. 'Will the bride soon be ready?'

'Oh yes, sir,' replied the one-eyed man guarding her house. 'It will only take a moment longer to finish her face-paint.'

'Iker hasn't bothered her, I hope?'

'I wouldn't have let him pass,' replied the guard. 'Everyone must learn to be patient, don't you think?'

Flesh-Eater was still guarding Iker's tent.

'Everyone else has been up for a long time,' said Amu, puzzled. 'Why is he sleeping so late?'

He went towards the tent, but the hound growled and bared its teeth.

'Wake up, Iker! Come on, wake up!' shouted Amu.

There was no reply.

Some of his men had heard his shouts and came running over. 'Push that dog out of the way with your spears,' he ordered them.

It was no easy task, but eventually the hound had to move. Amu went into the tent and re-emerged almost immediately. Flesh-Eater had suddenly grown calm.

'Iker has gone,' Amu announced.

'We must pursue him and bring him back,' demanded an onlooker.

'It would be pointless. Sooner or later he'd run away again. I'd forgotten that an Egyptian can't live far from his country. But Iker will never see it again – it's too far away, and the way there is full of danger.'

18

As Isis emerged from the library of the House of Life at Abydos, a temporary priest handed her a letter bearing the royal seal. Fearing that it brought bad news, she went to Senusret's temple to find a little peace.

Surrounded by the gods depicted on the walls, and hieroglyphic inscriptions celebrating a deathless ritual, she relived the stages of her initiation. But she could not forget Iker. She would never have thought that she could be so troubled by the absence of someone she was not even certain she loved. If this letter informed her that he was dead, would she have the courage to continue fighting against the enemy?

When she left the temple she, who ordinarily smiled all the time, barely greeted the temporary priests whom she met and who wished her a good day by saying, 'Protection for your *ka*.'

She found a place where she could be alone, in a little garden planted before a small tomb. In the garden rested stelae enabling those to whom they were dedicated to participate magically in the Mysteries of Osiris. Trembling, she broke the seal and unrolled the papyrus.

Senusret told her he had received a coded message signed by Iker.

Iker was alive . . .

Isis held the letter tightly to her heart. So her intuition had not deceived her. But where was he, and what perils was he facing? To have survived proved that he had a remarkable ability to adapt and a talent for avoiding danger. But how much longer would luck and magic protect him?

General Ibcha looked distinguished in his coloured kilt and black sandals, a sword in his hand. At his side, the tribal chiefs greedily observed their prey: the town of Sichem, soon to be the capital of free Canaan. Each man was already thinking of seizing power by eliminating his former allies; but first they must win a crushing victory by killing as many Egyptians as possible.

'What a stupid mistake, shutting themselves up in the city,' said Ibcha. 'Nesmontu really is too old to command. We shall launch a massive attack on the south side, which is unfortified. I remind you all of the order: no prisoners are to be taken.'

The howling mob charged forward.

'Here they come,' said Nesmontu's assistant.

'Only to the south?' asked Nesmontu.

'Yes, sir.'

'Their first mistake. Have they kept any forces in reserve?'

'No, sir.'

'Their second mistake. Where are the tribal chiefs?'

'Together in the vanguard, sir.'

'And that's their third. Are all our men at their posts?'

'Yes, General.'

'This should be a good day,' said Nesmontu.

Ibcha had expected to meet fierce resistance, but when the Canaanites entered Sichem they encountered no obstacles at all. They poured along the streets and alleyways, searching in vain for an enemy to kill.

While they were regrouping here and there, and getting

their breath back, in one instant hundreds of Egyptian archers leapt up on the terraces and roofs. Their accuracy aided by the nearness of their targets, in a few moments they had wiped out half the Canaanite army.

Seized by panic, the survivors tried to escape from the trap. Two regiments of spearmen barred their way.

'Attack!' roared Ibcha, trying to ignore a spear-wound in his leg.

The fighting was brief and bloody. The archers went on firing, decimating the enemy; and not one fugitive got past the wall of spears.

'Don't kill me! I am your ally!' cried Dewa, terrified. 'You owe your victory to me!'

Nesmontu had not thought it advisable to tell the traitor what he planned to do. Dewa had intended to slip away from the fighting and return later to claim the fee for his collaboration, but the turn of the battle had condemned him. Shot through and through by arrows, the dying General Ibcha still had the strength to plunge his dagger into the traitor's back.

Then silence fell broken only – and only for an instant – by the panting of a survivor trying to escape; which was ended by a shot from an archer.

The Egyptians themselves were astonished by the ease and speed of their victory.

'Long live Nesmontu!' shouted a footsoldier, and his cry was taken up by all the rest.

The general congratulated his men on their success and excellent discipline.

'What are we to do with the wounded Canaanites, sir?' asked his assistant.

'Treat their wounds and interrogate them.'

A tribal chief had fallen dead on top of Thirteen-Years, thus saving his life. The boy knew that if he moved he would be killed instantly.

Out of the corner of his eye, Thirteen-Years saw Canaanite corpses littering the main road into Sichem, and became aware of the full extent of the disaster. Worse even than that was the knowledge that he had failed in his mission, had failed the Herald.

But destiny was smiling on him! A group of Egyptian officers were coming towards him, and in the lead was Nesmontu himself. He heard the general order the bodies of the dead Canaanites to be burnt and the town to be cleansed.

A few more steps, and Nesmontu would be within reach – his triumph would end in disaster, and the Canaanites' sacrifice would not have been in vain.

Thirteen-Years gripped the handle of his dagger and prepared to plunge it with all his strength into the general's chest.

When a soldier moved the dead body that had saved him, Thirteen-Years leapt up like a snake and struck.

At that moment, terrible pain tore through his back. His vision swam, yet he could make out Nesmontu.

'But I . . . I killed you!' croaked Thirteen-Years.

'No,' replied the general. 'You're the one who's dying.'

Thirteen-Years spewed out a jet of blood, and his eyes rolled back.

Nesmontu's assistant had blocked the dagger-blow with his own body, and saved his commander's life. He had taken Thirteen-Years' dagger in his forearm, and a spearman had killed the boy.

'I thought I saw something moving under there,' explained the assistant.

'Decoration and promotion for you,' decreed the general. 'For this poor lad, only nothingness.'

'Poor lad? With respect, sir, no, he wasn't: he was a fanatic,' said his assistant, tying a cloth round his arm. 'We're facing an army of utter darkness, prepared to enlist a child and instil into him one single aim: killing.'

*

As he was entering Memphis with Bina and Shab the Twisted, the Herald suddenly stopped and his eyes took on a bright red hue.

'The Canaanite army has been wiped out,' he said, 'and there will be severe repression. Senusret knows now that his enemies are capable of uniting, which means the next rebellion may be even larger. He will therefore have to station as many soldiers as possible in Syria and Canaan. That will leave the field open for us, and we shall strike at the heart of the Two Lands.'

'Did Thirteen-Years succeed?' asked Bina in a strange voice.

'He obeyed me, but I cannot make out the result of his actions. If Nesmontu is dead, the army's morale will be profoundly affected. As for Ibcha, he is certainly dead. He will not trouble you again.'

Crooked-Face and his men entered by other routes, mingling with the traders. They all easily passed the guards' checks, for the guards were searching for weapons. But they would never find the weapons the Herald would soon be using.

A wildcat crouched on top of a dead tree growled at Iker. After several days' hard march through woods, marshes and plains, he was almost at the end of his strength. If the cat pounced on him, he would be done for.

Angrily, he seized his throwing-stick and brandished it. Frightened, the wildcat slunk away.

Go on . . . He must go on. The Royal Son moved on again, and his legs carried him despite himself, as though they had a life of their own. But in the end they gave way. Iker lay down and fell asleep.

He was awoken by birdsong.

A few paces away lay a vast pool whose surface was covered in lotus-flowers. Astonished to have survived, he ran down to it, plunged in, and bathed with a childlike joy. There were clumps of papyrus nearby, and as he chewed a sweet-tasting stem he began to regain hope.

Suddenly the sun was blocked out by a black cloud: hundreds of crows with sharp beaks.

One of them emerged from the flock and dived at him, barely missing him. A dozen more followed suit, forcing Iker to lie flat in the reeds. The furious birds wheeled above their prey, cawing stridently.

The Royal Son got up and flung his throwing-stick into the sky. It was charged with magic. Would it dispel the curse that had taken possession of the crows' souls?

A beak pecked his left shoulder, drawing blood. Another brushed past his head. Then the whole flock flew in widening circles before flying away. The throwing-stick fell back to earth at Iker's feet.

Fearing another attack, he hastily left the accursed place.

The desert was never-ending: cracked red earth, the few plants all dead of thirst, not a single well or oasis.

Where was Egypt? Far away – too far away. No more cardinal points, no more horizon, no more hope. Only heat and thirst. Iker was going to die alone, without a ritual, without a tomb. The tragedy of the *Swift One* was beginning again, but this time no giant wave would carry him off to an Island of the *Ka*, and nobody would come to his aid.

Heedless of being burnt by the pitiless sun, Iker sat down in the scribe's position. Death lay before him like recovery at the end of an illness, the smell of an exquisite perfume, the return to one's homeland after exile, the sweetness of an evening under an awning at the end of a burning-hot day. Iker was giving up.

Then a bird flew towards him out of the light. It had a human face: his own.

'Stop pitying yourself,' it told him. 'To kill yourself like this would be an act of utter cowardice. You must pass on to the pharaoh a message which is vital for the survival of Egypt. Do not abandon yourself to nothingness.' Its wings beating strongly, the bird returned to the sun.

'What direction must I take?' cried Iker. 'Everywhere is desolation and wandering.'

Then he saw it: a four-sided column, each of whose sides bore Isis's serene and smiling face.

'I love you, Isis. Tell me which way to go, I beg you.'

The south-facing side shone most brightly.

Jaw clenched, the Royal Son walked towards the south.

19

Every single person in Memphis had heard about Nesmontu's triumph. Medes's secretariats had sent out to all the provinces the announcement that the Canaanite rebellion was over, thanks to the valiant general's feat of arms.

However, it was a morose victor who presented himself before the pharaoh.

'Sichem is still under control, Majesty,' he reported, 'and several tribes of hotheads have been partially wiped out. But there is nothing to rejoice about.'

'Why this gloom?'

'Because it was not a real army, just a collection of boasters. They headed straight into disaster without even realizing it.'

'Who was commanding them?'

'Nobody. They were merely a mob, incapable of attacking intelligently or even of beating a retreat. We should not call it a battle, merely an execution.'

'Was that not what you expected?' asked the king.

'Among the Canaanites lies and treachery are the rule, and I had taken precautions. All the same, I had not expected such an easy victory.'

'How do you explain what happened?'

'Those imbeciles were deliberately sent to their deaths. Someone wanted to make us believe that the Canaanites were assembling an army of liberation and that it represented a real danger.'

'Did you not do everything possible to lure it out of its safe territory and towards Sichem?'

'Indeed, Majesty, and I ought to be glad that I did. However, I have the feeling that I myself have been tricked.'

'But you put down the rebellion, did you not?'

'In the short term, yes. But the truth is that we are being deluded.'

'Will the Canaanites raise another army?'

'If they ally with the Syrians, perhaps. But I have little faith in that particular union.'

'Nevertheless, ought we to keep as many troops as possible in Canaan?'

'That is the vital question. Either we believe that this ridiculous attack on Sichem was intended to prove that the rebels are no threat, and we lower our guard, exposing ourselves to a real attack on our bases; or else we remain on guard and garrison the whole region. But, Majesty, if we do the latter we may lay ourselves open to a fatal blow elsewhere.'

'Have you received any more messages from Iker?'

'No, Majesty. Unlike Sobek, I am certain that his message is a valuable clue. Unfortunately, though, without more accurate information I cannot risk the lives of my soldiers, even experienced ones, by sending them to such a dangerous region. Unless the Royal Son can obtain more details about the Herald's lair, we shall not move.'

Sobek the Protector was triumphant. 'As I supposed, Majesty, Iker's message had only one goal: to deceive us. He wanted to make us disperse our troops while the Canaanite tribes attacked Sichem. Fortunately, General Nesmontu did not take the bait.'

'My reading of the message is different,' argued Sekari.

'Iker was being used to send us false information. As soon as he realized that, he escaped, hoping to rejoin us and tell us the truth.'

'Either the Royal Son is dead or else he is betraying us,' snapped Sobek. 'Sekari's friendship with Iker is preventing him from thinking clearly.'

'I have faced many dangerous situations and I have never allowed my feelings to cloud my judgment,' Sekari snapped back. 'I know Iker well, and I am certain that traitors here at court sold him to the enemy. However, he will return.'

'If he does,' promised Sobek, 'I shall throw him into prison myself.'

'Why do you hate him so much?' asked Sekari.

'It is a question of clear-sightedness, not hatred. The traitor can be no one but Iker himself. Although I hate most of the people at court, my investigations have found nothing untoward anywhere. They're flatterers and much too cowardly to take dangerous risks, whereas Iker wanted to kill His Majesty.'

'But he's proved his innocence.'

'No, he hasn't. He has rejoined his allies and is now fighting us from the outside. If he comes back to Memphis, he'll again try to kill the king. But that snake won't bite, because I'll crush its head.'

'The future will prove you wrong, Sobek.'

'You're the one who's wrong, Sekari.'

The pharaoh remained silent. Each of the two adversaries considered his silence to be approbation.

At last he was getting somewhere! Sekari had almost despaired of finding a chink in the loyalty of the guards close to Sobek. They seemed to form an unyielding barrier. However one of them, a greying fifty year-old officer, had agreed to a meeting in great secrecy.

'Are you investigating Sobek?' asked the officer.

'That's a very big word,' Sekari corrected him. 'No one doubts his honesty.'

'Then what is your criticism of him?'

'His hostility towards certain notables. Sometimes he's too thoroughgoing and harms the search for the truth.'

'You can say that again!' exclaimed the officer. 'When Sobek gets an idea into his head, nobody can make him change his mind. But he isn't always right.'

'About the Royal Son, for example?'

'Yes, that's right.'

'Is he using illicit means to harm the Royal Son?'

'I fear he may be.'

'Can you be more precise?'

The officer hesitated. 'It's difficult. Sobek is my commander, and I—'

'This is an affair of state, not a deal between two smugglers! If you talk, you will be doing the pharaoh a great service.'

'Will I at last get the promotion Sobek has been refusing me?'

'I did not know about that. What reasons has he given?'

The guard lowered his eyes. 'Mere trifles.'

'Such as?'

'I'm not a man out in the field, that's all! The violence, the arrests, the risks—'

'Go away.'

'Don't you want to hear what I have to say?'

'All you're thinking about is sullying your commander's name, and you have nothing important to tell me. Be content with your post and stop this unjustified bitterness.'

Ashamed, the officer did not protest.

Sekari's investigation was not going well.

As he put down his heavy leather bag of remedies, Gua sighed in exasperation. None of his famous patients was easy to treat, but Medes's wife would have worn out a whole regiment of doctors.

He was thin, with a weak constitution, and looked frail beside this ample, over-excitable woman who thought she suffered from every possible and imaginable ill.

'Here you are at last, my dear doctor! My body is nothing but pain, my life is torture! I need remedies, lots of remedies.'

'Stop waving your arms around and sit down. If you carry on like this, I shall leave.'

Medes's wife obeyed with the air of a little girl.

'Now, answer my questions honestly. How many meals do you eat every day?'

'Four . . . perhaps five.'

'I said: "honestly".'

'Five.'

'With cakes at every one?'

'Almost . . . Yes.'

'And fats?'

'Without them,' confessed the patient, 'food would have no taste.'

'Under these conditions,' said the doctor, 'no medicine will work. Either you at last change the way you eat or I shall place you in the hands of a colleague.'

'But I'm racked with constant anxiety, Doctor. Without the comfort of food, I shan't survive long. Eating calms me and helps me to get to sleep.'

Gua frowned. 'You have a good husband, a beautiful house, and you're rich. Why are you so anxious?'

'I don't know.'

'You don't know or you refuse to tell me?'

Medes's wife burst into tears.

The doctor sighed again. 'Very well. I shall prescribe you some calming pills, made from poppies. All the same, you must eat better and less, then find out what is causing your anxiety.'

'You're my saviour, Doctor, my saviour!'

Fearing the sort of excess that horrified him, Gua hastily opened his bag and took out a small bag. 'One pill in the morning, two when you go to bed.'

'When shall I see you again, Doctor?'

'The treatment will take several weeks. You are to follow my prescription strictly.'

Gua was thoughtful as he left Medes's house. If this woman was not mad, she was suffering because of a secret too heavy to bear. If he could free her from it, he might perhaps succeed in curing her.

Medes regarded his wife with astonishment. 'You seem very cheerful today.'

'Thank Doctor Gua. That man is a genius.'

Medes's gaze hardened. 'You haven't been saying too much, I hope?'

'Oh no, don't worry. All he cares about is treatments and remedies. He doesn't enjoy conversation at all.'

'So much the better, my darling, so much the better. Never, ever talk to him about me or about your gift for imitating other people's writing. Do I make myself clear?'

She nestled against him. 'I am your staunchest supporter, my love.'

Medes was beginning to feel reassured. Neither Sobek-Khu nor Senankh had any hold on him. It was natural for them to suspect him, because anyone and everyone would be under suspicion in a court buzzing with rumours. The poison distilled by the Herald was spreading little by little. It was eroding the confidence and undermining the foundations of the pharaonic state, which was unable to defend itself.

He congratulated himself every day on having formed an alliance with the Herald. But he did not enjoy violence: he preferred to travel by indirect routes to achieve his ends.

141

Alerted by a coded message, Medes went to the house of the Phoenician trader, taking the usual precautions. Having made sure he had not been followed, he handed the doorkeeper a piece of cedarwood bearing the hieroglyph of the tree.

To his astonishment, there was not a single pastry or sweetmeat on the low tables in the reception chamber, and the Phoenician had lost his air of joviality.

'The goods will arrive within a few days,' said the merchant.

'You mean the . . . ?'

'The quantities are even larger than we planned, so we are ready to act.'

Medes rubbed his chin. 'Has the Herald really ordered this?'

'Are you by any chance afraid of the consequences?'

'Well, they'll be appalling, won't they?'

'That is the aim of the operation, Medes. If you're afraid, you had better give up now.'

'The Herald would not forgive me if I did.'

'It's lucky for you that you understand him. But clear thinking won't be enough. Make sure all the necessary administrative measures are in place so that we can begin the greatest rebel operation anyone has ever dreamt of.'

20

As he did every evening, the priest in charge of the lamps at the Temple of Hathor in Memphis went to fetch oil from the storeroom outside the building. A large quantity had just been delivered.

The priest was a fussy man, who always followed exactly the same routine when he performed his duties. He loved to gaze upon the results of his work, when a gentle light bathed the goddess's dwelling.

Slowly and solemnly, he carried the flame to the lamp known as the 'house of the ship', the one he always lit first. Conscious of the importance of what he was doing, he lit the wick.

Instantly, the oil flared up into a blaze and fierce flames devoured his hands, his chest and his face. As he staggered back, howling in pain, the fire reached the sacred ship and then began to spread.

As usual, the principal scribe in charge of the capital's supplies of fruit and vegetables wore a suspicious expression.

'Can you guarantee the quality of your oil? All my offices must be lit perfectly.'

'The producer is categorical about it.'

'I should like to count the jars again.'

'I've already done it three times!'

'Possibly, but I have not.'

Only when he himself had checked did the scribe at last consent to apply the seal that would permit the carrier to be paid by the tjaty's office.

The days to come were likely to be difficult, for it would take the scribe many hours of extra work to make up for the delays affecting his secretariat. In view of Tjaty Khnum-Hotep's insistence on efficiency, this situation could not go on. So the scribe had told his employees they must give up the forthcoming period of holiday in order to show that they were up to their job.

With extremely bad grace, and concerned that a reprimand would compromise their careers, they had bowed to his demand and would be working late.

The daylight began to fade.

'Light the lamps,' ordered the principal scribe.

A dozen of them blazed up uncontrollably. Cries of fear were succeeded by panic. The flames caught the papyri, the writing materials, the wooden chairs, then the walls.

One young scribe managed to get out of the furnace. To his horror, he saw other columns of smoke rising from the centre of the capital. Several offices were on fire.

The master-cook let out a string of curses. A banquet for thirty guests to provide, and his delivery of prime-grade oil had still not arrived!

At last a procession of heavily laden donkeys reached the house.

'I don't know you,' he said to the donkey-driver, a man with a moustache.

'My employer is ill; I'm taking his place.'

'If you cause delays like this, you're liable to be dismissed.'

'I'm very sorry, but I was told that you're very demanding. I spent a lot of time choosing the best oils.'

'Show me.'

One by one, the donkey-driver opened the jars. 'Moringa, olive and balanite oils, all of the finest quality.'

Suspiciously, the cook tasted them. 'They seem all right. But make sure there are no more delays in future.'

'Don't worry. I'll see there aren't.'

The master-cook hated rushing his work, and he didn't feel very well. Nevertheless, he succeeded in preparing a three-course banquet that was relatively satisfactory. The guests ate heartily and were lavish with their compliments.

And then everything went appallingly wrong.

A woman vomited. Servants took her to one side, but soon two more guests showed the same symptoms. Soon all the diners had been affected, and some of them lapsed into unconsciousness.

Doctor Gua was summoned urgently, but all he could do was note that there had been several deaths. After examining the survivors, he gave his opinion, which terrified the master-cook.

'The food was poisoned.'

The steward of the chief archivist of Memphis was delighted to be able to give his employer's wife her favourite luxury: a flask of ladanum, with its warm, ambergris scent. Thanks to information from a cousin, he had been able to procure some from a previously unknown vendor in the capital.

The archivist's wife was indeed thrilled. She thought she would make her best friends green with envy, unaware that they had all obtained exactly the same perfume from exactly the same source. She applied a few drops of the ladanum to her throat, and almost immediately she felt dizzy and swayed. Trying desperately to hang on to a wooden chest, she fell forward.

Surprised by her absence at the evening meal, her husband went to her bedchamber. The unfortunate woman's neck was one huge wound, eaten away by acid.

*

'You don't look well, sir,' the officer said to his captain. The captain was half-heartedly handling the steering-oar of a heavy cargo vessel, laden with wheat, which was destined for Faiyum.

'Don't make a fuss. I'm fine, just a bit tired.'

'What did you eat this morning?'

'Some bread and dates.'

'Did you forget your medicine for the pains?'

'Certainly not. Actually, the doctor gave me a new potion containing ladanum from Asia, and my back has completely stopped hurting.'

At that moment, the Nile began to swim before the captain's eyes. Suddenly, he thought he saw ten war-boats bearing down upon him. 'Abandon ship!' he shouted. 'We're under attack!'

Letting go of the oar, he tried to jump into the water. His officer seized him round the waist.

'We are lost! We're all going to die!' The captain's head lolled back, and his body grew limp.

The officer laid him down on the deck and slapped his cheeks. 'Captain, wake up! There is no danger.'

'He's dead,' said one of the crew.

Pretty Water-Lily was filled with happiness. Not only had she married a handsome, wealthy man, but the prospects for the forthcoming birth of her first child were excellent. She lived in a pleasant house in the southern part of Memphis, and her two servants, whom she cheerfully spoilt, were happy to do anything for her.

And her husband had just given her a wonderful gift, one she had dreamt of so often that she could scarcely believe it was real: a magnificent pregnancy flask shaped like a pregnant woman suckling her baby. It contained oil of moringa, and her maid was about to rub it into her body. All the energy channels would open, and both the mother's and the child's defences would be strengthened.

Expert hands kneaded her skin, producing a marvellous feeling of well-being. She was dozing when, suddenly, an atrocious sensation of burning made her cry out in pain. The maid jumped back in alarm.

'My body is on fire!' screamed Water-Lily. 'Bring water, quickly!'

But the remedy was worse than the ill. Less than an hour later, the young woman died in terrible agony. And her child would never see the light of day.

More than a hundred similar cases were reported to Gua. Although he did his utmost, he could not save even one of the victims.

The cargo vessel moored at the quay in Abydos. Ten soldiers lined up at the bottom of the gangplank.

Their commander, who had been appointed by Sobek himself, went aboard and asked the captain, 'What are you transporting?'

'Special cargo from Memphis: oil of moringa for personal use and cooking, lamp-oil and flasks of ladanum. Do you want to see my authorization?'

'Of course.'

The documents seemed in order. 'Who is responsible for this consignment?' asked the commander.

The captain rubbed his chin. 'I don't know, but it's not my problem! Can we unload?'

'Very well.'

Puzzled, the soldier checked the list of boats' movements, going back to the beginning of the month. This vessel was not mentioned, but that was probably nothing to worry about, because special cargos were not rare. And the seal of the tjaty's government on the bill of lading ought to have dispelled his suspicions.

147

But he had been put in charge of security at the port precisely because he was always suspicious. He summoned about twenty additional soldiers, and told them that none of the sailors was to leave the vessel.

The officer went back on board while the dock-workers finished unloading.

'Are you a native of Memphis?' he asked the captain.

'No, I'm from a village in the Delta.'

'Who's your employer?'

'A ship-owner in the capital.'

'Is this your first trip to Abydos?'

'That's right.'

'And you weren't worried by the thought of the assignment?'

'Why should I be?'

'Abydos isn't like any other destination.'

The captain shrugged. 'You know, in my profession you don't ask that sort of question.'

'Can you vouch for all the members of your crew?'

'Each unto his own, Commander. Myself, I get on with my work and don't worry about anything else.'

The commander had hoped that the flurry of questions would disconcert the captain into letting slip some significant details. But the captain was not disconcerted in the least; he remained imperturbable.

'When can I leave?' he asked.

'As soon as the usual formalities have been completed.'

'Will that take long?'

'I want to inspect your boat.'

'Is that usual?'

'By order of the pharaoh, the safety of Abydos requires exceptional measures to be taken.'

'Very well, go ahead.'

Surprised by this lack of resistance, the commander searched the boat thoroughly, but found nothing. Was he wrong, or should he heed his instinct?

'Wait here,' he said. 'I have some final administrative tasks to take care of.'

The vessel and its crew were under close guard, so there was nothing to fear. Yet the officer was still worried, so he summoned a temporary priest.

'I'd like a specialist to examine the oils before they're distributed. Fetch one as quickly as possible.'

When Isis arrived, the commander looked at her dubiously. Could this young woman really provide him with valuable expert information?

'What is the matter, Commander?' she asked.

'This delivery worries me.'

'Have you any good reason to be worried?'

'Only my intuition.'

Isis poured a little moringa oil on to a piece of fabric, then on to a flatcake and finally on to a small fish, which a soldier had just caught. A few minutes later, suspicious patches appeared.

'This oil is not pure,' she said. 'It may even be harmful.'

'Let us move on to the lighting oil,' said the commander.

'Fill a lamp with it,' advised Isis.

The officer did so, and prepared to light the wick.

'Wait,' cut in Isis. 'Use a long stick and stand well back.'

The commander did so. It was well that he did, for as soon as the oil felt the flame it exploded. If he had been close to it, he would have been badly burnt.

Pale-faced, he said to Isis, 'You saved my life!'

'Are there any other suspicious products?'

'One more, ladanum.'

Made cautious by the results of the first experiments, the commander handled the flask very delicately.

'I think it best if I take it to my workshop and examine it there,' said Isis.

When he saw her carrying the flask away, the captain of the cargo vessel dived into the river. Knowing what the result of the tests would be, he had no choice but to try to escape.

But he was a poor swimmer. Just as the archers began to fire, he was caught by a current, and he panicked. Struggling vainly, he swallowed a great deal of water, sank, rose to the surface, shouted for help, sank once again and drowned.

21

Iker ran and ran. His stride looked short, but it was tireless. He was profoundly grateful for the military training he had had to undergo in the province of the Hare when the province had been governed by Djehuty.

Confident that the vision of Isis had not deceived him, Iker ate up the space. There was plenty of water to be found. He ate berries, slept for a few hours and then set off again. His exhaustion and despair were forgotten. Each stride was taking him nearer to Egypt.

At last, in the distance, he made out the first fort of the King's Walls. He quickened his pace. In less than an hour, soldiers would greet him. Then he would return to Memphis and give his report to Senusret, and his country would avoid the Canaanite trap.

An arrow plunged into the ground at his feet, recalling him to reality. To the lookouts, he must seem like a rebel bent on trying some underhand trick. He stopped and raised his arms in the air.

Five soldiers armed with throwing-spears emerged from the fort and came to meet him, eyeing him suspiciously.

'Who are you?' asked their leader.

'Iker, the Royal Son.'

This declaration caused consternation, but the officer

recovered quickly and asked, 'Have you got the seal proving your status?'

'I have just come from Canaan. On His Majesty's orders, I infiltrated the enemy, and I could not carry anything that might compromise me. Please take me to Memphis.'

'First of all, you must see the commander of the fort.'

The commander was a red-faced man, full of his own importance. 'Stop lying, boy, and tell me who you really are.'

'Iker, the Royal Son.'

'The word is that he is dead.'

'I am very much alive and must speak to the king as soon as possible.'

'Well, you're a bold one, I'll give you that. Canaanites don't usually hold up so well.'

'Give me something to write with.'

Curious, the commander granted the request.

In fine hieroglyphics, Iker wrote the first of Ptah-Hotep's Maxims. 'There,' he said. 'Is that enough to prove that I'm an Egyptian scribe?'

The officer was not yet convinced. 'That isn't the Canaanites' style . . . Very well, we shall examine your case more closely.'

The Phoenician trader had good reason to be satisfied. All the rebels' operations had been successful and had spread panic throughout Memphis. Insane rumours were circulating, and Senusret's throne had been destabilized. The sinister emissaries of the goddess Sekhmet had spread their poisons, miasmas and sicknesses by firing deadly arrows, both visible and invisible.

The Phoenician's network was functioning smoothly. Each man delivering the contaminated oil had followed his orders to the letter. Nobody had been stopped, and there was no trail for the guards to follow.

The Herald's predictions were coming true. All his followers would now regard him as their absolute master, for he was defying the pharaoh at the very heart of his kingdom.

But one problem remained, and it was as delicate as it was irritating: Abydos. The success in Memphis had been built on a patiently implanted network, which his swift action had placed out of reach of the authorities. The situation of the sacred domain of Osiris seemed very different. So the Phoenician had grave doubts about the possibility of introducing ladanum and poisoned oils into Abydos. However, one of his best employees, a seasoned sailor, leading a crew unaware of what it was transporting, had accepted this difficult mission in exchange for an enormous bonus.

The Phoenician's most skilled spy, a water-carrier, came to see him secretly.

'There's very good news, sir. Memphis has been put to fire and the sword. Several uncontrollable blazes have damaged temples, destroyed offices and claimed many victims. Not to mention all the pregnant women of the nobility who've died.'

'Any more news about Abydos?'

'Failure has been confirmed. The cargo aroused the army's suspicions, and because of stringent checks nothing got through the security cordon.'

'What happened to the captain?'

'He drowned while trying to escape.'

'At least he he didn't talk. Are our other agents safe?'

'Those from outside the town have already left to rejoin the Herald. The others are following their usual trades and mourning with the rest of the populace.'

Senusret's face was even more grave than usual.

'These are not accidents, Majesty,' said Khnum-Hotep, 'but a controlled attack carried out by well-organized rebels.'

'My worst fears have been realized,' said Sobek-Khu tensely. 'The network of spies in Memphis has been

153

reactivated. Its lighting- and cooking-oils have caused many deaths and a series of fires. The damage is considerable.'

'The horror does not stop there,' went on the tjaty, his voice breaking. 'Many women were poisoned by the oil in the pregnancy flasks. Despite the best efforts of Doctor Gua and his colleagues, not one was saved.'

'It is Egypt that they want to murder,' said Sobek. 'They are killing our scribes, our priests, our leading citizens, elite and even our future children.'

'Restore calm and see that the sick and the wounded are cared for,' ordered the king. 'Medes must get me news of Abydos with all speed.'

Medes set all his scribes to write calming messages to the Northern and Southern provinces, and to ensure that they received them as a matter of urgency. While secretly rejoicing in the Herald's success, he again demonstrated his efficiency in the service of the pharaoh.

True, many innocent people had lost their lives, but their innocence counted for nothing in Medes's eyes. The only thing that mattered was taking power, and on this winding path his allies were obliged to strike hard.

As he was about to send a fast boat to Abydos to gather reliable information, Medes was informed that a priestess from there had arrived by boat. He hurried to the port straight away.

It was Isis, accompanied by North Wind.

He greeted her and asked, 'Is your visit a matter of protocol, or—'

'Please take me to the palace.'

'Has something serious happened in Abydos?'

'I must see His Majesty immediately.'

Medes was under strict orders to be careful, so he had had no contact with the Phoenician since the beginning of the rebel operations. As a result, he knew nothing about the fate of Abydos but, judging by Isis's solemn expression, it seemed that the site had not been spared.

'We narrowly escaped disaster, Majesty,' said Isis. 'Had the commander Sobek appointed been less alert, the oils and poison would have been distributed throughout Abydos. We would have had many deaths to mourn.'

'Your own skill and knowledge were not unimportant.'

'I was lucky, and the Shaven-Headed One confirmed my findings. Majesty, has . . . has Memphis been affected?'

'It did not escape this appalling attack. Many of its citizens are dead.'

Although the sovereign's voice did not shake at all and his gaze remained steady, she could tell that he was suffering deeply. Both man and king were gravely wounded, but nothing would prevent him from continuing the struggle.

'These atrocities must have been committed by the demon of darkness who is trying to kill the acacia,' ventured Isis.

'The Herald? Yes, you are right. He has demonstrated to us the extent of his powers; and he will not stop there.'

'Is it really impossible to identify him and find out where he is?'

'Despite all our research, he remains out of reach. I had hoped that Iker would uncover his trail.'

'Have there been any more message from the Royal Son?'

'No, Isis.'

'But he is alive, Majesty.'

'Remain in Memphis for a few days. The priestesses of Hathor are treating those who suffered burns, and your knowledge will be useful.'

Senankh and Sehotep were using every means at their disposal to help the Herald's victims, restore the temples and rebuild the offices and other buildings destroyed by the fires.

Meanwhile, Sobek organized the questioning of the few

155

witnesses who were still alive. They all said the same thing: they had not known the men who delivered the deadly oils. Sobek concluded that either the criminals lived in other parts of the city, or else they had come from outside. In the latter case, they must have had support from accomplices who knew the capital well. But these accomplices were as elusive as their leader.

Unfortunately, the information gathered was vague and contradictory. No one had paid much attention to the friendly, discreet and hurried delivery men. There was not a single thread to follow, not a single suspect.

Sobek's powerlessness filled him with such despair that he felt like bellowing in rage and hitting the first suspect who came along. He wished he could throw all the capital's bad lots into prison and hit them with a club until he learnt some useful information. But the Law of Ma'at forbade torture, and the pharaoh would never forgive such a deviation from it.

Why had he failed so completely? The only possible explanation was that the enemy had identified all his informants. The rebels used seasoned men, who blended perfectly into the background and obeyed their leader with incredible discipline. He had found not a single traitor, nor anyone with a loose tongue, not even anyone who could be bought. Punishment for disloyalty must be so terrible that none of the cohort of darkness dared do anything but play his role, slavishly obeying his leader's orders. Sobek was sickened, but knew he must be patient. One day one of the rebel spies would make a mistake, however small, and the Protector would exploit it to the full.

In the meantime, he had all the oils and medicines in the city checked. Once it was done he felt confident on that front, but how could he guess the nature of the next attack?

'Sir,' one of his men told him, 'the rumours are growing. People say the king used some of the poisoned oil and is dead. Groups are forming here and there, and we may face riots.'

Sobek hurried to the palace to inform the king.

Senusret immediately summoned his head steward and the guardian of the royal regalia.

Watched by astounded crowds, the pharaoh's travelling-chair was borne through every district of the capital. Senusret wore the Double Crown and a large kilt decorated with a griffin striking down his enemies. His chest was covered by a broad golden collar evoking the creative Pesedjet; and he held both the Sceptre of Power, the *was*, and the 'Magic' sceptre, which enabled him to restore multiplicity to oneness. His face was as calm as a statue's, and it reassured all those who saw it.

The king was not dead, and his appearance proved his unshakeable determination to re-establish order. Loud cheering rose up from the crowds, and Sobek felt greatly relieved: the Herald's hideous victory would be only brief. And when Senusret returned, unharmed, to his palace after giving back hope to his people, the Protector understood the value of the enormous risk the king had taken.

One of his men hurried up to him and said in a low voice, 'Sir, you're going to be very pleased.'

'Have we got the beginnings of a lead?'

'Better than that.'

'You've arrested a suspect?'

'I won't spoil the surprise for you, sir.'

22

Iker was unrecognizable. Unshaven, his hair as long and matted as a marsh-dweller's, dirty, and dressed in a filthy, ragged kilt, he would have horrified any courtier.

His return to Egypt had not lived up to his hopes. A patrol had brought him from the King's Walls to Memphis and then, without interrogating him, had thrown him into a cell in the prison to the north of the city. Ignoring his protests, the guard refused to exchange a single word with him and confined himself to bringing him cold flatcakes and water once a day.

On whose orders was he being kept in prison secretly? Iker was beginning to form escape plans when the wooden door burst open. On the threshold stood Sobek the Protector.

'So you claim to be the Royal Son, do you?' he demanded.

Iker got to his feet. 'Although I am not very presentable, you ought to recognize me.'

Sobek walked round the prisoner. 'To be honest, I don't. Here, we lock up deserters, those who try to escape from conscripted labour, and foreigners who are here illegally. Which category do you belong to?'

'I am Royal Son Iker, as you very well know.'

'I met the Royal Son at court, and you don't look at all like him. The unfortunate fellow died somewhere in Canaan.'

'Did my message not get through?'

'It was a forgery, or perhaps a trick to lure our army into an ambush.'

'Stop this play-acting, Sobek, and take me to His Majesty. I have very important information to pass on to him as a matter of great urgency.'

'The wild ramblings of a rebel won't interest the king. Instead of wasting your breath telling lies, tell me why you attacked the King's Walls.'

'Don't be ridiculous! I managed to escape from the Canaanites and the Syrians, and I want to tell my father what I have discovered.'

Sobek folded his arms, a sarcastic smile on his lips. 'Not even the greatest of heroes could return from that hell. There are only two possibilities. Either you're a rebel trying to pass yourself off as the Royal Son in order to murder the pharaoh, or else you really are him – in other words, a traitor with precisely the same intention. It's up to you to decide which you are before you're sentenced to forced labour for the rest of your life.' The Protector stalked out and slammed the cell door behind him.

Isis had treated many burns victims, and fortunately most of them would survive their injuries. At last she could return to Abydos. She was preparing to board the boat when North Wind brayed loudly several times. He flatly refused to walk up the gangplank.

Isis stroked him. 'Are you ill?'

The donkey pricked up its left ear, signifying No.

'We must leave, North Wind.'

No, insisted the donkey.

'What do you want?'

North Wind turned and started trotting back towards the palace. Isis walked quickly, for fear of losing him. When he neared the palace, he sniffed the air for a long time, then galloped off at top speed, forcing passers-by to stand aside. Isis could not keep up with him.

'Is there a problem?' asked Sekari, who was discreetly ensuring the young priestess's safety.

'North Wind refuses to return to Abydos. It's the first time he's ever behaved as strangely as this.'

'Did you ask him why?'

'I didn't have time.'

'Well, I have a little idea.'

By questioning passers-by, Sekari was able to follow the donkey's trail.

'Still no clues, Sobek?' asked Sekari.

'If I had any, His Majesty would be the first to know. And what about you?'

'It seems that a Canaanite bandit is being held in the prison to the north of the city. I'd like to question him.'

'Why?'

'As part of my own investigation.'

'I'm sorry, but that villain's being held in secret. Only the tjaty can authorize you to see him, and I'm not sure he's still in a position to do it.'

'What's happened to him?'

'Carry out your own investigation.'

Sekari returned immediately to the palace. There he met Sehotep, who was visibly worried.

'The king has summoned the tjaty,' he told Sekari.

'Do you know why?'

'To judge from Khnum-Hotep's expression, there are serious problems.'

Senusret read out to the tjaty the report from the commander of the port of Abydos, which Sobek had passed on to him.

Khnum-Hotep was appalled. 'The seals of my government used by a murderer! I can think of nothing more dreadful,

Majesty. Of course, I shall resign immediately. Before I withdraw to my native province, will you grant me a final privilege, and permit me to ask you one question: did you think, even for a moment, that I was guilty?'

'No, Khnum-Hotep. And you shall remain in your post at this stormy time, when each servant of Ma'at must think only of the country's survival.'

Deeply shaken, and showing his age for the first time, the tjaty was so moved by this mark of confidence that he swore to work to the very end of his strength and to fulfil his duties to the very best of his ability.

'I have been guilty of negligence, Majesty,' he confessed, 'for the seals were much too easy to imitate and use. From now on I shall be the sole holder of them. Even my closest colleagues will no longer have access to them.'

'Will it not be difficult, or even impossible, to identify the thief?'

'Unfortunately so, Majesty. It has taken this disaster for me to become aware of a laxity for which I consider myself solely responsible.'

'Dwelling on past mistakes will not lead anywhere. Make sure the enemy cannot exploit such a weakness again, and make the tjaty's government exemplary.'

'You can rely on me, Majesty.'

Sekari found Khnum-Hotep looking older and very preoccupied, but he did not beat about the bush.

'I need an authorization.'

'Of what sort?'

'I wish to question a prisoner.'

'Sobek will hand him over to you.'

'He refuses.'

'Why?'

'He says the prisoner's identity must remain unknown.'

'Perhaps you should explain yourself, Sekari.'

161

'I will when I've questioned this man.'

'And you're so stubborn that you won't say anything until you have your authorization.'

'That's right.'

Armed with the precious document, Sekari ran to the prison, in front of which he found North Wind kneeling. Nothing and nobody could make him move. And if the donkey was behaving like that, Iker could not be far away.

The members of the King's House listened closely to Sobek-Khu's report, which covered every aspect of the tragedy. Thanks to the efforts of Sehotep's work teams, the buildings' wounds would soon be healed, though those of the humans would not. However, the large numbers of guards and soldiers deployed throughout the city were beginning to restore the people's confidence, particularly since hundreds of scribes were checking every product the citizens used.

'We know how the rebels operated,' said Sobek. 'They murdered the delivery men and took their places. The customers suspected nothing.'

'Ladanum is no ordinary product,' said Senankh.

'Indeed not, and I was hoping to trace the leaders of the ring by tracking the delivery back to its source, but the bills of lading were falsified. The doctors received the usual quantities in the usual way, so they had no reason to suspect anything was wrong.'

'What about the pregnancy flasks?' asked the tjaty.

'They were smuggled in in great secrecy. They're very costly, so only wealthy families could afford them. By using the witnesses' statements, I've traced the seller's storehouse. Unfortunately, he's disappeared, and nobody can tell me anything about him, apart from the fact that he came from Asia.'

'We should worry about minor matters,' advised Nesmontu. 'The real culprit behind these terrible crimes is the Herald.

Despite all the difficulties, he must be unearthed in his lair. Sobek and his men should guard Memphis. I and the army will see to that demon.'

'Has such a strategy any chance of working?' asked Senankh worriedly.

'We must strike fast and hard,' said the general. 'In view of the difficult terrain, I shall need all my troops.'

'General Nesmontu shall prepare a plan for an attack on Canaan,' ordered the pharaoh.

Recognizing Sekari, North Wind stood up and allowed himself to be stroked.

'You look very well,' said Sekari. 'Abydos suits you, it seems, and Isis is obviously taking good care of you.'

The donkey stared fixedly at the prison.

'Is Iker locked up in there?'

The right ear pricked up.

'Shall we go and fetch him?'

The animal's big brown eyes shone with hope.

The guard on duty looked closely at Sekari. 'I don't know you. What do you want?'

'To question the Canaanite bandit.'

'On whose authority?'

'Will Tjaty Khnum-Hotep's do?'

A good prison guard's main concern was preventing problems. Commander Sobek might have given strict instructions, but you couldn't argue with an order from the tjaty.

'It won't take too long, will it?' asked Sekari.

'Of course not.'

'Then get on with it.'

The guard unlocked the cell door and opened it.

Having thought of no solution but to knock out his jailer and try to escape, Iker charged. Trained to parry this kind of attack, Sekari blocked the arm of his attacker, who, however, did not let go. Locked together, they rolled on the ground.

'It's me – Sekari!'

Iker disengaged himself and stared at his adversary. 'You . . . Is it really you?'

Sekari sat up. 'I haven't changed much. You, on the other hand . . . It'll take an enormous amount of work to make you look presentable again.'

An incredibly loud braying made the two men jump.

'That's North Wind!' said Iker.

'He led me to your prison and he's waiting impatiently for you outside.'

'Sobek accused me of treachery and he wants me dead.'

'We'll settle that score later.'

As they emerged from the cell, three guards barred their way.

'The tjaty authorized you to question the prisoner, not to free him.'

'This young man is Iker, the Royal Son,' declared Sekari.

'He's already told us that story. You and your friend had better behave yourselves and stay here.'

'I must take him to the palace.'

'I don't like your attitude, boy. Obey my orders or you'll get a taste of my staff.'

Sekari could not leave Iker to rot in jail. At two against three, they had a chance, even if it was regrettable to beat up the representatives of public order.

A menacing growl rooted the five men to the spot. Out of the corner of his eye, one of the guards saw a gigantic hound, its jaws open to reveal its sharp fangs.

'Flesh-Eater!' exclaimed Iker. 'How did you manage to find me again?'

'A friend of yours?' inquired Sekari.

'Yes, fortunately. It would take much more than three opponents to stop him. A sign from me, and he'll attack.'

Caught between the devil and the deepest desert, the three

guards decided that the odds against them were too great. They were not paid to die for nothing.

'You won't get far, you and your monster,' said one of them.

'You needn't waste time searching for us,' replied Iker. 'We shall be at the palace.'

23

A few paces from a side door of the palace, the guards stopped a strange quartet made up of Sekari, a poor, repulsively dirty fellow, a big donkey and a ferocious hound.

'Call the Bearer of the Royal Seal,' demanded Sekari.

Sehotep consented to see what was going on.

'They say you have the best barber in Memphis,' said Sekari. 'My friend is in urgent need of his services.'

'Your friend? Who is he?'

'Don't you recognize him?'

'I don't . . . Come closer.'

'He doesn't smell very good, I warn you.'

Sehotep stared at the filthy wretch. 'No, it's impossible . . . It can't be!'

'Yes, it is, but he needs to be made presentable again.'

'Come to my house.'

North Wind and Flesh-Eater were getting along famously. The donkey regarded the hound as a useful colleague, who, by helping Iker to get out of prison, had proved his mettle and could therefore join the circle of close friends. For his part, Flesh-Eater understood that the donkey, being both intelligent and Iker's oldest friend, had the right of precedence during discussions. Now that these problems of protocol had been sorted out, they would watch over the Royal Son together. Side by side, they enjoyed a hearty meal provided by Sehotep's servants.

The barber examined his client cautiously. He had known difficult cases before, but this one outdid them all by a long way. He chose his sharpest bronze razor, which was as long as his hand and of two thumbs' width. It was shaped like an elongated pentagon, and presented two convex sides and three concave. The two first had sharp blades, to be used with care. Holding the wooden handle fixed to the razor's blade by copper rivets, the barber cut away the worst of the hair.

'Not too many tufts, supple skin, good quality . . . I may be able to rectify this disaster.'

Hot water, soapy lather, lotion to take away the sting of the shave, an elegant haircut suited to the shape of his face: Iker enjoyed the careful attention of a highly skilled man who was determined to create a masterpiece.

'Splendid,' said Sekari. 'You look far better than you did before you left for Canaan. Barber, you're a genius.'

The man turned pink with pleasure.

'But good looks aren't enough,' Sehotep reminded Iker. 'You need health, too. After such a long journey, I shall put you in the expert hands of one of my servants.'

On Iker's back, buttocks and legs, the servant spread a protective ointment made from powdered coriander, bean and wheat flour, sea salt, ochre and terebinth resin. Then he kneaded and relaxed each muscle of this overtaxed body.

After an hour's treatment, Iker felt reinvigorated. All his aches and spasms had disappeared and energy flowed round his body again.

'All you need now is clothes befitting your station,' said Sehotep, and he provided the Royal Son with a kilt, tunic and sandals.

The palace guards, who had been hand-picked by Sobek, did not know what to do. Refusing admission to Sehotep would have serious repercussions, but Iker the Royal Son – if it really was him – was not authorized to cross the security cordon.

'Call your commander,' demanded the Bearer of the Royal Seal.

The Protector was not long in coming.

'You recognize Iker now, I assume?' said Sehotep sarcastically. 'Perhaps he no longer resembles the dangerous Canaanite you threw into prison?'

'This criminal has only one idea in his head: to kill Pharaoh. By believing his lies, you are placing the king's life in danger.'

Iker gazed defiantly at him. 'You're wrong, Sobek. On the name of Pharaoh, I swear that you're wrong. I must tell him the results of my mission. Take all the precautions you need to, but think first of Egypt.'

Iker's determination shook the Protector. 'Follow me.'

'We shall accompany Iker,' decided Sehotep. 'You might be tempted to put him in some cell or other and forget him again.'

Sobek shrugged.

'The Bearer of the Royal Seal is right,' said Sekari with an approving nod. 'One can never be too careful.'

At the entrance to the royal apartments stood General Nesmontu. He said, 'When Iker has been purified, His Majesty will receive him.'

The Royal Son was taken to the Temple of Ptah. Two priests undressed him, washed his hands and feet, then led him into a shrine where a single lamp burnt. Senankh and Sehotep stood on either side of the young man, and Khnum-Hotep faced him.

'May the water of life purify,' chanted one of the priests, 'bring the energies back together, and refresh the heart of the man who respects Ma'at.'

The priests lifted a vase above Iker's head. Light poured out, bathing the whole of the young man's body.

Iker remembered the ritual celebrated in Djehuty's tomb and the words of General Sepi: 'You who wished to know the

Golden Circle of Abydos, see it at work.'

Today, by an incredible privilege, the Royal Son was standing in Djehuty's place.

Was the Circle opening its door to him a fraction? Trying not to think about it, he bathed in the gentle, regenerative rays of light.

General Nesmontu handed back to the Royal Son the guardian spirit's knife. 'I was certain you would return,' he said. 'Never again be parted from this weapon.'

Khnum-Hotep hung a narrow golden collar about the young man's neck. On it hung an amulet depicting the Sceptre of Power. 'May its magic protect you and grant you the courage of the righteous.'

Smiling, Sekari stepped forward in his turn. 'Here are your writing-materials, my friend. Not a single brush is missing.'

Iker enjoyed these small joys and, even more, the trust he was being shown. But Sekari had told him about the tragedy that had struck Memphis, so how could he be happy?

'His Majesty is waiting for us,' said the tjaty.

Iker would have liked to tell the king how immensely happy he was to see him again, but the solemn council chamber was hardly the place for it. He saw with dismay that Senusret had aged. But otherwise he was still the same: distant, stern and resolute, and with no hint of weakness in his gaze.

The Royal Son related his adventures in detail, omitting neither his fears nor his mistakes, and voicing his bitter regret at not having found any clues to the murderer of General Sepi. But he did not speak of Isis; she would know how much she had helped him.

Sobek asked a thousand and one questions, in the hope that Iker would contradict himself. But the young man did not become flustered, and Nesmontu confirmed the major part of what he said.

'What are your conclusions, my son?' asked the king.

'Syria and Canaan are a ruse, Majesty. The Herald no longer lives there, but he wants to draw our army deep into the region and immobilize it there. While our soldiers are far away, he will spread more terrible misfortune in Egypt. That demon knows the Canaanites are incapable of waging a proper war against us, still less of winning one. They will confine themselves to raids and minor attacks in order to wear out our soldiers, whose presence there will prove useless.'

'We were on the point of launching a vast offensive,' said Nesmontu.

'That region will always be uncontrollable,' said Iker, 'and will never accept the Law of Ma'at. The tribes will never stop fighting and tearing one another apart, alliances will dissolve, and thieves and liars will continue to dispute power. Attempts to transform their ways of thinking, no matter how generous those attempts may be, will always fail. The best we can do is impose a fragile peace on the main cities, like Sichem, and prepare for any invasion attempt by strengthening the King's Walls.'

'That would mean giving up our sovereignty,' grumbled Sobek.

'It does not exist and never will. The Herald has realized that, and is hoping to catch us in precisely that net.'

'Those are the words of a Canaanite collaborator!' exclaimed the Protector. 'They conclusively prove his duplicity.'

'Quite the contrary,' cut in Sehotep. 'I have been of that opinion for a long time, but I lacked the means to support my argument. Iker has just provided the necessary information.'

'Does General Nesmontu not advocate the invasion of Syria and Canaan and all-out war?'

'Only in the absence of any better plan,' conceded the old soldier, 'and if it enabled us to catch the Herald. If he is no longer there, deploying our forces would clearly be pointless.

Let the tribes weaken each other – that's all to the good, because it will prevent the formation of a Canaanite army. If a few tribal chiefs in our pay were to foment local disturbances, Egypt would benefit. It seems to me that the time has come to adopt this new strategy. It will take time, but I don't doubt that it will be effective.'

'The main question is still unanswered,' said Senankh. 'Where is the Herald hiding? And are we certain that he committed these abominable crimes? If he had, would he not have claimed responsibility for them?'

'His signature,' commented the tjaty, 'is the very extent of the disaster. Who else could have devised and carried out such a plan, if not the man who is attacking the Acacia of Osiris?'

Senankh had feared this reply, but he had to face the facts.

'Iker, did you really find no clues at all to the Herald's lair?' Sehotep asked.

'None at all, I regret to say. Most of the Canaanites and Syrians regard him as a fearsome shadow, a spectre whom one obeys on pain of terrible reprisals. The Herald's extraordinary aim is this: to become absolute master of the enemies of Ma'at and Egypt by insinuating himself into their minds. He does not even have to appear to convince them. I repeat: Syria and Canaan are merely a ruse. The Herald will abandon his rebels to their fate, while he causes devastation elsewhere. And that "elsewhere" began with Memphis.'

'We are in full control of the city,' declared Sobek.

'Let us hope so,' said Sehotep. 'What about the other cities?'

'Royal decrees will place the mayors on a state of alert,' promised the tjaty. 'However, local manpower will not be enough to guarantee security, so a military presence will be necessary throughout the country. We face a pressing decision: either Nesmontu combs Syria and Canaan again, or else he ensures the protection of the Two Lands.'

171

'At the end of his report, the Royal Son gave us the answer,' said Senusret. 'There is one last point to clarify: Sobek's attitude.'

'I consider that I was right to imprison a suspect, Majesty.'

'Iker, do you think your imprisonment was unjust?'

'No, Majesty. I also think Sobek-Khu did right. However, he should now examine the true facts and rid himself of his prejudices. One of the Herald's plans has been thwarted but we are still very far from victory, and we shall never achieve it unless we are united.'

'To work,' ordered Senusret. 'A plan for protecting the Two Lands is to be presented to me first thing tomorrow.'

Medes was devastated. Iker was alive! How could he possibly have escaped, alone and friendless, from the Canaanites and the Syrians?

But all was not lost. The fact that Iker had been summoned before the Great Council suggested that grave accusations had been made against him. If his testimony was not convincing, he would regret returning to Egypt. In the wake of the Memphis tragedy, his punishment would be heavy. The length of the meeting inclined Medes to hope again. Sobek-Khu disliked Iker, and he carried sufficient weight with the King's House to obtain a harsh penalty.

At last, Senankh emerged from the council chamber. 'If your administration really is efficient, my dear Medes, now is your chance to prove it. You are to send out a royal decree, official messages, confidential letters to mayors and village headmen, and orders to the garrisons – and all with the utmost speed.'

'It will be done, High Treasurer. What is the main objective?'

'To make Egypt safe from the rebels.'

24

Sharing the early-morning meal with Senusret in the palace garden was a privilege whose value Iker fully appreciated. Every dignitary dreamt of being shown such favour, and the entire court, which was still reeling from the shock of his return, would be seething with jealousy.

The king watched the sunlight playing in the treetops.

Despite the respect and awe he felt, Iker dared to break the silence. 'Majesty, did the Golden Circle of Abydos purify and regenerate me?'

'Egypt is not of this world. Directed by Ma'at, she conforms to the plan of work conceived at the beginning of time. Our country gives it concrete form here on earth. The Invisible has chosen its kingdom, and we worship it as our most precious treasure. When Osiris is reborn, the eye becomes complete: it lacks nothing. Then Egypt sees and creates. If not, she remains blind and sterile. That is precisely the threat confronting us.'

'How can we avert this disaster?'

'Success will depend on our clear thinking and our willpower. Either we shall submit to time and history, and the work of Osiris will be lost: or else we shall situate ourselves at the origin, before the creation of the heavens and the earth, and we shall once again know how to reconcile opposites, unite the Red Crown and the White, create brotherly feeling between Horus and Set. The gods, those of just voice, the pharaoh and human beings form a whole to which only Osiris brings oneness, thanks to the Law of Ma'at. If even one of these components is absent or rejected, the whole structure crumbles.'

'Would the sacred not remain a significant bond?'

'The sacred separates the essential from the useless, lights up and frees the way, dispels mirages and mists. Only the act of offering makes celestial harmony enter human society. It extracts the vital elements from matter and nourishes the soul of Osiris.'

'Majesty, will . . . Do you think that one day you will judge me worthy to know his Mysteries?'

'Only you alone can pronounce that judgment, through your deeds. Then Osiris will call you. Here is your new official seal, which brings with it both power and danger. Use it wisely.'

Senusret handed Iker a seal-ring bearing his name and his title.

For the first time, the young man understood how heavy a burden he must carry. He was no longer a rebellious young adventurer but one of the representatives of the pharaonic institution, without which the Two Lands would suffer disorder and injustice.

'Majesty, will I be . . . ?'

'Nobody is worthy of such an office. However, you must take it on. The great serpent of the Island of the *Ka* could not save its world, which was devoured by flames. Memphis almost suffered the same fate, but it survived. We shall not deliver Egypt into the hands of the Herald.'

Iker contemplated the seal. It was different from the Royal Son's, which he had never dared use. Today, only today, he was beginning to realize the extent of his responsibilities.

'Attend Nesmontu's council of war,' ordered the king, 'and do not hesitate to participate. But before the council begins, go to the main landing-stage. Someone is waiting for you there.'

The boat for Abydos was about to cast off. Dressed in a long red gown, Isis was standing on the quay, gazing down at the river.

Being preceded by North Wind and Flesh-Eater, Iker did not escape her notice. She greeted him, then her attention was claimed by his companions. As she stroked the donkey, the hound whined jealously, eager for the same attention. Despite the dog's size and impressive jaws, she was not in the least afraid.

'Flesh-Eater has adopted you,' declared Iker. 'In Canaan he was both my prison-guard and my protector. I had to leave him behind when I escaped, but somehow he found me again.'

'North Wind seems to enjoy his company.'

'They have even become friends. But tell me, are you . . . are you leaving Memphis?'

'I am going back to Abydos. I was certain you would survive your ordeal.'

'Only because of you, Isis. When I despaired, you appeared to me. You enabled me to overcome despair and return to Egypt.'

'You credit me with too many powers, Iker.'

'No, I don't, for you are a magician from Abydos, aren't you? Without your help, without your protective thoughts, I would have died. How can I convince you of my sincerity and show myself worthy of you? In offering me his teaching, the king opened my eyes to the duties of a Royal Son: to fill one's mind with righteous thoughts, to be reserved, to respect the solemnity of one's word, to face up to fear, to seek out the truth, even at the risk of one's life, to exercise an upright and entire willpower, not to yield to greed, to develop one's perception of the Invisible . . . I do not have those qualities, but I do love you.'

'After your great exploits, a brilliant career lies ahead of you, whereas I am only a priestess who hopes never to leave Abydos again.'

'My only ambition is to live beside you.'

'Does love still have any meaning in these turbulent times, when the future of our whole civilization hangs in the balance?'

'I offer you my love, Isis. If it were shared, would it not make us both stronger in the face of adversity?'

'What is your next mission to be?'

'To work with the King's House and ensure the country's security. As we have seen the truth of the Canaan ruse, the Herald will strike again, probably within Egypt itself.'

'Abydos is still under threat,' said Isis. 'The people nearly suffered the same fate as those in Memphis. That demon wanted to kill as many ritual priests as possible and weaken the sacred domain of Osiris.'

'Then you yourself were in danger!'

'The only thing that matters is the Tree of Life. If the gift of my life could heal it, I would not hesitate to give it.'

Watched attentively by the donkey and the dog, Iker went closer to her. 'Isis, are you sure that you do not love me?'

She hesitated. 'I would like to be sure, but I reject falsehood. During a ritual, I was made to climb onto a plinth, the symbol of Ma'at, and I swore always to confront the truth, whatever it may be.'

'I have undergone that ritual, too,' said Iker, 'and I took the same oath. After I defeated the false Herald, Amu wanted to marry me off. I could not bear the thought of being with another woman, so I decided to escape, even though it meant risking death. Whatever you decide, Isis, you will be the only woman in my life.'

The captain of the boat coughed loudly: he was getting impatient. He wanted to take advantage of a brief lull in activity on the river to raise the anchor.

'When shall we see each other again?' asked Iker.

'I don't know.' Isis climbed the gangplank slowly, as if she was sorry they could not talk for longer.

Iker watched her until the boat carried her out of sight. Was he merely deceiving himself by not giving up hope?

Nesmontu's report was convincing. Showing surprising adaptability, the old general had – in record time – thought up a new way of taking the enemy by surprise.

The occupying forces in Syria and Canaan would be reduced to the minimum needed to maintain the current situation. They would confine themselves to arresting troublemakers and to spreading false information designed to stir up ill-feeling among the tribes and clans.

In Egypt, the national army would take the form not of a single massive unit, which would be too unwieldy to move fast, but of a collection of small forces, each comprising forty archers and forty spearmen, placed under the command of an officer assisted by a standard-bearer, a boat captain, a scribe, provisioners and a map-maker.

The officers would take their orders only from Nesmontu, who would permanently coordinate the troops' actions and deployment. In particular, they were charged with watching strategic points and landing-stages. The local guards forces were to ensure the safety of towns and villages. And another army, an army of scribes, would check deliveries of all products. The tragedy of Memphis must never happen again.

'Is the Double White House able to bear the necessary costs?' asked the tjaty.

'Assuredly,' replied Senankh. 'Our armed forces will have everything they need.'

'For my part,' promised Sehotep, 'I shall attend to the ports and docks. Mooring will be made easier.'

'Does the Royal Son approve of these measures?' inquired Sobek with pointed sarcasm.

'If the cooperation between the guards and the army is wholehearted, the results will be excellent.'

'Are you suggesting I may be less than wholehearted?'

'That is not what I said! I meant merely that perfect coordination will require a great deal of effort.'

'Indeed it will,' agreed Nesmontu. 'And we shall supply it.'

Working at the tjaty's side, Iker learnt a great deal about how the various state secretariats worked. The latent threat encouraged the scribes to do their work thoroughly so that no attack, however serious, could prevent the ministers from ensuring that Ma'at was respected.

As the Royal Son was consulting a document provided by Nesmontu, which he would propose to the king that evening, Sobek interrupted him.

'His Majesty wants to see you immediately.'

Under the close protection of Sobek-Khu's hand-picked officers, Senusret left the capital. Iker followed them to a canal, where they took a boat heading south.

This time, the Royal Son did not allow himself to disturb the king's thoughts, for the atmosphere was heavy. However, when he saw the outline of the pyramids at Dahshur, the young man felt a deep serenity. Pharaoh Snefru's monuments seemed indestructible, anchored in the desert's eternity, and Senusret's pyramid, although smaller, expressed the same majesty.

The priests and soldiers responsible for the site's security assembled to welcome the king; Iker held back, a few paces behind him.

Head lowered, a priest came forward and bowed to the king.

'When did Djehuty die?' asked Senusret.

'Yesterday, at dawn. As soon as we realized he had passed

away, we sent you a message. Yesterday was a great day, Majesty, because Djehuty considered the work finished. The sculptors had just completed the final wall-carving depicting Atum, the creative principle, and he was planning to ask you to bring it to life and to confer full power upon your great work.'

The pharaoh and Iker went to Djehuty's official house. His body, wrapped in a large cloak, lay on a bed with feet shaped like bull's hooves. His face looked calm and peaceful.

'I was with him to the end,' said the priest. 'His last thought was of Your Majesty: he wished to express his gratitude to you, for his task as a builder lit up his old age. Djehuty knew that the radiance of Dahshur would serve Osiris. His last words were: "Now, I shall never be cold again."'

The priest withdrew, leaving the king and his son alone with the dead man.

'The hour of judgment is drawing close,' said Senusret. 'It is up to us to pronounce it. What do you wish for this traveller in the afterlife, Iker?'

'That he may cross the darkness of death and be reborn in the light of Osiris. Dhehuty was a good and righteous man. I thank him for his help and have nothing to reproach him for.'

When the monarch was slow to speak, Iker feared that he held a grievance against Djehuty, perhaps arising from the time when the then provincial governor had refused to rally to the crown.

But Senusret said gravely, 'Priest of Thoth and servant of Ma'at, initiate of the Golden Circle of Abydos, Djehuty experienced the Mysteries of Osiris. May he journey in peace.' Then he ordered the embalmers to mummify his spiritual brother and to prepare his house of eternity.

Iker felt a profound grief. Djehuty had welcomed him to the Hare province, enabling him to learn his trade as a scribe and to decipher the arcane mysteries of the sacred language, under the direction of General Sepi – who was also dead. It was thanks to those two wise men that Iker's destiny had been made clear, at a time when he was groping his way through the darkness.

As Senusret and his son stood before the king's pyramid, dazzling white and the creator of a light which would protect the Acacia of Osiris, they asked themselves a threefold question: where, when and how would the Herald attack next?

25

The Belly of Stone was an area forgotten by the gods, a mass of enormous, blackish stone blocks, and islets obstructing the course of the Nile. It almost blocked the Second Cataract, and proclaimed a desolation of granite and basalt resolutely hostile to all forms of life. Furious rapids attempted to force open this blockage, causing a constant, roaring turbulence in the river. The savage war between water and stone never ceased.

On a rocky promontory looming over this chaotic battleground, stood the Herald, Bina, Shab the Twisted and Crooked-Face. After a long journey across the desert, they had reached this, the most fascinating and dangerous place in Nubia.

'We'll never be able to cross the cataract,' said the Twisted One, deeply impressed by so much violence.

'Anyone would swear that giant arms were pushing the banks apart and amusing themselves by torturing the rocks,' remarked Crooked-Face.

The Second Cataract extended over a vast stretch of the river, almost equal to the distance between Memphis and the Great Sea. It allowed through a trickle of blue water which formed a powerful contrast with the ochre sand of the desert and the green of the palm-trees; in the Belly of Stone, no water-plants could survive in the raging waters.

'The death that will strike Egypt will arise from here,' predicted the Herald.

He climbed back down from the promontory and went to where Crooked-Face's fighters were waiting, a little way off.

'Memphis was sorely wounded,' he told them, 'and the pharaoh has not succeeded in healing the Tree of Life. Every Egyptian dreads our next attack. The enemy army is searching for us in Syria and Canaan, where rebel operations will weaken it day by day, for the clans and tribes remain loyal to me. The fires of the heavens and the earth will consume the traitors. Our network in Memphis remains intact, and Sobek's men will not arrest any of my followers. However, our past successes are nothing. Here, the energy we have at our disposal will increase our powers considerably. And it is not a human army that will invade the Two Lands.'

'But, my lord, there are only about a hundred of us,' said Crooked-Face, looking around.

'Look more closely.'

'I can see whirlpools and yet more whirlpools.'

'There they are, our invincible troops.'

Shab the Twisted stared at him in amazement. 'But how are they to be used, my lord?'

'Are we not capable of wielding powers thought to be uncontrollable?'

'Do you mean . . . Can you move those huge rocks?'

The Herald laid his hand on the Twisted One's shoulder. 'See beyond appearances: do not stop at material limits. Thought can go beyond them and bring out resources hidden in the heart of the rocks or the furious waters.'

He turned back towards the Belly of Stone. Suddenly he seemed to grow taller, and his followers spontaneously prostrated themselves.

'Egypt survives thanks to the Mysteries of Osiris. While they are celebrated, the land of the pharaohs will resist us, so we must seek out supernatural weapons. Osiris himself offers us one: the creative tide, the flood of celestial origin that gives prosperity and food to the Egyptians. Every year they are gripped by anxiety: what will be the level of the flood? Too low, and famine threatens; too high, and the damage is endless. It is precisely this flood that we shall use. Never before will it have been so enormous, so devastating.'

Although deeply awed, Crooked-Face was the first to get to his feet. 'You . . . Are you thinking of taking control of the floodwaters?'

'Have I ever disappointed you, my friend?'

'No, my lord, but—'

'The Belly of Stone itself will unleash this cataclysm. It is up to us to bring it to life so that it may express its destructive anger.'

The Herald and his followers set up camp near the promontory. They had brought plenty of provisions with them, so nobody went hungry. The Herald was content with a little salt; he never took his eyes off the fearsome spectacle, the key to his coming victory.

Bina stayed awake. Since her master's blood had been flowing within her, she needed hardly any sleep. She, too, had yielded to the fascination of the deafening chaos that never rested for a second.

The Herald opened his large acacia-wood box and took out two bracelets decorated with cat's claws. 'Put these round your ankles,' he ordered.

Very slowly, she did so.

'You are not a woman like other women,' declared the Herald. 'Soon you will act.'

Bina bowed.

The sun rose. In less than an hour, the heat became suffocating.

Suddenly, the Twisted One ran up to the Herald. 'Master, there are Nubians coming, dozens of them!'

'I have been expecting them.'

'They look threatening.'

'I am going to talk to them.'

While Crooked-Face and his men readied themselves for battle, the Herald moved out a little to face a tribe of about a hundred black warriors dressed in leopard-skin kilts. They wore coloured beads about their necks and heavy ivory rings in their ears, bore tribal scars on their cheeks, and were brandishing spears.

'Let your chief step forward,' demanded the Herald.

A tall, thin man with two feathers in his hair stepped out of the ranks. 'You speak our language?' he said in astonishment.

'I speak all languages.'

'Who are you?'

'The Herald.'

'And what are you heralding?'

'I have come to liberate you from the Egyptian occupier. For too many years, the pharaoh has been oppressing you. He kills your warriors, pillages your wealth and reduces you to misery. I, however, know how to strike him down.'

With a gesture, the chief ordered his men to lower their spears. Crooked-Face did likewise.

'Do you know Nubia?' asked the chief.

'The fire of this land is my ally.'

'Are you a sorcerer?'

'The monsters of the desert obey me.'

'Our Nubian sorcerers are the greatest in the world.'

'But their lack of unity renders them ineffective. Instead of confronting each other in pointless duels, they should join together to fight their true enemy, Senusret.'

'Have you looked closely at the fort of Buhen, which overlooks this cataract? It marks the border with Egypt. If we attacked it, the reprisals would be ferocious.'

'I did not know that Nubians were cowards.'

The chief's lips quivered with anger. 'Either you kneel

before me and beg my forgiveness, or I shall smash your skull.'

'On the contrary, you shall kneel and swear allegiance to me.'

The Nubian raised his club high.

Before it could touch the Herald's head, the talons of a falcon sank into the chief's arm, forcing him to drop his weapon. Then the falcon's beak put out his eyes with terrible precision.

The black warriors stared in disbelief as the dying man writhed in pain.

'Obey me,' said the Herald in a calm voice, 'or you will all die the same death as this coward.'

Some still hesitated, while others wanted to react with equal violence.

'Let the lioness of the desert exterminate the unbelievers,' ordered the Herald.

A terrifying roar stopped the Nubians in their tracks. In horror, they saw the huge creature charging towards them. It bit, tore, clawed and feasted on the tides of blood, not sparing a single warrior.

From the acacia-wood box, the Herald took the queen of turquoises, which he exposed to the sun's light before presenting it to the blood-spattered lioness. Almost immediately, she grew calm. A heavy silence fell upon the place of slaughter.

Beautiful and haughty, Bina stood at the left hand of her lord. There was a red patch on her brow, which the Herald wiped away with a fold of his woollen tunic.

'The other tribes will react quickly,' said Crooked-Face.

'I hope so.'

'Will we be able to drive them back?'

'We shall persuade them, my friend.'

It was not warriors armed with spears and clubs who emerged

from the desert and came towards the Herald's camp, but some twenty elderly Nubians, their bodies covered in amulets. They were led by an old man with very black skin and white hair. He moved with difficulty, supporting himself on a stick.

'Is this all they can send against us?' laughed Crooked-Face.

'There is no more dangerous regiment in the world,' replied the Herald.

'How can these little old men be dangerous?'

'I warn you, don't anger them or they'll reduce you to ashes. These are the flower of Nubian sorcerers, capable of casting worse curses than anything you can imagine.'

The old man addressed the Herald. 'Was it you who wiped out the tribe of the Hyena's Son?'

'I was forced to punish a band of insolent curs.'

'Do you wield dark forces?'

'I, the Herald, use all forms of power in order to strike down Pharaoh Senusret.'

The Nubian shook his head. 'Those of us here have considerable powers, but we have not succeeded in ridding ourselves of the occupier.'

The Herald smiled condescendingly. 'You confine to your own defeated land. I am going to spread a new faith throughout the entire world. And you will help me set free the violence this land bears. The fire of the Belly of Stone will ravage Egypt.'

'None of us would risk provoking its anger!'

'You and those like you have slumbered because you fear the pharaoh. I have come to awaken you.'

Angrily, the old man struck the ground with his cane. 'Have you brought the Terrifying One to life?'

'The lioness obeys me.'

'Nonsense! Nobody can contain her rage.'

'Unless he possesses the queen of turquoises.'

'That's only a foolish legend.'

'Would you like to see it?'

'You are mocking me!'

The Herald showed his treasure to the sorcerer.

The old man gazed for a long time at the enormous turquoise, with its blue-green reflections. 'So it is not a legend . . .'

'Obey the precepts of God, and obey me. If not, the Terrifying One will slay you.'

'What have you really come to do here?'

'I shall say it again: to free you from a tyrant. But first you must be converted and become my followers. Then, you shall unite your magical powers to mine and we shall cause a cataclysm from which Egypt will never recover.'

'It seems indestructible.'

'In Syria and Canaan, and again at the very heart of Egypt's capital, Memphis, I have already inflicted deep wounds.'

The old man was astonished. 'Memphis? You dared . . . ?'

'Senusret has paralysed you. Now he and his people know fear. And their torments will only become greater.'

'Is this king not a giant of a man, with a giant's strength?'

'Yes, he is,' agreed the Herald, 'so it would be pointless and stupid to attack him from the front. My spies are working in the shadows, out of reach of his guards and his army, and their bites catch the Egyptians unawares. With the help of the Nubians and the Belly of Stone, I shall strike Senusret with a blow of unheard-of force.'

The old man looked at the Herald with new eyes: this man spoke with formidable calm, as if nothing could prevent him from carrying out his insane plans.

'Since the first Senusret built the fort of Buhen,' said the Nubian, 'Egypt has left us in peace. The army does not come beyond this border, and our tribes share power.'

'Soon, after spreading terror in Canaan, the pharaoh will

go beyond this limit. He will ravage your whole land and lay it waste. You have only one chance left: to help me unleash the tide that will prevent him from acting.'

Perplexed, the old man leant on his stick. 'I must consult all the sorcerers. We shall deliberate and give you our decision.'

'Be sure not to make the wrong one,' advised the Herald.

26

To the east sat Pharaoh and the Great Royal Wife; to the south were High Treasurer Senankh and Sekari, to the north General Nesmontu and Royal Seal-Bearer Sehotep, and to the west Tjaty Khnum-Hotep and the Shaven-Headed One. After celebrating Djehuty's funeral rites, the Golden Circle of Abydos was aligning its perceptions towards the future.

'The beautiful Goddess of the West has welcomed our brother,' declared Senusret, 'and he will be reborn eternally in the east. Like Sepi, he will be present among us for ever.'

He would have liked to prolong the ritual and strengthen the bonds between the Golden Circle and the Invisible, but a serious problem must be put to the brotherhood.

'Since the Memphis tragedy, the Herald has been quiet. This apparent calm must betoken a new storm, of whose nature we are unaware. The measures taken by Sobek-Khu and General Nesmontu have strengthened the whole country's security, but the enemy will, of course, have foreseen our reaction.'

'He has been silenced and rendered harmless,' said the tjaty.

'No, that is only what he wants us to believe,' argued Sekari. 'A criminal of that evil stature doesn't give up.'

'Thanks to Iker, we know that the next field of battle will not be Syria and Canaan,' General Nesmontu reminded them. 'In Memphis the close watch being kept by Sobek-Khu's men means that the Herald's network cannot operate, so he will take action elsewhere.'

'This summer is a particularly hot one,' observed Senankh, 'and the drought will be at its height before the flood – not a good season for moving around and trying to mount a major operation. That means we have a little time in hand.'

The Great Royal Wife described the work of the priestesses of Abydos and the care they were lavishing on the Tree of Life. The Shaven-Headed One then spoke of his priests' meticulousness in performing the necessary rites. He had nothing untoward to report. Despite all the anxiety, Osiris's sacred domain was holding fast against the enemy.

'Is young Isis making progress along the path to the great Mysteries?' asked the tjaty.

'She is advancing step by step, at her own pace,' replied the queen. 'Despite our desire to raise her further, we must not move too hastily, for that would be harmful to her.'

'In view of the role she will have to play,' said the king, 'her training must be exceptional.'

'Like Iker's?' suggested Sehotep.

'I am directing him, as my own spiritual father directed me.'

After the royal couple had poured water and milk at the foot of the acacia, the Shaven-Headed One burnt incense before it while Isis played the sistra. She had acquired such mastery of the instruments that she could make them produce an incredible variety of sounds.

'The archives of the House of Life have provided me with what may be vital information,' she said when the rite was over. 'Gold is indispensable to Osiran alchemy, for the flesh of the Reborn One is made of pure metal, a synthesis of the other elements. In it, the light solidifies and reflects the immaterial aspect of the divine powers. Its radiance becomes that of Ma'at.'

The king, the queen and the Shaven-Headed One had known all this for a long time, but it was good that Isis had learnt it for herself. She was following the path that would lead her sooner or later to a discovery of paramount importance.

'According to the ancient texts,' she went on, 'Pharaoh is the prospector, and also the goldsmith who works the gold so that its brilliance lights up both gods and humans and maintains the harmony between heavens and earth. The report of an explorer dating from the age of the great pyramids gives this clue: the gods themselves apparently buried their greatest treasure in the far-off lands of the South, in Nubia. What could this marvel be, containing all their energy, if not the gold destined for Osiris?'

'Without it,' said the Shaven-Headed One, 'it is impossible to restore the objects that serve in the celebration of the Mysteries. Deprived of it, they would become inert. And then there is the great secret about which my lips must remain sealed.'

Nubia, thought Senusret: a savage, poorly controlled land, peopled by both visible and invisible dangers. Nubia: the killing-place of General Sepi, whose murderer still went unpunished. Yes, Isis saw the truth. It was there that the gold of the gods was hidden. But in these troubled times, organizing a sizeable expedition there would be far from easy.

'Did you find any more details?' he asked the priestess.

'Unfortunately not, Majesty. I shall continue to search.'

The pharaoh was preparing to leave Abydos when Sobek the Protector brought him an urgent message from Sarenput, formerly governor and now mayor of the great trading town of Elephantine on the border between Egypt and Nubia.

'I shall not be returning to Memphis,' declared the monarch after reading the message. 'Summon the members of the King's House immediately.'

The meeting was held in the main courtyard of Senusret's temple, safe from prying eyes and ears. The decisions to be taken would have weighty consequences.

'Can Sarenput be considered a loyal servant?' asked the king.

'His record is unblemished,' replied Senankh, 'and I have found no trace of abuse of power or of dishonesty. Your decrees are rigorously applied.'

'For my part,' added Sehotep, 'I have no criticisms to make. Sarenput is a tough, straightforward fellow, who does not scorn the pleasures of life but who is content with his high office.'

'I have nothing to add,' said the tjaty.

'I have some reservations,' said Sobek, 'because I have not forgotten his past. And if we have to ride roughshod over him to take decisive action in Elephantine, he may react unfavourably.'

General Nesmontu nodded in agreement.

'If the information in Sarenput's letter is correct,' went on the pharaoh, 'we may know where the Herald wants to open his new front.'

The old soldier grunted with satisfaction. 'The army is ready for immediate action, Majesty.'

'Sarenput has had a report from the commander of the fort of Buhen, which was built by Senusret I to mark Egypt's border and to contain the warlike Nubian tribes. The report says a whole tribe has been slaughtered at the Belly of Stone.'

'The Belly of Stone? That place is a hell on earth!' exclaimed Sobek.

'Our garrison at Buhen are afraid. There is talk of monsters which can tear apart any living being, and some claim to have seen a terrifying lioness, much too large to be an earthly animal, which could not be killed even by an army of hunters.'

'I detect the mark of the Herald,' ventured Sehotep. 'In other circumstances, one would like to believe it was simply a local incident. Today that would be culpable foolishness.'

'Nubia is no ordinary country,' said Senankh emphatically. 'Your predecessors, Majesty, had the greatest difficulty in imposing even a semblance of pacification, and it was a long way from real friendship.'

'I have some Nubian archers among my soldiers,' said Nesmontu. 'They're skilful, brave and disciplined. If they are ordered to fight their blood brothers, they will. They have chosen to live in Egypt, not in Nubia.'

'I don't find their warlike qualities reassuring,' said Sehotep. 'Canaanites and Syrians are only too happy to flee before our troops, but Nubians defend themselves fiercely. And I am worried about their sorcerers, whose reputation frightens most of our men.'

'I shall lead the expedition myself,' declared Senusret.

Khnum-Hotep shuddered. 'But, Majesty, may the Herald not be trying to lure you into a trap?'

'Direct confrontation seems inevitable. And let us not forget the quest for the gold of the gods. Isis is right: it is in Nubia. General Sepi gave his life for it, and his offering will not be in vain.'

The pharaoh had taken his decision, and further discussion was pointless. Despite the enormous risks, was there any other way?

'Tjaty Khnum-Hotep, I charge you with governing the country during my absence. Each morning, in company with Senankh, you will consult the Great Royal Wife. She will rule in my name, and if I do not return from Nubia she will ascend the throne of the living. You, Sehotep, will come with me. You, Nesmontu, are to assemble your regiments at Elephantine.'

'That will mean leaving the provinces undefended, Majesty,' pointed out the general.

'I shall run that risk. You, Sobek, are to go back to Memphis.'

The Protector said angrily, 'Majesty, your safety—'

'My personal guards will see to it. Now, let us consider the worst that may happen. If Nubia is a trap Memphis remains the principal target, so you must concentrate all your attention there. If the decisive battle takes place in the Great South, the Herald's network may perhaps be a little less wary. Just one mistake, and you will trace it back to its source.'

The king's arguments were irrefutable. Nevertheless, at the thought of being far from him, the Protector felt regret and sadness.

'You will order Royal Son Iker to join me at Edfu,' added Senusret.

'Iker will go with you? Majesty, I think—'

'I know what you think, Sobek, and you are still wrong. During our Nubian campaign, Iker will do things which will at last convince you of his absolute loyalty to me.'

Since the dawn of civilization the sacred falcon – incarnation of Horus, protector of the pharaonic institution – had reigned over the temple at Edfu. Its wings spanned the universe; its gaze saw the secrets of the sun. And when it rested upon the nape of the king's neck, it endowed him with a sustained vision of the world beyond.

A priest greeted Isis at the landing-stage and took her to a forge not far from the shrine. In the presence of the pharaoh, two craftsmen fashioned a statue of the god Ptah, a blue skullcap on its head and its body wrapped in a white shroud, from which its arms emerged holding several sceptres, symbols of life, power and stability.

'Gaze upon the work of Ptah, master of craftsmen, which is linked to that of Sokar, lord of subterranean spaces. Ptah creates through thought and the Word. He names deities, humans and animals. The Pesedjet is embodied in his teeth and his lips, which make real that which its heart conceives and what Thoth expresses by means of his tongue. His feet touch the earth, his head the distant heavens. Through his own power, he raises up the work that has been accomplished. The name "*Sokar*" derives from the root "*seker*". It means "to beat metal", but refers also to the transportation of the body of resurrection across the underworld. When you ritually clean your mouth, *sek-r*, you open your consciousness to Sokar. And when Osiris speaks to the initiate in the depths of the darkness, he uses this same expression whose meaning is then "Come to me." Belief and piety will not lead you to Osiris. The right guides are knowledge and the alchemical body of work. On the eve of the battle against the Nubian sorcerers, I ask Ptah to fashion my spear and Sokar my sword. Watch them emerge from the fire.'

The first metalsmith brought to birth a spear so long and so heavy that only Senusret could wield it. The second fashioned a sword of such dazzling brilliance that the priestess had to shield her eyes.

The pharaoh picked up the weapons, which were still hot from the forge. 'The war against evil forbids cowardice and prevarication. We are leaving for Elephantine.'

27

The Herald fed on the formidable energy of the Belly of Stone. He became each whirlpool, each furious assault by the rapids upon the rock. Sitting silently at his feet, Bina gazed vacantly at the impressive spectacle.

From time to time, when the wind was in the right direction, they heard snatches of the Nubian sorcerers' discussion. At last, after long hours of intense debate, the old man with the white hair reappeared.

'We have chosen not to help you but to drive you from our lands,' he said.

The Herald displayed neither surprise nor anger. 'You were not all of the same opinion, I believe.'

'The most skilful among us, Techai, did indeed vote in your favour. But the majority prevailed, and he yielded.'

'Did you not speak out and sway them?'

The old man looked angry. 'I exercised my prerogative as the senior sorcerer, and I do not regret it.'

'You are making a grave mistake. Recognize that, persuade your friends to change their minds, and I shall show mercy.'

'It is useless to insist. You must leave Nubia immediately.'

The Herald turned his back on the old man. 'The Belly of Stone is my ally.'

'If you persist, you will die.'

'If you stand against me and my followers, I shall be obliged to punish you.'

'Our magic is stronger than yours. Persist in your stubbornness, and we shall take action this very night.' The old man struck the ground with his stick, then went to rejoin his fellows.

'My lord, would you like me to get rid this rabble for you?' asked Crooked-Face.

'I need some of them.'

'Should we really fear them?' asked Shab the Twisted.

'Follow my instructions to the letter and you will not be harmed. For three days and three nights, the Nubians will block out the eyes of the sky, the sun and the moon, which, instead of their usual radiance, will send us waves of deadly energy. Cover yourselves with woollen tunics. If even the smallest piece of your flesh is exposed, fire will consume you. The crackling of the flames will terrify you, and you will think you are burning at the heart of a furnace. Do not try either to look or to run away. Keep absolutely still until calm returns.'

'And what about you, my lord?' asked Shab worriedly.

'I shall continue to gaze upon the Belly of Stone.'

'Are you certain you have nothing to fear from these Nubians?'

The Herald's gaze hardened. 'It was I who taught them all they know of magic. Before their glory faded and they behaved like cowards, I was there. When my armies are unleashed upon the world, whether tomorrow, the day after tomorrow, or centuries from now, I shall still be there.'

Even Crooked-Face did not try brave things out, but obediently did as he had been ordered. The Herald himself protected Bina with two tunics firmly bound together with belts.

As soon as night fell, the Nubians launched their attack. Leaping forth from the promontory on which the Herald

197

stood, a flame enveloped him before growing in size at an insane speed. Its crackling and roar even drowned the din of the cataract. The bodies of the faithful disappeared into the brazier, and the rock grew red. Black clouds hid the newborn moon.

For three days and three nights, the torture continued.

Only one of the Herald's followers, losing hope, threw off his garments and ran. A tongue of fire curled round his legs, consuming them in a few seconds. Then his torso and face were reduced to ashes.

At last, the sun shone once again. The Herald untied the knots on the belts and freed Bina.

'We have triumphed,' he proclaimed to his followers. 'Stand up.'

Exhausted and haggard, they had eyes only for their master.

His face was calm and rested, as if he had just emerged from a restorative sleep.

'We must punish these foolish fellows,' he decreed. 'Do not move from here.'

'But what if they attack?' asked Crooked-Face, eager to be rid of them.

'I am going to seek them out.'

The Herald took Bina behind an enormous rock pounded by the waters, where the men could not see them.

'Undress.'

As soon as she was naked, he stroked her back, which took on the colour of blood. Her face became that of a lioness, with flame-filled eyes.

'Go, Terrifying One, and punish their disobedience.'

A ferocious roar petrified every living being within a large area, as far as the fort of Buhen. The great lioness sprang forward.

The first to die was the old, white-haired man. Incredulous at the failure of the best sorcerers in Nubia, he was exhorting them to blot out the sun and moon again when the lioness silenced him by closing her jaws round his head. A few brave men tried to speak words of conjuration, but the slaughterer give them no time. She tore, lacerated and trampled them underfoot. Only five of the Nubians escaped her claws and her teeth.

When the Herald showed her the queen of turquoises, the lioness grew calm. Little by little the pretty brown-haired young woman reappeared, with a supple and delicate body, which the Herald hastily covered with a tunic.

'Step forward, Techai, and prostrate yourself before me.'

The sorcerer, a tall, thin man covered in tattoos, obeyed.

'Techai . . . That name means "Looter", does it not?'

'Yes, my lord,' the sorcerer whispered in a shaky voice. 'I have the gift of stealing dark forces and using them against my enemies. I voted for you, but the majority did not listen to me.'

'You and those who did likewise have been spared.'

The other survivors also prostrated themselves.

The Herald's eyes flamed brilliant red, and he seized one of them by the hair and tore off his kilt. The naked body thus revealed left no room for doubt.

'You have hardly any breasts, but you are a woman!'

'I will serve you, my lord!'

'Females are inferior creatures. They remain children all their lives, think only of lying, and must submit to their husbands. Only Bina, the Queen of the Night, is permitted to assist me. You are nothing but a shameless temptress.'

The sorceress kissed the Herald's feet.

'Techai,' he ordered, 'stone her and burn her.'

'My lord—'

The Herald's eyes, like burning coals, made it clear to the Nubian that he had no choice.

He and his three colleagues collected stones. The unfortunate woman tried to run away, but a stone struck her on the back of the neck, and another in the hollow of her back. She got up again only once, trying in vain to protect her face.

The four Nubians threw dried palm stalks on top of her bloodied, still quivering body. Techai himself set fire to it.

Still trembling, the sorcerers thought only of surviving. Techai tried to remember two or three incantations which ordinarily stopped even the worst demons in their tracks. But when he saw the Herald slake his thirst with salt while staring at him with his red eyes, he admitted defeat and realized that any attempt at resistance would lead to his death.

'What do you require of us, my lord?' he asked.

'Announce my victory to your respective tribes, and order them to assemble in a place which is inaccessible to the Egyptian scouts.'

'The scouts never venture into our lands. As for our chiefs, they respect magic. After what you have done, Triah, the powerful Prince of Kush, will be forced to accord you his respect.'

'That is not enough. I demand his absolute obedience.'

'Triah is a proud man, and easily angered. He—'

'We shall resolve that problem later,' promised the Herald in a soft voice. 'When you come back, bring food for my men. Bring women, too: they are to stay in their huts except when needed to give my men pleasure and to cook. Afterwards, I shall talk to you about my plans.'

As he watched the sorcerers leave, Crooked-Face was sceptical. 'You are too lenient, Lord. We shan't see them again.'

'Oh yes we shall, my friend, and you will be surprised at how soon.'

The Herald was not mistaken.

Two days later Techai reappeared, visibly tired, at the head of a small army of black warriors armed with spears, daggers and bows.

'Here are four tribes who are already determined to follow

the supreme sorcerer,' he said. 'Prince Triah has been informed, and he will not fail to send you an envoy.'

Crooked-Face examined the Nubians' muscular frames. 'Not bad,' he conceded. 'These fellows should make good recruits if they survive my training.'

'What about food?' asked Shab the Twisted.

Techai signalled to the bearers to come forward.

'Grain, vegetables, fruit, dried fish . . . This is a poor region, but we have brought you our best.'

'Taste everything,' the Twisted One ordered a bearer.

The man ate a little of each kind of food. None of it was poisoned.

'And what about women?' demanded Crooked-Face greedily.

There were twenty of them. Twenty pretty and very young Nubian girls, their breasts bare, who were dressed only in kilts made of leaves.

'Come, my beauties,' he said. 'We've built you a big hut. I'm going to sample you first.'

While Shab was organizing the building of their camp, at a safe distance from the Buhen, the Herald took the sorcerers close to the turbulent heart of the cataract. Even for them, the heat was almost unbearable.

'According to the state of the river and the natural signs,' he said, 'what type of flood do you foresee?'

'Strong, very strong,' replied Techai.

'That will make our task easier. By concentrating our powers on the Belly of Stone, we shall loose a raging torrent.'

'You mean . . . Are you going to drown Egypt?'

'Instead of the Nile fertilizing the thirsty banks as it covers them, its fury will ruin that accursed country.'

'It will be very difficult, because—'

'Are you saying you cannot do it?'

'No, Lord, no!' said Techai hastily. 'But we must beware of the backwash.'

'Are you not the greatest sorcerers in the world? Since you wish to drive out the occupier and liberate your land, the Nile will not turn against you. And it is not the only weapon we shall use.'

'Have you . . . a sort of security?' asked Techai.

The Herald said smoothly, 'There are some Nubian archers serving in the enemy army, are there not?'

'Renegades, my lord, traitors! Instead of staying in their homeland and fighting for their tribes, they chose an easy life by enlisting in the enemy's forces.'

'Their easy life will prove illusory,' said the Herald. 'We shall make them pay for their treason by disrupting the Egyptian ranks.'

'Are you capable of destroying the fort of Buhen?'

'Do you think that mere walls can stop me?'

Aware that he had insulted the Herald, Techai hung his head. 'For too long we have been behaving like a defeated race. Thanks to you, we shall regain our pride and confidence.'

The Herald smiled. 'Let us prepare to awaken the Belly of Stone.'

28

Medes's wife was having an attack of hysterics. Insulting the maids who dressed her hair, painted her face and rubbed her feet, she rolled about on the ground. It took her husband's intervention and several good slaps to quieten her. Even after he seated her on an ebony chair, she continued to twist and turn.

'Have you lost all your dignity?' he demanded. 'Pull yourself together immediately!

'You don't understand! I've been abandoned – Doctor Gua has left Memphis.'

'I know.'

'Where is he?'

'In the South, with the king.'

'When will he come back?'

'I don't know.'

She leapt up and flung her arms round her husband's neck. Fearing he'd be strangled, he slapped her again and forced her back down on to her chair.

'I'm lost!' she wailed. 'He's the only one who knows how to treat my illness.'

'Not at all. Gua has trained some excellent pupils. Instead of one doctor, you shall have three.'

The sobbing stopped. 'Three? Are you making fun of me?'

'The first shall examine you in the morning, the second in the afternoon, and the third in the evening.'

'Is this true, my darling?'

'As true as my name is Medes.'

She rubbed herself against him and kissed him. 'You are the best of all husbands.'

'Now go and make yourself beautiful.'

Leaving her in the skilled hands of her maids, he went to the palace to receive the tjaty's instructions.

The first person he met was Sobek, who said, 'Ah, I was just about to summon you.'

Medes concealed his irritation. 'I am at your service.'

'Your boat is ready.'

'My boat . . . ?'

'You are leaving for Elephantine; the pharaoh is waiting for you there. Gergu will be responsible for the vessels transporting grain, which will be vital to the expedition being prepared.'

'Would I not be more useful in Memphis?'

'His Majesty wishes you to oversee the work of the scribes. You will write the ship's journal, the daily reports and decrees. I believe hard work does not frighten you?'

'On the contrary, very much on the contrary!' protested Medes. 'But I detest travel – I am always unwell on boats.'

'Doctor Gua will take care of you. You leave tomorrow morning.'

Was this mission meeting a real need, or did it conceal another purpose? Was Sobek keeping watch on him, as on the other notables, hoping he would put a foot wrong?

Whatever the case, Medes must not take any risks and so must not contact the Phoenician before leaving. His accomplice would understand his silence, but it was unfortunate, because a cargo of precious wood from Byblos was due to be eased past the trade-control officials, and Medes could neither delegate this delicate task nor pass on the news of Iker's return.

*

The Phoenician's network was still dormant. Shopkeepers, itinerant traders and barbers carried on their occupations and chatted with their customers, expressing their anxieties about the future and praising the pharaoh. Sobek's guards and informants were still searching fruitlessly. Until he had new instructions from the Herald, the Phoenician would devote himself to his business activities and increase his own wealth, which was already considerable.

He was surprised to receive a visit from his best agent, the water-carrier.

'Is something wrong?' he asked.

'Medes has just embarked on a boat heading south.'

The Phoenician frowned. 'We were to meet tonight.'

'Gergu is going, too. He is taking charge of vessels laden with wheat for the army.'

That was a natural precaution: Senusret was leaving Egypt and heading into Nubia, where there might be a shortage of food. The Herald's plan was working wonderfully well. There was just one annoying detail: Medes had been conscripted.

'What is happening at the palace?' he asked.

'The queen is ruling, while the tjaty and Senankh handle affairs of state. Sobek has increased the checks on all goods coming into the city, and his men are patrolling everywhere, as well as keeping a close watch on all the leading citizens. It is obvious that the king has ordered him to double his efforts.'

'That Protector is a real pest!'

'Our groups are kept strictly separate,' the water-carrier reminded him. 'Even if he did catch one of our men, it would lead him to a dead end.'

'You've given me an idea . . . When hunting, the best way to catch a wild animal is to set out some bait, isn't it?'

'That's a daring ploy!'

'Weren't you just saying how strictly separated our groups are?'

'Well, yes, but—'

'I'm the head of this network, and don't forget it,' said the Phoenician angrily. 'Now, if Medes is away, who's going to deal with the trade-controllers? The next delivery of wood is planned for around the time of the full moon.'

'Sobek has tightened security on all the quays,' said the water-carrier.

'That man is really beginning to annoy me! It means our ship must remain in Byblos with its cargo. Can you imagine the loss of profit? And we don't know when Medes will return from Nubia – or even if he'll return at all.'

The Herald's religious vision preoccupied the Phoenician less than the development of his own trade. The current government and the nature of its power mattered little, so long as trade flourished and his secret profits were considerable.

The Protector and his men were becoming a hindrance to trade, but the Phoenician was not going to let himself be ruined.

If the situation got any worse, Gergu would throw himself into the water! Red-faced, sweating and vociferous, he no longer knew which god to swear allegiance to. The prospect of travelling to the South had been enjoyable, but managing the grain-vessels was turning into a nightmare. One ship's cargo was missing and did not feature on any of the lists, and there was also a phantom vessel which could not be found in the port. Until these mysteries had been cleared up, the fleet could not weigh anchor. And he, Gergu, would be held responsible for the delay. It was pointless to hope for help from Medes, for the two men must maintain a discreet distance from each other.

'Is there a problem?' asked a voice behind him.

He turned and saw Iker standing there.

'There's no end of problems,' confessed Gergu gloomily.

'And I've checked and checked again.' He was on the verge of tears.

'Can I help you?'

'I don't think so.'

'Explain it to me anyway.'

Gergu handed the Royal Son a papyrus, which was crumpled from repeated consultations. 'First, the contents of one grain-store have vanished into thin air.'

Iker examined the document. It was written in cursive script which was particularly difficult to decipher. Not until he read it for the third time did he see the solution.

'The scribe has counted the same quantity twice.'

Gergu's coarse face brightened. 'Then I actually have all the grain the king requires?'

'No doubt about it. What else?'

Gergu's face fell again. 'The ship that's disappeared – I won't be forgiven for that.'

'A ship doesn't evaporate like a cloud in spring,' said Iker. 'I shall investigate at the port offices.'

At first, the inventory of the grain-carrying cargo vessels seemed in order. But appearances were deceptive. A careless scribe, or one who was in too much of a hurry, had mixed up two documents. This error had led to the disappearance, on papyrus, of a ship from the trading-fleet, because it had been listed under the wrong name.

Gergu was beside himself with gratitude. 'You're a genius!'

'My training as a scribe accustomed me to this type of mistake, that's all.' But Iker was thinking about *Swift One*. In her case, too, a switch like this been used to erase a ship from the royal fleet.

Gergu finally emerged from the mist. 'Are you Iker, the Royal Son?'

'The pharaoh has granted me that title.'

'Forgive me. I have only glimpsed you from a distance, at

the palace. If I'd known, I wouldn't have dared to . . . to inconvenience you like this.'

'Let there be no formality between us, Gergu. I know your work well, for I took charge of the granaries when I lived in Kahun. It is difficult but vital work. In a crisis or if the annual flood is poor, the survival of the population depends on the reserves that have been built up.'

'I think of nothing else,' lied Gergu. 'I could have had a lucrative career, but working for the common good is more noble, is it not?'

'I am certain it is.'

'The court is buzzing with your remarkable exploits in Syria and Canaan – and here we have another, which has benefited me. Shall we drink some good wine to celebrate?'

Without waiting for the Royal Son to agree, Gergu removed the stopper from a wine jar and poured a fruity red into an alabaster cup, which he took from the pocket of his tunic.

'I have a second one for emergencies,' he murmured, displaying it. 'To our pharaoh's good health!'

The wine was a real pleasure to drink.

'They say you killed a giant,' Gergu went on.

'Beside him,' agreed Iker, 'I did look like a dwarf.'

'Was he the Herald, whom everyone's so afraid of?'

'Unfortunately not.'

'If that monster really exists, we'll soon flush him out. No rebel will put Egypt in peril.'

'I am not as hopeful as you are.'

Gergu did his best to look astonished. 'What do you think there is to fear?'

'No argument, not even a powerful army, will convince fanatics to give up their plans.'

North Wind came up to them and dipped his tongue into Iker's cup.

'A wine-loving donkey!' exclaimed Gergu. 'What a fine travelling-companion.'

A look of annoyance from Iker dissuaded the animal from doing it again.

'Are there any other problems, Gergu?'

'No. For the time being, all is well. Allow me to thank you again. The envious members of the court never stop criticizing you, for they don't know you. But I've had the immense good fortune to meet you. Be assured of my respect and my friendship.'

'You may rely upon mine.'

The captain gave the signal to cast off. At the last moment, Sekari clambered aboard the leading boat, where the high-ranking officials had taken their places. He went to join the Royal Son, who was trying to explain to North Wind that alcoholic drinks would endanger his health.

'I've nothing to report,' said Sekari. 'There aren't any suspicious characters on board, but I'll keep checking everyone and everything.'

'Are you worried about anything in particular?'

'This fleet cannot possibly go unnoticed. A member of the rebels' Memphis network may have been told to cause problems for us.'

'Bearing in mind how closely the guards are watching everyone, that would be very surprising.'

'We have already had several surprises – and horrible ones, at that.'

Sekari went off to search the boat the boat again, and a green-faced Medes came up and greeted the Royal Son.

'You have been so busy with all your obligations, my lord,' he said, 'that I have not yet had an opportunity to congratulate you.'

'All I did was carry out my mission,' said Iker.

'And risk your life doing so. Syria and Canaan are not peaceful places.'

'Unfortunately, we are still far from dispelling the most serious threats.'

'We have great assets,' ventured Medes. 'We have an exceptional king, a reorganized and well-led army, and an efficient force of guards.'

'Yet Memphis was seriously harmed, and we still cannot find the Herald.'

'Do you really believe he exists?'

'I often ask myself that question. Sometimes a phantom can sow the seeds of terror.'

'Indeed,' said Medes, 'but His Majesty appears to think this spectre has taken bodily form, and he sees far beyond the range of common men – without him we would be blind. In re-establishing unity in Egypt, the king has given her back her former vigour. May the gods grant total success to this expedition and peace to our people.'

'Do you know Nubia?'

'No,' replied Medes, 'and I don't want to.'

29

There were many soldiers on the main quay at Elephantine. At the foot of the gangplank stood General Nesmontu.

'Did you have any trouble during the voyage?' he asked Iker.

'No, none at all.'

'His Majesty has taken grave decisions. He is convinced that the Herald is hiding in Nubia.'

'Isn't that land inaccessible?'

'In parts, yes, but the gold of the gods is probably there. You will be in the front line alongside the king. After extricating yourself from the Canaan wasps' nest, now you find yourself plunged into the Nubian cauldron. You really are blessed by the gods, Iker!'

'I hope that this way I shall win Sobek's trust.'

'As long as you succeed: Nubian warriors and sorcerers are formidable. At my age, this is an unhoped-for chance to deploy a real army in the heart of enemy territory, with a thousand dangers every day. I feel younger already, and this is only the beginning.'

As the two men left the quay, they saw that there was intense activity everywhere in Elephantine. Despite the overpowering heat, preparations were being made for the expedition. Everything must be checked: the state of the war-fleet, the soldiers' equipment, the hospital ship, and the administration.

'If the Herald thinks he's safe,' said Nesmontu, 'he's going to have to think again.'

North Wind led the way and Flesh-Eater followed. The donkey chose exactly the right way to Sarenput's palace.

When they reached the main entrance, trouble threatened.

Good Companion and Gazelle, the mayor's two dogs, were standing guard outside. The first was dark, lean and fast. The bitch was small and plump and had prominent teats. They were always together, each protecting the other. They growled when they saw the giant hound.

'Quiet, Flesh-Eater,' ordered Iker. 'This is their territory.'

Gazelle approached first and walked round the new arrival, watched closely by Good Companion. As soon as she licked the hound's nose, the atmosphere became more relaxed. To celebrate this meeting, the three dogs began playing – running around and barking joyfully. Good Companion raised a hind leg and then Flesh-Eater urinated in the same place, sealing their friendship. Eventually they grew tired. Gazelle lay down in the shade, and the two males stood guard.

'Let us hope Sarenput will be as friendly,' commented Nesmontu. 'You are summoned to the decisive meeting, just before noon.'

With its low forehead, firm mouth, prominent cheekbones and jutting chin, there was nothing pleasant about Sarenput's face. Energetic and rugged, the former governor lived in a sparsely furnished palace where the air was agreeably fresh, thanks to artfully situated high windows.

The inner council consisted of Sarenput, Nesmontu, Sehotep and Iker. When he was introduced to the mayor as the Royal Son, Iker felt a critical, almost scornful, gaze upon him.

'The demon who is trying to murder the Tree of Life has gone to ground in Nubia,' said Senusret. 'He calls himself the Herald and has caused great harm in Memphis. Iker enabled us to avoid the trap he had set for us in Syria and Canaan. I have decided to confront him face to face.'

'The Nubians need a good lesson,' remarked Sarenput. 'I've received a new and worrying message from Buhen. There are disturbances in the region, the tribes are growing more and more restive, and the garrison fears it will be attacked.'

'The Herald is probably trying to organize an uprising,' suggested Nesmontu. 'We must take action with all speed.'

'Communications between Egypt and Nubia are still extremely difficult,' said the king, 'so we shall dig a canal which is navigable all year round. Then neither the annual flood nor the rocks of the cataract will hinder us, and both war- and trading-boats will be able to sail in safety.'

What would be the reaction of Sarenput, who knew the region better than anyone else? If this plan seemed unrealistic to him, he would be extremely uncooperative, even hostile. An innovation like this was liable to shock him; or he might be angry at not having thought of it himself.

'Majesty,' he said, 'I approve wholeheartedly of your decision. Before the Two Lands were reunified such a canal would have been very dangerous for this province, but now it is vital. Of course, the quarrymen and stone-cutters of Elephantine are entirely at your disposal.'

'Here are the results of my calculations,' said Sehotep. 'The canal must be a hundred and fifty cubits long, fifty wide and fifteen deep.'[1]

'The success of the enterprise depends on the agreement of the gods of the cataract,' declared Senusret. 'I must consult them without delay.'

Since the desecration of the sacred islet of Biga, it had been strictly guarded. Everyone except the pharaoh and his

---

[1] 78 metres long, 26 metres wide and 8 metres deep.

representatives was barred from going there, so that the work of Isis might continue to revive Osiris in secrecy.

Clear water, a calm and shining sky: far from the noise of the city, the islet seemed to belong to another world. The king rowed rhythmically and in silence. At the prow of the boat sat Isis, gazing at the beautiful resting-place of one of the aspects of the Reborn One.

Soundlessly, the skiff touched land. The three hundred and sixty-five offering-tables of Biga rendered the year sacred. There, the goddess daily poured a libation of milk from the stars.

The young priestess followed the pharaoh to the cave housing the leg of Osiris and the vase of Hapy, the god who launched the annual flood. At the summit of the rock were an acacia and a jujube tree.

Isis took a ewer containing water from the previous year's flood, and purified the monarch's hands.

'Sovereigns of the cataract,' she prayed, 'be favourable unto us. The king is the servant of Osiris and the incarnation of his son Horus. Goddesses Anuket and Satet, grant him life, strength and vigour so that he may reign according to Ma'at and dispel the darkness. May his courage be victorious.'

On the threshold of the cave appeared two women of incredible beauty. The first wore multicoloured feathers upon her head, the second the White Crown with gazelle horns. Anuket presented the king with the sign of power, and Satet handed him a bow and four arrows.

Senusret fired the first arrow to the east, the second to the west, the third to the north and the fourth to the south. In the azure sky, they were transformed into streaks of light.

When he looked again, the two goddesses had disappeared.

'We may return to the other side of reality,' he told Isis, 'and begin to dig the canal.'

Sehotep was very glad of Iker's presence. The tireless young scribe could handle an enormous amount of work, checking calculations, organizing the construction site, solving a thousand and one problems or motivating the craftsmen while heeding their complaints.

Medes was not idle, either. He set to work on the decree, dated Year Eight of Senusret III, which announced the creation of the Elephantine canal linking the first province of Upper Egypt with Nubia. But even as he worked he was worrying about the future: their departure would necessarily take place before the start of the flood, and he had no news of the Herald. Luring Senusret into these inhospitable parts, populated by dangerous tribes, was not a bad idea, but the fighting was liable to go on for a long time. Medes hated travelling, nature and the heat, and he was afraid he might be hit by a stray arrow or even a Nubian warrior's club. Instead of being close to the fighting, he would much have preferred to stay in Memphis. Should he resign? No, that would ruin his career and attract the Herald's fury. Whatever happened, he would have to follow the venture through to the very end.

Gergu was also unhappy. Obliged to work extremely hard, he was drinking too much.

When he presented himself to Medes in a dishevelled state, the latter realized that Gergu needed to be taken in hand.

'Stop behaving so irresponsibly,' he snapped. 'You are to play a major role in this expedition.'

'Do you know where we're going? To a land of savages who love killing and torturing people. I'm afraid. And when I'm afraid, I drink.'

'If one of your subordinates lodges a complaint about your drunkenness, you will be dismissed from all your offices – and the Herald would not forgive you for that. When he provoked this war, he foresaw that we would be brought here with Senusret's army.'

The reminder abruptly sobered Gergu: he was even more

afraid of the Herald than of the Nubians. 'But what does he expect of us?'

'He'll send us our orders when he is ready. If you fail him in any way, he'll exact his vengeance.'

Gergu collapsed on to a straw-seated chair. 'All right, I'll make do with light beer.'

'Have you succeeding in making friends with Iker?'

'I certainly have. He's a friendly, warm-hearted boy, very easy to deceive. And he's incredibly efficient. He's already extricated me from several sticky situations.'

'We'll have to kill him sooner or later. He doesn't know it, but we're the ones he's searching for. If he ever found out the truth, we'd be dead men.'

'There's no risk of that. He hasn't got a devious mind – he'll never realize.'

'Make him talk as much as possible,' said Medes. 'Being so close to the king, he must have information that would be extremely useful to us.'

'He doesn't indulge in much idle talk, and he puts work before everything else.'

'Find a way to make him confide in you.'

At the end of a tiring day, Iker took a boat, crossed the Nile and reached the western bank. Sarenput's house of eternity was nearing completion, and he had recommended Iker to inspect the site. It was late in the evening, and the craftsmen would have gone home after closing the door of the tomb. The young man drank in the peace of the sunset and the splendour of the surroundings.

The expedition was preparing to leave. Everyone had been working hard in the scorching heat, and he needed to relax. The donkey and the hound were tired, too, and were sleeping side by side. They had shown no wish to accompany their master, so he could not be facing danger. And as for his other guard, Sekari was enjoying some leisure in feminine company.

In distancing himself from activity and daily concerns, Iker rediscovered his feeling for writing. Facing the magnificent landscape, which the sun was bathing in a soft gold, his hand ran over his palette, drawing the signs of power composing a chant to the evening light.

But happiness remained beyond his reach. Many courtiers would have been more than content with the much-envied rank of Royal Son, but Iker could never forget Isis. Because of his title, many beautiful and charming women flocked around him, but none of them found favour in his eyes – indeed, they might as well have been invisible – for only Isis reigned in his heart.

She was beyond feeling and passion. She was love. Without her, Iker's destiny, however brilliant it might seem, would be nothing but a painful void.

With a heavy heart, he headed for Sarenput's tomb. When he neared it he halted, surprised. Its door was still open and light was shining from it.

Iker entered. There was a first chamber, with six sandstone pillars. Then a staircase, and a sort of long corridor with beautifully decorated walls, leading to the shrine where Senusret's *ka* would be venerated. He was depicted six times as Osiris.

By the light of the lamps with their smokeless wicks, Isis was painting hieroglyphs.

Fascinated, Iker dared not interrupt. He would gladly have stayed there his whole life, gazing at her. Beautiful, calm, graceful in her every movement, she must be communing with the gods. He hardly dared breathe as he tried to engrave these miraculous moments in the deepest part of himself.

She turned round. 'Iker! Have you been here long?'

'I . . . I don't know. I didn't want to disturb you.'

'Sarenput asked me to check the texts and add the words of Osiris. He wishes to ensure that his house of eternity is flawless.'

'Will he become an Osiris?'

'If he is recognized as being of just voice, this place will be magically brought to life and will enable his body of light to live again.'

Isis put out the lamps, one by one.

'May I carry them for you?' asked the Royal Son.

She paused before one of them. 'Isn't this text remarkable?'

Iker held up a lamp so he could make out the inscription: '*I was filled with joy when I succeeded in reaching the heavens; my head touched the firmament, my belly brushed the stars, for I myself was a star, and I danced like the planets.*'

'Is it only a poetic image, or has someone really lived through this experience?'

'Only an initiate into the Mysteries of Osiris can tell you that.'

'Isis, you live at Abydos and you must know the truth.'

'I am travelling towards it, but there are still many doors to pass through. Outside initiation and the discovery of the creative powers, our existence would be meaningless. However harsh the ordeals may be, I shall not give up.'

'Do you consider me an obstacle on your path?'

'No, Iker, no . . . but you trouble me. Before I met you, the study of the Mysteries of Osiris occupied all my attention. But now some of my thoughts always remain with you.'

'Although the knowledge of the Mysteries is also my goal, I must obey the pharaoh. He is the only one who could grant me access to Abydos. But that does not prevent me from loving you, Isis. Why should this love hinder our quest?'

'I ask myself that every day,' she confided, moved by his devotion.

If only he could have taken her hands, held her in his arms . . . But that would have shattered the slender hope that had just arisen.

'I love you more and more every day,' he said. 'For me

there can be no other woman. It will be you, or no one.'

'Is that not going too far? Are you not endowing me with imaginary virtues?'

'No, Isis. Without you, my life has no meaning.'

She turned away and said, 'We must go back to Elephantine.'

Iker rowed very, very slowly. She was there, so close and yet so inaccessible. Her mere presence made the sun shine in the darkening sky.

On the bank Sekari was waiting for them. He said, 'We must go to the palace at once. The pharaoh has had some very bad news.'

30

The scribes who watched the river-gauge at Elephantine were in great consternation. All the signs were that the annual flood was going to be so enormous that it would bring danger and devastation. Everyone knew the figures and what they meant: twelve cubits high brought famine; thirteen, hunger; fourteen, happiness; fifteen, the end of all cares; sixteen perfect joy.[1] Any higher than that and problems began.

'What is the extent of the danger?' the king asked the head scribe.

'I hardly dare tell you, Majesty.'

'To hide the truth would be a serious mistake.'

'I may be wrong, and so may my colleagues, but . . . We fear there is going to be a cataclysm, a gigantic tide higher and more powerful than anything we have known since the First Dynasty.'

'In other words, a good part of the country is in danger of being destroyed.'

The scribe murmured a barely audible 'Yes' through shaking lips.

The pharaoh immediately called a meeting of the inner council composed of Sehotep, Nesmontu, Iker and Sarenput.

'Sarenput,' he ordered, 'you are to move all your people

---

[1] 16 cubits = 8.32 metres.

into the hills and the desert, and ensure that they take with them all the food, clothing and other things they will need. You, Sehotep, are to strengthen the fortress, for the enemy may take advantage of the start of the flood to attack, and you are also to finish the canal as quickly as possible. Nesmontu, you are to strengthen our military defences. Iker, you are to coordinate the work of the scribes and the craftsmen, and dictate to Medes the warning that must reach every town in Egypt. The tjaty must take urgent measures immediately.'

Medes was unconvinced. 'Are we really in danger?'

'The scribes are quite clear,' replied Iker.

'The country has known strong floods before, and we haven't panicked.'

'This one is going to be unprecedentedly severe.'

'Messengers will leave first thing tomorrow. Thanks to my new organization and the fast boats now at my disposal, the news will be spread quickly.'

'The messengers must go to even the remotest villages and take with them orders for the people to leave for higher ground. The headmen must carry out those orders at once. His Majesty wants as many lives as possible to be saved.'

Medes set to work immediately.

So this was the Herald's signal. Either it was a deception, designed to frighten the authorities and disrupt Egypt's defences, with a view to a Nubian invasion, or else the Herald was going to transform the Nile into a weapon of universal destruction. In either case, this was the start of the major offensive, and the rebels in Memphis would strike there once again.

But even while he secretly applauded the future, Medes had one concern: to find a safe hiding-place so that he himself did not become one of the victims.

Even Crooked-Face was afraid. The din rising up from the Belly of Stone was worse than deafening. The battle of the

221

enraged water against the rock intensified still more, and the river continued to swell and rise.

The Nubian sorcerers kept up a ceaseless chant, whose words Crooked-Face could not understand, while the Herald gazed northwards with red eyes shining with ferocious brilliance. At his feet, Bina was contemplating a chaotic sky, dominated by the wrath of Set.

Shab the Twisted drew Crooked-Face back from the river. 'Don't stand so close, or a wave might sweep you away.'

'Well . . . The chief really is amazing!'

'So you're finally beginning to realize that, are you?'

'He's greater than the pharaoh, isn't he?'

'Senusret's still a formidable enemy, but our lord's always one step ahead.'

'To succeed in using the Nile like this!'

'The true faith will be like that. It will inundate the whole world and destroy all the unbelievers.'

The maddened waters gushed out of the Belly of Stone and forged an unusually broad way through.

In a few days from now, thought the Herald, Osiris will emerge from his silence and take the form of the flood. This time, it will bring Egypt not life but death.

From the top of the cliffs on the western bank, Elephantine looked peaceful as it dozed in the strong summer sunshine. The heat was overpowering, the green of the palm-trees glinting, the blue of the Nile iridescent.

This delightful landscape was experiencing its last hours before desolation. After disappearing for seventy days, the ritual duration of a pharaoh's mummification, the constellation of Orion would reappear. As it rose in the night sky, it would mark the resurrection of Osiris and the moment at which the waters began to rise. They ought to have provided the country with happiness and prosperity, but they had become its worst enemy.

'The dew is changing in nature and consistency,' said Isis. 'The flood will begin tomorrow.'

'It is not Osiris who is turning against his people in this way,' said the pharaoh, 'and it is not only nature that is being unleashed.'

'Are you thinking of the Herald, Majesty?'

'Angered by the Tree of Life's resilience, he is launching a new form of attack.'

'Can one single man really call up such forces?'

'He has the help of Nubian sorcerers. If we survive this attack, we shall have to prevent that land from doing more harm in the future.'

'How are we to fight?' she asked.

'The earthly river is born of the celestial Nile, which itself issued forth from the *nun*, the primordial ocean. The Herald has stirred up this tide, but cannot attain its true source, the mother and father of the Pesedjet, hidden at the heart of the fertilizing water. It alone calms the flood, and it alone may still save us. So I must go to the cave at Biga and invoke the Pesedjet.'

'The country and its people need your presence, Majesty. People clamour all the time for your instructions. If you are not seen, if they think you are dead, everything will fall apart. The Herald will have won.'

'There is no other way of checking the Nile's fury.'

'If you think me capable of doing it, I will act in your name.'

'The cave will flood very quickly. I have no right to endanger your life.'

'All our lives are in danger, Majesty. If I hide away, far from the cataclysm, I shall not be doing my duty as a priestess. Since you have granted me the privilege of passing through the first stages of initiation into the great Mysteries, I should like to prove myself worthy. And since it is too late to appeal to my superiors, and your duties summon you elsewhere, my path is traced out before me, is it not?'

Iker rolled up the last papyrus and closed the last wooden chest, which an assistant scribe immediately took away. All the archives of Elephantine would be saved: he had checked that no documents had been forgotten.

Under Sarenput's firm hand, the people were being evacuated in a calm and orderly manner, taking their most precious possessions with them. They tried in vain to comfort one another. Distress caused spasms in their bellies, though it was eased by the presence of the pharaoh. Instead of leaving the region, he was standing in the line of battle, confronting the danger head on.

'The canal is finished and has been strengthened,' Sehotep told Iker. 'Even the most violent flood will cause no more than scratches.'

'Let us rejoin His Majesty at the citadel,' suggested Sekari, who, as was his custom, had hunted here and there, fearing one or more rebels might be among the town's people. But then, when he thought about it, why would the enemy infiltrate a town which was about to be annihilated?

Following Sehotep's plans to the letter, the artificers had worked well. Although a little dilapidated, the ancient building had been transformed into a fortress, the lower part of which was composed of solid blocks of granite.

From the top of the main tower, the king gazed down at the First Cataract. Foaming water was beginning to cover the rocks. Soon, they would no longer be visible.

'This tower should resist the pressure of the waters,' said Sehotep, 'but I am not absolutely certain. It would be better if you were somewhere safe, Majesty.'

'On the contrary, my place is in the forefront of the battle. It is different for my loyal companions.'

'That is not so, Majesty,' retorted Nesmontu. 'My soldiers

occupy this building, and I am their leader. To abandon them would be the equivalent of desertion. Do you consider me capable of such cowardice, at my age?'

'The spectacle is not without a certain grandeur,' observed Sekari. 'I wouldn't want to miss it. And His Majesty may perhaps have urgent orders for me.'

'Either I am a skilled master-builder and have nothing to fear,' declared Sehotep, 'or I am incompetent, and the river will punish me.'

'A son's place is at his father's side, is it not?' asked Iker.

'If we die,' said Nesmontu, 'the queen and the tjaty will not give up the fight. If we are together, at the king's side, there is no risk. Pharaoh is immortal.'

Not wishing to waste words in pointless debate, Senusret accepted their decision. His face betrayed no sign of the deep emotion produced by this display of brotherly affection.

The waters rumbled more and more loudly. Never had the flood swollen so quickly.

'Majesty,' asked Iker, 'do you know where Isis has taken refuge?'

'She is speaking the words of pacification in the cave of Hapy, the spirit of the flood.'

'A cave? Won't it be submerged?'

'Isis is our last bulwark. If she does not succeed in awakening the Pesedjet hidden at the heart of the tide, we shall all die.'

An anxious silence fell, broken only by the grim barking of Flesh-Eater and North-Wind's strident complaints.

An enormous wave launched the attack by a maddened river the colour of blood.

Isis invoked Atum, the creative principle, whose name meant both 'He Who Is' and 'He Who Is Not'. From the master of the Pesedjet came the primordial couple, Chu, the light-filled air, and Tefnut, the flame. From them were born the sky-goddess, Nut, and the earth-god, Geb. Their children completed the Pesedjet: Nephthys, mistress of the temple, Set, the dangerous power of the skies, Isis and Osiris. At the moment when the priestess spoke Set's name, a deafening clamour drowned her voice.

The tumultuous waters were about to invade the cave and drown her.

However, she went on chanting the prayer to the Pesedjet that the pharaoh had taught her.

The enormous snake hidden at the back of Hapy's cave came forward and formed a circle round the entrance by swallowing its tail. In this way, it drew the symbol of cyclical time, eternally renewed from its own substance.

The furious tide broke over the snake's body, but did not break the circle. The flood laid waste the islet of Biga, sweeping away the offering-tables.

Isis kept on praying to the Pesedjet to pacify this destructive anger.

'The tower is shaking,' whispered Sekari.

'It will hold,' promised Nesmontu.

The sight before them was like a hallucination. This was no longer a river but a succession of monstrous waves which covered the town, carried away whole houses of sun-dried brick and ravaged the fields.

'Are the people far enough away?' fretted Sehotep. 'If the river keeps on rising like this, it will reach even the hills.'

Outwardly imperturbable, the pharaoh thought of the young priestess. He, too, was reciting the ritual words celebrating the happy return of the flood, the vital meeting between Isis and Osiris, and the presence of the Pesedjet, charged with transforming the waters' rise into a beneficial force.

Iker had thoughts only for Isis. Had her courage and self-denial led her to her death?

And the tower of the fortress shook again.

31

Gergu was dead drunk. He pulled the hood of his cloak down over his face and wept uncontrollably. He had taken refuge on top of a hill, where he had thought he would be safe. Like everyone else, he had been appalled by the ferocity of the flood. He was convinced he would soon be swallowed up, and was terrified of looking death in the face.

Someone tapped him on the shoulder – the guardian of the otherworld had come to slit his throat!

'I'm innocent!' he howled. 'I had to obey orders, I—'

'Calm down,' ordered Medes. 'It's over.'

'Who . . . who are you?'

'Wake up!'

Gergu uncovered his head and recognized the Secretary of the King's House. 'Are we alive?' he asked.

'Only just.'

The water-level had stabilized, a mere handspan below Gergu's shelter. The whole region around Elephantine was now one immense lake, over which thousands of birds were flying. The only thing visible above the surface was the main tower of the citadel.

Iker and Sekari paddled furiously towards Biga. The tide was calmer and the waves were subsiding, to be replaced by a swift-flowing Nile. There were still many whirlpools and eddies, so that river travel was still difficult, but Iker could not wait for conditions to improve. The flood had entirely covered Biga. How could Isis possibly have escaped?

'The islet was here,' said Sekari, his face sombre.

'I'm going to dive down,' said Iker.

Near the surface the water was muddy and opaque, but it grew clearer as he dived deeper. He saw a glow of light and swam towards it. It came from a cave round whose entrance a huge snake was coiled in a circle.

He swam nearer, and he saw her: calm and collected, Isis was still speaking the words of pacification.

He called to her, swallowed water and had to surface to breathe.

'She's alive!' he shouted to Sekari. 'I'm going back to find her.'

Sekari shook his head in sorrowful disbelief.

Iker easily found the the cave again, and this time Isis saw him. When she emerged from her refuge and took the hand he held out to her, the snake melted away and the Nile invaded Hapy's cave.

Isis was a good swimmer, but allowed Iker to help her. When they surfaced, side by side, near the boat, Sekari thought the flood must have disturbed his mind.

'Is it . . . is it really you, Isis?' he said.

'I told you she was alive,' said Iker.

Sekari helped them both into the boat. Isis's linen robe clung to her graceful curves, making him suffer from a different kind of disturbance. He turned his head away and fixed his eyes on his oar.

'We're going back now,' he said, 'and I'm not going to do all the rowing.'

Iker began rowing at top speed; he dared not look at Isis, either.

The flood's destruction was considerable, but only about a

228

dozen people had died: peasants who had been so frightened that they had left their places of safety and been caught by the tide.

As the persea fruit opened, celebrating Isis's and Osiris's rediscovery of each other, the people set to work again, and over the following weeks and months the flood would be transformed from a disaster into a blessing. Under the direction of Iker and Sehotep, new islets were created, designed to be farmed. Month after month, retaining-pools would supply precious water until the next flood. Because of the incredible quality of silt deposited by the Nile, the next harvest would be exceptional. Canals with strong banks had to be created, while preserving the marshy areas used for hunting, fishing and the raising of livestock.

'You are to rebuild the town,' the king ordered Sarenput.

'It will be more beautiful than it ever was before, Majesty.'

'Begin by restoring Biga. New offering-tables are to be set up there.'

Senusret's prestige soared. Some compared him to the pharaohs of the Golden Age, and nobody doubted his ability to protect Egypt from calamities. Indifferent to praise and suspicious of flatterers, the king knew well that he owed this victory over the Herald's evil magic to Osiris and to a young priestess who had not hesitated to risk her life.

The Phoenician paced up and down. Usually he had himself well under control, but now he was ravaged by anxiety. In Medes's absence it was impossible to carry on the lucrative trade in timber, because only Medes knew how to bribe the trade-control officials.

Simply being a wealthy merchant was no longer enough for the Phoenician. He could well have contented himself with his riches and led a comfortable life, enjoying a thousand and one pleasures, but since his contact with the Herald he had acquired new ambitions and discovered new horizons.

Power. The power of shadows: to see without being seen, to classify people, know their opinions and habits without their being aware of it, to spin a spider's web, and make his puppets dance as he pulled their strings. These things intoxicated him more than the finest wine. The Phoenician hated happiness and equilibrium, and thoroughly enjoyed his mission: to erode Memphis from inside.

As he was stuffing himself with pastries, the water-carrier asked to see him.

'The palace is in uproar,' he informed the Phoenician. 'This year's flood is terrifying. It has already drowned Elephantine and will soon destroy the whole of Egypt – it will reach Memphis in two weeks at the latest.'

'Is the pharaoh dead?'

'Nobody knows, but there must have been innumerable deaths. Here is a message from Medes, though it is already old.'

The message was in code. It gave details of Iker's incredible return, and told the merchant the vital news of the devastating flood.

The Herald's plan continued to unfold implacably. From Nubia, he had managed to cause a cataclysm and break the back of his enemy before he attacked. Panic would soon overtake Memphis.

The Phoenician's orders were clear: he must reactivate his network of spies, to add to the confusion and the fear, and to prepare for the invasion of the capital.

The Queen of Egypt took steps to restore a measure of calm to the court, which was rife with alarming rumours.

'Stop behaving like cowards,' she commanded the principal state officials whom she had summoned to the palace. 'The Two Lands are being governed; the tjaty is carrying out his duties and I mine.'

'Majesty,' said the principal archivist worriedly, 'has King Senusret been killed?'

'Certainly not.'

'But you have no proof that he has survived the disaster.'

'It will be several days before the river is navigable. Then we shall receive accurate news.'

'The inhabitants of Elephantine have all been drowned, Majesty, and soon we shall suffer the same fate.'

'The floodwaters have not yet reached the Theban region, and the tjaty is taking the necessary precautions. Canal banks and retaining-walls are being strengthened.'

'But will those measures be adequate?'

'Why can you not trust the pharaoh and gods?' cut in Khnum-Hotep. 'The throne of the living holds firm, and the Law of Ma'at remains in force.'

'Everyone must remain at his post,' ordered the queen. 'When I know more, I shall summon you again.'

The inner council was immediately assembled.

'Have there been any messages from Abydos?' the queen asked Senankh.

'The Tree of Life's condition is unchanged, Majesty.'

'Sobek-Khu, are things calm in Memphis?'

'Only on the surface, Majesty. I believe that when the disaster strikes, the rebels' spy network will be revived. My men are on the highest alert.'

'Senankh, what food reserves have we?'

'We could bear two years of famine.'

'It is pointless deceiving ourselves,' said Khnum-Hotep. 'There is nothing natural about this flood. Only the demon who seeks the acacia's death could have made it huge enough to destroy a good part of the country. Almost our entire army was at Elephantine and may have been wiped out. If it has, the only place still protected is Abydos.'

'In other words,' said Senankh, 'Memphis has become easy prey.'

'You're forgetting my men,' protested Sobek.

'For all their courage, they could not fight off a massed

231

attack by Nubian warriors,' said the tjaty. 'Invasion has been threatening for a long time. We thought we had contained it, by means of the forts between the First Cataract and the Second, but in fact there are not enough of them. Unfortunately, the enemy has realized this, too.'

'Senusret is not dead,' declared the queen. 'I can feel his presence.'

'Whose turn is it?' asked the travelling barber.

A thickset fellow emerged from the waiting queue and sat down on the three-legged stool. 'Very short at the neck, with my ears uncovered.'

'What about your moustache?'

'Tapered.'

'Do you like summer in Memphis?'

'I prefer spring in Bubastis.'

Once the code words had been exchanged, the two Libyans, who belonged to the Phoenician's network, were able to talk with confidence. The waiting customers were a safe distance away and were chatting or playing board-games.

'We're being awakened,' said the barber.

'More transporting of goods?'

'No, direct action.'

'Another attack on the palace?'

'That would be impossible – we wouldn't take Sobek by surprise a second time. We've been studying his security measures for several weeks, and there are no weak points.'

'Then what are we to do?' asked the thickset man.

'The flood will cause serious damage in the capital. All the inhabitants, including the guards, will be ordered to strengthen the riverbanks and the retaining-walls. If things go well, the Herald will lead the Nubian troops here. What we must do is disrupt the city's defences.'

'How?'

'By destroying the people's illusion of safety.'

'That sounds a good plan,' agreed the thickset man, 'but I would like some definite details.'

'We're to attack a guard-post.'

'You're mad!'

'The leader's orders.'

'Then he's mad!'

'On the contrary, Sobek won't be expecting anything so dramatic. He'll be humiliated, perhaps even dismissed, and the town will be defenceless.'

'The guards will defend themselves fiercely.'

'If we prepare our strike well, we won't give them the time. Additional order: there must be no survivors.'

The thickset man shook his head. 'It's too risky.'

'I've already found the most vulnerable guard-post. It's in the northern quarter and there are only ten or so men, two of them scribblers and four old men. At dawn, before they're relieved, they'll be tired and thinking mainly of their morning meal.'

'If you put it like that . . .'

'After the success of our attack, even the guards themselves will be afraid.'

32

Iker supervised the installation of the royal bed on the flagship, which would lead the war-fleet towards Nubia. The bed was a marvel of the craftsman's art – at once simple, spare and strong enough for anything – and would enable the king to sleep in perfect comfort. The base was composed of criss-crossed skeins of hemp, fixed to the frame and held in place by two straps, making the whole thing flexible. The four feet, shaped like lions' paws, guaranteed stability, to which was added the lion's vigilance, which would protect the king while he slept; as would the god Bes, armed with knives to cut the throats of bad dreams.

Iker laid his father's clothing in sycamore-wood chests and checked that nothing undesirable had been placed inside. He satisfied himself as to the quality of the sandals, with their triple leather soles and reinforced stitching.

Unit after unit, Nesmontu's soldiers boarded the warships, led by their standard-bearers. The troops observed especially strict discipline, for they were watched closely by the old general. The scribes in charge of supplies worked with Gergu to ensure that the boats carrying provisions were loaded properly and nothing was forgotten. They also oversaw the loading of weapons: bows, arrows, shields, spears, throwing-spears, axes, daggers and short-swords.

'Our army does not only embody strength,' Nesmontu told

Iker. 'It is also one of the expressions of the worldly order that Pharaoh fashions, for it is not enough to shout the words "love", "peace" and "brotherhood" to make them respected. Man is not born good. His natural inclinations are envy, violence and the desire for domination. The Creator does battle against the darkness, and the Lord of the Two Lands is inspired by his example.'

Doctor Gua, carrying his heavy leather bag as always, came up to the Royal Son and asked, 'Where is the hospital ship?'

'At the rear.'

'Will I have enough remedies, bandages and operating-knives?'

'Come and check for yourself,' suggested Iker.

They were greeted by a silver-haired man of average height, with a serious face. He was busy sorting out bags of medicinal herbs.

'I am Principal Doctor Gua. Who are you?'

'Remedy-maker Renseneb.'

'What training have you had?'

'I was educated at the House of Life of the Temple of Khnum in Elephantine, and I know how to prepare potions, infusions, pills, ointments and suppositories.'

'Have we enough remedies and healing substances?'

'I have prepared for a long stay and many patients.'

'Let us examine everything together.'

Iker left the two men and went back to the quay. There, assisted by the priestesses of Satet and Anuket, Isis was filling jars with the water of the new year.

'It contains the greatest possible amount of *ka*,' she explained, 'and makes living beings more youthful by removing fatigue and minor ailments. The interior surfaces have been covered with clay to make them impermeable and to ensure that the water does not become stagnant. One sweet almond in a small jar will prevent any unpleasant surprises.

235

The most delicate matter is the stoppers, which are made using the buds from date-palms and wads of green grass. For the large jars, we use a cone of clay on a basketwork disc the size of the neck. This keeps the jar watertight while allowing the water to breathe.'

Each jar bore a number and the date on which it was filled. Even deep in the Nubian cauldron, the soldiers would not go short of water.

'Isis,' said Iker, 'once again we are parting, perhaps for ever.'

'Our duty must come before our feelings.'

'You did say "our feelings"; does that include your own?'

She gazed into the distance. 'While you're risking your life in Nubia, I shall care for the Tree of Life in Abydos and carry out my duties as a priestess to the best of my ability. The present crisis does not allow us time to dream. And I have something important to tell you.'

The young man's heart began to beat very fast.

'This conflict will be no ordinary one: you are preparing to fight a battle like no other. It is not a matter of merely driving back an invader or conquering a territory; what is at stake is saving the Mysteries of Osiris. The enemy feeds on darkness and takes many forms in order to extend the reign of *isefet*, and the Nubians are unwitting instruments of his evil ambitions. When you believe you are far from me, you are in reality close to Abydos. The geographical distance matters little; all that counts is the communion experienced in our common fight.'

Isis no longer seemed so distant. 'May I . . . may I kiss you on the cheek?'

As she did not answer, he dared to do it. Her perfume possessed him; the softness of her skin intoxicated him. Never would he forget the intensity of this too-brief moment.

'We are leaving!' boomed General Nesmontu's strong voice. 'Every man to his post!'

The quay was immediately a hive of activity. The last chests of weapons and provisions were rapidly loaded, for the old soldier took discipline very seriously.

'Be exceptionally vigilant,' Isis warned Iker.

'If I come back alive, will you love me?'

'Come back alive, Iker. And never forget for a single moment that the survival of Osiris hangs in the balance.'

Did her eyes, so solemn yet so gentle, betray a feeling to which she would not yet admit? But the flagship was already weighing anchor, and Iker's absence was the only thing preventing the gangplank from being withdrawn. He climbed aboard just as Senusret appeared at the prow.

On his brow, the king wore a golden cobra decorated with lapis-lazuli and with eyes of garnet: the fearsome snake would precede the fleet, driving enemies from its route. In addition, he was brandishing a spear so long and so heavy that nobody else would have been able to use it.

'In this eighth year of my reign,' he declared, 'we are setting off along the new canal named "The Power of the Divine Light Appears in Glory".[1] Thanks to it, from now on Egypt and Nubia are permanently linked, and supplies will reach us easily. However, our task promises to be a difficult one. This time, we shall truly extinguish the flames of this rebellion.'

Calmly indifferent to the rolling of the boat, North Wind watched Medes as he vomited.

'Come with me,' said Dr Gua sympathetically.

Green-faced and barely able to stand, Medes felt ridiculous. He would have swallowed anything in order to regain his martial bearing.

As for Iker, he was studying the Nubian landscape. It was the hot season again, but it was made bearable by a northerly

---

[1] *Kha-kau-Ra*, one of Senusret's coronation names.

breeze which also aided sailing. The sun was drying out the few cultivated fields, and the dates were ripening – at each stop the soldiers gathered thousands of them, for they were nourishing and full of goodness. The fruit of the doum-palms, whose branches were shaped like a sorcerer's wand, was inedible, but the god Thoth and scribes loved to meditate in the trees' shade. Doum-palms were not so common in southern Egypt, but in Nubia they were everywhere.

Iker felt a malaise which derived neither from the heat nor from the journey. A strange, oppressive atmosphere reigned over this land. Right at the start of the canal a new world began, very different from the Two Lands.

'You seem preoccupied,' observed Sehotep.

'Can you feel the presence of a negative magic?'

'Ah, so you feel it too.'

'I don't think it is natural. I think evil forces are on the prowl.'

'The Herald, perhaps? Could his powers be so extensive?'

'It is wise to expect the worst.'

'The king agrees with you. It was around here that General Sepi was murdered. We are heading towards the forts of Ikkur and Kuban, whose garrisons watch several tracks, notably Wadi Allaki, which leads to an abandoned gold mine. Elephantine has received no reports from either fort in the past two months. Perhaps their messengers got lost, or perhaps the soldiers have been killed, but Ikkur and Kuban are to the north of our main base in Nubia, Buhen, which is apparently intact. Well, we shall soon know the reason for their silence.'

Flesh-Eater began barking furiously, signalling danger.

'Hippopotami in sight!' shouted the lookout.

The animals hated being disturbed during their interminable naps and did not hesitate to attack boats, often capsizing them. With their long canine teeth, they could bite through thick wood.

The archers were taking up position when the sound of a slow, sweet melody was heard.

Seated at the prow, Sekari was expertly playing a flute some two cubits long. Using a series of holes pierced in the lower part of a thick reed, he produced a rich range of sounds, whose intensity he could vary.

The hound grew calm at once, but the hippopotami gathered together and their leader, a monstrously large animal, opened its jaws wide in anger.

'Let's harpoon it,' suggested a soldier.

Sekari kept on playing his flute.

The leader stopped dead and his fellows stayed still, with only their eyes, nostrils and ears visible above the water, for their skin was too sensitive to bear the burning sun.

Unexpectedly, another creature appeared on the riverbank.

'The white hippopotamus!' cried a sailor. 'We're saved.'

The male, its back covered with blood-like secretions, was regarded as red. An incarnation of Set, it ravaged the fields. On the other hand the female, which was considered white, contained the benevolent power of Tawarct, 'She Who Is Great', protector of fertility and birth. Each year the pharaoh, wearer of the Red Crown and victor over the dangerous male, celebrated the festival of the white hippopotamus.

The leader of the herd was the first to emerge from the river, but the other members immediately followed suit. Completely docile, they followed the female as she disappeared into the reeds. Once its way was clear, the fleet set off again.

The troops' spirits, already high, soared to the sky, and everyone began to recall Senusret's successes. He had subjugated the provincial governors, one by one, without losing a single soldier, hadn't he? Under the leadership of such a king, the Nubian campaign was bound to be successful.

Sekari finished his melody with airy, joyful notes in honour of Senusret.

'Another of your hidden talents,' said Iker. 'Does that tune always calm hippopotami?'

'Actually, it attracts females, and with a little luck they calm down the males.'

'Where did you learn to play music?'

'In my profession, you encounter a thousand and one dangerous situations, and violence isn't always the answer. Unfortunately, though, the flute isn't a universal peace-bringer: less receptive opponents than hippos are barely sensitive to it.'

'Did the Golden Circle of Abydos teach you the secrets of music?'

'During his earthly reign, Osiris taught human beings to emerge from barbarism by building, sculpting, painting and playing music. We are moving closer to Abydos by a dangerous route and we won't be fighting an ordinary war. The resurrection of Osiris depends upon this one.'

Sekari's words echoed those of Isis. Suddenly, Iker was certain that he was taking part in a supernatural expedition. The clash of weapons would hide another conflict, one which would determine the future of the human race to whom Osiris had offered the sense of a certain harmony, now under threat.

'I'm worried about our Nubian soldiers,' Sekari went on.

'Why? Because of possible treason?'

'No, because they're well-paid and they have no wish to go back to their tribes, who regards them as traitors. But their behaviour has changed. Usually they're cheerful and relaxed, but now they're becoming edgy and irritable.'

'Could a rebel have infiltrated them and be causing the trouble?'

'No. I'd have spotted him.'

'Have you told General Nesmontu?'

'Of course, and he's as puzzled as I am. He's known these men for a long time and trusts them.'

'So traditional defences will be no use. If treason does occur, it will be unlike anything we know.'

'Probably.'

'I'm going to ask His Majesty to take exceptional preventive measures immediatcly. I shall make some clay figurines and . . .'

While Iker was describing his plan to Sekari, the fleet came within sight of Ikkur and Kuban. Both forts seemed intact, but not a single soldier appeared on the battlements of the guard-towers.

'This reeks of an ambush,' declared Sekari.

33

In normal times, Ikkur and Kuban had sheltered caravans and prospectors in search of gold, and gold destined for the temples of Egypt had been stored there. They were constructed according to a simple plan: a rectangle of brick walls relieved by bastions, from which a covered passageway led down to the river. The soldiers could thus draw water without being exposed to an attacker's arrows.

Now, however, vultures and crows were wheeling above both forts.

Nesmontu ordered the fleet to anchor in midstream. 'I shall send out scouts,' he said.

Ten men landed on the eastern bank, and about twenty on the western one. They dispersed and ran off towards their various objectives.

Sekari, who had moved across to the Nubian soldiers' ship, did not even glance at the scouts: he was watching his vessel closely.

Suddenly, some of the Nubians howled, others tore at the sails, and several of the best archers broke their bows.

An officer hurried to the trouble-spot. 'That's enough!' he ordered. 'Calm down immediately.'

As he was walking through the ranks, intending to punish the most over-excited men, a tall black warrior plunged his knife between the Egyptian's shoulder-blades. Animal-like cries rang out.

Unable to contain the rebellion single-handed, Sekari jumped into the water and swam to the flagship, which he boarded with the aid of a rope.

'The Nubian archers have gone mad,' he told Iker, who had hurried to meet him. 'We must take urgent action.'

'That we should have to fight one of our own regiments . . . It's terrible,' mourned Nesmontu.

'If we don't act quickly, they'll do irreparable harm.'

The rebel boat was bearing down on the flagship. 'Rise up against the king!' roared the murderer. 'A fierce spirit is within us; victory is reaching out to us!'

Senusret laid on a travelling-altar the clay figurines Iker had made. They represented vanquished soldiers deprived of their legs, their hands tied behind their backs. On each one's head was an ostrich feather, the symbol of Ma'at. Words of conjuration covered their chests. The pharaoh read the words out in a voice so solemn and so powerful that he made the attackers tremble.

'You are the tears from the divine eye, the multitude, which he must now contain so that it does not become harmful. May the enemy be reduced to nothing.'

With his white club, the pharaoh struck each figurine, which he then threw into the fire of a brazier.

But the rebels' boat continued on its way, the Nubians dancing and chanting.

The archers on the flagship took up their positions.

'Wait for my order and aim carefully,' ordered Nesmontu. 'In hand-to-hand fighting, these men have no equal – and in their frenzy they will be even harder to beat.'

The leader was parading himself at the prow, roaring insults at the Egyptians. Suddenly, to his fellows' terror, his head burst open like an over-ripe fruit. The dancing stopped abruptly. Most of the Nubians collapsed; a few staggered about like disjointed puppets, and then fell into the water.

'We must re-take control of that vessel,' said Nesmontu.

A party of sailors obeyed. They were rather nervous, but they met no resistance: not one of the Nubians was still alive.

'Someone must have put a collective spell on them,' concluded Sehotep.

'It won't happen to the other regiments, will it?' asked Iker worriedly.

'No,' replied the king. 'The Nubian sorcerers responsible for this crime exercised a special influence over the spirits of these unfortunate men, their brothers in blood. The sorcerers intended to weaken our army.'

Nesmontu ordered the ships to moor along the riverbank, and shortly afterward the first scouts returned.

'Both Ikkur and Kuban are empty,' reported an officer. 'There are traces of dried blood everywhere, so the garrisons were probably killed, but we didn't find a single body.'

'Did you find any clues to the attackers' identity?' asked the king.

'Just this piece of woollen cloth, Majesty. It must come from a very thick tunic, but the Nubians don't wear tunics like that.'

Senusret rubbed the fabric between his fingers. It was like the fabric he had found on Biga when the islet had been profaned by a demon who mocked the rites and wanted to disrupt the flood.

'The Herald,' he concluded. 'He committed this latest crime, and he is waiting for us deep inside Nubia.'

Everyone shuddered. What hell was awaiting the expedition?

'Look over there, General,' shouted a sentry. 'A Nubian – he's running away.'

An archer was already drawing his bow.

'We must take him alive,' ordered Nesmontu.

Several soldiers at once set off in pursuit, accompanied by

Iker. The soldiers ran too fast and were soon panting for breath. The heat burnt their lungs and made their legs buckle.

Although he seemed to be lagging behind the others, Iker did not quicken his pace. Trained in running long distances, he conserved his strength while remaining in the chase. Little by little, the gap narrowed.

Eventually the Nubian fell, and he could not get up again. When Iker reached him, he saw a horned viper slithering away. The unfortunate man had been bitten on the foot; he had not long to live.

His eyes were already glazing over. 'The gods are punishing me,' he panted. 'I shouldn't have robbed the dead men in Ikkur and Kuban . . . I didn't know she'd come back to eat them.'

'She? Who do you mean?'

'A lioness – a gigantic lioness. She slaughtered the garrisons . . . Their arrows didn't touch her, and their daggers couldn't wound her . . .' The dying man tried to go on, but his breath failed and his heart gave out.

Iker ran back to the flagship and made his report to the king. 'The Nubian was telling the truth, Majesty,' he said when he had finished.

'The situation is much more serious than I thought,' admitted Senusret. 'The Nubian tribes have rebelled, under the Herald's leadership. He has prepared a series of traps and ambushes, in order to wipe us out and then invade Egypt, and one of them is the awakening of the lioness. No army can destroy the Terrifying One, so if she is haunting the Great South we are defeated before we begin.'

'Is there no way of controlling her?' asked Sehotep.

'Only the queen of turquoises can calm her and transform her ferocity into gentleness.'

'That stone does exist,' Iker reminded him. 'I found it in the mine in Sinai.'

'Unfortunately, the Herald has it,' said the king.

'And so the trap closes,' said Nesmontu. 'He wants to lure us to Buhen, if not beyond, to the gathering-point of the Nubian tribes. Then, with the Terrifying One's aid, they will crush us and he will have no more obstacles to overcome.'

'Should we not go back to Elephantine,' suggested Sekari, 'and fortify it?'

The king shook his head resolutely. 'This is not the first time I have faced an enemy's apparently overwhelming superiority. If I had given in to fear and despair, what would have become of Egypt? You can all see it. Our enemies are not just human beings who wish to conquer a territory. It is Osiris they want to destroy, by preventing the Mysteries from being celebrated. Only his teaching can enable us to act righteously.'

'I shall send a troop of miners to gather as much red jasper and cornelian as possible,' said the general. 'Each soldier must have some pieces in order to keep the lioness at a distance. She has a horror of the blood of the eye of Horus, fixed in jasper, and of the flame hidden at the heart of the cornelian. It will not be enough to defeat her, and poorly equipped men's lives will be at risk, but at least we shall be able to make progress.'

'You know the lioness well, General,' said Iker.

'At my age, my boy, one has travelled around a good deal. I am not sorry to face her again – and this time, I hope to make her swallow her own tail!'

'There's one thing I don't understand,' said Sekari. 'Why did the Herald attack Ikkur and Kuban, and so warn us of the dangers ahead? Surely it would have been better to let us advance and then take us by surprise?'

'He has foreseen our reaction,' said Iker, 'and he hopes to make us leave as soon as possible.'

'Why? What secret does it hold?'

'The track to Wadi Allaki leads to a gold mine,' replied the king, 'and it was on that track that the Herald murdered General Sepi.'

'A worked-out mine and an impassable route, according to the experts' reports,' said Nesmontu.

'They have been known to make mistakes,' Sekari pointed out sarcastically.

'I volunteer to explore the area,' announced Iker. 'General Sepi must have made an extremely important discovery.'

'The ultimate goal of our expedition remains the discovery of the gold of the gods,' said the pharaoh. 'In it, the fire of resurrection materializes. It is a synthesis of and bond between the elements that make up life, and it encloses the light that passes on the Mysteries of Osiris. Go, my son, and travel to the end of the track.'

'I shall go with him,' declared Sekari.

The two men disembarked and walked along the riverbank to another ship.

'You look worried, Nesmontu,' said the king.

'Iker does not belong to the Golden Circle of Abydos, but now knows some of its secrets. Should we not plan to admit him?'

'He still has a long road to travel, and I do not know if he will succeed.'

'Are you feeling better, my lord?' Gergu asked.

Medes was less green in the face, and had even started eating again. 'Since this accursed boat dropped anchor, I am alive again.'

'The Herald has wiped out the garrisons at Ikkur and Kuban,' whispered Gergu. 'Our Nubian archers rebelled and were all killed. The pharaoh must be despairing of the cause. He's consulting his closest advisers, and in my opinion he's thinking of beating a retreat. What humiliation! The army will be demoralized and Egypt will be severely weakened.'

'Try to find out more.'

Gergu looked around and saw Iker deep in conversation with Doctor Gua. He went over to them and asked, 'Are you ill, my lord?'

'No, I'm merely consulting the doctor before taking a walk in the desert.'

'A walk? Is that quite the right word? I loathe these desert places – they're probably populated by venomous creatures.'

'Precisely,' said Gua. 'I am giving the Royal Son a powerful remedy for stings and bites. It is a balm made from sea salt, edible reeds, ibex fat, moringa oil and terebinth resin, and the Royal Son and Sekari must smear it over their skin several times a day.'

'Where are you going?' asked Gergu.

'I'm sorry, I cannot tell you. Our mission is secret.'

'Secret . . . and dangerous?'

'Of course – we are at war.'

'Be careful, Iker, very careful. No road is safe.'

'I have known worse.'

Gergu saw a group of miners collecting their tools and stores of food and water. So an expedition was being organized. But asking questions might arouse suspicion, so he rejoined Medes, who was writing the ship's journal.

'A liaison scribe is overwhelming me with rough notes,' complained Medes, 'and they have to be put into the proper form. The king has decreed that Ikkur and Kuban are to be enlarged, and their garrisons doubled. There is no question of retreat.'

'The fleet will remain here until Iker returns from a secret mission,' said Gergu. 'I don't know what it's about, but it seems to be important.'

34

'The map is wrong,' decided Sekari. 'It's directing us away from the probable location of the old mine. We should bear east.'

When consulted, North Wind agreed. He headed a detachment of twenty donkeys bearing food and water, and was taking his new role very seriously. His assistant, Flesh-Eater, was permanently on guard.

Because of the extreme heat, the expedition made many brief halts so that men and animals could have a little water. Fortunately, there were no sandstorms to hamper their progress.

'Before we left,' Iker told Sekari, 'the king told me of something Isis discovered: one of the ancient documents mentions a City of Gold in this region, though it gave no precise location.'

'According to my inquiries, there was only one mine in this region. It was worked for a time, then abandoned when the seams ran out.'

'Could that be false information spread by the Herald?'

Sekari shook his head. 'If you're right, he wants to keep us away from this place by sending us along false tracks.'

'This is where he murdered General Sepi. Why should he do that unless the general was getting close to the treasure?'

Ahead of them the track was blocked by a heap of black

stones covered with rough drawings of demons of the desert with wings, horns and claws.

'We should turn back,' advised the miners' leader.

'We are close to our goal,' objected Iker. 'Even if we accept that the map is only approximate, the mine cannot be more than a day's march away.'

'No miner has gone beyond here for three years. If you go any further, you disappear.'

'I have a mission to accomplish.'

'Don't rely on us.'

'That's clear insubordination,' noted Sekari. 'We are at war; you know the punishment.'

'There are six of us against two of you. You'd better be reasonable.'

'And threats as well.'

'Let's not vanish into nothingness. Let's go back to Kahun.'

'You and your colleagues, you can go. When you're arrested, I shall take great pleasure in commanding the archers who execute you for cowardice and desertion.'

'The desert monsters are no joke. You and the Royal Son are making a fatal mistake.'

Obeying North Wind's orders, the donkeys refused to follow the deserters, and Flesh-Eater's menacing snarl deterred the men from insisting. The miners set off into the distance, and did not look back.

'Good riddance!' said Sekari contemptuously. 'Cowards and incompetents can cause even the best-prepared expedition to fail.'

'Is ours really well prepared?' asked Iker doubtfully.

'Weren't you advised several times to arm yourself?'

The Royal Son remembered the warnings given him by the mayor of Kahun and by Heremsaf, a priest of Anubis who had later been murdered by one of the Herald's henchmen.

'The monsters drawn on these stones are watching us from

250

the other side,' said Sekari. 'The Herald has cast a spell on the region. Unless we retreat, the monsters will tear us apart with their claws and beaks. The reason why General Sepi didn't turn back is that he knew the magic words that render them powerless.'

'But he died all the same.'

'The Herald knows the words, too, so he altered the monsters' behaviour and made Sepi's words ineffective.'

'Have we lost before we start, then?'

'I come back again to those famous weapons.'

From one of North Wind's leather bags, Sekari took out two sturdy fishing-nets.

'Would those be the nets that must be placed between sky and earth in order to capture the wandering souls of evil travellers?' asked Iker.

'You're going to learn how to use them.'

'They come from Abydos, don't they?'

'No more talking. It's time for training.'

At first Iker was clumsy, but he soon learnt how to throw the net. He also made use of two other weapons, his knife and his throwing-stick.

'I think there will be three of them,' said Sekari. 'The first two will attack face-on and the third from behind.'

'Who will deal with them?'

'Flesh-Eater. He isn't afraid of anything.'

'And what if there are more than three?'

'We shall die.'

'Then tell me about the Golden Circle of Abydos.'

'Talking about it is pointless. Watch it at work.'

They skirted the piles of stones and went on. Iker had never seen Flesh-Eater so on edge, and all the donkeys except North Wind were trembling.

The attack came almost immediately.

There were five monsters, winged and lion-headed. As one, Iker and Sekari deployed their nets, imprisoning two of the creatures, which tore at each other as they struggled. Flesh-Eater sank his teeth into the neck of a third.

Sekari leapt aside just as claws grazed his cheek. Lying on the ground, Iker sank his knife into the beast's belly, then rolled aside to avoid the gaping jaws of the fifth monster, which was drunk with rage. Getting to his feet, the Royal Son aimed his throwing-stick. It flew up towards the sun, and Iker feared that he had missed his target. But it fell back at lightning speed, and shattered the head of the monster threatening him.

A light wind began to blow, raising a cloud of sand. When it cleared, there was no trace of the attackers, nor of the nets, nor the guardian spirit's knife, nor the throwing-stick.

'Did they actually exist?' Iker wondered.

'Look at Flesh-Eater's mouth,' said Sekari. 'It's full of blood.'

The dog's tail was wagging eagerly. Knowing that he had done well, he revelled in his master's praise.

'But my weapons have disappeared,' said Iker.

'They came from the other side, and they've returned there. You were given them so that you could fight this battle and pass through this door. Without your courage and speed we'd have lost. Now, let us continue along General Sepi's path; he must be pleased with us.'

Before long they reached the abandoned mine; its installations were in good condition. Sekari explored one of the galleries and found a promising seam. Above ground, Iker discovered a small shrine. On the altar was an ostrich egg, which was so heavy that he could not lift it. With much effort, he and Sekari managed to get it outside.

'We must break it,' said Sekari. 'According to tradition, it contains marvels.'

Iker picked up a stone which was half buried in the sand nearby. As he did so, a huge scorpion stung him on the hand and then scuttled away.

Sekari knew what was to come: nausea, vomiting, sweating, fever, breathing difficulties and heart failure. Given the size of the killer, Iker might well die within a day.

Sekari smeared the injured hand with Dr Gua's balm and spoke the words of conjuration: 'Spit your venom; the gods will throw it back. If it burns, the eye of Set will be blinded. Crawl away, disappear, be annihilated.'

'Do I have a chance of survival?

'If you suffocate, I'll make an incision in your neck for you to breathe through.'

North Wind and Flesh-Eater came to Iker and licked his face, which was covered by an unpleasant sweat.

'That was no ordinary scorpion,' said Sekari. 'It was the sixth monster, set to guard the treasure.'

Iker was already having difficulty in breathing. 'Will you tell . . . Isis . . .'

Descending from high in the sky, a vulture with white plumage and a black-tipped orange beak landed close to him. With a flint gripped in its beak, it struck the top of the egg, which shattered into a thousand pieces, revealing gold ingots. Then the great bird flew away again.

'You're saved, Iker!' cried Sekari. 'That was the incarnation of Mut, whose name means both "death" and "mother". You'll live.'

He laid an ingot on the wound, and before long Iker's breathing returned to normal and the sweating ceased.

'This is indeed the healing gold,' he said.

Protected by a hundred soldiers, a team of miners began working the seams of gold. After being extracted, washed, weighed and formed into ingots, the gold would be sent to Abydos by special caravan and under heavy guard.

Iker and Sekari had been received as heroes by the army, and had thought their discovery would ensure Egypt's triumph over evil.

The pharaoh brought them back to harsh reality. 'You have

won a fine victory, but the war continues. The gold is vital to us, but by itself it is not enough. To be fully effective, we must find its essential complement, which is hidden deep inside Nubia in the lost city whose traces Isis discovered. I, too, would have preferred to return to Egypt, but the threat is still formidable – we must not let the Herald assemble the tribes against us. In addition, we must pacify the Terrifying One or the annual flood will never be normal again: in the place of regenerative water, blood will flow.'

The fleet sailed on southwards. When it reached the fort of Miam,[1] the soldiers expected an enthusiastic welcome from the garrison but, as at Kuban and Ikkur, they heard nothing but a heavy silence, and not a single defender appeared on the battlements.

'I'm going to take a few archers and investigate,' said Sekari.

He did not take long. 'There are no survivors, Majesty, and traces of blood and fragments of bone everywhere. The lioness has been here, too.'

'She is not attacking us directly,' Sehotep pointed out, 'and she is luring us southwards. By allowing her to do so, are we not taking too many risks?'

'We shall continue,' decided the king. 'I shall finalize my plans when we reach Buhen.'

Buhen was the most forward post in Nubia, and formed a barrier at the Second Cataract, preventing the Nubians from setting out to invade Egypt. But Buhen had sent no messages for a long time.

Anxiously, the crew of the flagship approached the fort housing the administrative centre of this far-off land. Despite evident damage, the high walls were still holding.

A soldier was standing on top of the main tower, waving his arms.

---

[1] Aniba, 250 kilometres south of Aswan.

'It may be a trap,' warned Sekari.

'We must disembark in force,' said Nesmontu. 'If the main gate does not open, we shall break it down.'

But it did open, and about thirty exhausted soldiers threw themselves into the arms of the new arrivals, describing murderous Nubians, vicious assaults and a bloodthirsty lioness. Buhen could not hold out much longer.

'Have Doctor Gua take care of these brave men,' ordered the general. 'We shall begin organizing our defences.'

Quickly and with good discipline, the army set to work.

Senusret was thinking about the Belly of Stone and the Second Cataract. His gigantic plan seemed impossible to realize. Yet it must be done.

35

All the Egyptians in Buhen listened attentively to the pharaoh's words. His solemn voice announced staggering decisions.

'It is not an ordinary enemy who seeks our destruction, and we shall therefore not fight him in the usual manner. At the head of the rebels, a demon is unleashing destructive forces and seeks to impose the tyranny of *isefet* by spreading violence, injustice and fanaticism. To oppose this, we are going to construct an impassable magic barrier, made up of many fortresses, from Elephantine to south of the Second Cataract. The ancient ones will be enlarged and strengthened, and we shall build several others. In reality, they will make up one whole, so powerful that it will discourage the invader. The work is to begin this day. Soon hundreds of craftsmen will come from Egypt, and I shall stay in Nubia with the army to protect the construction sites and fight off all attacks. Every man will be equipped with amulets and must never be separated from them, on pain of falling victim to the lioness. Let us set to work.'

The king's vision aroused great enthusiasm. The artificers would dig ditches, and thousands of bricks would be produced to build high, thick walls topped with crenellations; covered passages and double entrance gates would give protected access. The distance between each pair of fortresses would be calculated so as to allow communication by visual signals, smoke or carrier-pigeons. Sheltered by the battlements, the archers would be able to aim at any attacker, including any boat that tried to force its way through the checkpoints.

Buhen was the first, and very spectacular, result of a rapid transformation handled in masterly fashion by Sehotep, assisted by Iker. Occupying an area of 54,000 square cubits, the stronghold, partially hewn out of the rock, looked like a little settlement divided into six districts, separated by streets at right angles to one another.

Each morning, the king celebrated the ritual at the temple dedicated to Horus, close to his residence, sheltered by walls twenty-two cubits high and sixteen thick. Every ten cubits there was a square tower or circular bastion. Two doors opened on to the quays where warships, supply-boats and vessels laden with raw materials were moored. The dock-labourers worked ceaselessly, and boats were constantly sailing up and down the Nile.

Medes, who had been provided with a comfortable office, ensured a smooth and frequent messenger service between Buhen, the other fortresses and Memphis, and checked that messages from his administration were correctly written. Gergu was drooping under the weight of work. Besides coordinating the movements of the grain-carrying boats, he had to oversee the filling of the granaries and the distribution of food. In the current circumstances it was impossible to cheat. Following Medes's example, he was obliged to behave like a devoted servant of the pharaoh.

'What are the Egyptians playing at?' demanded Crooked-Face impatiently. 'They weren't supposed to stop at Buhen, they were supposed to come straight to the Belly of Stone.'

'They will come,' predicted the Herald.

'They have enlarged and strengthened the fortress,'

grumbled Shab the Twisted. 'It's impossible to attack it from the river – we'd be struck down before we got near the walls.'

'It's no better from the desert side,' said Crooked-Face. 'A drawbridge runs to the great double door, across a deep ditch.'

'My faithful friends, do you not understand that they are afraid, and are hiding behind defences which will turn out to be illusory?'

Suddenly, there were shouts of joy from the Nubian camp.

'Here is the man I have been waiting for,' said the Herald.

A tall black man, whose face was marked with many tribal scars, walked heavily towards them. He was wearing a red wig, heavy gold earrings and a short kilt, held up by a broad belt. He was surrounded by ten sturdy warriors, and his gaze was filled with a rare violence.

'I am Triah, Prince of Kush, the land beyond the Third Cataract. Are you the one they call the Herald?'

'I am indeed.'

'I was told that you want to liberate Nubia and conquer Egypt.'

'That is true.'

'Nothing can be done without me.'

'I am convinced of that.'

'Have you really awakened the demons of the Belly of Stone, and the Terrifying One?'

'They have already struck hard at the enemy, and will continue to do so.'

'You know sorcery, and I know war. I shall therefore lead my tribes to victory and will then reign over all Nubia.'

'No one contests your right to do so.'

Triah said arrogantly, 'Hundreds of warriors obey me without question. Do not, under any circumstances, attempt to play me false.'

'The choice of the moment of the attack is vital,' said the

Herald. 'God will tell me, and you must fall in with it, or the attack will fail. Only my powers can bring down Buhen's walls and break down its doors. If you disobey me, you will die and your province will fall into the hands of the pharaoh.'

The change of tone took the prince aback. 'Are you daring to give me orders?'

Triah was a brute, but had a keen sense of danger. When he saw the Herald's eyes flame red, he sensed that he was facing a particularly formidable sorcerer, whose capacity for harm must not be underestimated.

'I tell you again, Triah, God speaks through my mouth. You will submit to him, because he will give us victory.'

The prince's glance fell upon the beautiful Bina, who was standing behind the Herald, her eyes lowered. He said, 'I want that woman.'

'Impossible.'

'Chiefs offer each other gifts. I will exchange her for several of my wives and several strong donkeys.'

'Bina is no ordinary woman.'

'What does that mean? A female is a female!'

'You are right, except as regards the Queen of the Night. She obeys no one but me.'

For the second time, Triah was humiliated. 'We are going to put up our tents,' he decided. 'Tell me when you want to discuss our plan of battle.'

Work had begun on several sites at the same time, and was advancing at a remarkable rate, thanks to excellent co-ordination between the civilian and military artificers. Medes was kept extremely busy sorting out all the administrative problems like a model official. But he was worried: how was he to get out of this trap and warn the Herald of the pharaoh's true plans? Where was the Herald hiding, and what was he preparing to do?

'I'm exhausted,' groaned Gergu, collapsing into a chair.

'Fortunately I still have some of the water from the flood left – it's an excellent restorative.'

'You drink water?'

'It sets me right in the morning, before the beer. I've never worked so hard, and this heat is exhausting. However, by good luck, I've just had a small success.'

'Have you done something stupid?' demanded Medes.

'As if I would! In the village of Buhen a few peaceable natives are settled, under close watch. I requisitioned their donkeys – spoils of war, you might say – and I'm starting up a business, all perfectly legal and very lucrative. Is there any news of the Herald?'

'No.'

'I don't find his silence reassuring.'

'He is not idle, you can be sure of that.'

Iker entered, and the two men stood up.

'A serious problem has arisen: several boats need refitting. To avoid cluttering the quays at Buhen, I am planning to set up a carpentry workshop on a nearby islet. There we shall group the men shown on this list. Prepare the necessary orders.'

As soon as Medes agreed, the Royal Son left.

'And it's like that every day!' complained Gergu.

'A grain boat is arriving this morning. Supervise the unloading.'

The sole inhabitant of the islet, a small green monkey, gazed in astonishment at the donkey and the giant hound, who were equally surprised but not at all aggressive. The monkey climbed a rock to safety, then cautiously allowed Iker to approach.

'You have nothing to fear,' he reassured it, offering it a banana.

The monkey delicately peeled the fruit before eating it, and then climbed on to Iker's shoulder.

'Don't be jealous,' he told North Wind and Flesh-Eater. 'You shall have some food too, as long as you respect our guest.'

The artificers approved of Iker's decision. Many vessels needed major repairs, from the caulking of a hull to the installation of a new steering-oar. Each man had a precise role, and nothing must halt Senusret's incredible plan.

'And we haven't even passed through the Second Cataract,' said Sekari. 'Mind you, when we do we're likely to have to face some fierce fighting. The Herald's waiting for us down there.'

Iker frowned. 'Isn't he making a mistake by letting us strengthen our rearward bases?'

'He doesn't think they'll be of any use. How can they be, if he wipes out most of our army?'

'The pharaoh will never lead us into such a disaster.'

'Sooner or later we'll have to pass through the Belly of Stone.'

'The pharaoh must foresee an easy victory.'

'If all we had to do was fight a Nubian prince, I wouldn't be worried. But it's the enemy of Osiris who's lying in wait for us.'

In the little village of Buhen, not far from the enormous fortress, animated discussions were taking place. Several Nubian families had gathered there in order to escape from the Prince of Kush, whose savagery terrified them. A great lover of human sacrifices, he did not even spare children. Everyone knew that he had established himself south of the Second Cataract. Only the Egyptians could prevent him from killing all the people in the surrounding areas.

Rebellion burned in the refugees. Why had an Egyptian official taken their donkeys, their main wealth? Until then they had been treated well and fed better than before, but they would not put up with this injustice. After a long debate, however, the Nubians decided to stay. If they returned home, Triah's warriors would cut off their heads and brandish them as trophies. It was better to submit to the Egyptian occupation, which was less violent and more remunerative, for trade was beginning to be organized. The pharaoh had promised a form of local government, by creating a mixed court, charged with preventing military blunders.

But one youth was rebelling against his parents, and refused to share these hopes. Cursing the villagers' cowardice, he left his hut and ran across the grasslands in search of the troops belonging to Triah, his idol. His knowledge of the region enabled him to reach his goal.

Seeing him running towards them, two archers immediately fired. The first arrow struck him in the left shoulder, the second in his right thigh.

'I am your ally!' he shouted, dragging himself towards them.

The archers hesitated.

'I come from Buhen and I want to see Prince Triah! My information will be useful to him.'

If he was telling the truth, the two soldiers would be rewarded, so they took the wounded boy to their chief's tent.

Triah had just taken his pleasure with two of his wives and was drinking date-wine.

'Prince, this prisoner wishes to speak to you.'

'Make him kneel and bow his head.'

The archers roughly shoved the youth to his knees.

'Explain yourself, and quickly.'

'My family has taken refuge in the new village, and the Egyptians have stolen our donkeys. Help us, my lord.'

In his anger, Triah slapped the boy. 'Nobody has the right to act that way. This time, it is enough! I shall punish the pharaoh.'

'Shall we enlist the lad?' asked one of the archers.

'I have no need of the powerless. Kill him.'

Triah summoned his officers and lavished a fiery speech upon them, vaunting the bravery of the Nubians and the cowardice of the Egyptians. Faced with an attack by the black warriors, Buhen would not hold out for long.

It was not necessary to obtain the approval of the Herald, since after his triumph the Prince of Kush would have him impaled. Nobody insulted a chief of his standing and survived.

36

Memphis was still asleep when the ten men from the small northern guard-post hailed the arrival of the flatcake-seller. After their morning meal, they would be relieved by the day shift.

They all came out of the whitewashed brick building, stood in front of the door and enjoyed the first rays of the rising sun. Although still sleepy, they were ravenous.

As planned, this was the moment the rebels chose. Ten easy targets. Their execution would spread terror through the capital and create a lasting climate of insecurity.

When the first attacker came up against Sobek the Protector himself, he was so surprised that he did not even think to parry the savage blow that stove in his face. His men had the will to resist, but the seasoned fighters chosen to replace the usual guards overcame them in a few moments.

'Over there, sir! Someone's running away!'

Sobek himself caught the leader of the band, seizing him by the hair. 'Well, well, it's our barber! So, you wanted to kill some guards, did you?'

'No! You're making a mistake!'

'Who is the leader of your network?'

'There isn't any network. I haven't done anything wrong. I was running away because I'm afraid of violence.'

'Listen, fellow, we've been watching you for several

264

weeks. You assembled a fine band of brigands and took your time preparing for this attack. If you want to keep your head, you'd better be talkative – very talkative.'

'You have no right to torture me!'

'That's right,' agreed Sobek, 'and I've no intention of doing so.'

'Then . . . are you going to let me go?'

'What would you say to a walk in the desert? I'll have water, but you won't. And you'll walk ahead of me. At this time of the year, the scorpions and snakes are rather bad-tempered.'

The barber had never ventured outside Memphis. Like most town-dwellers, he was afraid of those dangerous, lonely wastes.

'It's illegal, inhuman, and you—'

'Get moving.'

'No! No, I'll talk.'

'I'm waiting.'

'I don't know much – almost nothing, in fact. I just got the order to organize this . . . operation. As there weren't many guards and they were mostly elderly, it should have been easy.'

The Protector was fuming. Ten murders these cowards had planned! But at least he now held one of the enemies who been hidden deep in the shadows and had committed so many crimes.

'Who gave you the order?' he demanded.

'Another barber.'

'What's his name?'

'I don't know.'

'Where does he live?'

'I don't think he's got a home. He travels from place to place, and passes on his orders to me when he sees fit. I don't do anything on my own initiative.'

'Why do you obey a piece of filth like that?'

The rebel's eyes filled with hatred. Suddenly, he was no

longer afraid of Sobek. 'Because the god of the Herald will soon reign over Egypt! You and the impious, blind servants of the pharaoh, you will all be killed. We, the followers of the true faith, will have wealth and happiness. And my native land, Libya, will at last have its revenge.'

'In the meantime, give me a list of your chief's hideouts.'

The Phoenician wolfed down two cream-filled cakes, one after the other. He would not be able to stop eating until the water-carrier told him the result of the attack on the guard-post. And his agent was late, very late!

At last he arrived. 'It was a complete failure,' he said in alarm. 'Sobek was there.'

The Phoenician went pale. 'Did the barber get away?'

'No, he was arrested.'

The fat man felt sick and had to sit down, dabbing his forehead with a perfumed cloth.

'It doesn't end there,' went on the water-carrier. 'Sobek has launched a huge operation, and all the barbers in town have been taken in for questioning.'

'Including the one in charge of our network?'

'He cut his throat before he could be interrogated.'

'Brave fellow! So the trail cannot lead back to me.' Reassured, the Phoenician poured himself a cup of white wine.

'At the moment,' said his agent, 'our groups can't communicate with one another. Sobek's guards are everywhere, so it will take time to re-establish secure links.'

'What about the travelling sellers?'

'I advise you to leave them dormant. Sobek's bound to take an interest in them.'

'That mad dog ought to be killed.'

The water-carrier shook his head. 'He's untouchable, because his men positively worship him. And after this latest exploit he'll be even more popular.'

'Untouchable, perhaps. Incorruptible, certainly not. This latest success is bound to swell his head and make him susceptible to suggestions . . .'

The inhabitants of the village near Buhen were building huts, granaries, enclosures for the livestock and palisades for protection. Becoming accustomed to their new and agreeable conditions of living, the refugees were taken unawares by the Kushites' attack.

The Egyptian officer in charge of supplying the village with water and grain was the first to die. Triah cut off his head and planted it on a stake. His warriors slaughtered their fellow countrymen, children included. In less than half an hour, the village had been wiped out.

'Now for Buhen!' shouted the Prince of Kush, rushing towards the great desert-facing gate of the fortress.

The Egyptians had no time to raise the drawbridge and block entry to the fort. A howling mob poured into it, sure of easy victory. Triah was already imagining himself cutting Senusret's throat, then displaying the body at the gates of his palace.

The Kushites were expecting a large courtyard, in which hand-to-hand fighting would turn in their favour. But they found themselves crowded together in a narrow, twisting passageway.

Nesmontu gave the signal, and the Egyptian archers stationed above, shielded by the crenellations, began to fire. The few Nubian survivors fired back, but did not hit a single one of their opponents.

'Forward!' shouted Triah, convinced that once out of this trap he would at last be in contact with the enemy.

A second passageway succeeded the first and led into a smaller courtyard, closed off ahead by a heavy door. Virtually imprisoned, the attackers were subjected to a rain of murderous arrows. Not one of them got away, for an Egyptian squadron, coming from behind, had raised the drawbridge. Triah was the last to die, his body bristling with dozens of arrows.

Shab the Twisted dared to awaken the Herald. 'Forgive me, Lord, but the Prince of Kush has attacked Buhen.'

'The fool! It's too soon – much too soon.'

'He had been taking drugs for hours, and decided to take revenge on the Egyptians because they had requisitioned some donkeys.'

'The degenerate imbecile! He's making an enormous mistake.'

'Perhaps he has succeeded and seriously damaged the enemy defences.'

Followed by Shab the Twisted and Bina, the Herald went to the area of desert near Buhen. They saw that the fortress was intact, and Egyptian soldiers were taking the Kushite warriors' bodies out of the fort and piling them up ready for burning. Triah's body was treated like any other. The Nubian army, which the Herald had been counting on to confront Senusret's forces, had been annihilated.

'An absolute disaster,' said the Twisted One bitterly. 'We mustn't stay here, Lord. We must go back to Memphis. You'll be safe there.'

'You're forgetting the Belly of Stone. Senusret will be so full of confidence after this easy victory that he'll try to cross the Belly and conquer the lands beyond it.'

'Even with the Terrifying One's help, will we be able to drive him back?'

'Don't doubt it, my brave friend. He is only a pharaoh, I am the Herald. His reign is ending, mine is beginning. Can a minor incident like this really shake your faith in me?'

Shab the Twisted felt ashamed. 'I still have much progress to make, Lord. Please don't be angry with me.'

'I forgive you.'

On his return to camp, the Herald questioned Crooked-Face about the Egyptian positions. Most of the soldiers were stationed in Buhen, but a detachment was guarding a nearby islet where boats were repaired.

'Kill all the soldiers on the islet and set fire to the boats,' ordered the Herald. 'Senusret will realize that the rebels are far from beaten. His administration will be disrupted, and this unexpected setback will alarm his troops.'

'I'm going to enjoy doing that,' promised Crooked-Face, delighted to be taking action at last.

37

Sekari awoke with a start. 'What a nightmare! I was chewing cucumber, which is a bad omen. Something bad's going to happen.'

'Go back to sleep,' advised Iker, who needed his sleep.

'Don't mock the key of dreams. Besides, look at Flesh-Eater and North Wind: they're awake and on their feet.'

The Royal Son glanced across doubtfully. The two animals were shaking themselves, eyes fixed on the river.

'That's unsual,' he said. 'Are the sentries at their posts?'

'Don't move. I'll go and check.'

Cautiously, Sekari approached the carpenters' workshop. There was no sign of the guard. He ran to the tent where the off-duty soldiers were sleeping.

'Get up,' he ordered, 'and disperse. We're under attack.'

Scarcely had the Egyptians dashed out of the tent when the attackers' torches fired it and it blazed up: the enemy had been sure they would roast the sleeping men alive. Fierce hand-to-hand fighting ensued, and for a time the outcome was far from certain.

Anxiously, Sekari rejoined Iker, who was being attacked by two Syrians. Using all his agility and speed, Iker dodged their dagger-blows. He knocked out the first one, while Flesh-Eater dragged the second to the ground and sank his teeth into his throat.

Already, three boats were burning.

As the rebels had lost the advantage of complete surprise, there were not enough of them to overwhelm the Egyptian garrison. Despite their losses, the soldiers were gaining the upper hand.

By the light of the flames, Iker recognised the brute who was setting fire to a fourth boat.

'Crooked-Face!'

He spun round. 'I'd like to see you dead, you damned little scribe!'

A dagger, thrown with vicious anger, grazed Iker's cheek. Then Crooked-Face dived into the water and disappeared.

The pharaoh himself led the funeral ritual for the Egyptian officer killed in the attack on the village of Buhen. After his body had been identified, an embalmer had reattached his head. The murdered villagers were also given proper burials.

Senusret's troops had been alarmed and horrified by Triah's cruelty, but the pharaoh's presence reassured them. The destruction of the Nubian army proved, they thought, that his strategy was right.

By the king's side was Royal Son Iker, who had driven off a surprise attack during the night. True, several soldiers had been killed, and three boats destroyed, but the attack failed.

'There will be no pause,' said the king. 'The moment has come to pass through the Belly of Stone.'

Anxious murmurs ran through the ranks.

'I shall be the first, accompanied by Royal Son Iker. Do not forget your protective amulets, and follow General Nesmontu's orders to the letter.'

Left alone with Senusret, Iker saw him write a few words on a golden palette, the symbol of his office as High Priest of Abydos.

The king's words changed and other signs appeared,

271

replacing those he had drawn. Then they faded away, and the palette was unmarked again.

'The invisible power is answering the vital questions,' explained the king. 'Tomorrow, just before dawn, our boat shall pass through the Belly of Stone.'

'But it isn't possible, Majesty.'

'At that hour it will be. Four forces nourish the righteous act: the capacity for light, generosity, the faculty of manifesting power, and the mastery of the elements.[1] The very essence of the universe's creative forces, light is their most subtle and intense manifestation. It passes through us constantly, but who is really aware of it? Ra, the Divine Light, opens up our spirit during successive initiations. When your soul-bird awakens, you can reach the heavens, pass from the visible world to the invisible and come back to the visible. Travelling from one world to the other enables you to free yourself from the slavery of human mediocrity and escape from the servitude of time. Look above and beyond events; discover how to discern the gifts of the heavens.'

'But isn't the lioness able to destroy a thousand armies?'

'She is Sekhmet, the queen of powers. You wear round your neck the amulet of the sceptre *sekhem*, the Mystery of Power, and I wield that sceptre to consecrate the offerings. It is impossible to destroy the lioness of Sekhmet. Instead, as her powers have been stolen by the Herald, I must give her back her rightful place.'

As he sat in the king's boat, Sekari was frozen to the marrow. In the middle of summer, an icy dawn was breaking over the Second Cataract, far from the gentleness of Egypt. Without any doubt, this was another of the Herald's curses.

Five explorers gazed upon the Belly of Stone: the pharaoh,

---

[1] *Akh, user, ba, sekhem.*

Iker, North Wind, Flesh-Eater and Sekari. The Egyptian army would not follow them, but would go round by way of the desert.

As an initiate of the Golden Circle of Abydos, Sekari knew how great the pharaoh's powers were, but even so, faced with this barrier of rocks and tumultuous waters, he could not help being doubtful of success. Still, when he took his oath he had sworn to follow the king wherever he went, and not even this monstrous landscape would make him hold back. One's word was not lent; it was given. He who broke his solemn oath suffered a living death.

'Look at that huge rock looming over the cataract,' Senusret said to Iker. 'What does it look like?

'Like the uraeus, the cobra that rears up on Your Majesty's brow.'

'That is why we shall be protected. Forget the rapids and the clamour.'

Wielding the steering-oar, the pharaoh sent the boat through a narrow gap, where raging waters crashed. Rocky chaos extended as far as the eye could see.

Soaked to the skin, Sekari hung on to the rail. The Nile became more and more ferocious, its spray forming a curtain around them, and the boat creaked everywhere, as though it were about to fall apart.

'Take the steering-oar,' Senusret ordered his son.

The king drew his gigantic bow. The point of the arrow was made of cornelian and sparkling red jasper. As it flew through the air, it cut through the curtain of mist.

'We did a fair bit of damage,' said Crooked-Face.

'How many boats were destroyed?' asked the Herald.

'Three, and a fourth was seriously damaged.'

'That's a disappointing result.'

'Three cargo boats fewer – that weakens their supply lines, my lord. And the troops will be afraid all the time. We can launch harassing attacks anywhere and everywhere. The further they go into Nubia, the more vulnerable they'll be.'

'The Nubian magicians ran away,' Shab the Twisted reminded him morosely.

'Those fellows always run away at the first sign of trouble. But my Libyans aren't afraid of any enemy on earth. And we've got the lioness. She'll put the Egyptian army to flight by herself.' Crooked-Face omitted to mention that he had seen the ghost of Iker.

'Let us go and rest,' said the Herald. 'Tomorrow we shall take the next step.'

A little before dawn, he emerged from his tent, with Bina close behind him. The air was icy, the death-throes of the darkness oppressive.

Bina swayed. 'Lord, I can't breathe.'

A trail of fire lit up the dying night. At first it seemed to lose itself in the sky, but then it fell back with incredible speed and pierced Bina's leg. She gave a roar of pain.

The Herald had no time to care for the wounded lioness, for with the first rays of the sun an immense falcon with golden eyes appeared and wheeled over its prey.

Immediately, the Herald's hands were transformed into talons and his nose into a bird of prey's beak. When the falcon let out a piercing cry, he thought it was giving the signal to attack. The incarnation of the pharaoh could see the invisible, and was not in the habit of giving its prey any chance at all.

This time, however, it would be defeated. Two cubits from the ground, the Herald's nets would ensnare it, and then he would cut off the head of the Horus Senusret.

The falcon flew back up into the sky, lit up by the reborn sun.

'My Lord,' said Shab, 'the cataract has become silent.'

A lookout ran up. 'We must run, my lord! The Egyptian army's coming!'

*

Never had river travel been so peaceful. The Belly of Stone was reduced to a mere jumble of rocks between which the Nile forced its way, carrying the royal boat.

'Now that,' conceded Sekari, 'I'd never have believed.'

'Neither North Wind nor Flesh-Eater had any doubts,' said Iker. The donkey and the dog were both lying at their ease on the deck.

'And what about you?'

'I was holding the steering-oar and I saw the king's arrow pierce the darkness. Why ask oneself pointless questions?'

Sekari's muttered reply was inaudible.

The king took the steering-oar again.

'Did the falcon Horus strike down the Herald, Majesty?' asked Iker.

'That was not its goal. Once the lioness was immobilized by her wound, the first bird soothed the river's torment. We shall dig another canal which will be navigable all year round. It will enable us to reach the strong fortresses we shall build beyond the Second Cataract. The evil forces of the Great South will not get past these advance posts of our magical wall.'

'Have the Herald and the lioness been rendered harmless?'

'Unfortunately not. We struck them hard, and it will take them time to recover, but evil and violence always find the foods necessary to be reborn and to attack Ma'at again. That is why we need so many fortresses.'

'Is the City of Gold near here?'

'You will soon be leaving in search of it.'

The Egyptian army emerged from the desert singing, and rejoined the pharaoh – Nesmontu gladly permitted this expression of relief, which chased away fears and strengthened unity. They were all astounded when they saw the calm waters of the Belly of Stone.

'Did you meet any strong resistance, General?' the king asked.

'It was mostly disorganized, though sometimes dangerous. A few remnants of Nubian tribes, and some Libyans and Syrians who were rather well trained.'

'What were our losses?'

'One dead, many men wounded slightly and two seriously – but Doctor Gua will save them. There were no enemy survivors. They fought in small groups and refused to surrender. I believe the Herald's strategy is one of constant raids and attacks by fanatics who are ready to die. We must be very alert and take rigorous precautions.'

A feast was held to celebrate the victory at the Second Cataract. Nesmontu made a speech in which he said that the man who loved Pharaoh was a most fortunate man, provided with everything he needed, whereas he who rebelled knew neither earthly nor celestial happiness.

A poem by Sehotep, destined for the scribes' schools, compared the king to the regulator of the river, to the retaining-walls holding back the tides, to the airy room where one sleeps well, to the indestructible rampart, to the warrior who helps others and whose arm does not weaken, to the refuge for the weak, to cool water during the summer heat, to a warm, dry dwelling during the winter, and to the mountain holding back the winds and dispelling the storm.

After the feast, the army watched attentively and with emotion as the king, wearing the Double Crown, raised up a red granite stele marking the new limit of Egyptian territory.[2] Its text proclaimed:

Southern border, established in the eighth year of Senusret. No Nubian may cross by water or by land, aboard a boat or with a group of fellow countrymen. The only ones authorized will be native traders, accredited messengers and those who travel with good intentions.

[2]The stele of Semna.

The Way of Fire

As soon as the festivities ended, they began to construct new fortresses, the furthest from Egypt and the most imposing ever built in Nubia.

38

Bega was worried sick. Why there was there no sign of life from his allies? Gergu was totally silent, and there had been no messages from Medes. The smuggling of stelae had stopped, and Abydos was cut off from all contact with the outside world, living under the protection of the army and the guards. According to the rare snippets of information that the temporary priests exchanged, Senusret was fighting major battles in Nubia. Would the Herald be able to trap and destroy him?

The more time passed, the bitterer Bega became, and the more his hatred for the king and for Abydos grew. He had been so sure that he had found a way of taking his revenge. Must he now give up hope? No, he must be patient. Thanks to the Herald's formidable powers, this uncertainty would soon end. Senusret's belief that the Great South had been subdued would lead him into over-confidence. And then he would meet unknown forces, far superior to his own. When the victors poured into Abydos, Bega would be its new High Priest.

At least today he had one thing to rejoice at: the reversal in Isis's fortunes. He had long been suspicious of her, for she was rising too quickly in the priesthood, a body which he believed should be reserved for men. Bega hated women, especially when they were involved in sacred matters, and he considered them incapable of entering the true priesthood. He agreed with the Herald's teaching: their place was at home, in the service of their husbands and their children. As soon as he was in charge of Abydos, Bega would drive the priestesses out.

Isis was often summoned to Memphis by the king, and she could have become the head of the priestesses, one of the most important people in the sacred city. However, the Shaven-headed One had just had dealt her career a big blow, stopping her in her tracks – she must have displeased the king – by assigning her to wash laundry in the canal. This lowly task was ordinarily reserved for the washermen, and even they never stopped complaining about it.

Bega suspected Isis of spying for Senusret, of watching the permanent priests and warning the king about anything untoward, no matter how insignificant. But she was an incompetent intriguer, a stupid girl suddenly reduced to the level where she belonged. Delighted to see her humiliated like this, Bega was careful to take no notice of such a menial servant, and concentrated on his ritual duties.

Isis carefully washed the tunic of white royal linen, using a little nitre foam to restore the precious relic's brilliance and purity. She would never have dreamt that the Shaven-headed One would entrust her with such a sacred task: washing the garment of Osiris that had been revealed during the celebration of the Mysteries.

Concentrating on her work, she paid no attention to the disdainful, contemptuous looks directed at her. The tunic had been woven in secret by the goddesses, and handling it, having direct contact with it, enabled her to proceed to another stage. Very few people, since the dawn of pharaonic civilization, had had the chance to set eyes on the tunic.

When the tunic was dry, she took it to the Shaven-headed One.

'So you've finished, have you?' he said, in his usual testy way.

'Are you satisfied with the result?'

Osiris's white tunic dazzled in the sunshine.

'Fold it,' he said, 'and lay it in this chest.'

The small chest, inlaid with ivory and blue glazed pottery, was decorated with open papyrus blossoms. Isis laid the tunic in it.

'Do you perceive the immaterial frontier embodied in this place?' the Shaven-headed One went on.

'Abydos is the gate to the heavens.'

'Do you wish to pass through it?'

'I do.'

'Then follow me.'

As instructed by the pharaoh, master of the Golden Circle of Abydos, the Shaven-headed One took Isis to a shrine in the Temple of Osiris. On a low table, a game of *senet*, 'passing over', was laid out, ready to begin.

'Sit down and play this game.'

'Who will be my opponent?'

'The Invisible One. Since you have touched the tunic of Osiris, you cannot avoid this test. If you win, you will be purified and your spirit will be opened up to new realities. If you lose, you will die.'

He closed the door of the shrine and stood in front of it.

The board was rectangular, and contained thirty squares arranged in three parallel rows. There were twelve gaming pieces shaped like spindles for one player, and twelve cones with rounded heads for the other.[1] The pieces were moved forward according to the number obtained by throwing little tablets bearing numbers. Some squares were favourable, others unfavourable. The player had to negotiate many snares

---

[5]In other versions of the game, each player had five or seven pieces.

before returning to the *nun*, the primordial ocean, in which he was regenerated.

On her first throw Isis reached square fifteen, 'the dwelling of rebirth', which contained the hieroglyph for life, flanked by two *was* sceptres.

The tablets turned over suddenly, and five opposing pieces moved together, blocking her progress.

Her second throw was unfortunate: square twenty-seven, a stretch of water in which one might drown. Isis had to move backwards, and her position was weakened.

When the Invisible One expressed itself again, she thought she was lost. But, she shought, why should she be afraid? Did she not try her utmost to lead a righteous life, in the service of Osiris? If the time came to appear before the court of the god, her heart would speak for her. She threw the tablets.

Twenty-six, the square of 'the perfect dwelling'. It was the ideal throw, giving access to the celestial doorway beyond the game.

The squares disappeared, for the crossing had been accomplished.

The Shaven-headed One opened the door again, and presented Isis with a gold ingot.

'Come with me to the acacia,' he said.

Once there, he walked round the tree as the ritual required.

'Take the gold, Isis,' he said, 'and lay it on a branch.'

A gentle warmth emanated from the ingot. Nourished by a new sap, the whole branch grew green again.

'The healing gold!' exclaimed Isis rapturously. 'Where did it come from?'

'Iker discovered it in Nubia. This is only the first ingot – we shall need many more, all of the greatest purity, before we can envisage a total cure. Nevertheless, we are making progress.'

Iker . . . So the Royal Son was taking part in the regeneration of the Tree of Life. Clearly he was no ordinary man, so perhaps it might be possible for his destiny to be linked to that of a priestess of Abydos.

Der-Wetiu, Dabernati, Waf-khasut, Uronarti, Semna and Kumma: from north to south, no fewer than six fortresses now formed a barrier along the Belly of Stone. Each day, Senusret visited the building sites organized by Sehotep, assisted by Iker and General Nesmontu. Seeing the walls rise, the builders forgot their tiredness and the harshness of the work. Well fed and with as much water and beer as they desired, the craftsmen were looked after by Medes and Gergu, who were obliged to cooperate, and were aware that they were taking part in a work that was vital in order to safeguard the region.

Der-Wetiu impressed even the most apathetic observer.[3] Standing upon a promontory which rose forty cubits above the Nile, 'She who drives back the people of the oases' was immediately west of the southern extremity of the Second Cataract. Surrounded by a ditch, the rectangular fortress had a double curtain-wall, and the entrances were protected by bastions. The walls were were sixteen cubits thick and twenty high, so Der-Wetiu could be defended by a garrison of no more than thirty-five archers and the same number of spearmen.

Shielded by its ramparts were a paved courtyard surrounded by pillars, living-quarters, offices, storehouses, granaries, an armoury, a forge and a temple. The armourers made and repaired spears, swords, daggers, throwing-spears, bows, arrows and shields.

There was an open town nearby, of comparable size. Here, houses of sun-dried brick had been constructed, along with bread ovens and workshops. The Egyptians irrigated the

---

[3]Der-Wetiu was also known as Mirgissa or Iken. It occupied an area of 8.5 hectares.

desert, enabling them to plant trees and create small gardens, much to the surprise of the local tribes.

Dr Gua and Remedy-maker Renseneb treated the sick efficiently, and a climate of trust was re-established. Der-Wetiu was growing, and becoming the main trading-centre of a disinherited land, enabling it to emerge from poverty: everyone had enough to eat now. The local tribes had all submitted to the pharaoh, and nobody spoke of rebellion or battles any more. Afraid of the sinister province of Kush, and easy prey for factions whose only interest was in killing each other, the people turned to the Egyptian protector. Far from being accused of tyranny, Senusret was seen as a liberator and a living god, for he guaranteed prosperity and security.

Sehotep's proudest innovation was a four-cubit-wide ramp for boats, made of beams covered with silt, kept wet when boats were being hauled out of the the water. The ramp meant that, when the water was low, boats could be hoisted on to heavy sledges and hauled across the land, avoiding the dangers of the Nile. Food and raw materials could transported in the same way.

From the top of Der-Wetiu's towers, lookouts kept permanent watch on the Nubians' comings and goings. Having learnt to identify the tribes and to know their usual customs, they passed on details of any major or minor incidents to the fortress commander, who immediately sent out a patrol. Each person was checked, and nobody entered Egyptian territory without a proper pass. Assisted by his team of scribes, Medes kept detailed records, copies of which he sent to the other fortresses and to Elephantine. In this way, clandestine immigration would be kept to the minimum.

Medes had a bad headache, and sent for Dr Gua.

'Doctor, I feel almost unable to work,' he complained. 'My head is on fire.'

'I shall prescribe you two complementary remedies,' said

the doctor. 'First, some pills prepared by Renseneb; they will unblock the channels of your swollen liver and ease the pain. Second, I shall apply the skull of a silurid caught this morning to your head. Your headache will pass into the fish's bones, and you will be cured.'

Although sceptical, Medes discovered that the treatment worked well and remarkably quickly. 'Are you a magician, Doctor Gua?'

'A medicine without magic would not work. I must leave you now, because I have a great deal to do. If the headache returns, I'll come back.'

Where did the small, thin man with his ever-present leather bag get all that energy? wondered Medes. During the pacification of Nubia, Gua and Renseneb had played a vital role. Not content with treating the tribal people, they trained some as doctors and remedy-makers, who would replace the two Egyptians when they left. Under Senusret's leadership, this vast land was at last emerging from lawlessness and poverty.

However, some things had not changed.

'I am missing a report,' a scribe told Medes.

'Administrative or military?'

'Military. One of the patrols has not handed in the required report.'

Medes went to General Nesmontu's headquarters. 'General, I must inform you of something. It is probably unimportant, but perhaps it ought to be checked. One of the patrol commanders has not written up his report.'

Nesmontu immediately sent a soldier to fetch the officer.

The soldier returned alone. 'I cannot find him, General.'

'And what about his men?'

'They are not in their quarters, sir.'

The truth was inescapable: the patrol had not returned. A council of war ensued, presided over by the king.

'Which way did they go?' asked Senusret.

'Along the western track,' replied Nesmontu. 'It was a routine patrol, a check on a caravan of nomads. The caravan did not arrive at Der-Wetiu, so I fear our men may been ambushed. We must find out if it was an isolated event or part of preparations for a major attack.'

'I shall handle it,' said Ikcr.

'The army has plenty of excellent scouts,' protested Nesmontu.

'We must not deceive ourselves: this is the Herald's work. While the necessary measures are being taken, I shall assess the situation. A few determined soldiers are all I need.'

Senusret raised no objection. In this new confrontation with the Herald, the Royal Son would be continuing his training, however risky it might be. For there was no other way to pass from darkness into light.

Sekari regretted leaving his comfortable bedchamber and the good food served to the officers. He definitely ought to have found a friend who moved about less. But his role was still to protect him, was it not?

39

General Nesmontu had insisted that all the members of the patrol, Iker included, must wear a coat capable of resisting arrows. This consisted of a magic papyrus, firmly attached to the chest by a cord. Its thickness counted less than the hieroglyphic texts, which could ward off danger.

They found the caravan of Nubians and their donkeys resting in the shade of some balanite trees. As the patrol approached, the traders raised their hands in a sign of friendship. But Flesh-Eater growled and North Wind refused to go any closer. Realizing that the enemy was suspicious, the Kushite archers stopped play-acting and fired, but the arrows all missed – Iker silently thanked General Nesmontu.

'There are more of them coming up behind us,' warned Sekari, 'and on our flanks as well. We're surrounded.'

'Get down on the ground,' ordered the Royal Son, 'and dig!'

In the time, they could dig only shallow trenches, so they would not be able to hold out for long. Triah's death had by no means deterred the Kushites if they were still capable of forming a plan like this.

'I don't wish to discourage you,' said Sekari, 'but the future looks rather bleak. We know how they ambushed our patrol, but we won't be able to tell the general in person. If you're thinking of attacking, don't. There are twenty times more of them than there are of us.'

Iker could not see any grounds for hope, so he devoted his last thoughts to Isis. She had saved him before. If she loved him a little, she would not abandon him to these barbarians.

'Do you hear that?' asked Sekari. 'It sounds like bees buzzing.'

And indeed a swarm was heading towards them, a swarm the like of which no bee-keeper had ever seen, so vast that it hid the sun. The bee was the symbol of the King of Lower Egypt, and the army of insects attacked the Kushites.

'Let's get away from here!' shouted Iker. 'We have nothing to fear from the bees.'

A tall Nubian tried to bar the pair's way but was stung dozens of times and collapsed. Ignoring the deafening buzz of its allies, the Egyptian patrol followed them and thus escaped from the trap.

Iker ran for a long time, often turning to check that none of the soldiers had fallen behind. Then the swarm seemed to be sucked up into the sky and it disappeared. The patrol stopped and looked around.

'We're saved, but we're lost,' said Sekari.

'As soon as night falls, we'll find our way by the stars,' said Iker.

The desert stretched as far as the eye could see, and there was not a sign of any vegetation.

'We'll shelter behind this dune,' said Iker.

As they were making camp, he spotted a stone object half buried in the sand. He dug it out, watched with interest by Sekari.

'I know what this is,' said Iker excitedly. 'It's a mould for making ingots! There was a mine around here.'

At the foot of the dune there were other traces. They explored further, and came upon the blocked entrance to a gallery. The soldiers unblocked it and found that it was still well shored up.

Iker and Sekari entered. Flesh-Eater and North Wind

287

remained on the surface, under orders to sound the alert if danger threatened.

At the end of the gallery was a sort of walk, bordered by stone huts containing scales, basalt weights and numerous moulds of varying sizes. Framing the door to a small shrine were two pillars, each topped by the face of Hathor.

The face of Isis.

Inside the shrine were small ingots, neatly laid out in rows.

'She has guided us to the City of Gold,' murmured Iker.

Bina was in such pain that she begged the Herald to kill her. Despite the seriousness of the wound, which ought to have resulted in her losing her leg, he managed to soothe her and treated her with plants provided by the Nubian sorcerers.

If the pharaoh thought he had halted the terrifying lioness, he was wrong. Placed on the wound, the queen of turquoises would soon heal her. The Herald was right. Almost at once Bina stopped giving those terrible cries, a mixture of her own voice and the lioness's. Given strong sleeping-draughts, she slept for a long time.

Despite the loss of Triah's army, the surviving Kushites and several Nubian tribes continued to obey the great sorcerer. Many warriors listened to his teaching, delivered in a smooth, compelling voice. The new god would enable them to drive Senusret's troops out of Nubia, destroy the fortresses, and then invade Egypt. For the Herald foretold an enviable future: all unbelievers would die.

'The Egyptians are building incredibly quickly,' said Crooked-Face. 'Now they're setting up a base at Waf-khasut! From that cliff, they'll be able to control the river and the desert even more tightly.'

'The work must not be allowed to continue.'

Crooked-Face felt reinvigorated. 'Seizing Waf-khasut will be a fine success, and we won't be easy to dislodge. We'll take no prisoners, of course.'

'What has become of our false caravan which trapped the enemy patrol?'

'It has disappeared in the desert – probably a counter-attack by Senusret. He won't give us any room to move and will return blow for blow. Nevertheless, we shall strike him down.' Crooked-Face's optimism galvanized his warriors.

The Herald was somewhat more circumspect. The more of Nubia Senusret conquered, the more magic entered him, making him as strong as the walls of his fortresses. Fortunately, though, there were still several weak points.

Sekari was sitting on a folding stool, sampling a fine wine. 'Another cup, Iker?'

'No, thank you, I've had enough.'

'You ought to study the *Key of Dreams*. If you see yourself drinking wine in a dream, you are nourished by Ma'at. It happens to me often. And in a sinister place like this one, I don't know a better remedy.'

There was nothing attractive about the fortress of Waf-Khasut, 'She who makes the foreign lands bend'.[1] At its foot the Nile was narrow, easy to keep watch on. The stronghold was of modest size, measuring only a hundred and sixty cubits by ninety, but it had walls ten cubits thick, and housed a small garrison and granaries. From the cliff, a staircase led down to the Nile. The only land entrance would be a narrow, well-defended gate. Because of their experience building other forts, the builders made rapid progress. Until the completion of the main wall, the only way danger could threaten was from the desert. So the site was guarded by a detachment of twenty archers under the Royal Son's command.

'Get drunk every day and every night,' went on Sekari, 'and make sure you always have the best wines. If you do

[1] Shalfak.

that, you'll be happy and serene, for they fill the household with joy and are united with the gold of the gods. Aren't that poet's words admirable?'

'Oughtn't one to see a symbolic meaning in them?' suggested Iker. 'Don't they describe a divine intoxication, when one communes with the Invisible?'

'A disembodied, pointless symbol! But tell me, what about the gold sent to Abydos? Will it work?'

Sekari began to play a lute, whose body was a turtle's shell covered with stretched gazelle-skin, painted red and pierced with six holes. Using three strings, he composed a melancholy melody to accompany his slow, solemn song.

'I have heard the words of the sages. What is eternity? A place where justice reigns, where fear does not exist, where turbulence is forbidden, where no one attacks his neighbour. There, the ancestors dwell in peace.'

Lying nearby, the hound and the donkey listened in delight to the singer.

As for Iker, he was thinking about Isis. In daily contact with the Mysteries of Osiris, close to the source of life, she must inevitably consider the love of a man derisory.

If Sekari had not been holding his lute against his thigh, the arrow would have gone straight through his flesh.

Flesh-Eater barked in fury and North Wind brayed loudly, instantly waking the soldiers. Prepared for this type of attack, they reacted like professionals, taking shelter behind the blocks of black granite that served as foundations for the fortress. Meanwhile, Sekari and Iker slipped round and attacked the Nubians from behind.

The warning given by the donkey and the dog alerted the reserve troops stationed not far from Waf-khasut, and they took immediate action.

Only the chief of the Nubian tribe managed to escape, by sliding down the slope to the river. He slipped into the water and hid among the rocks. A little later he heard footsteps and thought he was lost, but the two Egyptians just looked out over the Nile.

'No boat,' observed Sekari. 'The fools came from the desert with only a small force and without noticing our security measures.'

'They were sent to certain death,' said Iker. 'The Herald probably assumed we were keeping the gold from the lost city at Waf-khasut. The pharaoh was right to take it to Askut for greater safety.'

With that, the two men walked away. The chief forgot about the deaths of his warriors. He had learnt a piece of vital information which would please the Herald.

40

'So,' said the Herald, 'the Egyptians have discovered the gold.'

'They're keeping it at Askut,' the chief revealed proudly.

'Why did you not destroy Waf-khasut?'

'Because . . . because there were not enough of us.'

'You attacked blindly, did you not? Before receiving orders from Crooked-Face?'

'The important thing is that we now know where they're storing the treasure.'

'The important thing is to obey me.'

With one blow from his club, Crooked-Face smashed the Nubian's skull. 'An incompetent fool, not fit to lead,' he sneered. 'All these Nubian fighters are the same. Training them would take months, and even then I wouldn't be sure of success.'

'It's impossible to get at Askut,' said Shab the Twisted. 'Since the fortresses of Semna and Kumma were built, every boat undergoes strict checks.'

'I must know if this gold is a real threat and if it must therefore be destroyed,' declared the Herald. 'Bina will recover fully, but it is still too soon to call upon her help. So this is what we are going to do.'

Suffering from heat and overwork, Medes was exhausted and

sweating. Semna, the southernmost fortress, was not the place for rest and coolness. Designed to contain Nubia once and for all, it was built in three parts: Semna West, bearing the name of 'Senusret exerts his mastery', with fortifications marked by alternate high and low towers; Semna South, 'She who drives back the Nubians'; and Kumma, built on the west bank and housing a small temple.

Never had the Egyptian border been secured so deep into these hostile lands. Standing on either side of a rocky passage through which the Nile squeezed its way with difficulty, the fortresses would easily block any attack. Under Sehotep's direction, the artificers had undertaken an enormous project: raising the lake from the Semna pass by piling up rocks in order to create a channel through which trading-boats could pass safely. To the north of Semna an immensely long wall was to be built, to protect the desert road.

Medes was writing up the decree appointing a hundred and fifty soldiers to Semna and fifty to Kumma. These troops would enjoy good living-conditions. Comfortable houses, paved streets, workshops, granaries, a drainage system, reservoirs of water, regular food supplies . . . The garrisons would have all they could want. And still Medes had to go on working for Senusret and against the Herald!

Carrying his heavy leather bag, Dr Gua entered the office, where a servant was fanning Medes rhythmically.

'What is wrong with you today?' asked Gua.

'My bowels. And I'm drying out.'

'This climate seems very healthy to me, and you have good fat reserves.'

After examining him, the doctor took out a measuring vase, identical to the one Horus used to treat his eye, in such a way as to procure life, health and happiness. It enabled doses to be measured accurately and also made them effective. Gua poured in a potion of fresh date-juice, ricin leaves and sycamore-milk.

'The veins in your thighs are silent, and your anus is overheated. This treatment will re-establish balance, and your bowels will function normally.'

'I'm exhausted, Doctor.'

'Take this potion three times a day, on an empty stomach, eat less, drink more water, and you will return to Memphis in good health.'

'Aren't you worried about the health of our troops?'

'Do you think Renseneb and I are idling our time away?'

'The idea never entered my head, but this heat, this—'

'Our soldiers are well cared-for. I cannot say as much for our enemies – that will make our victory so much the easier.' And Dr Gua hurried off to the hospital at Semna, where several serious cases awaited him.

As soon as he had left, an officer came into Medes's office and said, 'I have just arrested a suspect. Do you wish to question him?'

As the most senior authority in the fort, Medes could not avoid doing so. To his amazement, the suspect was none other than Shab the Twisted.

'Why was this man brought in?' he asked.

'Because he had no pass.'

'Explain yourself, fellow,' ordered Medes.

'I belong to the messenger service in Buhen,' replied the Twisted One, humbly and submissively. 'I didn't know about this new rule that I need a pass. I've brought you orders from headquarters.'

'Leave us,' Medes told the officer.

As soon as the door closed behind him, Medes complained, 'It's been an eternity since I had any news!'

'Don't worry,' said Shab. 'All is well. The Nubians are unreliable allies, but the Herald is using them to best effect.'

'There is no way through the line of fortresses Senusret has built. We're heading for disaster, and I'm trapped here. And Iker – he's still alive!'

'Calm down, and give me a pass that will enable me to go everywhere.'

'Will the Herald actually dare to attack Semna?'

'Whatever you do, don't leave this office. You will be safe here.'

The atmosphere in Semna market was cheerful. Buyers and sellers were haggling around stalls of fruit and vegetables, fish and local craftwares. A good portion of the garrison was enjoying this trade. As for the market traders, they were enjoying growing rich.

All the men turned to gaze when there suddenly appeared among them a beautiful woman, her waist encircled by a belt of cowrie shells and pearls. On her ankles she wore strange bracelets shaped like the talons of a bird of prey.

Now that her wound had scarred over, Bina felt strong enough to carry out the first part of the Herald's plan.

'You aren't from here,' remarked a soldier.

'And where do you come from?'

'From Elephantine. What are you selling, my beauty?'

'Shells.' She showed him a magnificent cowrie shell, its shape evocative of the shape of the female sex.

The soldier smiled. 'Pretty, very pretty . . . I think I understand. What do you want in exchange?'

'Your life.'

The man scarcely had a chance to laugh. The pointed part of Bina's ankle-bracelet pierced his lower belly. At the same moment, the Kushites disguised as traders took out the weapons they had hidden in their baskets and slaughtered both the genuine traders and their customers.

From the top of the main watchtower, a lookout sounded the alert. Immediately, the gates of Semna West closed, and the archers rushed to their firing positions.

Medes emerged from his office and called to the commander, 'What's all this shouting about?'

'We're under attack by a wild band of Kushites.'

'Warn Der-Wetiu and Buhen.'

'We can't, sir. The enemy is blocking travel by river, and our messengers would be killed.'

'What about visual signals?'

'The sun is against us, and the wind would blow distress smoke away.'

'In other words, we're besieged and cut off.'

'Don't worry, sir, the problem won't last long. The Kushites won't have time to seize our strongholds.'

When Medes peered cautiously out from behind a crenellation and saw the mass of excited warriors, he was not so sure. Was he going to die stupidly, at the hands of barbarians sent by the Herald?

In view of the modest size of the fortress of Askut, which was built on an islet south of the Second Cataract, Crooked-Face was leading only about thirty well-trained men. They would strike fast and hard.

With Semna under attack and powerless, the three light boats encountered no opposition. Over-confident in the effectiveness of their measures, the Egyptians had not stationed a single war-boat between Semna and Askut. Mooring was easy: not a guard on the horizon.

The raiders took up their planned positions. Crooked-Face scaled a rock and discovered a fort with unfinished walls. It even lacked its wooden door.

Always wary, Crooked-Face sent a scout to explore. The Libyan went into the building, and returned very quickly.

'It's empty,' he said.

Crooked-Face went to check for himself. He found equipment for washing gold, a number of grain-stores and a small shrine dedicated to the crocodile-god Sobek. Askut housed large reserves of food and everything needed for treating the gold. So why did the place seem abandoned?

'The garrison have been warned about the attack on Semna,' ventured a Nubian, 'and have taken refuge in Der-Wetiu.'

'Search everywhere and find the gold, if there's any left.'

'There's somebody over there!'

Crooked-Face instantly recognized the young man who came out of the shrine.

'Don't fire!' he ordered. 'I want this one alive.'

Iker stopped ten paces from him.

'You again, you damned scribe! Why didn't you run away with the others?'

'Do you take Senusret's soldiers for cowards?'

'There's not a single one around. Give me the gold, and I might let you live.'

'You really do have falsehood ingrained in your soul. Your disgraceful career ends here.'

'One against thirty? Do you think you can defeat us?

'I see only you, a Libyan and a Nubian – the rest of your men are prisoners. You've been with the Herald so long, and have obeyed him so blindly, that your instinct is failing. Sekari and I fed false information to one of your allies, a tribal chief, and he passed it on to your leader. Nubian gold was indeed worked here, but it's out of your reach now. I'd have liked to catch a bigger fish, but at least your capture and that of your best men will weaken the Herald.'

Suddenly there were Egyptian soldiers everywhere.

As Crooked-Face unsheathed his dagger, Sekari's arrow passed through his wrist. His two men tried to protect him, but they were killed almost at once. Taking advantage of a moment's confusion, Crooked-Face ran to the bank and dived into the river.

'He's escaping from us again!' said Sekari furiously.

'Not this time,' said Iker, 'for the god Sobek protects this site, and the sacred crocodile is my ally since I descended with him into the depths of a lake in Faiyum.'

Enormous jaws with razor-sharp teeth closed round Crooked-Face's back. The crocodile's tail thrashed the blood-stained water. Then calm returned, and the waters bore away all traces of the drama.

Iker and Sekari went immediately to Der-Wetiu, where Senusret, General Nesmontu and the bulk of the troops were awaiting their arrival.

'We are about to fight the last battle of Nubia,' announced the pharaoh. 'May we succeed in pacifying the Terrifying One.'

41

The Servant of the *Ka* came to find Isis in her quarters and took her to Senusret's temple of a million years. He did not speak a word, and she asked no questions. Each new stage of the initiation into the Mysteries of Osiris began in this way, with silence and contemplation.

The previous day, the new gold from Nubia had made three branches of the acacia grow green again. It was another small step in the Tree of Life's recovery. The remedies found so far worked only slowly, but nevertheless these results gave grounds for viewing the future with a little more hope.

On the threshold of the temple stood the Shaven-headed One. He said, 'The time has come to know if you are of just voice and worthy to belong to the community of the living who are nourished by the Light. So you must appear before the court of the two Ma'ats. Do you accept?'

Isis knew the outcome: either a new birth or annihilation. Her previous ordeals represented only a preparation for this formidable progression.

She thought of Iker, of his courage and of the dangers he constantly faced. And then she realized that she felt more than simple friendship for him. Like the Royal Son, she must defeat fear. 'I accept,' she said.

Anointed with olibanum, dressed in a long gown of fine

linen and white sandals, Isis was shown into a huge chamber where forty-two judges were seated, each wearing the mask of a god or goddess.

Two incarnations of Ma'at presided over the court, one feminine, the other masculine.

'Do you know the name of the door of this chamber?' asked a judge.

'The Scales of Justice.'

'Are you capable of separating yourself from your faults and your iniquities?'

'I have committed no injustice,' said Isis. 'I fight *isefet*, I abhor evil, I respect the rites, I do not profane the sacred, I do not betray secrets, I have neither killed nor caused anyone to kill, nor have I inflicted suffering on anyone, or mistreated any animal, or stolen the possessions and the offerings of the gods. I have neither added to nor taken away from the bushel, nor falsified the scale.'

'Verify these declarations by weighing your heart.'

'I wish to live by Ma'at. Heart of my celestial mother, do not rise up against me, do not bear witness against me.'

Jackal-headed Anubis took Isis by the hand and led her to a golden scale. It was guarded by a monster with a crocodile's head, a lion's chest and the hindquarters of a hippopotamus.

'Your heart must be as light as the feather of Ma'at. If not, the Devourer will swallow you down and the component parts of your individual existence will be scattered and will return to nature.'

Anubis brushed the priestess's belly. From it he took out a little vase, which he placed upon one pan of the scale. On the other, he laid the goddess's feather.

Isis did not close her eyes. Whatever the sentence, she wanted to see her destiny.

After swaying a little, the two pans remained in perfect balance.

'The Osiris Isis[1] is of true and just voice,' declared a judge. 'The Devourer will spare her.'

Within the priestess's chest beat a new heart, unchanging, a gift from the forty-two divinities in the chamber of the two Ma'ats.

'Now you are ready to pass through a new door,' announced the Shaven-headed One.

Isis followed her guide.

At the entrance to a shadowy shrine the priest removed a red linen cloth that covered a glazed pottery lion.

'The fire springs forth from my mouth,' he chanted. 'I protect myself. My enemy will not survive. I punish grovelling humans and all reptiles, male or female. Advance, Isis, since you are of just voice.'

A gigantic snake appeared. Its body was made up of nine circles, four composed of fire.

'Do you dare touch this spiral?'

The priestess did so.

The circles united and formed the rope attached to Ra's ship. It led up to the heavens in the form of a golden flame, strewing turquoise, malachite and emeralds, which gave birth to the stars. Linked to the birth of the universe, Isis experienced the creation of the world.

When the dazzling light abated, she made out the walls of the shrine, which were decorated with scenes of Pharaoh making offerings to the gods.

The Shaven-headed One tied a knot in a red belt. 'This is the life of the goddesses and the stability of the gods. Within them Osiris is reborn. This symbol will protect you from attacks by evil people, will deflect obstacles and give you the chance to travel one day along the Way of Fire.' He placed the magic knot upon the priestess's navel.

At once she saw a luxuriant, sun-drenched land.

---

[1] The righteous man or woman became 'Osiris Such-and-such'.

'Gaze upon the green gold of Punt. Only it will enable us to heal the acacia completely.'

Medes had gone to ground in his office, and was sweating profusely.

The garrison had just repelled the third attack by the Kushites, who outnumbered the Egyptian defenders of Semna tenfold. Medes was in danger of being killed by his own allies. Despite the soldiers' fierce resistance, the outcome seemed obvious. At the Herald's chosen moment, the walls would tumble.

The garrison commander, who had been wounded on the forehead, put his bandaged head round Medes's door and said, 'The pharaoh is coming!'

'Are you sure?'

'See for yourself.'

'I must stay here and protect the archives.'

The commander returned to the fight.

The Kushites were stunned by the sight of Senusret standing tall in the prow of his flagship. One chief ordered his warriors to give battle – two boats were enough to block the Nile.

The king's heavy spear travelled gracefully through the air in a long curve, and sank into the chief's chest, causing immediate chaos.

Agile as a young man, General Nesmontu was the first to leap on to the enemy vessel. With discipline and accuracy, the footsoldiers and archers wiped out the besieging forces. The Egyptian army's superiority was such that the Kushites were completely routed. Soon Semna would be liberated.

Nevertheless, the king was not in the least exultant.

Medes realized why when he at last emerged from his shelter, watched in alarm by the soldiers.

'You . . . you haven't got have a shadow any more, and neither have we!' exclaimed one of them.

It was the same for every Egyptian.

Despite this apparent victory, Nesmontu feared that a cruel defeat lay ahead. Without a shadow, the human body was exposed to a thousand and one hurts. Without it, it was impossible to unite with the *ka*. Energy was diluted, and the soul was condemned to darkness.

Senusret thrust his flaming sword towards the sky, and Sekari whistled the song of a bird.

A cloud of swallows appeared in the blue sky. One the bank, a hundred ostriches began running in a southerly direction.

'Follow them,' ordered the king. 'The symbol of Ma'at is derived from their plumage. They will destroy the Herald's curse.'

The Nile was too narrow, there were menacing rocks, and a black cloud was hiding the sun . . . If the pharaoh himself had not taken command of the expedition, not one brave fellow would have dared explore such a fearsome world.

Taking advantage of a strong wind, the fleet moved forward. The cloud drifted, and the banks grew further apart.

Bathed in light, the ostriches were dancing.

'Our shadows have come back!' declared Sekari.

'But the battle continues,' the king reminded him. 'Now the Herald will make use of the Terrifying One's fury. Doctor Gua and Remedy-maker Renseneb, bring what is needed.'

The two men had prepared jars of red beer, to which rye-grass had been added.

'The lioness enjoys human blood,' explained the monarch. 'We shall try to deceive her and intoxicate her, but only the queen of turquoises can pacify her.'

The island of Sai lay halfway between the Second Cataract and the Third. At its northern end Nubian troops loyal to the Herald were gathering, ready to fight the Egyptians.

As the flagship approached, Bina gave a terrifying roar.

The black warriors drew back, to give the enormous lioness as much room as possible. Neither arrow nor spear could stop her.

From the prow, several sailors threw dozens of jars, which broke on the rocks. The smell of the spilt liquid attracted the savage creature, and she lapped it up greedily. Sated, she growled contentedly, then lay down and fell into a doze.

Then Senusret's boat touched land.

Hoping to kill the pharaoh, a tall Kushite brandished his throwing-stick. The king merely stretched out his arm towards the attacker, who staggered and fell, struck down by a unknown force.

'A magician! This king is a magician!' shouted a tribal chief.

It was every man for himself. Nesmontu's troops were ready for fierce hand-to-hand fighting, but they found no one to kill but fugitives: to a man, the Nubians fled.

A huge falcon soared above the southern part of the Isle of Sai, where the Herald was standing, following the battle at a distance. With anger and disgust, he witnessed the rout of his alllies.

The falcon's sudden dive took him by surprise. Before he could react, the bird seized the queen of turquoises and flew back up towards the sun.

'What are your orders, my lord?' asked Shab the Twisted nervously.

'We must find shelter. These Nubians are incompetent fools.'

'And Bina?'

'We'll try to get her back.'

When Senusret approached her, the lioness emerged from her torpor and bared menacing fangs.

'Be at peace,' said the king, 'you who have the power to slaughter humankind. May your violence become gentleness.'

Ignoring the danger of being attacked, he laid upon the beast's brow the queen of turquoises, which the falcon had given him. 'Pass on your strength to the children of the Light. May they triumph over misfortune and weakness.'

In a dazzle of green and blue, the lioness was transformed into a slender she-cat, with a glossy black coat, and golden eyes. A few paces away lay the body of Bina, in the middle of a pool of blood.

Transfixed by the change, the soldiers did not spot Shab the Twisted hidden behind a rock. He drew his bow. Iker's back was to him, presenting a perfect target.

Despite his fatigue and the excitement of the victory, Sekari was still alert. Instinctively, he sensed the arrow's trajectory. Leaping like a gazelle, he seized Iker by the waist and pulled him aside.

Too late: the arrow plunged into the Royal Son's left shoulder.

'A fraction further over,' said Gua, 'and you would be dead. As it is, you will have only a small scar.'

After giving the wounded man a pain-relieving draught made from poppies, he delicately extracted the arrowhead, using a lancet with a rounded blade. Then he joined the edges of the wound together with sticky cloth, and covered it with a dressing soaked in honey and safflower oil.

'I owe you my life yet again,' Iker told Sekari.

'I've given up counting! Unfortunately, your attacker escaped by boat. Still, Nesmontu has scoured the entire island and there isn't a single rebel left, so the area is safe now. They're starting work on building a fort this very day.'

'I thought I caught sight of a woman's body, near the lioness. If I am not mistaken, it was Bina.'

'She's dead, too.'

'And the Herald?'

'No trace of him,' replied Sekari. 'Apart from the woman

305

and the archer who fired at you, there were only Kushites fighting here. The future looks difficult for that demon. The Kushites will never forgive him for leading them into such a disaster.'

42

Beyond the Third Cataract, the burning sun was drying out the hills, which were being eaten away by the desert. Clouds of midges attacked everyone's nose and ears. Even the rapids produced not a breath of coolness.

However, the Herald was still wearing his long woollen tunic. On the islet where he had taken refuge along with his few remaining followers, he continued to care for Bina, whose breathing was still barely perceptible.

'Can you save her?' asked Shab, who was utterly exhausted.

'She will live and she will kill. She was born to kill. Although she can no longer transform herself into a lioness, Bina is still the queen of darkness.'

'I trust you, my lord, but have we not suffered a terrible defeat? And that man Iker is still alive.'

'I have planted the seed of the new belief in this land. Sooner or later, it will invade the world. It matters not if it takes a hundred, a thousand or two thousand years. It will triumph, for no mind can resist it. And I shall spread it once again.'

Several canoes were heading for the islet, filled with Kushites shouting and brandishing spears.

'There are too many of them, my lord! We won't be able to fight them off.'

'Don't worry, my friend. Those barbarians are bringing us the boats we need.' The Herald stood up and faced the river. His eyes grew red, and a flame seemed to blaze out of them. The waters foamed and, despite their skill, the Kushites' boats were overturned. A freak wave drowned all the men. But the boats floated intact on the water.

The Herald's followers saw that their master had lost none of his powers.

'Where are you intending to go?' asked the Twisted One.

'Where no one expects us: Egypt. The pharaoh imagines me wandering across this miserable country until some Kushite tribe captures and executes me. He's drunk with success after subduing the lioness, and the discovery of the healing gold has given him back his confidence. However, he still lacks an essential part of the gold. Even if the Tree of Life recovers – which is unlikely – that won't stop us. Our Memphis network is intact, and soon we shall use it to strike at the soul of Egypt.'

'You mean . . . ?'

'Yes, Shab, you understand me. Our journey will be a long one, but we shall reach our true goal: Abydos. We shall destroy it and prevent Osiris from being reborn.'

This inspiring vision drove away Shab the Twisted's tiredness. Nothing would divert the Herald from his mission. Besides, he had an invaluable ally at the very heart of Osiris's dwelling-place: Bega.

Into a cauldron, the pharaoh threw clay figurines of Nubians kneeling, with their heads bowed and their hands bound behind their backs. When he touched them with his sword, a flame flared out. The soldiers thought they heard the moans of tortured men as their bodies sizzled.

Medes changed the hieroglyphic sign on the official decree announcing the pacification of Nubia. It had been a black warrior equipped with a bow; now it was a seated woman. In this way, the magic of writing removed all virility from any rebels.

Senusret turned towards the clan and tribal chiefs, who had come to lay down their arms and swear allegiance to him. He spoke to them in his strong, grave voice. Medes noted down every word.

'I make my words effective. My arm carries out what my heart devises. Since I am determined to vanquish, my thoughts do not remain inert in my heart. I attack anyone who attacks me. If people remain peaceable, I establish peace. Remaining peaceable when one is being attacked encourages the attacker to persevere. Fighting demands courage, and the coward draws back. And he who does not defend his territory is still more cowardly. Defeated, you run away, showing your backs. You behaved like bandits devoid of conscience and courage. Continue in that way, and your women will be captured, your flocks, your harvests and your wells destroyed. The fire of the royal cobra will ravage all of Nubia. After adding to the heritage of my ancestors, I establish my border here. He who maintains it will be my son; he who violates it will be a troublemaker, and as such will be severely punished.'

Happy to have got off so lightly, the Nubian chiefs swore fidelity to Senusret, whose statue was placed on the border. Inside each fortress and outside their walls, stelae would recall the monarch's words and symbolize the vow making the region welcoming and peaceful.

'This pharaoh fires arrows without needing to draw his bowstring,' Sekari whispered into Iker's ear. 'His word is enough to frighten his enemies, and he won't need a single blow of the staff to ensure order. When the king is just, everything is just.'

The Egyptians had no time to enjoy their victory at leisure, for the monarch ordered the immediate establishment of a government capable of ensuring prosperity. Having calculated the length of the Nile as far as the border, Sehotep coordinated the work to be done on water supplies and irrigation, designed to make a great deal of land cultivable. Soon famine would be a thing of the past.

Senusret had not led a devastating raid. As well as the security guaranteed by the fortresses, a local system of trade would be developed, in which everyone would have a part to play. The pharaoh seemed not a conqueror but a protector. At Buhen, Semna and in many other places, people began to worship him and celebrate his *ka*.[1] Before his arrival, the people had suffered from lawlessness, violence and tyranny; now Nubia had become a favoured protectorate. Many soldiers and administrators would be staying there for a long time in order to reconstruct the region.

'Is there any information about the Herald?' the king asked Iker.

'Only rumours, Majesty. Several tribes claim to have killed him, but no one has put his body on show.'

'He is still alive. Despite his failure, he will not give up.'

'But won't Nubia be very hostile to him now?'

'Certainly the magical barrier of the fortresses will render his words inoperative for several generations. But, alas, the poison he spread will last for a long time.'

'If he manages to escape from the Kushites, the Nubians and our army, what will he try to do?'

'The part of his network in Egypt is still a threat, and the Tree of Life is still in danger. This war is far from over, Iker. We must not relax our vigilance or resolve.'

'Are we going back to Memphis, Majesty?'

'We shall stay for a while in Abydos.'

Abydos, the place where Isis lived!

'Your wound seems almost healed,' observed the king.

---

[1]More than a thousand years after his death, Senusret III was still venerated in Nubia.

310

'Gua is an excellent doctor.'

'Take charge of the preparations for departure.'

The protectorate was transformed into a haven of peace. There was no more tension between Nubians and Egyptians. Marriages were celebrated, and Sehotep was not the last to yield to the charms of a young village girl with a slender body and graceful bearing. As for Sekari, he spent all his time with her sister.

'Are we leaving already?' he complained. 'I was enjoying myself here.'

'Inspect the fleet meticulously. The Herald may try to attack us again, and your instinct may be all that saves us.'

'You didn't cast a single glance at all the beautiful women around here,' said Sekari in astonishment. 'What kind of man are you?'

'For me, there is only one woman.'

'But what if she doesn't love you?'

'It must be her, and no one else. I shall spend the rest of my life telling her so.'

'And suppose she gets married?'

'I shall make do with the few thoughts she's willing to grant me.'

'A Royal Son shouldn't be without a companion. Can you imagine all the rich damsels pining for you?'

'Little good will it do them.'

'I've got you out of several dangerous situations, but as far as this one goes I'm weaponless.'

'To work, Sekari. We mustn't keep His Majesty waiting.'

Rejuvenated by this formidable military campaign, General Nesmontu took personal charge of the voyage back to Egypt.

Medes was green-faced and could keep nothing down save Gua's potions: they stopped him vomiting for a few hours. Gergu, who was relieved and happy to have survived, went back to the strong beer. As the contents of the grain boats had been transferred to the granaries of the fortresses, he could afford a little free time.

'Do you like travelling by water?' Iker asked him.

'It's my favourite pastime. And this time we can really enjoy the voyage.'

'Do you know the area around Abydos?'

Gergu froze. If he lied, Iker might notice and stop trusting him, so he would have to tell part of the truth. He said, 'I've ɔeen there several times.'

'Why?'

'To deliver supplies to the permanent priests when they need them. I've become a temporary priest, which makes thing easier.'

'Then you've seen the temples!'

'No, I'm afraid I haven't. I'm not authorized to, and my duties are purely administrative. Frankly, I find the work rather dull.'

'Have you met a young priestess by the name of Isis?'

Gergu thought for a moment. 'No. What's special about her?'

Iker smiled. 'You definitely haven't met her.'

As soon as Iker went away, Gergu rushed to see Medes. He took a writing-tablet with him and pretended to be asking for advice. 'I was obliged to tell the Royal Son about my links with Abydos,' he said worriedly.

'You didn't say too much, I hope?'

'As little as possible.'

'Try to avoid the subject in future.'

'Iker seems very fond of the priestess called Isis.'

Isis, the pharaoh's messenger, whom Medes had met in Memphis . . .

'Why don't we give up and become Pharaoh's men?' said Gergu. 'Now the Herald's dead, let's not take any risks.'

'There's no proof that he's dead.'

'But all his followers have been killed.'

'Only two things are certain: the defeat of the Kushites and the colonization of Nubia. The Herald will find other allies.'

'Let's not end up like Crooked-Face, eaten by a crocodile or some other predator.'

'That lumbering idiot made stupid mistakes.'

'And what about the Terrifying One's submission? Senusret's invulnerable, Medes. Attacking him would be madness.'

Medes felt sick. 'You're right, and this triumph increases his power still more. But if the Herald has survived, he won't give up.'

'May the gods ensure that he has been killed and—' He broke off as he felt a fierce pain in the palm of his right hand: the tiny figure of Set was burning, red hot, into his flesh.

'Stop blaspheming,' Medes warned him.

General Nesmontu checked the findings of the scribe whose job it was to check the depth of the Nile with a long pole.

'Four cubits,' he said 'Four cubits? That's terrible! Only a little shallower and the hulls will be grounding on the rocks.'

He had to order a halt, for fear of serious damage. The entire fleet was stuck between the Second and First Cataracts, under a merciless sun.

'Another of the Herald's curses, I suppose,' he growled. 'After trying to flood us, now he's drying us up. This would not be a pleasant place to set up camp, and we might run short of water, too.'

'Wouldn't the Nile's water do?' asked a soldier.

'No, because it looks an unhealthy colour.'

The pharaoh displayed no anxiety, but the news spread quickly from boat to boat.

Alarmed, Medes immediately checked that he had enough full water-skins. If they were stuck here for a long time, and no wells were found nearby, how would they survive?

People began to doubt and to be afraid that this triumphant campaign was going to end disastrously.

Iker noticed that Senusret was staring at a large grey rock on the riverbank. To his astonishment, he saw that the rock was moving, very slowly, towards the river.

'That's not a rock,' declared Sekari, 'it's a turtle – an enormous turtle. We're saved!'

'Why are you so optimistic?'

'Because the pharaoh has put order where there was disorder. The turtle symbolizes both heaven and earth. In its earthly office, it's a vase filled with water, and the vase was raised up to the heavens to form the sources of the Nile. Since the sky and the earth both consider the king's actions just, the turtle will spit out the river it swallowed, and make the ground fertile.'

Watching from the bow of the flagship, Iker saw the imposing animal do so, unhurriedly. Little by little, the level of the Nile rose, and its colour changed. Soon it would be navigable again.

43

The deputy head of trade-control at the port of Memphis was a tall, lanky, rather flabby fellow with a friendly manner. He had just accepted an extremely well-paid job for one of the Lebanese trader's agents: to approach Sobek, man to man. The Protector must have his little weaknesses behind his rough, unbending façade.

Although he was involved in the timber-smuggling, the trade-controller knew neither the people behind it nor the buyers. He was content to falsify the official records: the less he knew, the better he felt. With what he had earned for this undemanding task, he had bought himself a new house near the centre of Memphis, and he was planning to acquire a field. But the problem of Sobek-Khu remained, and he had undertaken to resolve it, so he was delighted when Sobek invited him to his house for the midday meal.

'It's a pleasure and an honour to be here, Commander,' he said. 'After the horrors our city suffered, you have succeeded in restoring calm.'

'Only in appearance,' said Sobek.

'You will catch the rebels, I'm certain.' He took another mouthful of the delicious leeks in cumin sauce. 'Work is still work, and we have no lack of it, but should one not also enjoy the pleasures of life? Wouldn't you like a comfortable, attractive place to live, for example?'

'My official residence is enough for me.'

'Of course, of course, for the time being. But one must think of the future. Your salary alone won't be enough to buy you what you want. Many leading citizens are businessmen. At your level, you should think about it.'

Sobek seemed interested. 'Think about what?'

The trade-controller sensed that the Protector was taking the bait. 'You have a small fortune in your hands without realizing it.'

'Explain what you mean.'

'The power to sign official documents. That signature is worth a very great deal, so you could trade on it: forget it from time to time or place it on more lucrative permits than the ordinary documents that bring you in nothing. The risks are minimal – even non-existent – and the profits are excellent. Do we understand each other?'

'Perfectly.'

'I knew you were an intelligent man. Let's raise our cups to a glowing future.'

But the trade-controller was the only one to drink.

'And this practice has enabled you to buy a superb house, well beyond your means?' asked Sobek calmly.

'That's right. I like you, so I want to help you take advantage of the system.'

'When I invited you here, I intended to question you about this discreetly and obtain your confession gently. In the current circumstances, the arrest of a corrupt trade-controller will hardly raise a stir. You have said more than I hoped for, but nevertheless you must undergo a detailed interrogation.'

Pale-faced, the trade-controller dropped his cup, whose contents splashed all over his tunic. 'Commander, you misunderstand me! I was only talking in theoretical terms – purely theoretical terms.'

'You moved on to the practical, too. I keep up-to-date files on everyone responsible for the security of this city, whatever their rank, and I am suspicious of anomalies. You have been behaving like a man who has suddenly become wealthy, which attracted my attention.'

Seized by panic, the trade-controller tried to escape. But he ran straight into the arms of four guards, who immediately took him off to his new home, an uncomfortable cell.

The interrogation disappointed Sobek. That sorry creature was nothing but a petty cheat, who didn't know the names of the people making use of him. Unless he had been lying, his only contact seemed to be a water-carrier, and there were hundreds of water-carriers in Memphis. The description he had given was so vague that it was useless.

Nevertheless, this might be the beginnings of a lead, so Sobek decided to follow it and to keep a close watch on the Memphis trade-control post. Was this attempt at corruption the result of fear among the rebel network? He might have a chance to discover how it was financed and to dry up the source.

'The trade-controller has been arrested,' the water-carrier told the Phoenician, who immediately gulped down a cake soaked in date-wine.

'Sobek the Protector, Sobek the Incorruptible! Is there anything human left in that man? Now you're in danger, too, because you were the trade-controller's only contact.'

'I don't think so, because he didn't think I was of any importance. That stupid fool was content to do as he was told and get rich.'

'Be especially careful.'

'There are many, many water-carriers in Memphis. At the slightest sign of danger, I'll do what's needed. But I'm afraid I have other news, and it isn't good.'

The Phoenician closed his eyes and leant his head back. 'Tell me the worst.'

'The royal fleet has arrived back in Elephantine. Senusret

317

has conquered and pacified Nubia, and has built a line of fortresses extending as far as the Isle of Sai, so no further rebellion is possible. The king's popularity has reached new heights – even the Nubians venerate him.'

'And what about the Herald?'

'He seems to have vanished.'

'A man like that doesn't just vanish. If the pharaoh had defeated him, he'd display the body at the prow of his ship. No, the Herald's escaped and will reappear sooner or later.'

'We still have the Sobek problem.'

'No problem is insoluble, and we shall eventually find the chink in his armour. As soon as the Herald returns, he'll tell us how to deal Sobek a death-blow.'

The first rays of sun were bathing the sacred domain of Osiris in light. It was not the kingdom of death, but the kingdom of another life. Isis enjoyed the gentle rays as they danced on her creamy skin, and thought of Iker.

No law forbade her to marry. But what attraction could a man exercise, however in love he might be, compared to the Mysteries of Osiris? Yet the Royal Son never left her. It was not an obsessive, tiring presence, more an effective support during the ordeals she was passing through. He was becoming her daily companion, attentive, faithful and loving. Would he return safely from far-off Nubia, the scene of murderous battles?

Isis was taken to the sacred lake by a permanent priest, He Who Sees the Secrets, and a priestess of Hathor. After her heart had been weighed, she must now experience the ordeal of the threefold birth. She waded out a little way into the lake.

'Gaze upon the *nun*,' the priest told her. 'All changes occur within this primeval ocean.'

'I desire purity,' declaimed Isis, using the ancient words. 'I take off my clothing, I purify myself, as did Horus and Set. I emerge from the *nun*, freed from my shackles.'

Isis would have liked to stay in the cool water for a long time. The previous stages of her initiation ran through her memory.

The priestess took her hand and made her sit down on a cube of stone.

The priest said, 'Here is the silver bowl cast by the craftsman of Sokar, falcon-god of the depths, who knows the way of resurrection. I shall wash your feet in it.'

The priestess dressed Isis in a long white robe with a red belt forming the magic knot at the waist, and put white sandals on her feet.

'Thus,' she chanted, 'the soles of your feet become firm. Eyes of Horus, these sandals will light up your way. With their aid, you will not stray. During this journey, you will become at once an Osiris and a Hathor; the masculine way and the feminine way will unite in you. Assisted by all the elements of creation, tread the threshold of death and enter the unknown dwelling. In the very heart of the night, see the sun shine. Approach the gods and look them in the face.' She presented Isis with a crown of flowers. 'Receive the offering of the Lord of the West. May this crown of the righteous ones cause your heart's intelligence to blossom. The great gateway opens before you.'

An Anubis appeared, with the face of a jackal. He took Isis's hand. The pair crossed the place of the ancient tombs, where the first pharaohs lay, then were confronted by guards holding knives, ears of grain, palm-fronds and brooms made of branches.

'I know your names,' declared Isis. 'With your knives, you cut through hostile forces. With your brooms, you disperse them and render them helpless. Your palm-fronds illustrate the emergence of a Light that the darkness cannot extinguish. Your ears of grain show the victory of Osiris over nothingness.'

The guards vanished.

Christian Jacq

Anubis and Isis went below ground, to a long, dimly lit passageway. It led to a vast chamber lined with massive granite pillars. In the centre there was an island. On it stood a gigantic sarcophagus.

'Cast off your former being,' ordered Anubis, 'and pass through the skin of transformations, that of Hathor, who was murdered and decapitated by the bad shepherd. I, Anubis, revived her by anointing her with milk and brought her back to my mother so that she might live again, like Osiris.'

Isis was wrapped in a cow-skin, to dress her as Hathor, then two priestesses took her elbows and laid her down on a wooden sledge, symbol of the creator, Atum, 'He Who Is' and 'He Who Is Not'. Using a ramp, three priests slowly pulled the sledge towards the island, where the Shaven-headed One was standing.

'What is your name?' he asked the first priest.

'The embalmer whose task is to keep the human being intact.'

'And you?'

'I am the watchman,' said the second.

'And you?'

'The guardian of the vital breath,' said the third.

'Go to the top of the sacred mountain.'

The procession circled round the sarcophagus.

'Anubis,' asked the Shaven-headed One, 'has the former heart disappeared?'

'It has been burnt, like the former skin and hair.'

'Let Isis enter the place of transformations and renewed life.'

The priests lifted the young woman and laid her inside the sarcophagus.

'You are the Light,' intoned the Shaven-headed One, 'and you are crossing the darkness. May the gods welcome you, reach out their arms to you. May Osiris receive you in the dwelling of birth.'

320

Isis experienced a space and time outside the visible world.

'You were asleep, and were awakened,' declared the voice of the Shaven-headed One. 'You were lying down, and have been raised up.'

The priests helped her out of the sarcophagus. Torches now lit the chamber.

'The single star shines, being of Light among the beings of Light. Since you come from the Isle of Ma'at, be enlivened by the threefold birth.'

As Isis was being stripped of the cow-skin, the Shaven-headed One touched her mouth, her eyes and her ears with the end of a staff made of three strips of the same skin.

'Daughter of the heavens, the earth and the stars' matrix, henceforth Sister of Osiris, you shall represent him in the rites. Priestess, you shall animate and bring back to life the symbols, in order to preserve the traditions of Abydos. You have one door still to pass through, the door to the Golden Circle. Do you wish it?'

'I do.'

'Be duly warned, Isis. Your courage and your will have enabled you to reach here, but will they be sufficient to triumph over formidable ordeals? The failures have been many, the successes few. Will your youth not be a severe handicap?'

'The decision belongs to you.'

'Are you really aware of the dangers?'

Iker's face appeared to her. Without that presence, perhaps she would have given up. So many treasures had already been offered to her! Because of this nascent love, she knew that she must go to the end of her journey.

'My desire has not altered.'

'Then, Isis, you shall know the Way of Fire.'

44

At last Medes disembarked at Elephantine, and found firm ground under his feet again. Dizzy and unable to eat normally, he nevertheless began to feel a little better. Suddenly an order came from the king: they were to leave immediately for Abydos. The thought of the gangplank, the boat, and that infernal rolling made him almost want to die!

But, despite his constant queasiness, Medes fulfilled his duties with devotion and skill. Messages were sent out constantly, and even the smallest and most remote villages would soon know that Nubia had been brought to heel. In the eyes of his people, Senusret had acquired the status of a living god.

Gua gave his patient a thorough examination. 'It's just as I thought: your liver is in a dreadful state. For four days, you must take a potion composed of extract of lotus-leaves, powdered jujube-wood, figs, milk, juniper-leaves and sweet beer. It is not a miracle cure, but it will give you relief. Afterwards, you must diet. And you will have to take this potion again if the troubles return.'

'As soon as I arrive in Memphis, I shall be perfectly well. River travel is torture to me.'

'You must at all costs avoid fats, meals containing butter, and strong wines.'

As he hurried off to treat a sailor with fever, Gua was thinking hard. Every good doctor knew that the liver determined an individual's character. Did Ma'at not dwell within the liver of Ra, the expression of Divine Light? By offering Ma'at, the pharaoh made that Light stable and Ra's nature benevolent.

Medes's liver was suffering from unusual ailments which were at odds with the open, jovial impression he liked to create. In a liver like that, Ma'at seemed reduced to a very small section. But probably the diagnosis ought not to be taken any further . . .

On deck, Gua bumped into the Royal Son. 'How is your wound?'

'Almost completely healed, for which you have my thanks.'

'You should also thank your good nature, and don't forget to eat plenty of fresh vegetables.'

Iker joined the pharaoh in the prow of the flagship. The king was gazing at the Nile.

'To combat *isefet* and enable the Light to reign,' said Senusret, 'the Creator does four things. The first is to form the four winds, so that all beings can breathe. The second is the birth of the great tide, which can be controlled by both great and small if they attain knowledge. The third is to fashion each individual in his own image. By committing evil voluntarily, human beings have transgressed celestial law. The fourth action is to enable the hearts of initiates to remember the West and to attend to making offerings to the gods. How can the Creator's work be made to last, Iker?'

'Through the rite, Majesty, for it opens our consciousness to the reality of the Light.'

'The word "Ra", the Divine Light, is made up of two hieroglyphs: the mouth, symbol of the Word, and the arms, symbol of the act. The Light is the Word in action. The right that gives life to the Light becomes effective. So the pharaoh fills the temple with radiant actions. Each day, there are numerous rites so that the master of the universe may be in peace in his dwelling. The ignorant think that thought has no weight, yet it plays upon time and space; and Osiris expresses thoughts so profound that an entire civilization was born out of them, a civilization that is not merely of this world. That is why Abydos must be saved.'

At the foot of the acacia tree lay the Nubian gold. The sickness was losing ground, but the Tree of Life was still far from being saved.

With the Shaven-headed One, Senusret attended the rite in which the sistra were played by young Isis. Then the king and the priestess went to the terrace of the Great God, where the *ka*s of the servants of Osiris participated in his immortality.

He said, 'Here you are at the opening to the Way of Fire. Many have not returned. Have you considered the dangers?'

'Majesty, might this course of action contribute to healing the acacia?'

'When did you realize that?'

'Little by little, in a vague way. I did not dare admit it to myself, fearing that I was suffering from illusions and vanity. If my commitment were to serve Abydos, would I not experience the happiest of destinies?'

'May clear-sightedness be your guide.'

'Majesty, we still lack the green gold of Punt. While consulting the archives I made a discovery: not the precise location of the divine land, but the means of discovering it, during the Festival of Min. If the person who holds the key is among the participants, he or she must be persuaded to speak.'

'Do you wish to try to discover the key-holder yourself?'

'I shall do my best, Majesty.'

Seated just inside the threshold of a shrine, Bega was feeling distinctly uneasy. Would Gergu dare to come here? Would he manage to avoid being seen by the guards?

Footsteps sounded. Someone was coming.

It was Gergu, bearing a basket of offerings, which he laid before a stele depicting a couple initiated into the Mysteries of Osiris.

'I would rather not show myself,' said Bega. 'What happened in Nubia?'

'The Nubians were utterly defeated, and the Herald has disappeared.'

'Then we . . . we're lost!'

'Medes and I are not under suspicion, and the pharaoh is completely satisfied with our work. Moreover, there's no proof that the Herald's dead, and Medes is convinced he'll reappear. Until something happens, though, we must be extremely careful. Have you anything interesting to report?'

'The pharaoh and the priestess Isis spoke for a long time. She is to lead a delegation which will take part in the Festival of Min at Kebet.'

'That's unimportant.'

'It may not be. Isis has carried out patient research, and I think she has found something. The Nubian gold has already enabled the acacia to recover somewhat, and she may be hoping to gather important information at Kebet.'

Kebet was a mining town where all sorts of minerals from the desert were bought and sold . . . Gergu would be sure to pass on the information to Medes. Could it be that Isis hoped to find another form of gold during the god's festival?

The king summoned together all the permanent and temporary priests of Abydos, and informed them that Nubia, which was now at peace, had become a protectorate of Egypt. Nevertheless, none of the security measures protecting the sacred land of Osiris was to be lifted, for the rebel threat had not altogether disappeared. The soldiers would remain in place, and would continue to screen everyone thoroughly until the danger had completely gone.

Iker had been ordered by Senusret to remain aboard the flagship, but he could not take his eyes off Abydos, which he was seeing for the first time. It was so close and yet so inaccessible! How he would have loved to explore the domain of the master of resurrection, with Isis as his guide; to pray in the temples and read the ancient texts. But one did not disobey the pharaoh. And the pharaoh did not yet consider him worthy to cross that frontier.

On the quayside Isis appeared, beautiful, graceful and smiling.

Iker rushed down the gangplank. 'Isis! Would you . . . would you like to see round the ship?'

'Very much.'

He led the way, constantly turning round. Was she really following him?

They stood at the prow, in the shelter of a sun-shade.

'Would you like a chair, something to drink, a—'

'No, Iker, I would just like to admire the river, which gives us prosperity and has brought you back alive.'

'You mean . . . you thought of me?'

'While you were fighting, I was also going through harsh ordeals. Your presence helped me and your courage in the face of danger was an example to me.'

Many people could see them, so he dared not take her in his arms. And besides, he was he probably interpreting those surprising words in too favourable a way. She would probably push him away indignantly.

Instead, he said, 'The pharaoh guided us both constantly. None of us, not even General Nesmontu, would have won even the smallest victory without his guidance. Before we arrived in Abydos, the king revealed to me the four deeds of the Creator. I realized that he himself acted in that way, too. Through spirit, not only through strength, he has ended the lawlessness and rebellion in Nubia, in order to transform that desolate land into a happy place. The fortresses are not mere buildings but a magical network capable of blocking negative energies from the Great South. Alas, though, we did not capture the Herald. You know, Isis; you know it well; ever since we met, you have been protecting me. Death has often come close to me, but you have driven it away.'

'You credit me with too many powers.'

'No, I am sure that I do not. I had to come back from Nubia to tell you that I love you.'

'There are many other women, Iker.'

'No, there is only you: today, tomorrow and for ever.'

She turned away to hide her emotions. 'The Tree of Life is faring better,' she told him, 'but we still lack the third type of healing gold.'

'Does that mean a return to Nubia?'

'No, because it is the green gold of Punt.'

'Punt! So, just as I thought, it is not just the product of the poets' imagination.'

'I have not been able to find its location in the archives, but it is possible that during the Festival of Min an informant will give us a vital clue.'

'"Us" . . . You said "us"?'

'Indeed. The king has entrusted this mission to both of us. If the person we hope for takes part in the ritual at Kebet, we shall have to persuade him to give us that precious piece of information.'

'Isis . . . am I nothing to you but a friend and ally?'

The longer she took to reply, the more his hope grew. Was her attitude changing? Was she experiencing new feelings?

'I enjoy our meetings,' she confessed, 'and during your long absence I missed you.'

Rooted to the spot, Iker thought he had misheard. Was his mad dream becoming reality? Or was it in danger of being suddenly shattered?

'Could we continue this conversation over the evening meal?'

'Unfortunately not. My duties are very demanding. In fact, the Festival of Min will probably be the last opportunity for us to see each other.'

The Royal Son's heart was in his mouth. 'Why, Isis?'

'Initiation into the Mysteries of Osiris is a perilous adventure. As I am sworn to secrecy, I cannot tell you about it, but I can tell you that I have decided to follow this quest through to its end. Many have not returned from the path I must take.'

'Is it necessary to take so many risks?'

She looked at him with a disarming smile. 'Is there any other way? You and I live for the permanence of Ma'at and to save the Tree of Life. To try to escape from that destiny would be as cowardly as futile.'

'How can I help you?'

'We are each following our own path, strewn with ordeals that we must confront alone. Beyond them, perhaps we may be able rejoin each other.'

'I love you here and now, Isis!'

'Is this world not a reflection of the invisible one? It is up to us to decipher the signs that wipe away borders and open doors. If you really love me, you will learn to forget me.'

'Never! I beg you not to do this, I—'

'It would be a fatal mistake.'

Iker hated Abydos, Osiris, the Mysteries; and immediately regretted his puerile reaction. Isis was right. Nothing directed them towards an ordinary, trivial existence; nothing gave them the right to plan for a happy, tranquil little life, sheltered from adversity. They would not be together again until they had both confronted the unknown.

Tenderly, their hands joined.

45

Memphis at last! Soon Medes would see the Phoenician again – he was sure to know what had happened to the Herald. But why was the pharaoh so set on celebrating the Festival of Min at Kebet, instead of returning to the capital, where a triumphal welcome awaited him? It was probably something to do with healing the Tree of Life.

Medes held a major trump-card: Gergu. He had become Iker's friend, and had offered to take over responsibility for supplies for the festival. In view of his excellent work in Nubia, his offer had been accepted immediately. He could thus spy on the main protagonists in the event and discover the reasons for their action.

Well cared for by Gua, Medes was feeling vigorous and determined again. There was no doubt that the pacification of Nubia was a crushing defeat for the Herald. However, was there really cause for despair? If Senusret had not adopted a triumphal attitude, and if he continued to speak soberly and with caution, he must fear that the enemy was in Egypt itself.

The Herald was an excellent tactician, and must be planning several angles of attack. Some might be disappointing, but others would be highly successful. His will to destroy the pharaoh and to spread his beliefs was clearly still intact.

*

All Kebet was celebrating. The taverns were serving countless cups of strong beer; the sellers of amulets, sandals, kilts and perfumes were run off their feet. Min, god of all kinds of fertility, from the most material to the most abstract, had set in motion a rush of revelry. Even women who were normally modest and reserved were flirting. At least, thought Sekari, who was already on excellent terms with a local hussy, our spirituality isn't weighed down with sadness and prudery.

Senusret was conducting a very ancient ceremony. Dressed in ceremonial robes and ornamented with gold, he crossed the town to the temple. Before him processed ritual priests bearing shields on which stood statuettes of pharaohs who had passed on to the eternal East. Beside the king was an effigy of Min, his penis erect to signify that the creative desire, characteristic of divine power, was never extinguished. Also there was a white bull, both a symbol of the pharaonic institution and the animal incarnation of the god. Bearer of the sparkling light, it spread strength over all.

Iker could not stop gazing in admiration at the beautiful priestess walking at the king's left hand. For the duration of a festival, Isis was representing the queen.

The statue of Min was placed on a plinth, and priests released birds. They flew off in all four directions, announcing that the pharaoh's actions were maintaining the harmony of both the heavens and the earth.

Wielding a golden scythe, Senusret cut a sheaf of spelt and offered it to the white bull, to his father Min and to the *ka* of his ancestors. Seven times, Isis walked round the pharaoh, speaking the words of regeneration.

Then a small black man appeared. In a solemn but warm voice, he sang a sacred song to Min, which sent shivers through the listening throng. The musician hailed the bull that had come from the deserts, he with the happy heart, charged with giving the king the emerald, the turquoise and the lapis-lazuli.

Min asserted himself as the reborn Osiris, giver of riches.

Once the main ritual was over, the episode everyone had been waiting for began: the erection of the mast of Min. Watched with much interest by a group of young girls, acrobats scrambled up it, eager to unhook the red vases used in the ceremony of re-founding the sacred shrine.

Isis led Iker to one side. 'The man I was hoping to contact is here.'

'Who is he?'

'The singer with the beautiful voice. Only he can tell us how to reach Punt – according to the ancient texts, he bears the title "Man of Punt". He has not been seen for several years, so we must take advantage of his presence here.'

Gergu watched them go. He would rather have downed several cups of strong beer, but he steeled himself to follow the couple.

The singer was sitting in the shade of a palm-tree.

'I am a priestess of Abydos,' said Isis, 'and this is Royal Son Iker. We have come to ask for your help.'

'What do you want to know?'

'The location of the land of Punt,' replied Iker.

The singer sneered. 'That way was cut off long ago. Finding it would require a navigator who has visited the Isle of the *Ka*.'

'I have,' said Iker.

The singer started. 'I hate liars.'

'I am not lying.'

'Whom did you meet on this island?'

'A huge snake. It had failed to save its own world, and asked if I could save mine.'

'Well! So you are telling the truth.'

'Will you take us to Punt?'

'The captain of the ship must have the Venerable Stone, otherwise the ship will be wrecked.'

'Where is it?'

'In the quarries of Wadi Hammamat in the Eastern Desert. But you'll never manage to bring it back from there.'

'Yes, I shall.'

Memphis's welcome outdid Medes's expectations. Senusret was seen as an almost legendary hero for having reunited North and South, and pacified Syria, Canaan and Nubia. His popularity rivalled that of the great sovereigns from the time of the pyramids; people composed poems to his glory and tellers of tales constantly elaborated upon his exploits. The king himself, though, was as stern as ever, as if he thought his great victories unimportant.

Medes's wife received him with hysterical delight. When at last she was asleep, calmed and soothed by Gua's sleeping-draught, he went to see the Phoenician.

He checked the whole area around the merchant's house but saw nothing unexpected, so he followed the usual procedure.

As usual, there were rich cakes and pastries set out in the reception chamber – his host had got much fatter.

'Are we safe here?' asked Medes.

'Sobek has had a few small successes, but there's no serious problem. Ny network is divided into strictly separate groups, precisely in order to protect us. But I'm afraid your long absence has affected our business affairs very badly.'

'I was virtually a hostage of the pharaoh's, but at least my exemplary conduct means that I'm now respected and considered irreplaceable.'

'All the better for us. What really happened in Nubia?'

'Senusret defeated the tribes, pacified the region and built a series of impregnable fortresses. The Nubians have abandoned up their plans to invade Egypt.'

'That's vexing. But what about the Herald?'

'He's disappeared. I was hoping he'd have contacted you.'

'Do you think he's dead?'

'No, because the sign on Gergu's palm burnt him when he voiced doubts. The Herald will soon give us new orders.'

'That's right,' said a soft, deep voice.

Medes jumped.

The Herald was standing there in front of him, with his turban, his beard, his long woollen tunic and his red eyes. He said, 'So, my brave friend, you have stayed loyal to me.'

'Oh yes, my lord!'

'No army will stop me, no strength will surpass mine. He who understands that is a happy man. Now tell me, why did the pharaoh stop at Abydos, and why did he make a point of presiding over the Festival of Min?'

Medes brightened. 'I've had a message from Gergu, carried by one of my fast boats, so I can explain that. The priestess Isis, who has made important discoveries in the library at Abydos, took the place of the queen in the festival. She's often been seen in the company of Royal Son Iker – I'd hoped he was dead but he seems indestructible – and one wonders whether it's simple friendship or whether they're going to get married. However, that isn't the important thing. What is important is that they spoke to a priest with a significant title: "Man of Punt". Why do such a thing, if not with a view to acquiring the gold hidden there? Unlike many people, I believe the land of Punt is a real place.'

'And you are right,' said the Herald. 'Is an expedition being organized?'

'Yes, but not to Punt. Officially, Iker is going to the quarries of Wadi Hammamat to bring back a sarcophagus and some statues.'

The Herald seemed angry. 'So the Man of Punt has told him to find the Venerable Stone, without which the way to Punt is impassable.'

Medes realized why the crew of *Swift One* had failed, even though they had offered Iker to the sea-god. 'Does he stand any chance of success?'

'I doubt it.'

'But with great respect, my lord, that damned little adventurer has already done us a lot of harm.'

The Herald smiled. 'Iker is only a man. This time his audacity will not be enough, but nevertheless we shall take the necessary precautions to prevent any Egyptian ship from reaching Punt.'

Bina appeared behind him, looking frail but beautiful. There were thick bandages under her tunic.

'Yes,' said the Herald, 'she has survived, too, and Senusret cannot imagine the blows her hatred will deal him.'

The Phoenician greedily ate a handful of grapes. 'Sobek-Khu is causing me a lot of problems,' he confessed. 'I've tried to re-form part of my network, ordering my men to be extremely cautious, but I've had to give up trying to bribe that damned commander – he's unbelievably honest, and his men would die for him. Only you, my lord, can rid us of him.'

'Your efforts have been praiseworthy, my friend. But now, since the usual methods have not worked, we shall use others.'

Sobek had wasted no time. The royal palace and the main government secretariat buildings, including the tjaty's offices, had been made absolutely secure. He had also checked all the scribes and other employees, and had transferred anyone he considered suspicious. Only experienced men, whom he had known for a long time, remained in their posts. All visitors were searched, and nobody was allowed to approach the king bearing a weapon.

Senusret's brief congratulations touched the Protector deeply, for they were as rare as they were welcome.

'How did Iker behave in Nubia?' asked Sobek.

'In an exemplary manner.'

'Then I must have been wrong about him.'

'Human beings rarely admit their mistakes. Still more

rarely do they choose the right path and hold fast to it, no matter what the obstacles. The Royal Son is one of those people.'

'I have no excuses to offer.'

'No one asks them of you – especially not Iker.'

'Is he to remain in Nubia?'

'No. I have entrusted the government of the region to Sehotep. As soon as he has appointed trustworthy officials, he will return to Memphis. As for Iker, I have charged him with a new mission, a particularly dangerous one.'

'You are not sparing of him, Majesty!'

'Are you defending him now?'

'I admire his courage. Even Nesmontu has not braved so many dangers.'

'That has proved to be his destiny. Even if I wished it, nobody could act in his place. Now tell me, what are the results of your investigations?'

'Your court consists of many vain, envious and pretentious people, imbeciles, plotters, and a few who are truly faithful to you. However, I reached one reassuring conclusion: there is not one ally of the Herald among them. For one thing, they are afraid of you; for another, they like their privileges and their comfort too much. So I had to search elsewhere. I found that barbers served as go-betweens for the rebels. Several of them have vanished, and the others are being closely watched. And we have a new lead: the water-carriers, though there are so many that it is not easy to watch them all. In addition, I arrested a corrupt trade-control official. That did not produced the results I hoped for, but it should at least have complicated the enemy's life. But it would be a big mistake to lower our guard. Memphis is an open city, and I believe it is still the main target.'

After Sobek had left, Senusret granted a long audience to Tjaty Khnum-Hotep. His running of the country – although overseen daily by the queen – had been exemplary. Tired and ill, the old man had been planning to hand the king his resignation, but once in Senusret's his presence he remembered his oath. It was for the sovereign, not him, to decide. An initiate of the Golden Circle of Abydos owed a duty to his country, his king and his ideal. In any case, he would not much have enjoyed long, lazy days, lolling in a comfortable chair.

Stiff-backed and heavy of limb, Khnum-Hotep set off back to his office. He would continue to fulfil an office which was as bitter as gall yet useful to the people of the Two Lands.

46

He was an alert, talkative fellow by the name of Khauy, who hailed from Kebet and considered himself no fool. An experienced soldier, he had led several expeditions across the desert to Wadi Hammamat and boasted of having always brought back his troops in good health.

Nobody got preferential treatment from Khauy. Iker might be the Royal Son, but he was going to hear what he needed to hear.

'Quarries? Those really are quarries – and Wadi Hammamat's no joke. I always make sure my men have beer and fresh food. I've even transformed part of the desert into fertile fields and dug reservoirs. Unskilled men won't get you what you want. I need ten scribes, eighty quarrymen, the same number of stone-cutters, twenty hunters, ten sandal-makers, ten brewers, ten bakers and a thousand soldiers who will also act as labourers. And food and supplies for all of them, down to the last water-skin, basket and jar of oil.'

'Granted,' replied Iker.

Khauy was astonished. 'Well . . . you have influence and no mistake!'

'I am carrying out the pharaoh's orders.'

'Aren't you rather young to lead such a large team?'

'I'll have the benefit of your advice, so I've nothing to

worry about, have I? What's more, Gergu, the principal inspector of granaries, is at your disposal and will make your task easier.'

Khauy scratched his chin. 'If you look at it that way, we can probably reach an agreement. But we'll do things my way and work at my speed.'

'Very well.'

Khauy had no other demands to make. All that remained was for him to gather together professional workers attracted by the excellent wages.

Djebel Hammamat was over thirteen hundred cubits high, and formed an impressive rocky barrier. Passing through the centre of a sort of gateway, Wadi Hammamat snaked through a rather flat valley which was easily accessible. Since the First Dynasty, Bekhen stone had been quarried: a variant of medium sandstone, black and resembling basalt.[1]

Despite its beauty the Pure Mountain drew fewer gazes than Isis, whose presence intrigued the members of the expedition. Some said she was a favourite of the king and had supernatural powers, which would be vital for driving away the desert demons.

Iker was in heaven. When Isis told him she would be going with him, the sky had become more radiant, the air filled with exquisite perfume. How welcoming the desert seemed, how friendly the heat! Leaving Khauy and Gergu to take care of supplies, he gave Isis a detailed account of his adventures, then they talked of literature and a thousand and one aspects of daily life, though Iker did not dare ask her about Abydos. They realized that they shared many likes and dislikes, and to him the journey seemed terribly short. North Wind and Flesh-Eater were discreet, the donkey merely carrying water if it was necessary.

[1]*Grauwacke* or *greywacke*.

'This is the place,' said Khauy. 'My men are going to set to work.'

Sekari disliked the place immediately, for it brought back bad memories of another, very similar mine.

'Anything wrong?' Iker asked him.

'As if you'd notice! When a man's as deeply in love as you are, he doesn't even see a horned viper slithering over his foot. Don't worry, everything's all right. Despite his big mouth, this fellow Khauy seems reliable and competent.'

'Sekari, tell me the truth. Do you think Isis—'

'You make a very fine couple. Now we'd better start looking for the Venerable Stone.'

The officials in charge of the expedition began by gazing upon the 'table of builders' engraved on a rock-face. The first named was Ka-nefer, 'Creative Power Accomplished'; the second, Imhotep, was the creator of the first stone pyramid. His genius had passed down from one master-builder to another, and tradition considered him the builder of all Egyptian temples across the centuries.

Isis offered water, wine, bread and flowers to Min, and asked him to bless the craftsmen's work.

The mine presented no special difficulties. The teams were properly housed and fed, and soon extracted some superb blocks of stone with red glints and others that were almost black.

'Will these do?' Khauy asked the Royal Son.

'They're splendid, but is this the Venerable Stone?'

'That's just a legend. A long time ago, a quarryman is supposed to have discovered a red stone that could cure all ills. The fellow had too much imagination. Surely you haven't come to look for that?'

'Yes, I have.'

'My specialities are statues and sarcophagi, not children's fables.'

'Let us explore the mountain.'

'Search all the galleries one by one, if that's what you want.'

Iker did just that, but had no success.

Meanwhile, Isis celebrated the ritual and made offerings. Soon afterwards a gazelle appeared, so heavily pregnant that it could no longer run, and all eyes converged on it.

'I'll bring it down with a single arrow,' promised a hunter.

'Don't fire,' ordered Isis. 'Min is sending us a sign.'

The gazelle gave birth. As soon as her little one was capable of moving, they went back into the desert together. At the place where the birth had taken place lay a red stone with golden flashes.

With the aid of a hammer and chisel, Sekari detached it from its rocky bed.

'Yesterday,' complained a quarryman, 'I cut my leg. If that's the Venerable Stone, it will heal my wound.'

Isis laid it on the injured leg for a few moments. When she took it away, there was nothing left but a small scar.

The craftsmen looked at her in amazement. Was this wonder owed to the powers of the young priestess or of the stone? Even Khauy was open-mouthed.

Iker handed him a rolled papyrus, marked with the official seal of the Royal Son. 'Take the expedition back to Kebet and give this letter to the mayor. He will pay you the men's wages and bonuses. I shall go on, taking only the carpenters and a few soldiers.'

So Gergu, much to his annoyance, was not to be a member of Iker's party, and he could think of no pretext for getting himself included. On the return journey, he fulminated.

At the first halt, he went off alone to answer a call of nature. A man lying hidden in the sand nearby called to him, and suddenly he lost the desire.

'So you escaped!' exclaimed Gergu.

'As you see,' replied Shab the Twisted. 'The Herald

protects true believers. They aren't afraid of death, because they know they'll go to paradise.'

'All the same, Nubia was not a pleasant experience.'

'The warriors were too undisciplined. Sooner or later the Herald will impose the true faith on that region. What happened at Wadi Hammamat?'

'Isis found a stone which can heal wounds. Then Iker decided to separate from the rest of the expedition and go off somewhere with a group of carpenters and soldiers. I was ordered to return to Kebet, then resume my work in Memphis.'

'Carpenters, you say . . . Is Iker going to build a boat?'

'I'm sorry, I don't know.'

'The Herald is watching you, Gergu. Make your report to Medes, and tell him to contact the Phoenician. I'm not going to take my eyes off Iker, and I'll stop him doing anything.'

Shab had become the leader of a band of particularly fearsome sand-travellers, a fine attack force. But before attacking the Royal Son and his companions, he wanted to know their plans.

'Who are we waiting for? asked Sekari.

'The Man of Punt,' replied Iker, who was sitting beside Isis on a rock-bed of basalt, facing the desert.

'Supposing he doesn't come?'

'He will.'

As they were reasonably well housed and fed, nobody protested about this rest period. Isis's presence reassured those who were anxious.

At sunset, the Man of Punt appeared. He walked calmly up to Iker and asked, 'Have you found the Venerable Stone?'

Isis showed it to him. The singer took a knife from his kilt.

Immediately, Sekari leapt forward.

'I must check,' said the singer. 'The Royal Son must stretch out his left arm.'

'No tricks, or—'

'I must check.'

Iker acquiesced. The black man cut into the muscle of Iker's upper arm, then placed the stone on the wound. When he withdrew it, the arm was unmarked.

'Perfect,' he declared. 'Who are these men?'

'Carpenters and soldiers who are used to fighting the sand-travellers. Tjaty Khnum-Hotep told me how to reach the port of Sawu, where we'll find the wood we need to build a ship.'

'You may be young, but you seem gifted with foresight. Sawu is the best point of departure for Punt.'

The deep valley hollowed out by Wadi Gawasis opened on to an open bay on the Red Sea coast. There, a small port housed a considerable number of pieces of wood, whose quality was much appreciated by the carpenters.

'Build a ship with a long hull and a raised stern, with two observation posts, the first at the prow, the second at the stern,' ordered the Man of Punt. 'A single mast will suffice. Make strong oars and a central steering-oar. The sail must be broader than it is tall.'

Sekari did not hide his concern. 'This place is dangerous.'

'If it's infested with sand-travellers,' objected Iker, 'why didn't they steal all this wood?'

'They're lazy and ignorant. For one thing, it's too heavy to transport; for another, they wouldn't know what to do with it. My instinct tells me we were followed. I'm going to post guards all round the site.'

On what was to be the prow, Isis drew a complete eye of Horus, which would enable the ship herself to determine the right course to sail. Her name was to be *The Eye of Ra*.

The Man of Punt was watching the carpenters work.

'Where is your land and what should our course be?' Iker asked him.

'Some say it lies to the south or the south-east of Kush and Nubia; others that it borders the Red Sea; others still that it's the island of Dahkak Kebin in the Red Sea. Let them talk. Punt, the Land of the God, will never feature on any map.'

'Then how shall we reach it?'

'That will depend on the circumstances.'

'Do you think you're well enough armed to face up to them?'

'We'll see. I haven't been back to Punt for a long time.'

'Are you making light of me and the destiny of Egypt?'

'Why do you think none of the texts says exactly where the Land of the God is? Its location varies constantly so that it can escape from the greed of humans. I used to know, but now I no longer do. You discovered the Island of the *Ka*, and the young priestess has the Venerable Stone. Insofar as I can, I will help you. But you, and you alone, hold the secret of this voyage.'

Shab the Twisted regretted having waited so long, for Sekari had posted soldiers round the port, so that he could no longer make a surprise attack. However, he congratulated himself on his patience, since he now knew what was happening: Iker was planning to reach Punt, following the old man's instructions. The carpenters were working fast. In a day or two's time, *The Eye of Ra* would be ready to sail.

At last, the news the Twisted One had been hoping for arrived.

'The pirates agree,' the leader of the sand-travellers told him, 'on condition that they receive half the booty.'

'Very well.'

'And will you give me something in addition?'

'The Herald will be generous.'

The sand-traveller struck himself on the chest with his closed fist. 'Not one of them will escape, you can take my word for it. Except for the woman – we'll take her alive and show her what real men are.'

Shab did not care what became of Isis. Let the sand-travellers have her.

47

A few minutes before the sand-travellers attacked, Flesh-Eater sounded the alarm. Sekari awoke with a start and roused the soldiers.

Two sentries were dying, mortally wounded by the pointed flints from slingshots. Shab the Twisted stabbed a third in the back of the neck, his usual way of killing. It was clear that the Egyptians could not hold out for long.

'Everyone to the ship,' ordered Sekari, 'and weigh anchor.'

The craftsmen were being attacked by a horde of sand-travellers. Iker wanted to stay with them, but first he must save Isis. Scarcely had he got on board with her, the Man of Punt, Flesh-Eater, North Wind and ten men, when Sekari pulled up the gangplank and unfurled the sail.

'I must go back and fight,' protested the Royal Son.

Sekari blocked his way. 'That would be madness. Our mission is Punt, and we must sail immediately or we'll all be killed. Look: there's hardly any resistance now.'

As *The Eye of Ra* left the port, a much larger ship barred her way.

'Pirates,' said Sekari. 'We'll never get past them.'

Iker turned to the Man of Punt. 'How can we escape from them?'

'Take the ways of the sky and the roads above. There, the

golden child born of Hathor has built its dwelling. You shall fly upon the wings of the falcon, if the insatiable sea receives the offering it demands.'

Iker thought of the terrible episode on board *Swift One*. Must he drown to save the crew?

'This time,' said the old man, 'you need not sacrifice yourself.'

When Iker looked down into the water, he thought he saw the face of his master, the scribe from Madu who had taught him hieroglyphs and the rule of Ma'at.

A sudden fierce squall overturned the ship, which rolled on to her side and drifted off course with remarkable speed before righting herself again.

'Is anyone hurt?' asked Sekari.

The crew had suffered only bruises and scratches, which were healed instantly by the Venerable Stone. As for the pirates, they had lost their ship and their lives.

At the prow of *The Eye of Ra*, Isis played the sistra rhythmically, and the music mingled with the voice of the sea. Iker held the steering-oar, while Sekari trimmed the sail.

And the ship herself chose the direction to take in order to reach the land of Punt.

In murderous rage, Shab the Twisted finished off all the wounded Egyptians. It was a bitter victory, because the sand-travellers had suffered considerable losses and the pirates' ship had been smashed to pieces by a monstrous wave.

'The Egyptians won't get far,' predicted a sand-traveller. 'Their ship must have been damaged and will soon sink.'

The Twisted One agreed, but uneasily: Iker seemed able to escape even the best-laid traps. 'Take anything you want from the port, then burn the place,' he said.

The marauders were more than happy to obey. Then they dispersed, hoping to find a lightly guarded caravan. Senusret's men were getting more and more vigilant, and if the sand-travellers weren't careful they would eventually find themselves shut up in the Arabian peninsula.

The Twisted One must return to Memphis and inform the Herald that he had more or less failed.

'My knowledge of navigation is rather limited,' said Sekari. 'Is yours any better?'

'I'm just holding the steering-oar,' admitted Iker. 'Actually, the ship's steering herself – the ship and Isis, that is.'

'Sea in front, sea behind, sea on either side . . . No sign of Punt. All this water depresses me, and we haven't got a single jar of wine left.'

'Look at Flesh-Eater and North Wind: they spend most of their time asleep, so we can't be in any danger.'

'Apart from dying of thirst, or sinking when the next storm comes – very reassuring.'

Isis did not move from the prow, her eyes fixed on the horizon. She often pointed towards it with the little ivory sceptre the king had given her.

At the dawn of a sunny day, the donkey and the dog got up and went to her.

Iker shook Sekari. 'Wake up.'

'To see all that water again? I'd rather dream about a cellar full of fine wines.'

'What about an island covered with palm trees?'

'It's a mirage!'

'Not judging by the behaviour of North Wind and Flesh-Eater.'

Reluctantly, Sekari opened his eyes.

It was indeed an island, with long beaches of white sand. The anchor was dropped a good distance away, and two sailors dived in. Once they reached land, they waved to signal that there was no danger.

'I'm going to join them,' decided Sekari. 'You and Isis stay here while we make a boat.'

The donkey and the dog enjoyed the warm water, and then gambolled about on solid ground. The place seemed idyllic. A constant breeze countered the sun's heat, maintaining a pleasant warmth.

When the boat was finished Sekari came to fetch Iker and Isis. Reunited again, the ship's crew ate a meal of fish, which some of the sailors had caught and grilled.

'Let's explore,' proposed Sekari.

Isis led the little group. She stopped at a stone sphinx the size of a lion. It looked like the work of an Egyptian sculptor of the highest skill. Decorating the base was a hieroglyphic inscription: 'I am the Lord of Punt.'

'We've done it!' exclaimed Sekari. 'We're here! And the islanders have chosen one of our most important symbols as the protector of their country.'

The sphinx had the head of a man and the body of a lion, and depicted Pharaoh as the watchful guardian of sacred places. Did its presence mean that the people of Punt were faithful servants of Senusret?

Iker was more cautious. 'It might have been captured in war.'

'The hieroglyphics are clear and intact, and there's no ambiguity in the inscription. The Man of Punt has proved to be a real friend, hasn't he?'

Sekari's arguments made the travellers more hopeful, but nevertheless it was with apprehension that they set off into the palm-grove. Iker thought of the Island of the *Ka*, but this one was much larger.

The luxuriant foliage gave way to an arid, mountainous region. Dry, pebble-strewn slopes made walking difficult, and everyone followed North Wind, who always chose the best path. Here and there, aromatic plants grew.

From the top of a hill, Sekari spotted a village beside a lake surrounded by frankincense- and ebony-trees. The people of Punt used ladders to reach their homes, which were huts built on stilts. Cats, dogs, oxen, cows and a giraffe were wandering about freely.

'How strange: there isn't a single person there. Do you think they ran away at our approach, or have they been wiped out?'

'If the Herald's reached here,' said Iker, 'the worst has probably happened.'

''We must go down to the village,' decided Isis. 'I'll lead the way.'

Sekari was not in favour of taking such risks, but she gave him no time to protest.

When they passed through the entrance, which was marked by two large palm trees, several dozen men, women and children came out of their homes, descended the ladders and surrounded them. The people of Punt were elegant and aristocratic. Some had long hair, others short, and all wore little striped or flecked kilts. They seemed well fed and in excellent health. One detail struck Isis: the men's beards resembled the beard of Osiris. None of them was armed.

A middle-aged man, obviously the village headman, stepped forward. 'Who are you and where have you come from?'

'I am a priestess from Abydos, and this is Royal Son Iker and his friend Sekari. We have come from Egypt.'

'Does Pharaoh still reign there?'

'We are the envoys of Pharaoh Senusret.'

The headman walked round her, both admiring and suspicious. Iker and Sekari prepared themselves to defend her.

'When Pharaoh appears,' said the headman, 'his nose is myrrh, his lips are incense, the perfume of his mouth is like that of a precious ointment, and his scent is that of a lotus in summer, for our land, the Land of the God, offers him its treasures. Alas, sickness has struck us, and our country is drying out. If nature does not grow green again, Punt will die.

The phoenix no longer flies over our land. Only one woman, she who carries the Venerable Stone and plays the sistra, can save us.'

'I carry that stone, and I have come to offer it to you and to let the music of the sistra sound, to dispel the curse.'

While the headman touched each of his people with the Venerable Stone, Isis took up the instruments of Hathor and made them sing. As far as the eye could see, the trees grew bright and the vegetation began to flourish again.

Everyone looked up: a blue heron, with shining plumage, was wheeling above the village.

'The soul of Ra has returned,' declared the headman, smiling. 'The perfumes are reborn, the Tree of Life rises once more atop the primeval mound. Osiris governs that which exists, both day and night.'

'Did you say "the Tree of Life"?' asked Iker in astonishment.

'The phoenix is born on the branches of the willow at Iunu. Its mystery is revealed in the acacia of Abydos.'

Iker was even more astonished. How could this island-dweller know so much?

The headman prostrated himself before Isis. 'The wondrous scents of the land of Punt re-emerge, thanks to the feminine sun, to the envoy sent by the golden goddess, filled with songs and dances. May they be offered to your *ka*, at this happy moment when the Land of the God grows green again.'

When it came to festivities, the people of Punt – from the oldest to the youngest – were experts, and their good humour was infectious. Relaxed at last, the Egyptians joined in a wild dance, punctuated by songs of welcome.

Although captivated by two young beauties whose warm demeanour promised many happy hours, Sekari still watched his host out of the corner of his eye. But the headman seemed to have only peaceful intentions.

Iker could not take his eyes off Isis, who was so radiant

that she had won the heart of every one of the villagers. The headman's wife adorned her with a necklace of amethysts, malachite and cornelians, and a beautiful belt of shells set in green gold. It must, he realized, be the gold of Punt that they needed to heal the acacia. When he looked more closely, the belt's inscription left him deeply puzzled: it was Senusret's coronation name.

'Have emissaries from the king already been here?' he asked the headman.

'No, you are the first.'

'But this belt . . .'

'It's part of our treasure. Do you know Punt's secret name? It is the Island of the *Ka*. The creative power of the universe ignores the human race's boundaries. Now, you and your companions must breathe in the perfumes of the Land of the God.'

The people of Punt gathered together a large number of brightly coloured vases and opened them. The scents of olibanum, myrrh and different types of incense mingled together. They filled the whole island with sweetness.

'Thus is appeased the One who is great in magic,' declared the headman, 'the fiery serpent that shines on Pharaoh's brow. Under the protection of these perfumes, the righteous may appear before the lord of the world beyond. These wondrous smells are creations of the eye of Horus and have become the lymph of Osiris. When the preparer of the ointment heats the incenses of Punt, he is fashioning divine matter, used when the Reborn One is embalmed in the temple of gold.'

Iker did not understand these enigmatic words, but he was sure that Isis would. Had she guided him all this way so that he could hear these revelations?

'Let us entertain our benefactors as they deserve,' ordered their host. 'Fill the cups with pomegranate-wine.'

According to Sekari, the juice from the seeds of ripe

pomegranates, reduced to a third of its volume by boiling, produced a rather mediocre drink, to be taken for its ability to prevent a watery flux of the bowels rather than for pleasure. Nevertheless, he did not decline it. After that eventful journey, he needed reinvigorating.

An open-air feast was held, during which everyone ate and drank too much, with the exception of Isis and Iker, who had not forgotten their mission.

'The green gold of Punt is vital to the survival of Egypt,' Iker told the headman. 'Will you give us permission to take away a few ingots?'

'Of course, but I don't know where the ancient mine is.'

'Does anyone?'

'Only the bark-stripper.'

48

Equipped with a hatchet and a basket, the bark-stripper collected gum resin at a sensible, comfortably slow pace. He liked talking to trees and listening to them, and had no taste for the company of humans. Sensing this, Sekari sat down a few paces away and laid on the ground a loaf of fresh bread, a jar of wine and a dish of dried meat. As if he were alone in forest, he began to eat.

The bark-stripper stopped working and came nearer. Sekari handed him a crust and, after hesitating for a long time, he accepted. Less wary now, he also accepted some wine.

'I've have known better but it's drinkable,' said Sekari. 'Enjoying your day?'

'It could be worse.'

'Your resins are of such high quality that you must be well paid. In Egypt people like ointments, and the ones from Punt are the best of all. Unfortunately, though, our country is in danger of dying.'

The bark-stripper sampled a slice of dried meat. 'Is the situation really that serious?'

'It's even worse.'

'What's happened?'

'A curse. You're our only hope.'

The bark-stripper choked, and Sekari patted him on the back.

'Why are you making fun of me?'

'I'm serious. A priestess of Abydos, the one here with us, did a lot of research and found that only the green gold of Punt can save us. And the only person who can get it for us is you.' Sekari allowed a long silence to elapse.

At least the bark-stripper did not deny it. Deep in thought, he finished the rest of his food. 'In fact,' he said at last, 'I'm not the one, and I can't tell you anything.'

'No one's asking you to betray a secret. Introduce your friend to me, and I'll explain the situation to him.'

'He'll never speak.'

'Doesn't he care about the fate of Egypt?'

'How can one tell?'

'I beg you, give me a chance to persuade him.'

'It would be no use, I assure you. None of your arguments will make any difference.'

'Why is he so obstinate?'

'Because the chief who rules over this forest is a bad-tempered, aggressive, bloodthirsty baboon. I'm the only person who can work here without sending him into a rage.'

'Does he really have the treasure?'

'According to tradition, that huge monkey has always kept the secret of the City of Gold.'

'Show me where you usually see him.'

'You won't come back alive.'

'I'm not easy to kill.'

When the group were still some distance from the baboon's lair, the bark-stripper refused to go any further. Accompanied by the donkey and the dog, Sekari, Isis and Iker passed through a tangle of greenery. Suddenly, North Wind lay down and Flesh-Eater did likewise, his tongue lolling out and his tail between his legs, in a posture of submission.

The baboon who barred their way was brandishing an enormous staff, and was clearly accustomed to using it. His grey-green pelt formed a sort of cape, while his face and the tips of his fingers and toes were tinged with red.

Iker knew that looking the baboon in the eyes was the equivalent of a threat, so he lowered his gaze.

'You are a king,' he told him, 'and I am the son of a king. You are the incarnation of Thoth, god of scribes: do not condemn the Two Lands to death. We are not thieves, nor are we driven by greed. The gold is for the Tree of Life: with this remedy, the acacia will be healed and grow green again.'

The animal's enraged eyes flicked from one unfortunate to another. Sekari sensed that it was ready to spring. It could kill a wild beast with its teeth. When a troop of baboons approached, even a starving lion would abandon its prey to them.

The baboon climbed to the top of a tree. Sekari wiped his brow, and the donkey and dog relaxed.

'Look,' said Isis. 'He's guiding us.'

The powerful monkey showed them the best path, avoiding places which were marshy or overgrown. When the vegetation thinned out, the baboon disappeared. To his surprise, Sekari found that he was standing on a paved road. Tensely, they followed it to an altar covered with offerings.

'There must be people around here,' said Sekari.

Grinders, picks, pins, polishing-stones and washing-tanks left no doubt as to the nature of the work done here. Sekari spotted wells and shallow galleries, easy to mine. The equipment was in good condition, as if craftsmen were still using it.

'Monkeys don't usually turn themselves into miners,' he said.

'The powers of Thoth are beyond our understanding,' said Iker.

'Let's hope they haven't taken all the gold. I can't see a single grain of it.'

Patient searching proved fruitless.

'It's strange,' remarked Iker. 'There isn't a temple or shrine here. I think each mine must be under the protection of its own god.'

'And there's something even stranger,' said Sekari. 'There are no flying or crawling insects and not a single bird in this forest.'

'The place must be under a spell.'

'So the Herald's been here, and we're too late.'

'I don't think so,' disagreed Isis. 'The king of the baboons hasn't betrayed us.'

'Then how do you explain these peculiarities?' asked Sekari.

'This site protects itself, by being outside the usual world.'

This did not reassure him. 'In any case, there's no trace of gold.'

'We don't know how to see it. The light of day may be acting as a protective veil for it.'

'If we spend the night here, we'll have to light a fire.'

'There's no need,' said Isis, 'because we aren't threatened by any wild animals. With guards like Flesh-Eater and North Wind, we'll be alerted to any danger, however slight.'

While Isis was trying to feel the spirit of the place more clearly, the two men explored the area. They found nothing, so at dusk they rejoined her. 'There isn't so much as a single stone hut,' complained Sekari. 'I'll make some beds of branches and leaves.'

'Don't fall asleep, whatever you do,' warned Isis. 'The mystery will be unveiled by the light of the moon, the celestial expression of Osiris. Its eye will give us illumination.'

Despite his tiredness, Sekari did his bit. This was not the first time a mission had obliged him to go without sleep.

Iker sat down beside Isis. He treasured each moment of this unhoped-for happiness, which allowed him to be close to her.

'Will we see Egypt again?' he asked.

'Not without the green gold,' she replied. 'Punt is a stage on our route, and we must not fail.'

'Isis, have you undergone the fearsome ordeal?'

'I know neither the day nor the hour, and the decision is not mine.'

He dared to take her hand. She did not draw it back. When his foot gently touched hers, she did not protest. The land of Punt was becoming a paradise. Iker prayed for time to stand still, for the two of them to become statues, that nothing would change this unspeakable happiness. He was afraid to tremble, to breathe, to break this miraculous communion.

The brightness of the moon altered and became comparable in intensity to that of the sun. It was no longer a silvery light but a golden one which flooded the mine – and only the mine.

'The transmutation is taking place in the heavens,' murmured Isis.

A few steps in front of them, the earth lit up from the inside, a fire within rising up from the depths.

Flesh-Eater and North Wind were motionless as they watched. Sekari did not miss one second of this awe-inspiring sight.

Isis pressed closer to Iker. Was she afraid, or was she silently confessing her true feelings? He did not question her, fearing that he might dispel too beautiful a dream.

Gold gave way to silver; the moon grew calmer, and so did the earth.

'Dig,' ordered Sekari. He took up two pickaxes, and handed one to Iker. 'What are you waiting for? I'm not doing this on my own.'

Iker had to move away from Isis, and the pain plunged him into something akin to despair. By accepting this intimacy, by sharing these moments of tenderness, by not refusing him her love, was she signifying that there would be a tomorrow?

The two friends did not have to dig deep. They unearthed seven sizeable leather bags.

'The prospectors use bags like these,' said Sekari.

Isis opened one. Inside lay the gold of Punt. The six other bags also contained gold.

In the village, the Egyptian sailors were taking their ease. Pampered and spoilt, they spent their time drinking, eating and seducing the pretty girls, telling them their stupendous exploits, from the conquest of an unknown sea to catching giant fish. Lost in admiration, the girls pretended to believe them.

'The celebrations are over,' announced Sekari. 'We're going home.'

This decision did not meet with unanimous enthusiasm. Nevertheless, who would complain about being back in Egypt? No other country, however delightful, could rival it. So in the end the crew willingly busied themselves with preparations for departure.

'Have you found what you came for?' the village headman asked Iker.

'Thanks to you, the Tree of Life will be saved. I ought to have thanked the bark-stripper, but he vanished before I could.'

'Did you see a huge monkey in the tops of the trees? Tradition says that he's the guardian of the green gold. As he looked favourably on you, let's celebrate with one last feast.'

Isis was its queen. Every child wanted to kiss her so as to be protected from bad luck.

But one question had still to be asked.

'Can you tell us the best course to set?' asked Iker.

'Punt will never feature on a map,' replied the headman, 'and it's better that way. Take the ways of the heavens again.'

They parted in good spirits, though not without a hint of sadness. Punt had grown green again, and the bonds of friendship with Egypt had been strengthened.

The Eye of Ra's sail was unfurled, and she set off across a calm sea. The sailors, not all of whom were sober yet, trusted Iker completely.

'What course did the headman suggest?' asked Sekari.

'We must wait for a sign.'

Soon the island disappeared. There was nothing to see but the ever-elusive horizon and the ocean's water, whose apparent calmness did not reassure Sekari.

'Here is our guide,' said Isis.

A huge falcon alighted on the top of the mast. When the wind changed, it took flight and showed them the way.

'The coast!' exclaimed Sekari. 'There's the coast!'

There were joyful shouts. Even for the most experienced sailors, the sight of land had a special magic.

'The falcon's leading us back to Sawu.'

'No,' observed Iker. 'It's content to fly above and lead us at a distance.'

Sekari's keen eyes made out men running towards the shore. So they were being watched – probably sand-travellers in the service of the Herald. They were regrouping, determined not to lose their potential victims.

'We've no water left,' said Sekari, 'and we can't stay at sea any longer. As soon as we touch land, they'll attack.'

'We must follow the bird of Horus.'

With regular beats of its wings, the falcon flew along the coast. As they neared the land, and *The Eye of Ra* came within range of enemy arrows, the sand-travellers were disrupted by a sudden panic. Several regiments of Egyptian archers and spearmen surrounded them.

'They're our soldiers!' cried Sekari. 'We're saved!'

Everyone was so emotional that the ship's docking was somewhat unconventional. Without waiting for the gang-plank, General Nesmontu climbed aboard as agilely as a young athlete.

'The pharaoh was right,' he said. 'This was the right place for me to greet you. Those sand-travellers were worthless cowards, but if you'd disembarked at Sawu they'd have killed you all. Since the divine falcon was guiding you, you must have found the gold of Punt.'

49

Although impulsive by nature, Sobek could be patient and methodical. None of his failures, however serious, discouraged him. And his first real success had made him even more determined to track down the rebel network in Memphis. It seemed to him that the attack on the guard-post and the attempt at corruption had been too crude to have been planned by the Herald. In the Herald's absence, one of his underlings had made an effort to shine, though he did not have his leader's stature.

Sobek was sure that water-carriers were involved. The place most at risk was the royal palace, so he began by having all its regular callers discreetly followed. One of his men, disguised as a water-seller, mingled with the real ones.

'I may have something interesting, sir,' he told Sobek after several days of this. 'At least thirty water-sellers move back and forth through the area, but one of them is particularly interesting. That fellow gets everywhere – it is incredible. But I can't give you a description of him.'

'That doesn't get us very far, then,' said Sobek.

'I wouldn't even have noticed him if a pretty girl hadn't come up to him. They left together, arm in arm, with lots of sweet nothings and significant looks.'

'That sounds utterly trivial.'

'Not as trivial as all that, sir, because of the girl. I

recognized her immediately, because . . . Anyway, you'll see.'

'Never mind the details. Who is she?'

'A washerwoman who's worked at the palace for a long time. She sometimes helps Her Majesty's personal maid.'

A broad smile lit up the Protector's face. 'Good work, my boy, very good work! You deserve promotion. And I'm going to question this young lady.'

Memphis was alive with an extraordinary rumour: the Royal Son had returned, bringing with him a fabulous treasure from the land of Punt.

Although sceptical, the water-carrier had passed on the information to the Phoenician before going off in search of more information to confirm or deny these rumours. He was bound to find out more from his mistress.

The little flirt was always late. After her duties were done, she loved to chat and collect all the gossip. Proud of her job and delighted to repeat what she heard, she provided the water-carrier – and therefore the rebel network – with a wealth of information.

At last she appeared, on the other side of the square where they usually met.

As soon as he saw her, several things aroused his suspicions. She was walking slowly, and looked tense and worried. The atmosphere of the square had suddenly changed: fewer people, less noise, passers-by converging on him.

The mistake. His only mistake. How could anyone have foreseen that Sobek would suspect this utterly anonymous servant?

Apparently unworried, he smiled at her. 'Shall we take our evening meal together, my sweet?'

'Oh yes, of course.'

In a sudden movement, he put his arm round her neck and began to throttle her.

'Move away,' he yelled at the guards, 'or I'll kill her!'

The square emptied. The only people left were the guards surrounding the couple, and they all began retreating slowly towards the nearest dwellings.

'Don't do anything you'll regret,' warned Sobek. 'Surrender, and you'll be well treated.'

The water-carrier took a dagger from his tunic and pricked his hostage's back with it. She cried out in fear.

'Stand aside and let us leave,' he demanded.

Archers were taking up positions on the terraces.

'Nobody is to fire,' ordered Sobek. 'I want him alive.'

The rebel pushed his mistress into a half-built building.

'You damned little fool, you told them about me, didn't you? Now you're nothing but a nuisance.'

Indifferent to her pleas for mercy, he stabbed her savagely, then climbed up a ladder to the roof. By jumping from that roof to the next and then the next, he had a good chance of disappearing in this district, which he knew extremely well.

Just as he jumped, an archer fired, determined not to let the suspect escape. The arrow grazed the water-carrier's forehead and he lost his balance. He tripped over a ledge, banged into the wall hard, and fell. When he hit the ground, he broke his neck.

'He's dead, sir,' said a guard.

'Fifteen days' close arrest for the man who disobeyed my order. Search the body.'

They found not a single document. Once again, the trail had been cut.

A scribe came hurrying into the square and told Sobek, 'You are wanted urgently at the palace, Commander. It has been confirmed officially: the Royal Son has arrived.'

In the presence of a court struck dumb with amazement, Senusret embraced Iker.

'I clothe you with stability, with permanence and with

completion,' said the king. 'I give you the heart's joy and recognize you as a Friend of the King.'

From that moment on, Iker belonged to the King's House, the very small circle of the king's closest advisers. He was almost overwhelmed by the honour, and could think of nothing but his new duties.

The courtiers all wanted to congratulate the new King's Friend and praise him to the skies over several cups of wine, but they were disappointed. The pharaoh and the Royal Son left them and withdrew into the palace garden. There the two men sat down under a wooden awning, whose lotus-shaped columns were decorated with heads of Sekhmet, the lion-goddess. On the roof was a uraeus crowned with a sun.

'Be wary of those close to you and of your subordinates,' the king advised Iker. 'Take no one into your confidence, and don't trust anyone, not even your friends. On the day of misfortune, there will be no one at your side. He to whom you have given much will hate and betray you. When you take your rest, may your heart, and your heart alone, watch over you.'

These stern words took Iker aback. 'Surely this wariness doesn't apply to Isis, Majesty, or to Sekari?'

'Sekari is your Brother, and Isis your Sister. Together, you have passed through formidable ordeals and special bonds have been formed between you.'

'Has she gone back to Abydos?'

'She must try different ways of using the gold of Punt.'

'Then the Tree of Life will soon be saved!'

'Not until Isis has travelled the Way of Fire – and no one knows if she will return from it alive.'

'So many demands, Majesty, and—'

'What is at stake is the fate of our whole civilization, my son, not the fate of one person. That which was born will die; that which was never born will not die. Life springs from the uncreated and develops in the Acacia of Osiris. Matter and spirit are not unconnected, any more than the Being and the primordial substance of which the universe is formed. Things of the mind establish borders between the mineral, vegetable, animal and human kingdoms. However, each one displays a creative power. From the ocean of energy comes a flame that Isis must pacify. There, at the heart of the *nun*, she will discover the first matter and experience the moment before death was born.'

'Will she have the strength she needs?' asked Iker anxiously.

'She will use magic, the power of the Light, which can turn aside the blows of destiny and fight effectively against *isefet*. She will have to use intuitive thought, work out the words of creation and overcome sterility by seeing beyond solidity and appearance. Learning is analytical and partial, knowledge global and radiant. Finally, Isis must pass on what she perceives, fashion her words as a craftsman fashions wood and stone. The correct word contains true power. When you are summoned to sit in council, be content to listen: avoid saying too much. Speak only if you bring a solution, for stating things precisely is harder than all other work. Place the right word upon your tongue, bury the wrong one deep in your belly, and be nourished by Ma'at.'

'Does her initiation mean that Isis will be able to fight off the Herald?'

'She is fully aware of the importance of her mission. The Herald wants to impose a dated, dogmatic belief, revealed once and for all. If he has his way, people will be locked in a prison and will have no chance of getting out, for they will not even see the bars. At the moment, creation is constantly renewed and each morning a new sun is born, which the celebration of the rites anchors within Ma'at. Believing in the Divine remains affective. To know it, learn different ways of applying it, put it into words, recreate it daily through civilization, art, thought: these are the teachings of Egypt. Its most important key remains Osiris, the perpetually Reborn One.'

'Isn't there anything I can do to help Isis?'

'You have already done it, by going to Punt.'

'She guided the boat and knew how to find the green gold. At her side, fear flies away and the darkened road grows bright.'

'Hasn't she advised you to forget her?'

'Yes, Majesty, because of the terrifying ordeal she is going to at Abydos. I know now that it is the Way of Fire. Either she will die or the Golden Circle will welcome her in.'

'That is correct.'

'Whatever happens, I shall lose her.'

'Why don't you give her up?'

'I can't, Majesty. At every stage, every danger, she was there. Since our first meeting, I have loved her devotedly with a love which goes beyond mere passion and builds a whole life. You probably think these are merely the words of an overwrought youth, but—'

'If I thought that, I would not have appointed you a Friend of the King.'

Iker asked another question which had been exercising him. 'Why do you keep me away from Abydos, Majesty?'

'Your training must carry you to a particular end.'

'Is that end still a long way off?'

'What do you think?'

'It's your teaching, not curiosity, which leads me towards Abydos. That is where the vital essence is found. If I turned away from it, I would no longer be your son.'

'Abydos is still in great danger, for the Herald's failures have not rendered him harmless. The Tree of Life is still his target.'

'But the healing gold will strike him down.'

'I hope you are right,' said the king. 'You will be one of the first to see it, together with the Shaven-headed One and Isis, if she returns safely from the Way of Fire.'

'You mean . . . ?'

'I shall soon have another official mission for you. It will take you to the sacred domain of Osiris. As a Friend of the King, you will represent me there.'

This wonderful news made Iker's head swim. But almost immediately anxiety brought him back to earth. "I can see the profound reasons for your decision about Isis, Majesty. However, I—'

'The decision is not mine but hers. The Shaven-headed One has also tried to dissuade her, but she will never give up. Ever since she was a child she has rejected half-measures. Instead of remaining at court and living peacefully here, in accordance with her rank, she chose the way of Abydos, with its dangers and its spiritual demands.'

A mad idea passed through Iker's mind. 'Majesty, if you have been watching her since she was a child, does that mean . . . ?'

'Yes, she is my daughter.'

The Royal Son and Friend of the King wished the ground would swallow him up. 'Please forgive my lack of respect, Majesty. I . . . I . . .'

'I don't recognize you, Iker. What has become of the adventurer who doesn't hesitate to risk his life to discover the truth? Loving my daughter is not a crime. Whether you be peasant, scribe or dignitary is of no importance. The only thing that matters is Isis's decision.'

'But how will I ever dare speak to her again?'

'May the gods permit her to travel to the end of the Way of Fire. When you go to Abydos, and if she has survived, no one will stop you speaking to her. And then you will know.'

50

Since the water-carrier's death the Phoenician could not eat a single mouthful of food. There was no surer way of dieting, it was true, but he would have preferred to lose weight in different circumstances.

'Knowing him, he will have died without talking,' he told the Herald.

'If he hadn't the guards would be here by now.'

'Our links have been broken, my lord, our men are isolated and can do nothing; my right arm has been cut off. And the smuggling that has been paying for everything has been interrupted.'

'Are you doubting that we shall succeed in the end, my faithful friend?'

'I only wish I could say no!'

'I appreciate your sincerity and I understand your concern. However, everything is proceeding according to my plan and your worries are unfounded. Our sole objective is Abydos and the Mysteries of Osiris. Why should I worry about a collection of Canaanites and Nubians? They'll be converted one day, and it doesn't matter at all whether or not Senusret subdues them. He spends all his time and effort maintaining order, and worries constantly that he may be attacked in the North as he was in the South. Our diversion has worked admirably, concealing our true goal.'

'But hasn't the pharaoh acquired the gold that can save the acacia?'

'That is a real success, I admit. Nevertheless, if Senusret is hoping the tree will recover fully, he'll be disappointed.'

The Phoenician's steward came in and bowed. 'You have a visitor, sir,' he said. 'The doorkeeper says he has given the password.'

'Very well. Show him in.'

Medes came in, taking off his hooded cloak. Despite his return to dry land, he looked no happier than the Phoenician. However, seeing the Herald again revived him. 'I've never stopped believing in you, Lord, and—'

'I know, my brave friend, and you won't regret it.'

'The news is terrible. First, the guards are scouring the city and questioning almost everyone. Second, we shan't be able to trade with Phoenicia any more, because the Protector has reorganized the entire trade-control service. Worst of all, Iker has brought back the green gold from the land of Punt, and he's been appointed a Friend of the King.'

'A remarkable career,' observed the Herald calmly.

'That boy's dangerous,' said Medes. 'According to the latest royal decree, he'll soon be going to Abydos as the king's official representative. What if he uncovers Bega's secret activities? Bega won't have the courage to keep silent. He'll talk about Gergu, and Gergu will talk about me.'

'But you know how to keep silent, don't you?' said the Herald.

'Yes. Oh yes indeed, my lord, you can be sure of that.'

'Deceiving oneself is a recipe for disaster: nobody can withstand an interrogation by Sobek. You and Gergu, under the Phoenician's direction, are to re-establish the links between my followers and cause regular disturbances in Memphis. That will show the pharaoh that we are still active at the very heart of his capital.'

'It's too dangerous, my lord!'

'The confederates of Set fear no danger. Remember the sign imprinted in your hand.'

Back to the wall, Medes wanted to know more. 'During this diversion, where will you be?'

'At the site of the final struggle: Abydos.'

'Why haven't you concentrated your efforts there?'

The Phoenician wondered if Medes's insolence would be severely punished, but the Herald seemed untroubled by it.

'I needed to strike a fatal blow, and the designated victim was not yet ready to receive it.'

'Whom do you mean, Lord?'

'The young scribe Iker, now Royal Son and King's Friend, who has escaped the voracity of the sea-god, reached the Island of the *Ka*, and survived a thousand and one other dangers. By sending him to Abydos, Senusret is undoubtedly entrusting him with a mission of prime importance. It matters little that the pharaoh himself is untouchable. We are going to destroy him through the spiritual heir whom he has patiently trained and prepared to succeed him, and whom he can never replace. Iker hopes to find happiness in the sacred domain of Osiris and attain knowledge of the Mysteries. But what awaits him there is death – and with it the shipwreck of Egypt.'

'Anyone can be wrong,' Sobek told Iker. 'If you bear a grudge, I shall understand. Your recent promotion won't make me produce a stream of apologies. I'd have done the same if you were a humble workman. Only your conduct and your deeds have made me see that I was mistaken.'

Iker embraced him. 'You were absolutely right to be so thorough, Sobek, and I shall never criticize you for it. Your friendship and your respect are treasured gifts.'

The rough-hewn commander cleared his throat to hide his feelings. Uncomfortable with declarations of friendship, he preferred to talk about work.

'Despite the death of the water-carrier, I'm uneasy. He was

a big fish, certainly, but there are bigger ones left.'

'You'll catch the network's leaders, I'm sure you will.'

A scribe interrupted them, asking for Iker's advice about a delicate case; then another came in, and another after that. When Iker at last escaped from them, he went to see the tjaty, who would tell him what his duties were within the King's House.

On his way to the tjaty's office he met Medes, who greeted him very warmly.

'My sincere congratulations, Friend of the King. And may I say, without the least flattery, that after all your remarkable exploits your appointment is a well-deserved reward? Of course, there will always be jealous people, but what do they matter? Now, I have here your authorization to enter the sacred land of Osiris. Has the date of your departure been set?'

'Not yet.'

'Fortunately, this mission will be less dangerous than your previous ones. Myself, I hope never to return to Nubia. The country has no charm, and the boat makes me ill. Please don't hesitate to ask for my help if you should want it.'

As they sat down to their evening meal, Sekari looked closely at Iker. 'How odd! You seem almost normal – surprising, for a Friend of the King. Am I still allowed to speak to you?'

Iker joined in the game by assuming a formal air. 'Perhaps you ought to kiss the ground in my presence. I shall consider the matter.'

The two friends burst out laughing.

'When I leave Memphis,' said Iker, 'I'll leave North Wind and Flesh-Eater with you.'

'And I'll be glad to have such excellent assistants. They thoroughly deserved their promotion to the rank of officers and their awards after their brilliant Nubian campaign. But why aren't you taking them with you?'

'I must go to Abydos alone. Afterwards, if things go well, they'll join me there.'

'Abydos . . . So you're going to discover it at last.'

'Tell me the truth: do you know who Isis is?'

'A young and beautiful priestess.'

'Nothing more?'

'That's remarkable enough, isn't it?'

'Do you really not know she's the king's daughter?'

'Well . . .'

'And you said nothing!'

'The pharaoh ordered me not to.'

'Do other people know?'

'Only the members of the Golden Circle. Secrecy is an essential aspect of its Rule, so no one would say anything.'

Iker said dejectedly, 'She will never love me. Oh, Sekari, has she survived the Way of Fire? I want to leave straight away. What a horrible journey it will be if misfortune—'

Sekari interrupted, hoping to comfort his friend. 'So far Isis has survived all the ordeals, however difficult, hasn't she? With her clear head, her intelligence and her courage, she has the right weapons.'

'Have you walked that terrifying path?'

'The doors are eternally the same, though they are different for each person.'

'Without her, life would have no meaning. But why should she be interested in me?'

Sekari pretended to think. 'As a King's Friend and Royal Son, you have a certain amount of experience. And you're a relatively skilful scribe – perhaps you could be useful to her, provided she isn't alarmed by your fine-sounding titles. They might frighten her off, don't you think?'

Sekari's cheerful humour heartened Iker, and a few cups of an excellent wine soothed his anxieties a little more.

'Do you think the Herald and his followers have left Egypt?'

'If he were a normal man,' replied Sekari, 'he'd have realized that he'd been defeated and taken refuge in Syria, Canaan or Asia. But he's neither a simple criminal nor an ordinary invader. He wants to destroy our country, and he still wields the weapons of darkness.'

'So you think there will be more trouble?'

'The king and Sobek think so, too, and that the rebels will probably attack again and kill more innocent people, so it's vital that we stay alert. At least at Abydos you'll be safe. There are so many soldiers and guards there that you won't run any risks at all.'

As he spoke those words, Sekari had a strange feeling. Iker's journey suddenly seemed threatening. Ill at ease and unable to explain his fears, Sekari chose to remain silent and not to alarm his friend.

Not once during the Herald's stay had the Phoenician been permitted to speak to Bina. When she came back to his house, her mission accomplished, she had veiled herself and shut herself away; only her master joined her from time to time.

Spirits were rising. Through the itinerant traders to whom Bina – who passed as just one customer among many – gave orders, contacts between the parts of the Memphis network had been re-established. Every one of the rebels now knew that the Herald, who was very much alive and in excellent health, was still spreading the true faith and carrying on the struggle.

Medes and Gergu had already put forward a few ideas for localized disturbances which would be likely to cause panic.

'It is up to you to choose the best,' the Herald told the Phoenician.

'But, my lord, I'm only a merchant, not a—'

'You want to be more than that, and I don't blame you – despite certain unfortunate actions of yours. If you want to become my right arm, the man who knows everything about every inhabitant of Egypt and who will separate the believers from the non-believers, you must make progress. Soon, my brave friend, you will head an armed force in the service of the new religion, and you will punish the slightest transgression.'

For a few moments, the Phoenician tried to imagine the power he would have. Compared to him, Sobek would be nothing. And this almost limitless power, which he had dreamt of for so long, was no mirage. The Herald really could offer it to him.

'Bina and I are leaving for Abydos,' the Herald went on.

'How many men do you want?'

'Bega will be enough.'

'Gergu says the place is very closely watched and—'

'He has given me all the details. Take good care of Memphis. I am going to lie in wait for Iker, and this time nobody will save him. I shall break the hearts of Abydos and Senusret simultaneously. Fragile Ma'at will fall apart, the torrent of *isefet* will be set loose, and no retaining-banks will be able to contain it. The Tree of Life will become the Tree of Death.'

51

Anubis, the jackal-headed god, led Isis to the circle of flames. 'Do you still wish to follow the Way of Fire?'

'I do.'

'Give me your hand.'

Isis trusted the priest with the muffled voice. No normal person would have dared approach the tall flames, which gave off a searing heat. Sure of her guide, she did not flinch once.

When her robe caught fire, she felt a sudden, unexpected peace. She was inside the Temple of Osiris.

'Nothing is left of your profane individuality,' said Anubis. 'Here you are naked and vulnerable. You are faced with two paths. Which do you choose?'

To her left was a waterway bordered by shrines guarded by flame-headed spirits. To her right was a path of black earth, a sort of dyke snaking between vast lakes. Separating them was an impassable channel of molten lava.

'Should one not travel them both?' she asked.

'The way of water annihilates, the way of earth devours. Do you persist?'

'Why should I fear them, since you are leading me where I must go?'

'Tonight we shall take the way of water. When day comes, we shall take the way of earth.'

The moon rose, and Anubis handed her the knife of Thoth. With its blade she touched each of the spirits, speaking their names. This took until daybreak. Then, in the brightness born into the ship of dawn, she set off along the way of earth.

The two ways crossed and recrossed without ever joining. At their end, a channel of lava fused them at the threshold of a monumental porch flanked by two pillars. Crouching guardians brandished snakes. 'This is the mouth of the world beyond,' explained Anubis, 'the junction between the East and the West.' And to the guardians, 'I am the master of blood. Open the way to me.'

The door opened slightly.

In the temple of the moon, a soft blue light enveloped Isis's body. The ship of Ma'at was unveiled.

'Since it has appeared to you, we shall continue.'

Seven doors, four leading into each other and three face-on, barred her way.

'Four torches,' said Anubis, 'correspond to the four easts. Take them, one by one, and offer them to the doors.'

Isis performed the rite.

'Thus the living soul travels this way, thus the great flame that emerges from the ocean gives life to your steps.'

The doors opened one after another, and the darkness melted away.

Isis saw the light of the first morning, whose eyes were the sun and the moon. A second circle of fire made it impossible to reach the Island of Osiris, which was surmounted by a hill of sand where lay the sealed vase containing the god's lymph.

'This is the final path,' said Anubis, 'and I cannot help you. You must pass alone through the fire.'

The young priestess approached the flames. A spark brushed her mouth. On her heart a star was imprinted; on her navel, a sun.

'May Isis become the follower of Osiris,' she prayed, 'may her heart not be distant from him, may her steps be free night and day, may this brightness be placed within her eyes and may she pass through the fire.'

'The way is set out for Isis,' responded the priest. 'The light guides her steps.'

For a moment, she stood motionless in the middle of the circle of fire, like a prisoner. Then, serene and unharmed, she stepped on to the Island of Osiris. She knelt before the sealed vase, the source of all energies.

When its lid lifted, she gazed upon life at its source. The whole temple filled with light.

'Your perfume mingles with that of Punt,' intoned the Anubis-priest, 'your body is covered with gold, you shine at the heart of the stars illuminating the hall of mysteries, you who are of just voice.'

He dressed her in a long yellow robe, and placed on her head a gold diadem decorated with carnelian lotus-flowers and lapis-lazuli rosettes. He put round her neck a broad collar of gold and turquoise, with clasps in the form of falcons' heads. Then he fastened red carnelian bracelets round her wrists and ankles, stimulating the vital fluid, and white sandals upon her feet.

When she looked back, there was no trace of the ways of water, earth and fire. But in the shrine of the Temple of Osiris the pharaoh appeared, accompanied by the Great Royal Wife. Around Isis stood Tjaty Khnum-Hotep, Sekari, High Treasurer Senankh, the Shaven-headed One, General Nesmontu and Sehotep, Bearer of the Royal Seal.

Senusret placed on his daughter's middle finger a ring of glazed blue porcelain. Its oval setting was decorated with a carved *ankh*, the sign for 'life'.

'You now belong to the Golden Circle of Abydos,' said the king. 'May our union with Osiris and the ancestors be sealed.'

Hands were joined, the circle was formed, and a moment of intense silent communion marked this final stage in the young priestess's initiation.

*

Isis laid the seven bags of green gold from Punt in seven holes dug by the Shaven-headed One at the foot of the Acacia of Osiris.

Watched by the king, she waited for the rising sun to appear. This morning, it pierced the darkness with particular brilliance. In a short time, the whole of Abydos, from the tombs of the first pharaohs to the landing-stage, was bathed in intense light.

As soon as Senusret uttered the ancient ritual words 'Awaken in peace', golden rays rose from the bags of gold and entered the acacia's trunk: its branches and twigs began to live again. When the day-star reached its zenith, the Tree of Life regained its full majesty, its foliage a glorious green.

For the first time in his life, the Shaven-headed One wept.

Iker was tense and impatient. The pharaoh and the queen were travelling, and so was the tjaty; Senankh was away on a tour of inspection; Sehotep was supervising irrigation works; General Nesmontu was on manoeuvres; and Iker was overwhelmed with work. That did not worry him, but he was tormented by one question: when would he receive the order to go to Abydos?

He could not find Sekari anywhere – he must be away on yet another secret mission. That suggested to Iker that, though Memphis was calm, there was trouble in store. Still, at least the Protector now trusted him and spoke to him every day. Sobek's men were working tirelessly, but they had come up with nothing. The commander was constantly in a rage, convinced that the rebel network was regrouping in order to strike hard.

At long last, Senusret returned to the capital.

He granted his first audience to Iker. Many courtiers already regarded the Royal Son as Senusret's successor. By associating the young man with the throne like this, the king was training him for royal office and guaranteeing the stability of the Two Lands.

Iker bowed before the pharaoh.

'Isis has travelled the Way of Fire,' said Senusret, 'and the Acacia of Osiris has come back to life.'

Iker could hardly contain his joy. 'Is she really unharmed, Majesty?'

'Really.'

'Then happiness reigns in Abydos once more.'

'No, not yet, for safeguarding the acacia was only a stage. The tree's sickness and the degradation of the symbols, deprived of energy for so long, have left deep scars. Your mission is to remove them.'

Iker was stunned. 'But, Majesty, I . . . I don't know Abydos.'

'Isis will guide you. You will see it with new eyes.'

'Will she accept this?'

'Whatever your feelings may be, and however difficult the undertaking, you must succeed. By decree, you are appointed prince, Guardian of the Royal Seal, and Overseer of the Double House of Gold and Silver. From now on, Sehotep and Senankh will work under your direction. In Abydos you will be my representative and will have the use of all the craftsmen you need. A new statue of Osiris and a new sacred ship must be made. Apart from its healing qualities, the gold brought back from Nubia shall be used to create these works. Ever since the tree became sick, the priests have detected disturbances: despite appearances, all is not righteous and perfect, so our victory could yet be reduced to a mere mirage. You have full powers to investigate, to dismiss any who are incompetent and appoint people who are capable of carrying out their tasks.'

'Majesty, do you really believe I can do all this?'

'While Isis was passing through the stages of initiation leading to the Way of Fire, you were following your own

379

way. It led to Abydos, the spiritual heart of our country, which the Herald may have corrupted. Even devoted servants of Osiris can be blind. You, however, will not be the slave of any customs or prejudices.'

'I am likely to meet strong opposition from the priests.'

'If your investigation is limited to conciliatory conversations, you will fail. Restore to the domain of Osiris its clarity and its unity, strengthen the acacia, banish weakness and compromise.'

Iker had expected his new rank of Friend of the King to entail heavy responsibilities, but this . . .

'Majesty, will the Golden Circle of Abydos be opened one day?'

'Go now, my son, and prove yourself worthy of your office.'

52

Medes was pleased with himself. Fully recovered from the Nubian campaign, he resumed his duties with an energy which exhausted all his subordinates, including the scribe who was in fact Sobek's spy. After much consideration, Medes had decided not to kill him but to let him continue to reassure the Protector that Medes was a conscientious official who served the pharaoh diligently.

And, much to his relief, his wife was benefiting from Gua's treatment and so was bothering him less. Powerful sleeping draughts had put an end to her attacks of hysteria.

In the middle of a moonless night, Medes went to see the Phoenician.

'The Herald is on his way to Abydos,' the merchant told him.

'But Iker hasn't left Memphis yet. Surely the Herald won't throw himself into the jaws of his worst enemy?'

'Don't worry. The Herald is always one step ahead of his enemies. Now, tell me, how do you plan to cause trouble in the city?'

'Fires, attacks on many citizens, thefts from the markets and from people's homes. Sudden, violent action will create a general feeling of insecurity, and Sobek will fear that a major incident is about to happen. In addition, it seems a good idea to attack a few unprotected scribes' offices. Make a note of their locations.'

The Phoenician wrote down the information. Since the water-carrier's death, he had had to use his doorkeeper to pass on his orders, but whereas the water-carrier had been able to go anywhere and everywhere, the doorkeeper could contact only a few rebels, who subsequently distributed the orders. After the Herald's success at Abydos and the death of Iker, he would have to work at an altogether faster rate.

Since the recovery of the Tree of Life, whose foliage gleamed in the sunshine, the domain of Osiris had almost forgotten the oppressive atmosphere that had filled everyone's hearts with dread.

Although the strict security measures were still in force, more temporary priests had access to the site and provided the permanent priests with considerable assistance. Stifling his bad temper, Bega continued to deceive his colleagues. They thought him austere, serious and totally devoted to his high office. Neither his words nor his behaviour gave any clue to his true feelings.

Despite periods of discouragement, Bega still harboured his longing for vengeance. It was all that enabled him to bear the humiliation.

As he stepped into his modest house, which no one else was allowed to enter, he sensed someone there.

'Who has taken it upon himself to—'

'I have,' replied a tall priest. He was beardless, with a shaven head, and wore a white linen tunic.

Bega did not know him, but that voice was familiar. When the priest's red eyes flamed, Bega shrank back against the wall. 'You . . . Are you . . . ?'

'Shab killed a temporary priest,' said the Herald, 'and I have taken his place.'

'Did anyone see you enter my house?'

'Relax, my friend, your time has come at last. I want to know everything about Abydos, before Iker arrives.'

'Iker? Coming here?'

'As Royal Son, Friend of the King and Senusret's special envoy, he has full powers. He may try to reform the college of priests and priestesses.'

Bega went white. 'He will discover our trade in stelae, and my links with Gergu!'

'He will not have time.'

'How can we stop him?'

'By killing him.'

'Here? Within the sacred domain of Osiris?'

'It's the ideal place to strike Senusret a fatal blow. He intends Iker to reign after him. Without realizing it, Iker has become the plinth upon which the country's future is built. By destroying it, we shall undermine the foundations of the kingdom. Even this pharaoh, for all his huge stature, will collapse.'

'Abydos is still under close watch – the guards and soldiers—'

'They are outside, whereas I am inside. Shab and Bina will soon join me. By knowing everything that goes on here, we shall be in a position of strength. This time, no miracle will save Iker.'

53

The separation was heart-rending. Neither North Wind nor Flesh-Eater wanted to be parted from their master, despite his explanations. Sekari also tried to reassure them, but the two animals displayed unusual nervousness, as if they disapproved of the Royal Son's journey.

'I can't sleep any more,' said Iker. 'Instead of a paradise, Abydos may turn out to be my hell. First, Isis will probably reject me; then, I'm bound to fail in my mission.'

While Sekari was trying to comfort his friend, Sobek arrived.

He told them, 'I've been informed of two attacks in the workers' districts and three cases of fires being set. So many things happening at once cannot be chance.'

Sekari frowned. 'The Herald's men are at work again.'

'They won't achieve anything,' said Sobek grimly. 'While my men are carrying out official and very visible investigations, will you keep your ears wide open?'

'Of course,' promised Sekari.

The Protector accompanied Iker to the port, and once more checked that there were enough highly trained guards aboard to protect him. Then he watched the Royal Son's departure, his boat preceded and followed by boats whose crews were well armed.

*

Iker stood in the bows, but he did not even see the gentle beauty of the countryside. He felt as though he was sailing between two worlds, unable to return to the one he had come from and knowing nothing of the one that lay ahead. His terrifying voyage on *Swift One* came back into his mind. Several puzzles had been solved, but the biggest mystery, that of the Golden Circle of Abydos, remained intact.

As they drew near to Abydos, all the archers suddenly rushed to the starboard rail.

'What is happening?' asked Iker.

'A suspicious boat,' replied the archer's commander, pointing to it. 'Unless it moves away immediately, we shall fire.'

Iker followed the direction of the captain's finger and saw that the boat's occupant was a heavily bearded fisherman, who looked so terrified that he could not move, let alone move out of the way.

'Wait,' he said. 'That poor fellow's no threat.'

'Orders are orders. He's come much too close, and you must not run any risks.'

Shab the Twisted pulled in his net and rowed away. He had wanted to test the soldiers' reactions and take advantage of any lapses, for he was ready to sacrifice his life in order to kill the enemy. Alas, there were no weak spots. He returned to the place where he was to contact Bega.

On the quay stood soldiers, guards, temporary priests and priestesses bearing offerings, and every single one of the temple's scribes, all nervous at the thought of welcoming the pharaoh's envoy. Nobody knew why he was coming here, but he had been preceded by a reputation for determination, incorruptibility and courage – witness his exploits in Canaan and Nubia. The most optimistic people were envisaging a simple protocol visit, although they were surprised by the absence of the Shaven-headed One.

As soon as Iker appeared at the top of the gangplank, everyone took the measure of him. Dressed with sober elegance, he did not look very fearsome. But his bearing and gaze commanded respect, and beneath his reserve true power was detectable. Disappointed, the flatterers swallowed their flowery compliments.

Bina had made herself wholly unrecognizable. She wore a large wig which hid a good part of her face, and her face had been thickly painted. She carried a big bunch of flowers which she was to present to the Royal Son. When he accepted it, two poisoned needles hidden among the flower-stems would prick him, and he would die in appalling pain.

She was not afraid of being arrested. The sole thought in her mind was to take her revenge on Iker, who had betrayed her by joining Senusret and fighting against the true god, the god of the Herald. She would take off her wig and spit in his face so that he would know where his punishment had come from.

The commander of the special guards stationed in Abydos greeted the king's envoy. 'Permit me, Prince, to wish you an enjoyable visit. I shall escort you to the palace where the pharaoh stays when he is here.'

Several young women offered Iker bunches of flowers. The most beautiful was that held out by Bina, who was in the front row of the crowd.

Iker wanted to take it, but the commander stopped him. 'I am sorry, my lord, but that is against the security regulations.'

'What is there to fear from a bunch of flowers?'

'I am under strict orders, my lord. Please follow me.'

Not wishing to cause a fuss, Iker simply smiled and nodded at the flower-bearers.

Bina could scarcely contain her rage. She wanted to run after the Royal Son, catch him, plunge the needles into his back . . . But it was impossible to get through the security cordon.

Abydos . . . At last, Abydos was opening itself to him! And yet Iker saw nothing. Until he had spoken to Isis, he would be nowhere.

She was waiting for him on the threshold of the palace.

The most sensitive and refined of poets could not have conveyed her beauty. How could one conjure up her exquisite features, the radiance in her eyes, the sweetness of her face and her royal bearing?

She smiled and said, 'Welcome, Iker.'

'Forgive me, Princess. The pharaoh told me who you are, and—'

'Are you disappointed?'

'My impudence, my audacity, must have—'

'What audacity?'

'I dared to love you.'

'You are speaking in the past tense.'

'No – oh no! If you only knew . . .'

'Why should I not know?'

The question left Iker speechless.

Isis smiled again and asked, 'Would you like to see your apartments? If you need anything, ask me.'

'You're Pharaoh's daughter, not my servant!' protested Iker.

'I want to become your wife, to form with you a couple more united than unity, and to fashion one life, which time and ordeals cannot destroy.'

'Isis . . .' He took her in his arms. It was their first kiss, the first communion of their bodies, the first intertwining of their souls.

It was also the first pain felt by the Herald, whose falcon's talons lacerated his own flesh. To see this pair becoming one was unbearable. Spattered with his own blood, he swore to put an end to their union, which was a threat to his final victory. He would not allow Iker any chance whatsoever of survival.

POCKET
BOOKS

The Tree of Life
Volume One in
THE MYSTERIES OF OSIRIS series

In the temple of Abydos, an acacia tree is dying. And its death
threatens all of Egypt. For this is no ordinary tree: it sprang
forth from the tomb of the god Osiris, the first ruler of Egypt,
as proof of his triumph over death. The great pharaoh Sesostris
III immediately joins battle against the invisible enemy who
wishes to lead Egypt to her doom. But unknown to Sesostris,
within his closest circle hides a traitor, a man who dreams of
power and glory, a man prepared to sell himself to the powers
of darkness in order to achieve his aim.

A young apprentice scribe, Iker, becomes an unwilling player
in the drama. Kidnapped by sailors who refer darkly to a 'state
secret', Iker does not know who is trying to kill him, nor
indeed who is trying to protect him. Haunted by a vision of a
beautiful priestess, Iker senses that he's being guided or
manipulated, and that he has set out on a path whose end he
does not know.

Will the two of them, Iker and Sesostris, the weak young boy
and the great man of power, succeed in preventing Osiris from
dying for the last time, thereby saving Egypt?

ISBN 978-0-7434-9225-6
PRICE £6.99

POCKET
BOOKS

The Conspiracy of Evil
Volume Two in
THE MYSTERIES OF OSIRIS series

The beautiful acacia tree of Abydos is dying.

But the beautiful priestess Isis has an idea: to save the 'Tree of Life', a new pyramid must be built in honour of Osiris. The pharaoh Senusret agrees to the plan – but what he doesn't know is that a triple conspiracy has been hatched against him.

On the one hand, the Herald, the bearded devil who preaches to the desert tribes, has decided to seize power by having the pharaoh murdered. On the other, within Senusret's own court, an ambitious, thieving traitor is plotting to get rid of his master. Finally, Iker the scribe, deceived by appearances, believes that the time has come to settle his scores.

Never has the pharaoh seemed so alone or so vulnerable. And never before has the future of Egypt been in such great peril.

'A melange of history, romance and adventure by an author who artfully combines story with truth' *Good Book Guide*

ISBN 978-0-7434-9224-9
PRICE £6.99

POCKET
BOOKS

Coming Soon from Pocket Books

The Great Secret
Volume Four in
THE MYSTERIES OF OSIRIS series

Unrecognisable, the evil Herald is hiding at the very heart
of Abydos, preparing to commit the supreme crime. By
bringing death into the kingdom of Osiris in order to prevent
his resurrection, he will at last be able to overthrow the
pharaoh Senusret, seize power and spread his wicked
doctrine far and wide.

Will young Iker manage to fulfil his mission, to celebrate the
mysteries of Osiris? In the face of misfortune, will the
priestess Isis bring her Quest for the Impossible to a
successful conclusion?

And if death could really be overcome . . .

After forty years studying the doctrines of Ancient Egypt,
Christian Jacq concludes this magnificent series by revealing
the Great Secret of resurrection. This mystery lay at the very
centre of Egyptian thought and pharaonic civilization – and
provides the key to our understanding of
Ancient Egyptian life.

ISBN 978-0-7434-9226-3
PRICE £6.99

POCKET BOOKS

This book and other **Pocket Books** titles are available from your local bookshop or can be ordered direct from the publisher.

9780743492256   The Tree of Life   Christian Jacq   £6.99

9780743492249   The Conspiracy   Christian Jacq   £6.99
                  of Evil

9780743492263   The Great Secret   Christian Jacq   £6.99

Please send cheque or postal order for the value of the book,
free postage and packing within the UK, to
SIMON & SCHUSTER CASH SALES
PO Box 29, Douglas Isle of Man, IM99 1BQ
Tel: 01624 677237, Fax: 01624 670923
Email: bookshop@enterprise.net
www.bookpost.co.uk

Please allow 14 days for delivery. Prices and availability
subject to change without notice